INSURRECTION

MONIQUE SINGLETON

VINCI

BOOKS

The Dominion Series

The Devil You Know

I AM the Storm

To Hell and Back

Insurrection

I would like to dedicate this book to everyone who has followed my journey, especially my family.

And then there were four.
Four books, and the prequel, in the Dominion series.
What had started out as a vague idea, has blossomed into a full story.
There is one more to go.

Vinci Books

vinci-books.com

Published by Vinci Books Ltd in 2025

1

Copyright © Monique Singleton 2025

The publisher and the author have made every effort to obtain permissions
for any third party material used in this book and to comply with copyright
law. Any queries in this respect should be brought to the attention of the
publisher and any omissions will be corrected in future editions.
A CIP catalogue record for this book is available from the British Library.
Paperback ISBN: 9781036709419
The EU GPSR authorised representative is Logos Europe, 9 rue Nicolas
Poussion, 17000 La Rochelle, France contact@logoseurope.eu

MIX
Paper | Supporting
responsible forestry
FSC® C018072

FSC
www.fsc.org

Printed and bound in Great Britain by Clays Ltd, Elcograf S.p.A.

Silence is the tyrant's best friend.

Chapter One

Five days.

It only took them five days to conquer Earth.

Humans tried to resist. Armies joined forces with previously internal and external enemies and attacked the invaders. Nothing like a common enemy to break down boundaries.

But the invader's overwhelming fire power and complete disregard for life—their own and that of the humans—quickly overwhelmed the Earthen forces. They targeted government cities in all major nations, devastating the seat of power and killing or capturing the heads of state, then made a streamed spectacle of their long and painful deaths. The message was clear. Anyone who dared to oppose them would be terminated in pain-filled agony.

Casualties were rampant and estimated to be just shy of a million. That number was lower than expected only because the stats were still coming in. The prognosis was at least double.

Cal-Tan was making a hell of a point.

'Is this our fault?' I whispered for the umpteenth time.

'He would have done it anyway,' Aaliyah answered. 'It was just a matter of time.'

I couldn't shrug off our involvement in this as easily as she could. It was my family that was responsible for this genocide, not hers. And I wasn't so sure he would have actually done it if we hadn't pushed his hand.

Who was I kidding? Of course he would have. He'd been planning this for a long time. Something like a mass invasion takes preparation and time.

'We could have warned them,' I continued my useless self-pity rampage. 'Told them the invasion was imminent.'

Jonah looked at me incredulously. 'How?'

I stammered. There had to have been been something we could have done.

'They wouldn't believe us. Didn't even buy into the whole Establishment thing until Ebony sent the last data. And even then, I don't think they actually understood what they were facing. And, not to forget, we didn't know.' He shrugged.

'We could have tried.' I sounded like a broken record and was just about as useful.

'Stop kicking yourself, Gabriel,' Aaliyah sighed. 'We've been over this countless times. There was nothing we could have done. Besides, it's moot. What's important is what we do now. How we combat this.'

'Can we even do that?' Jonah asked.

'We can sure as hell try.'

That summed it up quite eloquently.

'I question whether we should jump in straight away or wait,' Jonah stated uncharacteristically.

Aaliyah and I both looked at him in surprise.

'Don't get me wrong, I want to kill as many invaders as possible. But…'

Never thought I'd hear a "but" in this context from the big man.

'But we don't really know what we're facing. How many there are. And how many of us—any form of resistance—are left. We should plan our response.'

He was right. Though I'd never expected restraint from him. Even Aaliyah had to reluctantly agree.

'What do we do in the meantime?' A small voice asked from the corner.

I'd forgotten Tajan was here, but he was as much a fugitive as we were. More maybe, his stay on Earth was still relatively fresh and he wasn't used to the dimension yet.

After the initial invasion, we'd quickly determined that —besides complete world domination—our team would be Cal-Tan's main focus. He wanted us dead or at least stopped. This blitzkrieg was designed to quell any resistance or rebellion in record time, and he couldn't use our stubborn obstruction or the hope we might perpetuate. He aimed for total command as soon as possible and our continued existence was a threat to him.

Delay was bad for business.

His strategy worked.

We had to go underground.

Most of us, that is.

Ebony and some of her crew stayed put. Their cover stories, whatever they were this time, were still intact and they monitored the situation from there. We reasoned Aaliyah, Jonah, Tajan, Kate and I were probably top of Cal-tan's most wanted list as well as some of Ebony's people who were too interesting for my father to pass up on. He wanted slaves, either dead—to be reincarnated—or alive. It wasn't safe up top anymore for the likes of Tyrone, Caleb and Nasheed. So they joined us, literally underground.

Thank goodness Cal-Tan had never unearthed the connection we had with Ebony. I hoped she would stay safe and out of harm's way. With the Thirty-eighth dimension now also accepting female slaves, she could be in the crosshairs. But I trusted her to stay out of trouble and there was always Sly to contend with, though he alternated between our group and Ebony.

Tajan was lost without her. Aaliyah tried to console him, to no avail. He'd found new reason and meaning for life working with our computer wizard on the inventions they'd created together, and now that was gone. He was effectively a lot worse off than he had been in Taxore. There he hadn't been actively hunted. And his family was on Taxore, he was terrified what would happen to them. I felt sorry for him. My choice had at least been my own. He was more or less pulled into the fray by Aaliyah and the rest of us.

Talking about my other reluctant Taxorian friend. Initially she'd wanted to go off on her own. A one-woman suicide mission to kill as many invaders as possible before they annihilated her. Jonah managed to talk sense into her and convince her anything would be a lot better than what was waiting if she went alone. Cal-Tan would love to get his hands on her, almost as much as he wanted to catch me. Reluctantly, she conceded.

Around us, homes were raided, people executed in the streets and others taken away. There wasn't a family left that hadn't been impacted in some painful and terrifying manner. Daily streams showcasing the invader's intentions dissolved human's resistance to the new order. They became numb to the blood and gore on the TV stations and all around them.

Cal-Tan effectively quashed the resistance by killing human spirit.

They had lost too much and capitulated.

Chapter Two

Underground was a parking garage in the centre of Los Angeles, right in the middle of the affluent financial sector.

After the first invasion wave, we'd moved out of town, but the need to help in whichever way we could, forced us to go back. This was where the invaders were harvesting their prisoners, the men and few women who would be sent off-world.

'Have you heard from your contacts on Taxore?' Aaliyah asked yesterday evening after yet another cold dinner, we didn't dare to start a fire, not even this deep underground.

I shook my head. 'The last communication dated from before the invasion. The coded message was short, only stating Cal-Tan's personal trip to the Thirty-eighth dimension. That alone is food for thought. He's always restricted his own transportation to the absolute minimum, reluctant to put his life in the hands of others.'

Understandable, that's how he himself ascended to power. His father had been reduced to a gooey mush of blasted cells in a blotched transport. I doubt it was an accident, no one believed that where I came from. It was just too convenient and coincided with the development of the Twelfth dimension—Earth—as a supply route for slaves, something his father had countered. Cal-Tan had a hand in it, I'm sure of that. Besides, it's no more than the enactment of a generations old tradition in our family. The son murders the father.

Aaliyah nodded; she'd heard about Cal-Tan's patricide as well.

I shuddered to think what that meant for me but recognised the same pattern happening between us. He tried to kill me, and I wouldn't hesitate to return the favour. After our last confrontation, it seemed like the only option. The brutal tradition would be perpetuated.

Cal-Tan's interest in the Thirty-eighth was starting to get to me. My mother had no idea why he was so engrossed with the new world; he'd never shown so much enthusiasm for anything before, let alone another dimension. She'd reported that vast amounts of grunts, materials and supplies were being transported there but nothing had come back. What could the business model be for that? My father never did anything if there wasn't a solid profit to be gained. He was single-minded in his pursuit of power though wealth, and this would be another important step in his masterplan. I just wish we knew why that dimension was so important.

'This Thirty-eighth,' Jonah asked. 'Can humans live there?'

I nodded. 'It makes sense for the prisoners here to be transported there. The atmosphere is conducive to human life as well as Taxorian. Probably quite like Earth's. And I can't imagine anywhere else, not with the last information. But the big question remains what his goal is. I feel it's important, because it could potentially help our efforts to thwart him.'

I missed my mother's communications. It was the one last link to my past that I wanted to perpetuate, but it had stopped right after the first invader set foot on Earth. Not only was it way too dangerous for all parties involved, but the method we used—coded public messages—hadn't been available due to the disruption of all media outlets. The invaders had shut them all down and now controlled the information sent out into the world. Personal ads and podcasts were not seen as essential. We were running blind because of that.

Our team undertook small forays into the city to hassle the invaders and to stock up on supplies.

Generally, the most difficult thing to acquire at the moment was gasoline. But that was another benefit of hiding in the parking garage. Many of the neighbouring building's permanent residents had left their vehicles in the garage in the lower, private levels, and we helped ourselves to the gasoline still in them. Yes, I felt bad, if anyone managed to leave, they would end up without fuel, but I reasoned our resistance efforts trumped the remorse I might feel, besides, we never emptied them completely.

There was little comfort underground, but staying alive was the priority. That and irritating the enemy. We stole out in the night and raided their depots, setting fire to anything we couldn't use ourselves, attacked outposts where we killed the grunts manning them, and did our best to disrupt the harvesting.

The kidnapped humans were initially held in large buildings in the city centre, but our frequent attacks pushed the containment facilities further out, first to the suburbs, then the industry segments. The large warehouses made it easier for the Taxorians to defend themselves and their precious cargo. Our efforts dwindled after one monumental attack when the risks became too high for both our team and the prisoners.

Seven of us besieged a warehouse on the outskirts of town next to a residential area. In earlier days it had been a distribution centre for vegetables trucked into the neighbourhood.

I saw three loading docks that offered entrance to the vast open, inner area of the building. There were no windows, just a few small ventilation points high up the wall covered in wire meshing and the three offices at the left side of the loading docks. The fenced area around the warehouse was flat with truck bays lining the space between the warehouse and the road and neighbours about twenty metres away on both sides. At the back, high mesh fencing was almost up against the warehouse walls. The proximity to other buildings made that our best entry point.

It went well, up to the point where we threw a smoke bomb into one of the open loading docks. Then, all hell broke loose. Blue laser beams peppered the outside area and pinned us to the walls of the warehouse, after which the invaders started shooting through the panelling itself, leaving massive holes where the material had been literally melted away.

We dove for the ground and scrambled away from the docks; our only real entry point which had just become a death trap. Retreat was our only option. I crept along the building edge and had almost reached the fence at the back just as the invaders swung their attention to the prisoners.

The screams of terror and pain from inside the building made me turn on my heels. I couldn't leave them. Jonah and Nasheed had already entered the building by the time I reached the dock and dispatched two of the invaders. A further two continued to train their weapons on the prisoners with absolutely no regard for their own or the human's lives. Jonah mowed one down. The other was taken out by fire from Tyrone and me. But not before they'd achieved their goal.

More than sixty young men lay at our feet, all of them dead or dying. The invader's firepower had been so extensive some of them had been literally dismembered in the onslaught. There was nothing we could do for them. Nasheed found one man alive, but he died moments later in terrible pain.

The only sound was the drip of a broken water pipe.

The silence was oppressive and pushed heavily on my hearts. This should have been a freedom mission, now it was a slaughter.

'Why did they do that?' Tyrone asked, his voice resonating in the empty hall.

'To safeguard the investment,' I answered, the words cold but true.

'How's that?'

'They will be reincarnated on Taxore,' I explained. 'The guards killed them so that they could be harvested.'

'Sick.'

I nodded.

Prisoners were valuable to my father, dead or alive.

Chapter Three

The hiding place had been compromised.

We had to move again. Preferably out of the city this time, there were no safe places there anymore.

'Load everything in the trucks.' Sly took control of the evacuation. He was back with the group and approached everything in his normal military manner. Exactly what we needed to evacuate.

The seven pickups from the underground parking garage we'd chosen for our hide-a-way stood ready, their tanks full. With its eight levels—five of which were under-ground—it was a warren of spaces to hide in.

The thick concrete and excessive use of steel in the construction protected us from heat sensitive locators as long as we were in the lowest levels. There were three stair-ways in addition to the five unused lifts. We couldn't rely on continuous electricity anymore and standing in a small metal elevator while under attack didn't seem like a good idea anyway.

The parking garage had three separate entrances for

vehicles. Two routes for customers and one for the employees and maintenance teams. The last one was our way in and out. We reasoned it would be the least obvious exit.

Ebony informed us the invaders were searching the city building by building. They used advanced scanning equipment and were quick to open fire on whoever or whatever they found. One thing you could say for the Taxorians, they were thorough.

'I've found you a new location,' her voice resounded on the phone speaker. 'It's about three hundred miles west in the Rocky Mountains. The trip will be hazardous to say the least. The hunt for the resistance isn't restricted to only the cities anymore, though it is concentrated in the more heavily populated localities.'

We decided to cut our odds and split the group into individual trucks. They would leave the underground garage one by one, half an hour apart and all under cover of the darkness. Jonah, Nasheed and Aaliyah were in the second truck, Caleb, Kate and I in the fifth. Sly would stay till everyone else had left and drive the final pickup together with Logan.

'You all have a different route,' she continued. 'It will bring you halfway to your destination.'

The final location would be transmitted only after an airtight coded signal was received when we arrived at the stop point, just in case anyone was intercepted. We hoped everyone would make it there but had to plan for a worst-case scenario and keep the final coordinates under wraps. It brought home how extensive the invader's control was.

We waited with bated breath. The first pick up left the building an hour after midnight. There was radio silence, and we had no idea after they left the structure whether

12

they would be okay, even Ebony was in the dark. Jonah, Nasheed and Aaliyah were next. We said our goodbyes and Jonah started the truck. The sound resonated loudly in the otherwise empty space. A shiver ran up my spine, surely the noise would alert someone, but it was unavoidable. They left in a slow assent to the surface.

We repeated the process another two times and finally it was our turn. Kate sat on the back seat while I took up a position in the passenger seat. Caleb drove. Sly slapped the side of the truck to indicate we should leave, and we were off. Caleb slowly circumvented the steep ramps up from the eighth level. I kept my eyes peeled, looking for anything out of the ordinary. We reached the fourth level without issues, and I started to breathe a bit. Prematurely, as it turned out.

A blue laser bolt narrowly missed us and slammed into the wall behind the truck, disintegrating the concrete and exploding shards everywhere.

'Lay down,' I screamed at Kate as the rear window shattered.

She quickly slipped off the seat onto the floor, hiding from sight and hopefully out of danger.

Caleb swerved for yet another beam which narrowly missed our vehicle. He floored the accelerator, and we sped up the ramp at neck-breaking speed. I peppered the area where the lasers had come from as we passed and was rewarded with a loud scream and the weapon losing its aim.

The truck wheels left the ground when we crashed out of the parking garage, hit the ground with a jolt and raced off down the access streets. More lasers attacked us from both sides as Caleb ploughed on into a grunt standing in the middle of the road aiming his weapon at us. The pure weight of the truck and the power behind the enhanced engine tossed him up into the air in a bundle of broken bones and flesh.

The truck swerved but caught its wheels again and we raced off into the night. Caleb cut the lights, and we descended into the deep darkness of the unlit city.

'What about the rest?' Kate's voice was full of the same worry I felt.

'They'll have heard the shots,' Caleb announced. 'Gone through one of the other exits.'

I sincerely hoped he was right. But we wouldn't know until we reached our final destination. The silence fell on us heavily. No one knew what to say, so we didn't try. We all searched the shadows in what little we could see of the streets and sped onwards.

Chapter Four

The halfway mark left us waiting under a copse of trees outside a small village. Like all other inhabited areas, street-lights were no longer lit, and the world was plunged into darkness.

I held onto Kate as she slept on the back seat of the pickup. The breakout had exhausted her, still unused to the adrenaline connected with a narrow escape. I softly stroked the hair from her face and thanked my lucky stars she was alright.

Caleb pulled the phone from his jacket and looked into the screen.

'We have coordinates,' he announced.

He moved to the truck and entered the coordinates into the sat nav. I looked over the backseat at the display and waited anxiously for the system to work out where we were headed.

A map finally covered the screen, and I saw we still had another hundred miles in an estimated ninety minutes to go. Caleb changed the route from the shortest option to a rural, more backroad one to keep us away from inhabited areas. That extended the trip with another forty miles and three hours. It would be worth it.

The night was quickly waning, and we decided to search for a place where we could hide until the next night. Driving around slowly we found a disused and abandoned barn. I dismounted from the car and carefully opened the broken doors wide enough for the truck to enter.

The barn's skeleton was completely constructed of rough, thick wooden posts. The dovetail connections between them were a work of art and I marvelled at the artistry. Thick wooden planks coated the roof and the sides. Some of them were missing and let fresh air into the musty area. Disused farm equipment and stacks of old hay balls were all we could find. I noticed traces of wild animals that had made the place their home but fled when we arrived.

A fire wasn't an option with all the flammable material and besides, we didn't want to alert anyone to our location. We pulled some of the hay bails out of the pile, broke the ropes and spread the contents out as a natural bedding. Caleb and I took turns on guard while the others slept reasonably comfortably in sleeping bags on top of the hay.

The weather had taken a turn for the worst, and it had poured down. Streams of cold water leaked through the holes in the roof, but it had the added benefit that it kept most people indoors. The incessant downpour receded later in the day, and we made plans to continue our trip. We shared a cold meal from our provisions before we left the barn at midnight.

The first part of the trip was uneventful. We stayed off the main roads and even occasionally took some dirt tracks. For the last thirty miles we left all civilisation behind and with it, good roads.

We decided to wait for sunrise before we tackled the more difficult trails up the lower mountains into the Rockies. The truck started to slip on the muddy trails, and we had some harrowing moments when the back wheels struggled for traction. Kate held on to my hand on one side and the door handle on the other. Her knuckles were white with the effort. She was terrified. I couldn't blame her. I was far from comfortable myself but trusted Caleb's driving skills. I squeezed her hand, and she offered me a half-hearted smile.

We made it up the mountain in one piece and the trail slowly flattened out. We started to breathe again and Kate's grip on my hand softened.

Caleb constantly checked the coordinates as we slowly continued our trip. I looked out of the window and marvelled at the beautiful scenery. The elevation on the mountain gave us a fantastic view over the vast forests that coated not only this mountain but the surrounding ones as well. The deep green of the fir trees were peppered with apple-green maple trees. Deep down in the valley, a river snaked through the gorge.

'It's beautiful,' Kate whispered beside me. I turned and smiled at the radiance on her face.

She was right. It was.

Caleb slowed the car and stopped on a large ledge where the track widened.

'I've lost the sat nav,' he announced.

I leant over the back of the passenger seat and observed the screen. It announced that we had arrived at our destination. That was alarming, because there was nothing there. I disembarked and walked to the edge of the ledge. From there I observed the area in more detail. Caleb and Kate joined me, and we all searched for any signs of a building or construction.

I couldn't see anything other than an endless forest and glanced at the others. They shook their heads.

'What do we do now?' Kate asked.

I didn't really have a clue. But we couldn't stay where we were, we were too visible.

. 'This could be another safety measure Ebony put in,' Caleb suggested. 'In case we were intercepted.'

'Sounds logical,' I answered. 'And she probably expects us to find it ourselves from here.'

'I think we should just continue on the trail,' Caleb continued. 'And see from there.'

We agreed, we didn't have any alternatives.

Back in the pickup we slowly made our way along the side of the mountain, descending with every turn.

An hour later the trail effectively stopped at the edge of the river we'd seen earlier. I could see it continued across the water. There was no bridge, and we couldn't really gauge the depth of the fast-running water.

'I'll get out and walk in front of the car,' I opted. 'Then at least we can see whether we can traverse it.'

'Why you?' Kate asked, her face lined with worry looking at the swift running water.

'I'm the strongest,' I answered. My Taxorian background was finally a bonus.

'We'll tie a rope to the front of the car as an extra security,' Caleb suggested, alleviating some of the concern in her features.

Ten minutes later I was up to my knees shivering in the cold mountain water. Progress was slow with me battling against the strong current. The car slowly followed me, keeping the rope around my waist slack so it wouldn't hinder me.

The river was only a foot and a half deep and we managed to cross it without issues. I rejoined the others, wringing out my socks and emptying the water from my boots. The heat of the car's interior was welcome, and I dried out quickly.

The only real option was to continue to follow the slowly disappearing track. Half an hour passed, and we entered a clearing losing the trail in the knee-high grass.

'Now what?'

I shrugged. I was out of ideas. Kate looked just as confused.

We scanned the clearing and the tree line beyond. Nothing.

I got out of the car and started to walk towards the centre of the open space. The warm rays of the sun were welcome on my still cold skin. My clothes were dry, but wading in the mountain water had chilled me to the bone. I estimated it to be almost mid-day, and the sun was almost at its zenith.

A movement to my right caught my eye and I swivelled, crouching down to minimise my target area.

I'd seen something from my peripheral vision but couldn't place what it was. I scrutinised the forest. Was there a movement?

In the trees to the right, I spotted a branch moving. Then another. I slowly made my way back to the truck; certain I wouldn't get to the cover before whatever it was came out. Maybe it was a bear, or a moose. Or worst-case scenario, an enemy.

Caleb had followed my gaze and pushed Kate back into the car where she once again lay on the floor of the vehicle behind the front seats. His gun was pointed at the movement between the trees.

We waited with bated breath.

Soft wind blew through the branches of the trees, birds called to each other, other than that it was silent. My hearts beat wildly in my ears, drowning out the natural sounds.

A figure materialised from the edge of the forest, then another and the tension seeped out of my muscles like the river we'd just crossed.

Jonah and Nasheed approached us with massive smiles on their faces.

I'd never been happier to see them.

We embraced and I turned to the car. Caleb and Kate had disembarked and were coming towards us. Kate rushed into Jonah's arms, and he enveloped her in his massive bear hug, lifting her off the ground. Caleb and Nasheed clasped arms and there were smiles all around.

'Good to see you all,' the big man declared.

'Same here,' I answered, my voice full of the relief that flooded my body.

Kate joined me and snaked her arm around my waist. I pulled her closer, my arm around her shoulder.

'Have the rest come in?' Caleb asked, the worry clear in his tense features.

Jonah shook his head. 'Not all of them yet,' he answered. His features softened as he acknowledged the intense nerves in Caleb's face.

'What happened?' Nasheed asked carefully, observing the damage to the car.

'We were attacked on the ramp driving up from the third floor,' I answered, choosing my words carefully. On the drive all our thoughts had been with the two teams still left in the underground garage when we escaped.

'Did the other teams make it to the halfway mark?' Caleb asked.

Nasheed glanced at Jonah. His worried look wasn't lost on Caleb and his brow creased even more.

'One of the teams called in,' the big man's announced, keeping an eye on Caleb's reaction.

'Do you know which one?'

He shook his head. 'No.'

Jonah clasped Caleb's shoulder in support. 'He'll be alright, Caleb. Ebony would have let us know if something had happened to him.'

Caleb attempted a smile; it didn't really work. He tried to nod. 'Yeah,' he acknowledged. 'The old man is hard to kill.'

We all chuckled at that. Sly did have a knack for getting out of tight situations.

The silence that followed was uncomfortable. We wanted to support Caleb, but there was nothing else we could do or say. Kate stroked his arm, and he covered her hand with his own in gratitude for the sentiment.

'You need to get you to camp,' Jonah announced. 'Get the car out of the open space. Nasheed will join you to show you the way.'

I nodded and turned to walk back to the car with Kate.

'You okay if I stay with you?' Caleb asked Jonah.

'Of course.'

Nasheed took the driver seat; I sat next to him with Kate behind me. We set off slowly to the edge of the clearing. Jonah and Caleb rearranged the grass behind us to hide our tracks.

I didn't envy Caleb. He was worried sick about his father. So were we, but his family bond was much closer. I hope he was right, that no one could kill him. Sly's stern and rough edges had grown on me, and he was a valued member of our strange and dysfunctional family.

Twenty minutes later we rounded yet another corner on the narrow trail and entered an area bordered with high cliffs on one side and deep dark forest on the other. The rock wall was almost sheer and towered up high above us with an overhang that initially made me nervous. It looked as though it could come down anytime. It also offered a natural cover for the caves and constructions that formed the camp, rendering it practically invisible from above. I understood the attraction the place had.

I stepped out of the pickup and looked up at the steep wall of rock. It was definitely impressive. There were caves on two levels, the upper ones accessible with rough wooden ladders made from local tree trunks and thick rope. I counted more than twenty openings at first glance. Some looked natural, but most I deemed man-made, their edges too regular and precise. The thirty metre by twenty metre area in front of the caves was flat. At the edge, under the foliage of the tall fir trees, I saw the four vehicles that left before us hidden under camouflage nets. Three more cars stood to their right, also covered with netting. Further on I spied a paddock with some horses, something I really hadn't expected.

'You made it,' Aaliyah's happy voice resounded, and I turned towards the sound. She approached us and hugged Kate—they got on like a house on fire—and then even did the same to me. I hugged her back; just as happy the family was coming together again.

'This place is amazing,' she voiced enthusiastically. 'The caves go on into the mountain and are very comfortable.'

'Was it already inhabited?' I asked, noticing some faces I didn't know.

'Yes, two families lived here. They've been very helpful and offered us a lot of information on how to live here.'

'How did they know about the caves?'

'Seems one of them was involved in the construction of what was supposed to be a shelter for the apocalypse. An eccentric millionaire owned the land, and he was convinced the end of the humanity was nearing,'

'Well, he wasn't far off.' I commented.

'No, but no one believed him.'

'Is he here?'

She shook her head. 'He died before the invasion. Built it all for nothing.'

'Well, good for us that he did.'

She nodded, her laughter warm and uplifting.

'Why did they welcome us?' I questioned, ever the pessimist.

'I think mostly because they're not warriors. They have no idea how to protect themselves, so our presence makes them feel safer. That and they just yearned for human contact.'

I raised an eyebrow. Aaliyah knew what I meant and shook her head slowly. Hmm, they weren't aware of our origins. Good idea to keep that secret. I resolved to tell Caleb and Kate to stay silent at the first possible option. The humans in our team were used to us being around and didn't really see us as aliens anymore, but I was under no illusion others would do the same. It was best to keep that piece of information to ourselves.

Laughter caught my attention, and I swivelled towards a group of small children playing with a dog.

I could imagine the parents valued protection for their families. It made sense and allowed me to lower some of my apprehension about sharing the new HQ with others.

'Ebony vetted them,' Aaliyah added, reading my mind.

I nodded. That was good enough for me.

I viewed the surroundings with a different perspective and could understand Aaliyah's initial comment. The place was beautiful. The soft grass under my feet, the tang of the forest heady in my nose, the sound of a stream in the background. It seemed totally fantastic.

Aaliyah took Kate's hand and pulled her along. 'Come on, let's introduce you to the others and get you settled.'

Kate smiled at me, pulling my own lips up in a mirror of her enthusiasm and I followed the two women to a waiting welcome committee.

An hour later we had a personal cave allocated to us and a tour of all the communal facilities. The millionaire had seriously loved his comforts and there was a cave that housed working showers, a kitchen with a beautiful Aga wood-range, storage rooms and lovely communal areas.

It really was a massive uplift to the previous location in the parking garage, and I loved the smiles it evoked on Kate's face. She was in heaven. And by proxy, so was I.

There was even a real bed. Not just a camping stretcher, or a military style air mattress. A real bed. Made of natural logs and sporting a more than comfortable mattress with matching duvet. He hadn't cut corners, our unknown and unintended benefactor. I silently thanked him for his paranoid ideas, or maybe just premonitions.

There was—spotty—electricity, thanks to the solar panels, but the fact that they had to remain hidden meant they didn't receive the maximum sun they could. It was safety above comfort. But candles had a lovely, even romantic effect in the closeness of the caves, and I definitely didn't moan about that.

Now the only worry we had was how the other two

teams had fared. We hadn't heard anything, and I was biting my nails hoping they would both arrive at this new location.

Three hours later we finally had closure. Sly and his team made it to the clearing and after a heartfelt reunion with Caleb they made their way to the caves where the process was repeated. Kate shed a tear, and I must say I had a challenge to keep myself composed, I was just so happy they'd made it.

But it wasn't all good news. The sixth pickup had blown up after a direct hit by the invaders, killing everyone in the vehicle. Four people had died. Four of our close friends. Our elation was seriously tempered by the realisation that we'd lost so many of our companions.

It also drove home how close we'd come to losing all of us. If we'd decided to leave just half a day later, well, I don't have to spell it out. It would have been devastating.

The power of the invaders was acutely obvious and very sobering.

Chapter Five

It was an easy life to acclimatise to once we'd mourned our dead friends.

The peace and quiet after the tension of the city was such a contrast that I sometimes had to stop and pinch myself. Were we really here? Every night I thanked our lucky stars as I held Kate in my arms. This was the most serene moment we'd experienced since way before the invasion. Honestly, since I'd decided to join Jonah in his quest.

I quickly settled into the laid-back routine of gathering wood for fuel, taking care of the compound and, surprisingly, working with the horses. I'd never really been exposed to the animals other than as a transport option in the Middle Ages. I loved interacting with them, their stubborn characters, yet they still looked to humans for attention and comfort. Horses are honest animals. They mirror what you present them. An eye opener.

Kate thrived in the compound. She loved the nature, the children and life in general. If it wasn't so cliche, I'd say she found her piece of paradise. Her pleasure was contagious, and I found myself smiling more and more. For the first time since my decision to change sides, I really experienced something close to peace.

The caves were basic, but comfortable. We had most of what we needed in the supplies the millionaire had stockpiled and supplemented where necessary with what we harvested from the forests. We had regular forays into the woods to gather edible herbs and plants. The two families turned out to be experts in living naturally and I learned a lot. Kate took in the information like a sponge and revelled in her new knowledge. For someone who'd lived in the city all her adult life, she finally flourished deep in the forests. Nature and Kate were made for each other. Her enthusiasm even rubbed off on me and I gained a renewed appreciation for what was all around me.

Life was good.

For us.

For the rest of mankind, it was hell.

The invaders continued their unbridled attack on anything that even dared to oppose them. Just a whisper of insurrection was enough to bring down the new power's wrath. They were lethal in their reaction, totally without empathy.

The Hashta were let loose on the human population, their actions streamed on every TV station. The level of brutality eclipsed even the worst human horror movie. No one could have predicted this kind of savagery. Humans were terrified by the seemingly randomness of the attacks and subsequent torture by the black clad devils. No one was safe, that much was clear.

Humanity was overwhelmed.

They had no natural resilience against the overpowering brutality that rained down on them. The only way to handle it was to give in. To close their minds to the barbarity and focus on the very few positives they could find within the dark bottomless terror they found themselves in. It was just too surreal to be true.

It took all of ten days for the guilt to resurface in our team.

We'd gone underground after the invasion not only to stay alive, but also to hit back at the enemy. We felt we were vacationing while the world around us burned. What had been peace became frustration, and we noticed short tempers in the group.

'We're warriors,' Aaliyah lamented one evening around the fire. 'Not farmers and gatherers.'

Her sentiment resounded in my mind. This inactivity was getting to me too. It felt wrong in every fibre of my being.

Thankfully we had Ebony. She'd searched the areas within a day's drive from our new home, looking for a new mission, a way we could put even a small dent in the invader's plans and came up with a potential target.

There was a containment facility four hours away. It housed the kidnapped humans and made them ready for transportation to wherever they were sending them. Ebs estimated there would be close to three hundred captives there. If we could free them, they would at least have a chance to go underground and hide. We couldn't take them back to our compound, there simply wasn't enough room, and we had to stay careful, but at least they would be free again.

The invaders had constructed multiple large transportation hubs all over the world. We'd counted more than eight in the US alone. Transportation hubs made it easier to move large amounts of humans. Individual transports were handled from the hubs on Taxore, but that was cumbersome and expensive, so my father had chosen to build larger versions on Earth that could transport a thousand humans a day. That in turn necessitated large facilities to house the people scheduled for the procedure. They were generally incarcerated within a hundred-mile radius of the transport hub.

The cities were still the main harvesting locations. It made sense, that was where the concentration of young men were. It was also where most of the small resistance groups like ours harassed the invaders endlessly. That had pushed the holding facilities out into more rural areas. The Taxorians weren't bothered about humane transport to and from the new facilities. They bundled the captives into the loading bays of large trucks and drove back and forth from the cities. If anyone was wounded on the way, they were singled out for termination and reincarnation. The dual opportunities made the invaders callous.

The facility we singled out was ninety-six miles from L.A at the foot of the Angeles National Forest. The hilly terrain and the dark forests would at least give the prisoners a chance to stay under the radar once we'd released them.

We knew it was a drop of water on a hot plate, but at least we would be hitting back and helping others.

We planned the attack meticulously and excitement once again filled our team. This could be the first of many forays and it felt good to be active.

Not for the first time, we completely underestimated our enemy.

Chapter Six

None of us expected what would happen.

Not even in our wildest nightmares.

We'd launched the attack on the containment facility. There were more than three hundred young men incarcerated in the old school waiting to be transported.

The blueprints Ebs sent us showed there were seven classrooms in the small complex. Three to the front, one on either side of the entrance hallway and another up the stairs. The remaining classroom, a large room that was probably used as an assembly hall and the bathrooms were situated in the extension to the right of the entrance. The smaller extension to the left housed a kitchen and pantry.

A soft breeze cooled my skin. Shivers ran up my spine from the temperature and the adrenaline. My legs wanted to propel me forward and get on with the mission.

Observing the complex from my position two hundred metres away in the tall grass, I saw the building had tall windows, now sporting strong bars to keep the new occupants inside. My location perpendicular to the complex allowed me to notice the mesh fence that closed off the space around the small playground courtyard at the back, the bike shed and the front reception area. Parking spaces for the teachers had been opposite the school in a small flat paved area. The road in front of the school ended fifty metres further out in a round-about to allow parents to drop off their children and turn their cars.

The invaders had added an electric fence to the plot and some large spotlights that effectively lit up the building making it difficult to approach without being seen.

Nasheed cut the electricity for the whole surrounding area at the distribution house three streets removed from the school.

The spotlights faded and went dark, the building immediately shrouded in deep shadows.

Two teams sped into action and stormed the front and the back entrances simultaneously, slashing the fences, pulling the sides apart and opening an escape route. Heat sensitive binoculars had identified where we would find the prisoners. They were concentrated in the assembly hall and the four rooms to the back of the property. One of the front rooms housed what we had determined were the guards, the majority of which were probably grunts. Expendable forces for my father.

I'd joined the team that attacked the front of the building, and we made our way immediately to the small room where we killed the grunts with excessive force. It felt cold, but they were unredeemable and had to be dealt with using maximum firepower. The team then made their way to the holding areas where they were met by the second group and hundreds of released prisoners.

'Move!' Jonah shouted, mobilising them. The relief on their faces changed to action as the young men were herded out of the building to the three big trucks Ebony had somehow organised that had pulled up to the old school-house, two at the back and one in front of the parking lot.

We ushered the prisoners out of the building. In doing so I noticed they were all dressed in identical sweaters and jeans. As one passed me, a glint of metal caused me to stop him. I pulled the neck of his sweater down and to my horror saw a thin miscian ring that circled his throat. It was Taxorian technology and unbelievably deadly. Miscian was a pliable but very strong material mined on Taxore, basically impossible to saw through or remove, but that wasn't what made my blood run cold.

'Stop!" I shouted, my voice carrying over the chaotic scramble.

Jonah looked at me, his brow creased in question.

'Don't let them leave the grounds!' I shouted to our teams.

They looked at me with disbelief, so did the prisoners, as I ran around and pulled at the neck of more sweaters. Each one of the prisoners wore the miscian collar. Each of them was doomed if they left here.

'What the fuck!' Jonah had come up beside me, his face a mask of rage. 'We don't have time to waste, we need to get everyone in the trucks.'

'We can't,' I answered.

'Why the hell not?' Sly called out angrily from the side.

I was about to explain when the first explosions rang out.

We ran out of the rear of the building into the court-yard into the swirling dust from the explosions that made it difficult for us to see what was happening.

My ears rang with the sound of more blasts, and I screamed at Jonah to get everyone back inside. I ran towards the explosions, completely counter to what my body was urging me to do. I was the only one who knew what was going on and it instilled terror in me for the prisoners.

Just in front of me the loading area of one truck exploded in a massive ball of fire as not one but all the miscian necklaces ignited at the same time. The pressure of the explosion hurled me back and I hit the ground hard, rolling up against the building wall.

Time stood still.

The dust slowly cleared, and we were faced with the destruction. A big block of something heavy took up residence in my gut as I looked around me. There was nothing left of the truck or anyone who'd been within ten metres of it. Other humans lay on the ground bleeding, crying out, including three of our second team.

More explosions, now from the front of the building, confirmed the helpless position we were in.

No one was leaving this place alive. Not with the miscian collars.

I struggled to my feet, looking around at the devastation. I pulled Caleb up and pushed him to help the others from the team.

'We need to get everyone back inside!' I shouted above the screams of the dying. 'No one can leave.'

Some of the prisoners had come to the same conclusion and were running back to the building. Another explosion which blew the head off a tall blond man just a few feet from me urged the rest to hurry. They ran back past us and took up their previous positions in the assembly hall hoping their return would save them.

It did. For now.

I rubbed the blond man's blood and brain matter out of my eyes with my sleeve.

'We've got to go!' Nasheed shouted. 'Now! Incoming!'

I grabbed Jonah's arm and pushed him out of the building towards the second truck at the back of the courtyard. None of the prisoners had reached it and it had been spared from the exploding collars. Our driver started up the truck, turned it around and put it in first gear. We jumped in the back as he sped away, leaving the prisoners and our dead behind.

We had no choice.

I could hear vehicles pulling up at the front of the school as we sped away.

'What the fuck happened?' Sly demanded once we'd put a good distance between us and the school, his eyes blazing.

'The prisoners all had miscian collars,' I answered dejected.

'A what?'

'A collar, made of a Taxorian metal.'

'With a bomb?'

'The collar is the bomb,' I continued, rubbing the dust and blood from my face with a piece of my t-shirt I'd ripped off. 'It's a metal that's highly explosive if it comes in contact with yeraah.'

'Yer what?'

Yeraah,' Aaliyah chimed in. 'It's another Taxorian resource. Separate, they're harmless, put them together and…well, you get the picture.' She was staring at her hands, rubbing them to remove the blood and gore. She'd been close when one of the collars exploded. The right side of her face was covered in blood, both red and purple.

She took a water bottle and soaked a rag to get rid of the Taxorian blood before we got back to the base. We hadn't informed anyone else about our heritage and wanted to keep it that way for now.

Sure enough, the first question came before she had been able to clean it all off.

'Are you hurt?' Jack asked carefully. He was one of the newer recruits to the resistance and thus oblivious that Taxorians were part of the insurgence.

'No,' Aaliyah waved it away. 'Just covered in other people's blood.'

'That purple stuff,' he continued, pointing to a big patch on the side of Aaliyah's jacket. 'That's alien blood?'

'Yes.'

'It's weird,' he commented, convincing me this was his first encounter.

I just nodded. What else was there to say?

The rest of the trip was covered in silence, all of us completely subdued by the unexpected turn of events. They probably felt the same guilt I experienced. If we hadn't tried to free them, they would all still be alive. Yeah, for as long as it took Cal-Tan's customers to work them to death. It was debatable, who was better off, those alive or those dead.

Chapter Seven

'What the fuck are we going to do now?'

Jonah eloquently voiced what we were all thinking. Cal-Tan had successfully ended our plans of releasing the prisoners. No doubt most of them would be wearing collars from now on and thus be untouchable for us and other resistance groups.

'How did they set them off?' Sly mused. 'We killed them all.'

'They probably rigged the collars to be within a specific radius of the building,' I suggested. 'There will be a trigger there somewhere that sends out a restricted signal. As soon as that's broken or interrupted the yeraah is released into the collar.'

'And that sets of the explosion?'

I nodded.

We were in the small meeting cave, Sly, Jonah, Aaliyah, Nasheed, Tyrone, Caleb and I. Here we could talk freely, we were among friends, all of which knew our history. All could be trusted.

'How can we identify the trigger?' Jonah asked, reluctant to write off any future missions.

I shrugged and glanced at Aaliyah. She shook her head.

'It could be anything,' she answered.

'And we can expect this to be the new reality? That all prisoners will have collars?'

'I think we should presume that, yes. This was a costly lesson.'

'I should have known.' Ebony's distorted voice resounded from the screen on the wall, one of the creature-comforts the millionaire had installed in foresight. There was no image of her, just in case anyone walked into the room, or the connection was intercepted. She was still our best asset and, along with Aaliyah and my heritage, the biggest secret.

'How could you?' Jonah tried to help.

'It was too easy,' she answered. 'Getting the blueprints, the open way they flaunted the locations. They didn't even try to hide it, not really. I thought we'd just struck lucky, but now I see we were played.'

'You think they lured us in there to make an example?'

'Yes. I do. Us or any other group.'

'Just to show us what our actions would cause?'

'I think they expected to take you out at the same time,' Ebony answered coldly.

Caleb took a deep breath. 'They did. We lost three people. And all the prisoners.'

'How many prisoners?'

We all looked at each other for an answer.

'How many?' Ebony repeated.

'We don't know,' the big man answered, his voice hard with anger that radiated from his massive form.

'There were at least twenty in the truck that blew up,'

Aaliyah added. She'd been outside near the truck when the collars exploded. The vehicle had just started on its escape out from the school grounds.

'And more that just ran out of the building,' Caleb's voiced softly.

'So more than forty, maybe even fifty. And then a lot of wounded.'

'What will happen to them?' Ebony's distorted voice whispered.

We stayed silent. No one wanted to say it out loud.

Wounded grunts would be terminated and reincarnated in my own dimension. There was no way the invaders would nurse them back to health. It wasn't financially viable. Besides, reincarnation was always an option, so the asset wouldn't be a write-off. Not entirely. I fully expected all the grunts to have been administered with nanites. Maybe they had even been the chosen sacrificial lambs for this lesson aimed at the resistance fighters world-wide.

'There was nothing we could have done,' I offered, but it lacked the conviction I tried to portray. We were all numb with the guilt we felt. The prisoner's deaths weighed heavily on our shoulders.

'We're going to have to find some way to counter the signals,' Jonah broke the silence.

'Were any of the collars recovered from the scene?' The metallic voice asked on the screen.

It seemed strange to talk to a comic-like avatar of a rotund man wearing thick glasses and sporting a patchy beard. I desperately wanted to see the real person behind the avatar: Ebony. Talk to her face to face. Hold her hand, feel her near us. She was such an integral part of our strange family, and I missed her. I glanced at Jonah and saw I wasn't the only one. We'd gone underground six months ago. He hadn't seen her in all that time. It was different for me, at least Kate was here. She would hold me and help to placate my feelings of guilt and shame. Jonah was alone, his soulmate far away. He ached for her, and he was worried about her safety, no matter how secure she insisted she was.

Sly wasn't much better off. He'd been her protector for so long and now, because of a blotched mission a week ago, he too was on the inter-dimensional hit list. Thankfully, Cal-Tan and his cronies hadn't linked him to Ebony. Caleb and his family were here with us, just in case they had been identified. Sly's other sons were in other underground facilities with their families.

They'd all tried to bring as many of their kin with them, and the facilities were overcrowded. It was impossible to keep everyone together under these circumstances.

Chapter Eight

The deterrent worked.

We didn't dare target the holding facilities anymore. A last attempt at freeing the prisoners before they reached that point revealed they were issued the collars earlier in the process. It had been heartbreaking to convince the prisoners they had to stay put once we killed the grunts escorting the trucks. One tried desperately to run away but met the same fate as those in the facility. His example stayed the others, and we had to leave them.

It was another failure. A massive one that crushed our resolve. Depression was just around the corner.

Other forms of insurgence met the same fate.

The constant barrage of attacks on what was left of the human military left them decimated. My father's troops, aided by the dreaded Hashta, hunted down resistance fighters and made public spectacles of their extended deaths. If they couldn't get their hands on the intended revolutionaries themselves, they substituted family members, a practice that often had even more effect. The backbone of the resistance was broken by pure brutality.

Human casualties were astounding, running in the millions. Removing the bodies had become one of the main concerns for the remaining government and Taxorians alike. Decomposing corpses lined the streets and bred diseases, which was bad for business. With the collapse of health care, contracting a disease amounted to a death sentence. The invaders acknowledged the risks, it also impeded the harvesting, and they assisted in the clean-up. Mass cremations were a daily occurrence, the families held back as they cried over their lost relatives. It was heartbreaking, but necessary.

The invaders made their point. life was cheap.

We could see the humans moving into an acceptance mode. They capitulated. There was little else they could do with the balance heavily in favour of the invaders.

I'd seen it all before.

It opened the doorway for my father to take whatever he wanted.

Chapter Nine

'How is that possible?'

Aaliyah's features were flushed with indignation and anger.

'Why do they believe him?'

Jonah and I exchanged glances.

'I don't think it's a matter of believing or not,' Jonah answered. 'More basic survival.'

'But they're promoting it to their constituents as an ideal compromise.'

'They might not have a choice.'

She bristled even more. 'There is always a choice.'

'Is there?' I joined the conversation, if you could call it that, sentiments were heated and the tension felt oppressive.

I'd walked in on Jonah and Aaliyah arguing a few minutes ago. The cause was a video on autorepeat streaming to every available TV station. I turned to the big screen on the wall above our make-shift conference table. Though grainy, the images were clear enough and so was the message.

There was a cease fire. The combined human authorities had struck a deal with Taxore. Literally a deal with the devil. In the current circumstances, humans were not in a position to demand anything. They had to swallow whatever my father offered them, no matter how devastating that could be. And believe me, it was.

'If there isn't a choice, there isn't a chance,' Aaliyah answered my question, her tone dripping with sarcasm. 'Then, what are we doing here?'

'Not everyone can just up and join the resistance,' Jonah tried, his own voice showing signs of fatigue and waning patience.

'They would rather just accept their new destiny like cattle?'

'Yes,' the big man sighed. 'They would. If they thought their families would be safe.'

'But it's all lies,' she wouldn't let it go, her arms extending out wildly, emphasising her emotions.

'They don't know that.'

'That's naive, stupid.'

'And the only thing they can do, given the circumstances. Everyone wants to believe there's a way-out, Aaliyah. But there isn't. Not for most people.'

'I found a way.'

He sighed audibly. 'Yes, you did. But not everyone is as courageous as you. Or has lost so much. Most want to avoid that. It's human nature.'

The ceasefire was a capitulation. Humanity was bowing to a stronger power; my father. I'd seen it before, and it was happening again. Only now I was on the other side. The side that lost and had to concede to whatever the tyrant wanted. It stabbed me in my deepest hearts that I'd ever been party to this kind of subjugation. This was what I'd perpetuated for so long. The only consolation I had, was that I'd finally opened my eyes and now opposed the complete lack of empathy that so characterised my kind. The realisation didn't change what my father did, but it stopped me from total depression.

'How can anyone just accept this as their fate?' Aaliyah continued. 'Can't we mobilise them. Get them to fight.'

'Don't count on it,' Jonah answered dejectedly. 'Humans are fickle creatures. They like their comforts, and perceived security is one of them. They will take what they think is the lesser of the evils.'

'Don't they know the power their silence gives Cal-Tan?' Aaliyah tried. 'If no one opposes him, then he has free rein.'

'That's where we come in.' Jonah's remark lacked the customary drive. Even he was tiring.

She ignored him, continuing her line of thought.

'The silence will damn them. They are suppressing themselves.'

'And that's exactly the idea.' I agreed despondently.

She looked up at me, her stare somewhere between just noticing my presence and an unspoken "what the hell are you doing here?"

I didn't need her dismissal. I already felt the heavy burden my family ties caused. Yes, I was working with the resistance, but Cal-Tan was still my father. And he was still behind all this, and more.

'He wants Earth to rule itself without using too many of his resources. He's done it before, in other dimensions. I've seen him do it.' I took a deep breath. 'I've helped him do it.'

There, it was said.

'What exactly is the process?' Jonah asked once the emotions had calmed down a bit.

I pulled a chair out from under the table and sat down heavily.

'He attacks a dimension using absolute force and brutality, wears the inhabitants down with death and destruction, then offers them an alternative that is at least better than total annihilation.'

I took one of the glasses on the table and filled it with the clear water from the jug.

'He breaks their spirit. Shows them how utterly helpless they are. Then brings in the people in power, or what's left of them, and sits them down to lay out how it's going to be from there on.'

Jonah nodded slightly.

'There isn't really a choice,' I continued.

'There always is,' Aaliyah repeated her earlier statement.

I sighed. 'No. There isn't. Not for the masses, and not for the leaders who have their best interests at heart. Refusal is an instant death sentence. Then he'll just replace that leader with someone more compliant.'

'Or scared,' Jonah chimed in.

I nodded, took a sip of water and continued.

'Cal-Tan has shown his strength. The leaders know they're helpless against his weapons, the deadly emotionless grunts and the Hashta. The example he made of the US president is fresh in everyone's mind, and probably their nightmares. He uses fear like no one I've ever encountered. And now he also has the Hashta to use in his reign of terror, no one will go up against him.'

'The leaders must think about their constituents, their country men and women. Cal-Tan's mass deportations have decimated many of the armies globally. The young men have gone, and no one knows where to. Families have been devastated and are scared to lose what little they still have left. In light of what has happened in the past months, the price for his new rule seems reasonable.'

'How is sending a quota of young men and women to be deported in any way reasonable?' Aaliyah spat out.

'It isn't,' I agreed. 'It's the lesser of two evils.'

I sipped the cold water again, secretly wishing it was something a lot stronger, like vodka.

'It's the way he addresses it. It gives them false hope.'

In a stream the invaders broadcasted worldwide, in every language known to man, Cal-Tan had calmly laid out his plan and the impact of possible refusal. He'd come across like an amicable uncle, albeit one with bad news. It was all a sham. But a deception desperate humans wanted to believe.

The combined leaders had agreed to conscript and supply three million fit and healthy young men and women —though mainly men—between eighteen and thirty in the coming five years, to spend what my father called a five-year tenure in another dimension. On the surface it sounded tolerable. They would return after their tour and be free to continue their lives here on Earth. In exchange for the steady supply of labour and materials, Cal-Tan promised he would not directly interfere in how the planet was governed. Ultimately, the to-be-instated Earth Government would report to him through his appointed governor.

Naturally these demands just scratched the surface, there would be many more: for additional labour, assets, raw materials, anything he needed or wanted. First, he had to make sure the humans were compliant, then he could do whatever he wanted with a minimum of Taxorian effort and resources. Earth would in essence govern itself and do exactly what my father intended. In the end, I was sure he would clean out this dimension until it was of no more use to him. All the natural resources would be taken along with a whole generation of young men, and now possibly women as well, though it eluded me what he wanted them for. The planet would waste away and eventually be discarded.

Cal-Tan had no regard for human life. They were assets, no more and no less. He had no reason to care about their lives because of the reincarnation technology, they were valuable dead or alive. Whichever was the least bother for him and made the most profit would be preferable, but the other was always an option.

We still had no idea why Cal-Tan needed so many grunts. According to Ebony's calculations he'd already shipped more than a million humans through the mass transportation hubs. We had no inclination of where they were headed, though it was quite a coincidence that the thirty-eighth dimension had an atmosphere compatible with human life. I assumed that was where they would end up. What for? I was clueless. There had never been such a massive shipment of grunts in Taxorian history. Maybe that dimension had a wealth of raw materials that Cal-Tan was mining. It was just a thought, but it was the only explanation I had.

The so-called Earth government issued frequent streams with all kinds of updates. The last one introduced the new Taxorian governor.

'Do you know this Man-Kayl guy?' Jonah asked, cocking his head at the screen.

I nodded. 'Yes, I know him. He's been in my father's inner circle for centuries. I guess he's as trusted as anyone can get with Cal-Tan, whose inbred suspicion makes for few close friends. Man-Kayl wormed his way into my father's circle with his psychopathic tendencies and was probably seen as a kindred spirit. He made quick progress in the family business because of his ruthlessness. He's charming on the surface, but brutal and narcistic. What I know of him doesn't bode well for Earth.'

Jonah's nostrils flared and he sniffed loudly. Not what he wanted to hear, I guess.

Man-Kayl's charismatic introduction soon won over the Earthen leaders who hoped the promises made would now come to fruition. He assured them that in time, everything would be as they had agreed, but there were some small issues that had to be taken care of before they could continue the implementation.

Small improvements for the humans were actually made, just to show the supposed Taxorian willingness to adhere to their pledges. Earthen leaders used these as proof that the cooperation was working, the bad days had passed and both dimensions were working well together. It also helped to still the questions from concerned and grieving families of the transported young men and women.

It would all be alright. Cal-Tan would keep his side of the pact. He would return the missing humans after their five-year stint had been completed.

I knew it for the window-dressing it was. Designed to keep the assets calm. To counter any kind of resistance.

When Man-Kayl announced that the revolutionaries—us—were a massive danger to the fragile peace between the two species, some humans even started to turn on their own. A complex system of snitching was set up and many people betrayed their family and friends, assured by the govern-ment that they were doing the right thing.

I couldn't really blame them. They were basically held hostage with all the sons and daughters that had been taken. All they wanted was their loved ones to come back safe and sound.

I knew no one would come home.

Ever.

Chapter Ten

And then there were the animals.

Not something I'd ever thought about, but under the circumstances, they were indispensable.

Dogs, horses and yes, even cats.

It made sense. The original underground facilities in the cave system we lived in had been abandoned by humans long ago, and rodents had filled the void. Any leftover food had been quickly devoured as they made themselves at home in the labyrinth of corridors and rooms now used by the revolutionaries.

The group that re-conquered the complex had brought in cats to combat the rodent infestation. It had worked. The half feral creatures took to the dark underground hunting grounds like fish to water. They kept the numbers under control and even, occasionally, sought the company of the human co-inhabitants.

Horses had become a renewed means of transport. Vehicles were traceable. Anything with a combustion engine might light up on the aliens radar, a horse was invisible, blending in with the forests that coated the area above and around us.

We had a collection of different breeds, fifteen animals in total. Most were the hardy quarter horses, at home in the mountains and deserts. There was also a contingent of smaller Welsh type ponies, used in the transportation underground. Pound for pound, they were worth their weight in gold. But it was the two shires I was pulled towards. A mare and a stallion. Both massive and impressive in their size and demeanour. Known as gentle giants, most people expected them to be passive and docile. But these two also had the temperament of the knight's war steeds of centuries ago. They were gentle, to a small group of us. But in the heat of battle, they used their strength and bulk to help us.

I asked John where they'd come from, it seemed like a strange collection in the middle of nowhere.

'I used to work for the man who built this complex,' he explained. 'He loved horses, especially the big draught ones. The small ponies he had for his grandchildren. He died just before the invasion and his family left the estate as soon as things got tough. It's about thirty miles from here as the crow flies. We were left to take care of the animals. A group of refugees settled in the big farmhouse and when food began to get scarce, they talked about killing some of the horses, starting with the Shires. Stupid really, with petrol at a premium we used them for all the heavy farming work, and they were extremely valuable. Anyway, one night we set the whole lot free and left. These came with us or were caught later on.'

We used the Shires frequently for their extraordinary strength and sure footedness. Whenever supplies had to be transported through the dark forests, to bring in what we'd hunted, or when were went out looking for firewood, we turned to the trusty animals. They were basically indispensable.

Monarch, the stallion was a beautiful big black horse with white feather, the brown mare Kayleigh wasn't as tall but made up for her hight in attitude. She was a force to be reckoned with, her stubborn nature legendary in our camp. I navigated to her automatically, as she did to me in her own way. It sounds corny—stupid really, when I think about it— but she probably saw a kindred spirit in me, at least if I believed Kate. Her recalcitrant nature forced me to concentrate, to empty my mind and focus only on her and on what the mission was. She brought me peace. I loved being around her.

And then there were the dogs.

On Taxore we have few animals that could be seen as a similar kind of pet, and nothing like dogs.

The fierce loyalty and protective nature of the canines in the camp never ceased to amaze me.

I had my preferences.

The small intense terriers were not my favourites. Sure, they were great at killing rodents, along with the feral cats, but I found their nervous nature and high yelps irritating.

My favourites were the big dogs. A mix of Mastiffs, Rottweilers and Kangals, they were massive and ferocious animals. Fierce in their protection of their pack, and as it turned out, us.

Kate was the quintessential pet lover. She'd grown up with them on her family's farm before she left for the city. Her job as a waitress with its irregular hours meant that she couldn't have a pet herself, and she'd dearly missed their companionship. In the compound she was known for her compassion towards everything that lived and regularly nursed wounded or young animals back to health, taking pleasure in the interactions with them. Throughout the months we'd been there, she'd never actually adopted one.

Not until we came across a scene we'd never expected so close to our camp.

On one of our firewood gathering escapades, we tracked halfway up the heavily wooded mountains five kilometres from our camp. Kate, Jonah, Nasheed, Caleb and I had both Monarch and Kayleigh with us to haul back whatever fallen wood we found. The weather had taken an unexpected turn for the worst in early spring and the ten-centimetre-deep snow hindered our progress. The horses had less of an issue, their broad hoofs almost acting as snowshoes as they plodded onwards, perfectly happy in their thick winter coats. For us it was much less of a fun outing in the crisp mountain air. My breath turned to white steam as soon as it left my mouth, the condense freezing on my moustache and beard.

Kate was the only one of us who seemed oblivious to the bad weather. Her perpetual good mood was infectious, and I found myself smiling at the constant conversation she kept up with Monarch. He was definitely listening to her, his ears facing the chatter and every now and then he rubbed his head against her shoulder.

I was walking behind them with Kayleigh when the mare suddenly pulled hard on the reins. I tried to calm the horse and noticed Monarch was acting out in the same manner. There was something very wrong. Their eyes were open to the max, the whites around them showing, Kayleigh's ears twitched from side to side and her nostrils flared, searching for what had spooked her. The snow flew up under Monarch's hoof as he stamped on the ground.

We coaxed the horses back fifty metres the way we'd come, and they calmed.

'What the hell happened?' Jonah whispered.

'Something spooked them. Something big.'

The horses weren't easily frightened, especially the stallion. Whatever they sensed was something we had to investigate.

Jonah, Nasheed, and I left them with Kate and Caleb and retraced our footsteps back to the spot where they became alarmed. We crouched down to minimise our silhouettes, even though that seemed redundant to me at that time as we'd just been there and spread out to search for whatever we could find. I went left, Nasheed continued straight on, and Jonah pushed on through the brush on the right side of the path we'd been following.

The shrubs were thick on my side, but brittle in the cold winter air. I was able to push through them without too much effort. The fir trees around me became denser and the canopy shut over my head, blocking out the light. My progress was hampered, and I was soon confronted with an impenetrable wall of tree trunks and brambles.

I turned to walk back when I heard a shrill whistle. It was Nasheed. The signal we'd agreed on if we found anything. I hurried back to the track.

Jonah stood there, alerted by the sound as I was, and we made our way forward down the track to where Nasheed stood.

He pointed to a clearing on the right side of the track, slightly lower on the mountain side. We pushed through the brush and were confronted with a scene right out of a horror movie that froze my blood.

I counted two bodies, one human and one Taxorian, easily identified by his purple blood. Next to the human I saw several dead dogs, most of them big Rottweilers and

Mastiffs. All were riddled with still smoking wounds I recognised as the aftermath of Taxorian weapons.

We were instantly cautious. A Taxorian this close to our compound was unsettling. What was he doing here? And who was the human?

Jonah walked to him, pulled off his glove and held his fingers to the downed man's throat, searching for a pulse. He shook his head. He was gone. The alien was clearly dead, his throat ripped out. The skin ragged and raw.

'Oh, my god.'

I turned to see Kate's shocked face. Her hand was up in front of her mouth and her eyes were opened wide at the scene in front of her. Shit. She should have stayed with the horses.

I went towards her and tried to turn her around, but she resisted.

'Are they both dead?' she whispered.

'Yes.'

'What happened?'

'Looks like he was surprised by the alien,' Jonah answered.

She turned her head from one side to the other, taking in the scene.

'Is he dead?' She nodded towards the alien.

'Very,' Nasheed commented. 'Looks like one of the dogs got him.

She took it well, and I had to remind myself this was regrettably not the first dead body Kate had seen since I came into her life. As usual, she was hypersensitive to my moods, and she squeezed my arm in support.

'Do we know the human?' she asked.

Nasheed shook his head. 'He doesn't look familiar.'

'We can't leave him here,' Kate commented. 'I'll get the horses.'

She returned minutes later with Caleb and the two skittish horses. Under constant reassurance by Kate, they were persuaded to come into the clearing and the man was hoisted up over Monarch's back.

We were about to leave when Kate stopped in her tracks, listening attentively.

She turned, her head moving from side to side to determine where the sound had come from.

I wanted to urge her to leave, we had no idea if the grunt had been alone. Whether there were more enemies around. A hasty departure seemed like the best course of action. But she was oblivious and shook my hand off her arm. Kate moved to the right, between the dead grunt and one of the dogs. She concentrated and stopped in front of what looked like yet another canine.

'Come on, Kate. We need to leave,' I tried.

She waved me away and walked closer to what she'd found. The animal stirred. A low growl reverberated in the silence of the clearing.

Kayleigh snorted but stayed stationary. I gave the reins to Nasheed and walked over to where Kate stood.

My gaze was pulled to a black dog lying on its side. It was big, that much was clear. But what breed it was, escaped me. To be honest it was difficult to see through the purple and red blood and gore that coated the animal's fur. I was pulled to the eyes. They were black. Jet black. And they followed my advance with what could only be called malevolence. He was badly wounded, but definitely not throwing in any kind of towel.

My attention was distracted when Kate knelt down, a

step from the wounded animal. The growl broke though the silence again.

'Careful,' I said, anxious for her.

'It's ok.'

I very much doubted that, but she just moved closer to the dog.

He followed her closely with his eyes, the lips twitching and showing a glimpse of long white incisors and bloody saliva. I thought it was his, but the purple sheen belied that.

She placed her hand softly on the dog's side and held it there despite the low growl that chilled me.

'It's ok,' she addressed him softly, 'It's ok.'

I held my breath, my body tense and ready to jump in and pull her away should the animal try to bite.

I shouldn't have worried. Her calming voice and soft strokes seemed to have a sedating effect on the dog, though he continued to watch her attentively. The growl subsided and his erratic breaths became deeper and more regular.

'We have to leave,' I tried softly.

'Yes,' she answered. And then added what I was dreading. 'We'll take him with us.'

'The most humane thing to do would be to end his suffering,' Jonah offered and was rewarded with a new deep growl and a castigating glare from my lover.

'No,' Kate exclaimed. 'I can heal him. And by the look of what happened here, he deserves our help.'

She always did that. Put her finger on the one thing that meant we couldn't disagree. Whatever had happened, the dog had killed the grunt. That much was clear.

I looked at the animal.

It was big, most likely heavy, and covered in blood. How the hell were we going to bring it back? Never mind alive.

'Kayleigh will carry him,' Kate announced.

I raised my eyebrows.

'She will,' she assured me as she continued to stroke the dog.

I looked at the animal. It was difficult to see what the actual damage was. He was shot in the upper chest, that much was clear, but whether he had any additional wounds was something I couldn't make out. He was at the least, incapacitated.

'Can you pick him up?' Kate asked.

'I'm not sure he'll let me,' I answered.

'You might want to muzzle him,' Jonah suggested.

I turned to look at him. 'And how do you want me to achieve that without losing my hand?'

He laughed. 'Carefully.'

Yeah, great help.

Kate opened her coat and unbuckled her belt. She pulled it out of the jeans loops and held it up to the dog's mouth. The animal pulled his lips up and growled deeply.

'It's ok,' she crooned. 'It's just for a while. I won't make it too tight.'

Hell yes, I thought, make it really tight, but kept my ideas to myself.

'Be careful,' Jonah suggested redundantly.

Kate ignored him and continued to reassure the dog. It finally calmed down and she was able to slip a loop over its nose, effectively closing the big maw. It stiffened as she pulled it tighter, so she stopped again.

I glanced at Nasheed and Caleb, their eyes flitted from side to side, and they constantly shifted their weight, uncomfortable with this development. We should be leaving. This was no place to dally. The grunt would no doubt already be reported missing by the handlers, the vital signs now showing up as terminated. They might send someone else to investigate. We wanted to be far gone by then.

Nasheed had cleared away any signs of the dead human and to all intents and purposes it looked as though the grunt had been attacked by a pack of feral dogs that had ultimately killed him. We wanted that impression to stick. The ground was thankfully hard and devoid of snow, and our boots and the horses hooves hadn't made any lasting impressions that could identify us.

The dog was quiet again and Kate indicated I come closer.

'Let him smell your hand,' she said.

Not exactly what I wanted to do, but I understood the reasoning.

The dogs nostrils flared, and the low growl reappeared, but he relented quickly. I stroked the side of his face, and he relaxed further.

I took off my coat and laid it over the dog, then pushed my hands under the dog's body at the height of his hips and just under the shoulder. He yelped in pain. I stopped and let him adjust.

'We have to go,' Jonah urged again, his tone short and compelling. 'Now.'

I gently picked up the animal and walked two steps towards Kayleigh. She eyed me suspiciously, her nostrils flared, and her ears turned flat in her neck, clearly not happy with what she assumed was going to happen.

Kate walked up to her and softly talked to the big mare. One ear swivelled towards her, the other stayed stubbornly facing backwards on her neck. I brought the dog closer. The smell of the blood obviously spooked the mare, but Kate's and my soft words held her flight reaction at bay.

'You should ride her,' Kate suggested. 'That will make her feel better.'

I wasn't sure about that, but it was worth a try. I was the only one she would let on her back. I carefully handed the dog over to Jonah and mounted Kayleigh. She jittered slightly but calmed quickly when the big man handed the dog up to me and I laid him over the horses harness in front of me. I patted the side of her neck, and she arched back to look at me and the strange object bundled in my jacket on her back.

She gave me a disapproving look that told me I owed her big time, then decided it would be acceptable, for now.

We made our way back to the compound in a round-about way. There was a balance to be struck between speed to take care of the dog and the assurance that we wouldn't be followed. Jonah and Nasheed stayed back two kilometres out, to ensure extra protection if needed.

Kate, Caleb and I, with the two horses and their strange loads, moved past the sentries and up to the caves that formed the backbone of our compound.

Kate held on to the dog while I dismounted, then I delicately lowered him from Kayleigh's back into my arms again. A short yelp indicated he was still alive, and we hurried into the cave Kate and I shared.

Hours later, after Kate had bathed the dog and tended to his wounds, we let him recover in front of the small fire at the back of the room. He slept soundly, his breathing deep and regular, helped by the pain killer and antibiotics we'd administered.

'How's he doing?' Jonah asked as he poked his head around the make-shift door.

'He'll be ok,' Kate answered. 'The shot missed the vital

organs, though he did lose a lot of blood and has some bad burns. There were no other wounds.'

The big man nodded and left us.

'Seems we have a dog,' I said.

Kate just smiled.

'What should we call him?' she asked.

I shrugged. 'What breed is he?'

'A bit of everything,' she answered. 'He's a mongrel. A mutt.'

'Mutt then?'

She smiled broadly.

Our new family member had a name.

Chapter Eleven

'I'm sorry I took your life away,' I started out of the blue.

Kate lifted her head from my chest and looked at me. 'Where did that come from?' she asked with humour in her tone.

We were lying in bed in the aftermath of soft and passionate lovemaking. As usual, we were both comfortable in the silence that usually followed our trysts. The deep darkness of our underground bedroom was broken only by the small candle standing in a glass container on the small crate doubling as a table opposite the bed. It shone a soft light on the rough cave walls.

I saw her lips were pulled up in mirth.

'I'm the reason you're not able to live your life as you want to,' I continued. My guilt once again spoiling the moment.

'I am living my ideal life,' she answered me as she stroked my cheek softly with her hand. 'This is exactly where I want to be. Here with you.'

'But you're hiding,' I continued. 'Your life is constantly in danger. We live in a cave, for goodness sake.'

She laughed, the sound full and warm, reverberating off the walls.

'I'm with you.' She placed her finger on my lips silencing me. 'And I love it here. So, we don't have all the creature comforts. So what? We have each other. We're safer than we would be in any city or town at the moment. I love the outdoors, and I love this family we have.'

'But I'm the reason why you're not safe. Why none of us are. It's my family that's doing this to the world.' I just wouldn't let it go.

'Yes. And that's why you're fighting them. I'm so proud of you, Gabriel. You chose the right path, not the easy one. You fight for us and for freedom.'

'If I hadn't been here nothing like this would have happened.' I was adamant in my self-pity.

'Even you don't believe that,' she answered with a chuckle, planting my feet squarely back on the ground. 'Your father has raided this dimension for centuries; this is a continuation of what already was. Whatever he needs all the labour for now would have happened anyway. You know that, why do you continue to torture yourself? You are not him, Gabe. Not even close.'

We'd had these discussions several times. My guilt overwhelmed every good moment I experienced. There was something in me that urged me to sabotage anything positive that happened to me.

'You have to let yourself be happy, my love.' As usual she read my mind. 'This is not your doing. And blaming yourself and knocking yourself down will not solve a thing. It will only make it more difficult for you.'

'And you.' I had to get my words in.

'And us.'

That shut me up. Kate had a gift for including anyone in the equation. Making them feel supported, no longer alone. I'd been on my own—given that it was in company, but still lonely—for so long I pushed everyone away. She wouldn't let me. I was truly and completely connected to her, and she refused to be intimidated by my bad moods or petty self-doubt. She was there to stay.

'That first day,' she continued. 'When you walked into the diner, my life changed. I'd convinced myself I was happy with a mediocre existence. I didn't need any more than a steady job, a house with a white picket fence and a few good friends. Boy, was I wrong.' She laughed at the memory.

'I never did that, you know. Take someone home with me. And definitely not someone I'd only just met.' She stroked my cheek.

'But I felt it was different. Meant to be. And it changed my life. You did. I opened my eyes and saw how uninspired my existence was. How much I'd compromised for a dream I didn't really want. Thank you for that. Without that one moment, I would still be only surviving, not living.'

A deep warmth started in my hearts.

'I watched the door every day, hoping you would be there. And when you finally came, I knew I would never let you go. No matter what.'

Her kiss was warm and full of the love I felt. 'Will you get it in that stubborn head of yours that I'm not going anywhere. I belong with you. You belong with me. There is no debate. This is the only thing that matters. And it brings me a joy I never thought I'd experience. So let yourself bathe in what we have, Gabe. Allow happiness in your life.

It doesn't have to be anguish and pain anymore. This is enough for me. Let it be the same for you.'

I kissed her passionately. The warmth rising from deep inside me fuelled by her words. Pin pricks started at the back of my eyes when the glow reached my face. I held on to her, basking in these emotions I felt.

I berated myself for doubting our relationship. For doubting her. And once again thanked my lucky stars that she was here, with me.

'I love you,' I murmured into her hair. 'I love you more than life itself.'

She squeezed me tightly. 'And I love you.'

'So, you're stuck with me,' I concluded.

I felt her laughter. 'Good.'

'Besides,' she answered. 'We're parents now. We have to stay together for the family.'

My laugher felt good, and all the tension flowed out of me and dissipated into thin air.

'Mutt?' I asked redundantly.

'Mutt,' she answered.

I heard a soft whimper of approval from the other side of the cave. Seems someone else had been listening in on our conversation.

Chapter Twelve

Mutt was a hand full.

He proved very resilient and improved quickly. Once he'd been fed regularly and administered the antibiotics—to the utter discontent of our medical personnel who wanted to reserve the medicine for humans—he healed in leaps and bounds.

Mutt's strength returned, and with it his independent nature. He was obviously not used to being indoors with people, and after the first two weeks resisted our attempts to keep him stationary.

'He's feral,' Sly commented after a particularly close call where he'd almost been bitten. 'Dangerous. You can't keep him here.'

'He'll be alright,' Kate insisted. 'I'll train him.'

'Doesn't look like the trainable type,' Jonah added his ten cents.

'He's just not used to so many people around him, he'll be ok.'

I hoped Kate was right. The dog was growing on me.

He followed us wherever we went. A silent shadow that scared away anyone who happened to be in our walking direction. He didn't really do anything specific; he was just there. His gaze was so intense even the most courageous man held his distance. Yet to us he was friendly. Well to me he was that, he was devoted to Kate. I put that down to the fact that she'd saved him. He'd reluctantly let her into his life and now he was smitten. Now where had I seen that before?

His strength and health improved every day, and he slowly started to find his place in the compound. People got used to him. Some—Aaliyah and a few of the children—even made friends with him and he turned out to be gentle with them. Though his moods could switch on a dime, going from gentle giant to hellhound in an instant, as one of the group found out.

No one pushed this dog around, or by extension, his family.

The other dogs in the compound were wary of him to start with. Even though he was wounded, the power he exhumed caused them to keep their distance. The pack was a hierarchy, and the leader was unsure what to do with this big menacing new recruit. Mutt stayed at a distance, not exactly ignoring them, but not joining in any of the pack mentality either.

The six-dog pack was led by a big Rottweiler. He was an imposing canine who kept the rest of them well in check. His owners—if you could call them that—left him to his own devices most of the time.

Every time we passed him with Mutt you could see the hackles on the alpha rise, and he uttered deep barks. Mutt ignored him. I think that made the dog even more insecure and angry. He was used to his dominance over the compound canines and this black mutt wouldn't even acknowledge him or respond to his challenges.

It was bound to come to a confrontation, and it did one afternoon when Kate and I were out foraging in the forest, Mutt as usual shadowing us the whole time.

We walked back to the compound, our backpacks full, and were stopped by the pack lined up across the path. The alpha was one step in front of the rest and observed us menacingly. Mutt was behind Kate and slowly pushed past her to take up position in front of us. He sat on his haunches, completely unimpressed by the dogs as his hard gaze travelled from one to another.

I saw a few waver. The Rotti of course, didn't.

Ok, this was the showdown. There was no escaping a fight. The leader had challenged Mutt countless times only to be disregarded.

Kate was about to intervene, but I took her arm. 'This has to happen, Kate. Let him.'

She stepped back to her previous position and we stood absolutely still.

Mutt yawned, probably the ultimate insult, and slowly stood up. The alpha barked loudly, renewing his challenge. A deep thundering growl started in Mutt's chest, and he took his first steps towards the pack. Three of the dogs faltered and stepped back. This was the leader's fight.

I'd never seen a dog fight like this before. In my visits to Earth, I'd once been an observer to an organised match between fighting dogs but had left the revolting scene in disgust. This was nothing like that. Here there was no one edging them on. It was just plain and simple natural behaviour. A new dog had come into the pack's territory and the hierarchy had to be decided.

They clashed like a train wreck, the sound of two

heavily muscled dogs colliding echoing in the forest. The alpha growled hard and snapped at Mutt, who stayed silent and proceeded to push his opponent backwards. The Rottweiler was big, but Mutt had almost a hundred pounds on him and combine that with a bone crushing bite force and it was clear who the winner would be.

Within minutes, Mutt had his opponent on the floor and the dog's throat in his massive jaws. Now it was up to the Rotti. Would he concede? Or would Mutt rip his neck open? Thankfully the Rottweiler stopped struggling and surrendered to Mutt's greater strength. His body became flaccid, and we all waited for what the winner would do. Seconds went by that felt like hours until Mutt finally let go of the other dog's throat and carefully, on stiff and poised legs, stepped back. The loser stayed where he was, not daring to move. Mutt sat down and casually looked at the rest of the pack. One by one they cowered.

Seems the pack had a new alpha.

Chapter Thirteen

'That thing is evil incarnate.'

'Don't be stupid. It's just a dog.'

'It's more dangerous than a pack of wolves.'

'You're overdoing it.'

The recurring discussions with Steve and some others were starting to bore me. They had it in for Mutt. Sure, he was a big dog, and he didn't like most people. And yes, he would let you know. He'd already bitten one person who tried to kick him, but that was well deserved in my books. Mutt didn't take any shit. Good for him.

I took a good look at our new family member.

Weighing in at more than two hundred pounds he was an impressive animal. His deep-black, thick coat made him look even bigger than his massive, muscled frame. He dwarfed Kate with his big body and powerful head. The depth of his black eyes seemed infinite. Midnight black, a window to hell. The way he observed you occasionally made even me feel uncomfortable. It wasn't so much malevolence as a deep kind of intellect that touched your soul with a cold spike. That combined with the strength and enormous white fangs was profound.

I understood people's trepidation.

But I saw the other side of him.

How gentle he was with Kate. He was acutely aware of his size and strength and never pushed her too hard, or pulled, or growled. With Kate his eyes turned soft and friendly, making me wonder who he'd loved before, who he saw in my partner. And what had happened to him to make him the dog he was today. He was the same with small children which convinced me he'd been a family dog at some point.

He tolerated me, liked me a bit even if he had a strange way of showing it. But he adored Kate. She turned the terror of the compound into a love-struck puppy every time she gave him a tummy rub. Something no one else would even attempt unless they had a very serious death wish.

The monster grew on me. A lot. I'd never had a dog before. We don't have pets on Taxore. There are very few animals anyway and what there are, are completely unsuitable to live with people. We'd killed most of our creatures hundreds of years ago and what was left stayed as far from inhabited places as possible.

In my dealings on Earth, I hadn't stayed for extended periods of time, always returning home every few weeks. Bonding with anything here hadn't been an option. To be honest, I'd never shown any inclination to try. There was a lot I'd learned in the past two years. Love was one of them, and not just for people.

When Mutt walked past the other dogs, they all fell silent. That much power exhumed from the animal.

I must admit I was proud of him. I loved the way he managed to dominate without doing anything. Just his presence was enough. And Kate, well she was blissfully unaware of the impact he made on the compound. She insisted he was a friendly, big, lug. Well, everyone agreed with the big part. They looked at her with utter disbelief about the rest.

I remembered the first time someone in the compound had tried to get rid of him.

'We have been asked to take care of it,' Alex announced, his nerves barely under control.

'What do you mean?' Kate asked.

'Shoot it.'

'Hell no.' I joined in the confrontation.

Kate was aghast. The shock clear in her face. Mutt immediately responded and sat between her and Alex, who cautiously took a step back.

'That's what we mean,' he said.

'What?' Jonah asked.

Alex waved his hand in the air in the general direction of Kate and Mutt causing the dog to emit a deep and threatening rumble. 'Exactly that.'

Kate rubbed Mutt's head, and he calmed, though only in sound. The hostility in his posture and black eyes remained.

'Nothing wrong with that,' Jonah beat me to an answer. 'The dog is just protecting its owner. That's what dogs do.'

'But he bit Stan,' Alex wouldn't give up. He'd been tasked with a mission.

Good luck with that.

'Stan tried to kick him. That's what you get. Clearly self-defence,' the big man explained.

'He almost bit his leg off!'

'Well, maybe Stan will be more careful around animals now.' Jonah was as calm as I'd ever seen him. I was surprised he stood up for Mutt, I'd never seen him with any of the dogs.

There was an edge to the big man's words. 'I don't condone cruelty to animals, Stan got what he deserved. No reason to take this any further as far as I'm concerned.' He looked at me, I shrugged my agreement and Kate just smiled, still rubbing Mutt's head.

Alex glanced from Mutt to Jonah and back again, I could imagine he was weighing which one would be the biggest threat. Probably both. He came to the right conclusion, nodded, and retreated, his eyes still on Mutt.

'What do you think he is anyway?' Jonah asked pointing to Mutt.

'A bit of everything,' Kate answered. 'Probably mostly mastiff and Newfoundlander, or maybe Sint Bernard.'

'And everything that escaped hell on the way,' Jonah joked.

We joined him in laughter.

Mutt just observed. Though I detected a sliver of amusement there.

Chapter Fourteen

We knew it was dangerous to let people into our group, but, if we wanted to really do damage we had to at least in part, join forces with other resistance groups or individuals.

The main issue was how to know whether the intended allies were genuine or maybe infiltrated by the invaders and sent underground to expose our teams.

Ebs helped where she could with screening, but many of the databases she'd always tapped into were compromised or gone. The invaders had targeted the data centres as one of their first goals to disrupt human civilisation. It had worked. Only the newly reinstated Establishment-controlled data was made available, and Ebs was forced to go to the dark web, which was potentially even more dangerous and less reliable. Criminals had been quick to access new opportunities in the changed world. Delivering wanted humans was lucrative, and they had no qualms about selling out their own kind. Their loyalty was awarded to the highest bidder.

So we were balancing risk with need and let some people join us. Mainly fighters.

Ebony, in her alter ego, found like-minded humans who attempted to do their part in the resistance to what was quickly becoming the new way of life on Earth.

There were stages in the initiation.

First, we identified specific humans. Most of which were underground somewhere trying to find security and a group to team up with.

Ebony screened them where possible. If no data was available, then a small committee assessed the potential danger through interviews and stress tests. The new recruits were restricted in what they were party to, everything was on a need-to-know basis.

Then they were directed to a mid-way location. From there we mounted small joint missions. Each of which was a test. A further assessment weeded out those people who were allowed to join. Others were helped on their way and sometimes directed to other resistance groups.

During their probationary period in the alternative location, we instructed them on how to fight the invaders. We shared what we could on the strengths and weaknesses in the hope that it would give them an edge.

One group in particular caused a large debate: Biker Veterans. They had the military expertise we wanted, but not the mentality to take orders or to keep their restraint.

In the end we parted ways. The differences too large, even with Caleb's help and his contacts. Only two stayed. Phil and Andy. Two of Caleb's old friends.

Chapter Fifteen

We became complacent in our perceived security and paid a hefty price.

The caves had been our homes for more than five months, and we'd settled into an uneventful and even mildly pleasant routine, only broken by our infrequent raids on the invaders. The issue with the collars halted our attempts to free prisoners and we had to sit back and wait for Ebony to come up with some kind of jamming device.

'We're close,' she informed us in the last call. 'What we've developed now jams most of the frequencies but not all of them. So, it needs more tweaking.'

We didn't dare chance it. Our goodwill was at an all-time low anyway. The outside world was slowly coming around to Cal-Tan's mentality and they accepted the supposed temporary loss of their sons and daughters in exchange for what they thought was peace. Some even became our enemies.

The resistance had to contend not only with the invaders but also humans actively searching for them.

Man-Kayl enhanced this by offering a "get out of jail free" card. A family could gain freedom for their son or daughter by basically betraying the resistance. This was bigger than it seemed. They not only sold out the one group of people who were fighting to keep their kin on earth, their treachery condemned the whole human race. It was another way my father kept a strong hold on the dimension. He let the humans do the work.

No one knew who to trust. It was a witch hunt as never seen before in the history of the planet. Desperate parents or partners ratted out anyone they could in the false hope their loved ones would be spared deportation. If they didn't know any secrets, they invented some. Anything to ensure the safety of their kin.

Though I understood the reasoning, it only resulted in a paranoid world with a much stronger hold by the invaders. Fear makes for a powerful prison. It keeps people in line. And now it had expanded from only the invaders to everyone around.

And still they kept silent.

Still my father's tactics worked, as he knew they would.

The desperate families would be bad enough, but the worst threat were the bounty hunters. In addition to the pardons, Man-Kayl had promised large sums of money to anyone who would bring in resistance fighters, dead or alive. The extensive list of people who were affiliated with the resistance was available online and plastered everywhere. If possible, there were photos, otherwise only descriptions which made it worse. Gangs of "head-hunters" roamed the country, eagerly searching for anyone they could pass off as a resistance fighter. As usual, some humans had found a way to turn the whole invasion into personal gain, no matter that it was at the detriment of their brother man. Next to fear, greed was a trait my father could count on and use to his advantage.

Man-Kayl elevated the bounty hunters to stardom, regularly praising them in the streams all stations had to air. There was even a reality show that followed some of the more famous ones.

Thousands of innocent people were imprisoned. Most disappeared, never to be seen again.

We kept our heads low, like most of the resistance. Survival was most important now. That and waiting for our opening where we could make a difference. It was a chore, with enemies all around, but the mountains and forests hid us well.

At least that's what we thought.

One of the only occasions people would leave our camp was to foray for food in the woods. Small parties would go out to hunt or to gather edible items. Though we were fugal, supplies were now low and sometimes we went hungry. The forest was our main larder, we didn't dare go into any of the towns on the outskirts of the vast forest. Any strangers were viewed with the utmost suspicion and often never made it back to their homes.

Summer had slowly traversed into Autumn in the mountains and supplied us with bountiful food. Wild berries, nuts, herbs, root vegetables, everything we could need. The ample wildlife brought us meat, and the rivers fish. This was the time to stock up on reserves for the coming winter and we went out into the forests for longer and more frequent forays.

I was part of a hunting party in search of elk or moose. The meat would be dried and stored in some of the dryer caves. The hides would be tanned and provide us with additional warmth. Jonah, Aaliyah and I were joined by two seasoned trackers as we set off for a four-day hike in search of at minimum two animals. We tried to hunt at least a day's distance from the compound just in case there were any nosey humans around. I threw the self-made saddle bags over Kayleigh's back, packed the nets we would use to contain the meat, kissed Kate goodbye, and we headed off to the north.

Our trip was initially uneventful, On the second day we found and harvested a magnificent elk. After butchering the animal and packing everything we could on Kayleigh and in our own packs, we decided this was enough meat. The animal had been large, so we decided to go back to the compound first and then maybe later go for a second hunt later in the week.

We set off back home again in the early morning of the third day. The crisp air already hinting at what would be a cold winter.

Large swaths of golden aspen softly waved in the slight breeze. Late summer flowers mingled with the autumn colours and created a magnificent scenery. We followed a small stream back the way we'd come, always on the lookout for potential enemies, both animal and humanoid. The deepness of the forest and the difficult terrain convinced us there would be few people around. Mutt was with us, along with another of the dogs and we trusted they would alert us to any dangers.

Sure enough. We barely avoided a run in with a young male grizzly bear who had probably picked up Kayleigh's scent along with the elk meat. The combination of us and the dogs shied him away from a confrontation. Good choice, bear meat and fur were also something we could use. Only the hefty load the horse already had to carry deterred us from shooting the young animal.

We stopped at a stream close to midday to rest and eat, secure in the knowledge that we were about three hour's hike from our destination. The sun was still warm and pleasant as we refilled our water containers in the stream.

The soft calls of the forest were broken by an incessant buzzing from our cell phone. I looked at Jonah, concern already on my face. This was the distress call. Only to be used if something really bad had happened at the compound.

Jonah pulled his vibrating phone from his pocket and opened the text application.

Aaliyah, the others and I waited with bated breath. Its wouldn't be good news. None of it. Not if they used the distress call.

Jonah's features hardened and paled at the same time. The knuckles on the hand holding the phone tensed and he inadvertently reached for his axe with the other one.

It was bad. Very bad.

'What is it?' Aaliyah asked.

'There's been an attack,' the big man answered.

'On the compound?'

'On a foraging party.'

He looked up at me intensely, sending shivers up my spine. A large block of concrete dropped in my gut, and I felt my legs turn to jelly as I recalled another foraging party.

'Kate.' It wasn't a question. She'd been so excited to go into the forest with a small team to harvest wild potatoes and medicinal herbs when I left. That was one of the reasons she hadn't accompanied us. That and she hated hunting.

Jonah refrained from comments. Aaliyah pulled the phone out of his hand and read the message. She too paled as she glanced my way.

'What?' I shouted, my voice breaking. 'What happened? Is she safe?'

Slowly Aaliyah shook her head.

The bottom dropped out of my life, and I felt myself crumble to the forest floor. One of the trackers caught me and gently lowered me to a sitting position on the bed of pine needles.

No, that was impossible. Not Kate. It couldn't be. My mind shut itself off. I couldn't take it. It had to be a lie. Not Kate.

'There was an attack on the foraging party,' Aaliyah softly explained, but I wasn't listening. The only words I wanted to hear was that it wasn't true. That there had been a mistake.

'Bounty hunters,' Jonah added, his voice barely a whisper. 'There were five of them. They killed three of the party, wounded two more before they could be overpowered.'

'But there's always security,' I stammered. 'The foray's always have guards.'

'Yes, they do, and they were the ones who killed the bounty hunters.' The big man looked broken.

'But not before they killed some of ours,' Aaliyah added softly.

'But Kate?' I could hardly speak.

Aaliyah nodded.

I looked at Jonah, reluctant to believe what she was telling me. He nodded too.

Mutt came up to me and laid his head on my lap, acutely aware of my pain. My hand automatically stroked his fur as he whimpered. He knew. At least he knew something was very, very wrong.

I jumped up and raced to Kayleigh, pulling at the ties that held the load on her saddle.

'We need to get back, now.' I pushed at the meat to get it off her so I could ride her back to the compound. So that I could get there quicker.

Jonah placed his hand on my shoulder. 'It won't help, Gabriel.'

'She's not dead. She can't be, it's a mistake,' I shouted and shrugged his hand off me. 'I must get there. I have to save her!'

'She's gone, Gabe.' His words cut me deeply and I turned to strike him. He easily caught my fist and pulled me towards him, his arms around me in a massive bear hug. I fought against his hold, beating him with my fists and screaming that I had to leave, to no avail. He held on. My screams became sobs, and all restraint fled my body as I let the emotions take over. My hands dropped to my side and my shoulders slumped into his chest. He held on while I wept, the realisation setting in that they would not lie to me, that she was gone.

We stood there for what seemed to me like an hour but was probably no more than a few minutes.

My body stopped its shaking and slowly Jonah let go, holding me at arm's length to make sure I didn't fall.

'We have to go, that's true,' the big man carefully suggested. 'But not in a mad dash. There are bounty hunters in the forest. We have no way of knowing whether that was the only group, or whether they got them all. We must be careful, Gabe. We can't lose anyone else.'

I nodded forlornly. What else could I do? I was broken. Devastated. Still in denial.

Kayleigh gently rubbed her nose against my arm and neighed softly, aware something was wrong. I couldn't acknowledge her, or anyone else for that matter. My body hardly reacted to my own commands. Not that I had any. My mind was in turmoil, the only recurring thought that it was my fault.

'I should have left Mutt with her,' I whispered. 'He would have alerted them.'

'It's not your fault, Gabe,' Allah tried.

'Of course it is.' I answered. 'I shouldn't have left her. I should have been there.'

There was nothing they could say that would make any difference, so they let me continue my guilty ranting. It wouldn't have helped. I was so lost in my pain that nothing could pull me out, not even their love.

Just when I'd finally opened my heart to love, it came crashing down around me.

Chapter Sixteen

By the time we got back to the camp my pain had morphed into a dangerous fury.

With every step on the return trip my thoughts became darker, more violent. I wanted, no needed, someone to hurt as much as I did. It wouldn't help, part of me knew that, but I wasn't listening to reason. That had gone out the window together with my love and any delusions of a future. I didn't care about that anymore, only about revenge.

'Where is she?' I asked, barely able to formulate the words. My throat was constricted with equal amounts of pain and anger.

'In the caves at the back, they all are,' Sly answered.

I nodded; it was the only way I could acknowledge him without lashing out.

I turned to the entrance of the caves. The big hole in the mountain wall that had felt warm and inviting just days ago now resembled the open maw of a terrible creature. The dark interior, only lit by occasional oil lamps and candles did nothing to alleviate the cold dread that gripped my spine. I forced one foot in front of the other and slowly made my way to the entrance. The crowd of people, almost all the inhabitants of our camp, parted in front of me, allowing me to progress. Just inside the threshold a tall man stepped out to bar the way.

'The dog can't go in,' John announced.

I looked up at him, then slowly at Mutt who stood next to me, the bristles on his back raised as he astutely read my demeanour. I side-stepped and pushed past John, not willing to say a word. He initially hesitated then stepped back in front of me. I stopped again. Mutt growled deeply beside me. John was clearly unnerved but reluctant to concede.

'Let them in,' Sly's voice carried over the silence.

John hesitantly stepped back and Mutt and I continued our slow and painful walk to the back of the caves.

It was cool there. Cold even. The best place to store food, and in this case dead bodies. My mind had gone into survival mode and clinically—even coldly—analysed everything as though it were a scientific experiment.

We trudged on. The distance wasn't much, but it felt like a marathon to me. My mind pushed my body every hard-won centimetre, emotions screaming at me to turn around and leave. Go away, no matter where to, as long as I could leave this nightmare, then maybe it wouldn't have happened.

The walls closed in on me, pushing me to acknowledge the voice in my head. I felt as if I should duck, even though the ceiling was still more than a metre over my head. The soft whimper beside me alerted me we were near. Mutt had picked up her scent, but it was wrong. He knew. I felt him leave my side as he quickened his pace and trotted into the left-hand cave at the rear junction. The whimpers intensified into soft barks when he found her.

I stood on the threshold, my feet refusing to take another step. Cold shivers ran down my spine that had nothing to do with the temperature. I felt drops of sweat on the back of my neck and I was powerless to halt the trembles that racked my body.

She looked peaceful, serene even in the soft candlelight. As though asleep.

Kate lay on a stretcher bed, next to the other two fatalities, another woman and a teenager. Their identity didn't register with me, my only focus on the other half of my hearts, the one person who had made me feel whole in my long life. Her pale features were calm, not at all what I'd expected. I'd thought she would seem broken, clearly deceased, but initially she just looked like she had every morning when I woke up. My eyes strayed from her face to the stained blanket that covered her from her neck to her feet. Big blackish red stains covered the area of her chest bringing home the realisation that she had sustained heavy fire. Whatever had killed her struck her there. In the chest, in her heart.

A deep intense howl pulled me out of my stupor. Mutt raised his snout and let of a wail that resonated throughout the caves and inside my mind and hearts. I wanted to scream with him. Let it out, but I was mute.

Bridging the distance, I sank to my knees beside the cot and gently stroked her face.

My hand gripped the blanket at her neck.

'You don't want to do that, Gabriel.' The voice behind me said. Sly had followed me into the cave, along with Jonah and Aaliyah.

'Don't presume to know what I want,' I bit back. Part of me knew he was right, and that he was looking out for me, but I was determined to see. I had to be sure. How else would I believe?

I lifted the cover and pulled it back, exposing the terrible damage that had been done. A shotgun blast had ripped open the flesh exposing shattered bone and muscle beneath. There were gaping holes where her heart should be. Entry wounds from multiple sides.

I lowered the blanket again.

There was no doubt. She was gone. No-one, not even my kind, could survive the damage that had been done to her. A door closed on my heart and a voice at the back of my head whispered that someone would pay for this.

It gained in volume and pulled my features into a hard mask. Someone would pay.

Mutt ceased his howl and laid his head on her shoulder, his snout close to her face.

'Gabriel,' Sly addressed me, his hand on my shoulder. 'I'm so sorry.'

I looked at his hand, then slowly lifted my face until I looked him squarely in the eye. Sly was not one to be easily intimidated, but what he saw in my features, in my eyes, momentarily stopped his breathing. He blinked and cocked his head.

'It shouldn't have happened.' My voice was accusatory to the extreme. He didn't flinch, but it certainly registered and he removed his hand.

'Someone will pay,' I added.

'They already have,' he answered. 'They're all dead.'

I pushed myself up from the floor. 'Bring me to them.'

Sly glanced at Jonah, who nodded almost imperceptibly.

We filed out of the cave, a reluctant Mutt following to walk through the congregated crowd into the woods. No one spoke.

Thirty minutes later we entered a small clearing deep in the forest. The attack had been close to the compound, too close for comfort. I didn't care about that. I needed to see who was responsible for my loss, and for that of the others. I reminded myself Kate had been one of three to die that day.

Seven humans lay dead in a line on the forest floor.

Six men and one woman. All dressed in camouflage hunting gear. An array of weapons lay on the ground in a pile to the right of them: shotguns, heavy-duty machine guns and even a compound bow.

I stared at them. Focussing on each face separately. They looked so normal. Nothing like what I'd imagined. My expectation had been a group of mercenaries. Big rugged men with battle scars and tattoos. These were just normal human beings. One probably in his sixties, two teenagers, barely sixteen, the others middle-aged. Nothing special, except that they were all dead. Like Kate, and the others.

Disappointment dug deeply in my gut. Mercenaries I might have been able to deal with. These were the very same people we were fighting for. How could they do this to us?

'What happened?' Jonah asked.

Nasheed, cradling his left arm where he'd been shot, answered, his voice broken. 'We went out this morning. Eight of us. Looking for wild potatoes and other root vegetables. Kate wanted to gather herbs too. The group spread out over the area. She and I went to the left of the trail, the herbs she wanted would be in the shadows of the big trees.'

He swallowed audibly his gaze straying to me every few seconds.

My fists were balled. He'd been there. He had been with Kate.

'We heard shots and made our way back. I stopped her on the track and told her to hide in the bushes. Then I went on and saw this lot.' He gestured towards the first three bodies.

'They'd herded Mary, Jack, Kale and Jimmy together and forced them on their knees. Joe came from the other side of the clearing, and we opened fire on the captors. They fell and we called to our people to get out of the clearing.'

He sat down on a fallen tree, the emotion too much for him.

'Kate moved up behind me. I shouted at her that she should have stayed in the bushes. Then the rest of their group opened fire with the machine guns and one of the teenagers had a double barrel shotgun. Jimmy went down, wounded and I grabbed Kate to pull her back, but she pulled free and ran over. I ran after her but got shot in the melee and went down. She grabbed Jimmy and tried to pull him backwards when the kid with the double barrel shot her. More gun fire struck her and Jimmy, and they both went down. Joe and I fired back and killed them.'

'Too late.' I remarked. 'You killed them too late.'

I knew I wasn't being realistic. But I felt a foul need to lash out. I didn't care who I hurt. My revenge had been stolen from me. The murderers were dead. I couldn't expend my rage on them, so I took it out on what was nearest.

'Steady, Gabe,' The big man walked up to stand to the side of us, just in case I attacked Nasheed. I wanted to. I felt I had to.

'You should have kept her out of the fight,' I shouted.

'I tried, Gabe,' Nasheed was close to tears. 'I tried, but she ran past me. She pulled free. I couldn't get to her on time.'

Jonah pulled me to the side, his hand gripping my arm painfully. I attempted to pull myself free, but he held fast. 'You don't want to do this. Gabe. You really don't. Nasheed did all he could.'

'It wasn't enough!' I shouted.

'No, it wasn't. But it was all he could do. He was shot too. He couldn't do more.'

I knew he was right, but my pain couldn't let me concede.

He slowly pushed me around and propelled me out of the clearing, away from Nasheed and Joe.

I pulled my arm loose and strode off in the direction of the compound. I'd seen what I needed. I knew what had happened. Nothing would change the outcome. Now I want to be with Kate. Talk to her, even if she couldn't hear me.

Aaliyah joined me later that night. I was angered at her presence. I didn't want anyone nearby. Just Kate, Mutt and me. I felt she was intruding on my pain. I'd already chased away Sly and others who had come to console me. My demeanour, comments and Mutt's growls kept everyone distant. Everyone except Aaliyah. Even Mutt stopped his growling and rubbed his head against her leg.

She sat down on a rock a metre from me. I shot her a chilling look, but she ignored it.

'I know you're hurting, Gabe. We all are. You can't go around hurting others, your friends. It won't help you. And it's not what Kate would have wanted.' She tried.

'You don't know what Kate wanted.' I replied coldly. Even to me it sounded weak.

'She was our friend too, you know. We loved her as well,

and we always will. You are not alone, but you will be if you keep pushing everyone away. Let us grieve together.'

'I don't want anyone.'

'No, but you might need someone.'

We sat in silence.

'What will they do with her?' I asked more than an hour later. My initial rage had subsided and was replaced with extreme longing and pain.

'They will all be buried in the subterranean caves,' she answered.

There were layers of caves in the mountain. The ones we lived in and layers deeper down. Those were colder, some even freezing. We'd buried one of our group who'd died of natural causes there a month ago. In a small cave that had been sealed with a rock face.

It made sense. Burial in the forest wasn't an option with all the wildlife. We couldn't go deep enough to be sure some predator wouldn't dig them up. Cremation was out of the question because the smoke would be visible for miles. The mountain was the only viable option.

'When?'

'Tomorrow,' Jonah's voice alerted me to his presence. 'They will all be buried tomorrow.'

'What about the killers?' Aaliyah asked.

'They'll be dumped in the canyon. Let the animals get rid of those.' The big man answered.

I was relieved. I didn't want Kate to be buried with her killers, even if they had been just simple people who were trying to save their families. This was the result of Man-Kayl's strategy. Of my father's strategy. He had done it again. Indirectly, he was responsible for the demise of my happiness, and the one person I wanted to grow old with.

Chapter Seventeen

I was lost without her, and that translated to the one thing I knew, aggression. I wanted to lash out. Preferably to my father and his cronies. But in the absence of a real enemy, I became impossible to be around. No one—not even Aaliyah or Jonah—could break through the wall of self-pity and rage I'd erected.

The only soul that refused to be impressed by my obnoxious behaviour was Mutt.

He stuck to me like a shadow, never more than one step behind me. Wherever I went, he was there and kept everyone away from me. Nothing like a hellhound to deter nosey people.

That's not fair. They were concerned. Wanted to help me. But I wouldn't let them, and as the extension of my disposition, neither would Mutt. I'm not sure what scared them away most, his or my demeanour, but it worked. After the initial attempts, they left me alone.

I wallowed in my pain, drinking excessively and staying in my cave, usually in the dark.

At some point I decided to leave.

'You can't go now,' Sly tried to convince me.

'Watch me.'

'We'll be leaving in the coming days. Lady E has found us a new location. We can't stay here. It could be compromised. It's only a question of time before we're attacked again.'

'So, leave.'

'We don't want to go without you,' Aaliyah tried.

I shrugged.

'We don't know where the new location is yet,' she continued. 'How will you find us?'

I turned to look at her. 'I won't. I'm done. I have to go.'

Jonah stood to the side and watched. He didn't try to intervene. I think of all of them, he understood that I couldn't stay anymore.

Aaliyah glanced at him and indicated he should say something. He shook his head, then looked me straight in the eye and nodded.

I took Kayleigh and left the compound, accompanied by the ever-present Mutt. I had no destination, no reason, I just had to get away from people. They were going ahead with their lives, and I couldn't accept that. Mine had imploded. Everything I thought I was fighting for died with Kate. There was no point anymore.

We travelled up the mountain and deep into the forests for days on end. Kayleigh was patient, though even she refused to take another step after an exceptionally long trek. I started a fire and stared into the embers, not interested in my surroundings or what would happen. Mutt brought me a dead rabbit, but I ignored it. He reluctantly ate the prize and settled down beside me. Kayleigh munched on a patch of grass three metres away.

I wasn't scared she would leave; she knew her safety lay with us.

I held up the last bottle of vodka I'd stashed in the sleeping roll. The light of the fire reflected on the dismal amount left in the bottom, less than half remained. I'd had enough. I knew, but I wanted more. I wanted to drink myself into oblivion, anything to forget. Not for the first time, I cursed my rapid metabolism that processed the alcohol at a much faster rate than humans. It nullified most of the effect and inflamed me even more.

I held the bottle to my lips and drank the remainder in one long haul. At least that should give me a buzz, just by sheer amount.

Mutt came closer and lay down beside me on my left. My hand found his thick fur and I absentmindedly buried my fingers in the warm pelt. He lay his head on his paws and waited for me to emerge from my stupor.

I just stared at the embers. I imagined I could see her face in them. Hear her voice in the calls of the nocturnal animals of the forest.

Memories flooded my brain unwelcome, I didn't want to remember. I didn't want to hurt.

―――――――――

Hours later I woke from my curled position against Mutt. The fire had long since petered out and the cold night air seeped into my body on my unprotected side. I curled up tighter and pushed myself even more into the warm and soft creature that was basically saving my life. A thick layer of snow coated the clearing and us all. Kayleigh and Mutt seemed indifferent, their thick winter pelts keeping them warm. I had no such luck, the snow slowly seeped into my wet clothes and made me feel even more pathetic.

Only the deep, even breaths of the dog kept me sane.

I couldn't stop the memories from flooding into my mind. I tried to think of something else, anything, as long as it wasn't Kate. Her love, her beautiful face, the way she made me feel whole. Nothing worked. Images of the good times inundated me. Even the very few arguments we'd had felt like a massive loss. The pain was overwhelming and without the alcohol I had no way of numbing it.

I felt a block of something heavy and immovable settle in my gut, making me feel even worse. My body started to shake, I thought initially from the cold, but that wasn't it. Pin pricks started at the edge of my eyes and tears formed. My breaths came in stuttered gusts, the oxygen hardly reaching my lungs. Hyperventilation was just around the corner.

I sat up in an attempt to regain control over my body.

Mutt raised himself onto his haunches and looked at me with what I interpreted as concern. A soft whimper emerged from his throat, throwing me even deeper into my pain and loosening my control over my emotions. I looked into the big black eyes and recognised the loss I saw mirrored.

I snaked my arms around his massive neck and buried my head in the thick black fur. He put his head on my shoulder, and I let go. All the pain and loss exploded out of me in the flow of tears that shook my whole body. The warmth he projected urged me to finally unburden myself and let the sorrow and despair out. I felt him push his big head even closer to mine and realised he'd lost Kate too. His distress was as large as mine. I held on to his shaggy neck and we sat like that for a long time, supporting each other. Sharing our pain.

When there were no tears left, I pulled myself together and restarted the fire. The cold mountain air and almost frozen ground had chilled me to the bone. No one would be helped if I became sick, so I had to take care of myself. Mutt watched me and seemed to agree.

I built a makeshift shelter from branches and a small tarp I'd brought along. Lined with fir twigs and directly opposite the fire, it quickly warmed up and the two of us settled down to what remained of the night.

I hadn't made my mind up on the next steps. I would cross that bridge when I came to it. At that point Mutt and the shelter, with Kayleigh munching on lichen and sprigs of grass in the background, were all I needed.

In the morning, I caught a rabbit, dressed it and cooked it over the fire. Mutt made short work of the carcass and what was left of the cooked meat once I was sated. Kicking out the embers, I dismantled the lean-to and saddled Kayleigh. We took a last look at the clearing and headed out.

I had no real destination, I just wanted to wander. I wasn't going back. Not yet. I was still too fragile and needed time to set myself back on the rails. Find out what I wanted to do. How I would fill the void Kate left behind.

Three days later I overlooked the camp again from a perch high up on the mountain. There was no one there. Understandable, it was probably compromised. They'd left, like they'd told me.

I felt abandoned. How could they leave me here, then

quickly berated myself. They'd warned me. It had been my choice to leave. I hadn't let anyone know where I was going or how I was doing. They couldn't wait. Not with danger around each corner.

I watched the camp for hours. Nothing stirred. It was deserted.

I tied Kayleigh to a tree near the entrance to the compound. She would be able to pull free if I didn't come back, but I wanted her to stay stationary. She looked at me with those deep eyes and snorted. I hoped she understood that I didn't want to put her in any kind of firing line.

Mutt walked in front of me, his head down to the ground, sniffing at scents. Every twenty metres or so, he would stop, raise his head and look around, flaring his top lip to pick up anything out of the ordinary. I followed him.

Another dog appeared to the right; he barked softly, and Mutt acknowledged him. This was one of the pack. Two more came out. Their presence comforted me, it also convinced me there were no enemies here.

All of us—me and my strange pack of dogs headed by the big black hellhound—traversed the camp. As I'd expected, the place was empty.

There were signs of a hasty departure all around and I was able to retrieve a few helpful odds and ends that had been left behind. But there was still no hint as to where they'd gone to. It made sense. They couldn't leave a calling card that would potentially alert the enemy to the new location. I figured it had to be somewhere Ebony would have vetted. But where?

I made my way to the cave Kate and I had shared. My throat constricted and I felt new tears drip down my cheeks. Her perfume drifted to me from the bed and my breath caught. It was just so raw. A whimper informed me Mutt was experiencing the same.

I rubbed his head affectionally, and he leaned into my leg.

I took a few things from our personal belongings. Not many. Just what I could handle. Each object brought back memories and with them a new stab of pain. I leant down to pick up a book and a photo of Kate, Mutt and I fell out.

I held it up.

I thought about throwing it back, the pain was too raw, when I noticed words on the back. I turned the photo around and read the cryptic message. "Let's go back to where we made a difference." The words were written in longhand that wasn't mine or Kate's.

Tingles ran up my spine. Someone had left this here for me—for us—to find so I could figure out where they'd gone to and maybe meet up with them again. A nervous exhilaration filled me. I left to be alone; I came back because I didn't want to stay that way. And now I had a chance to find my family again.

With renewed energy I quickly picked up a few things, pushed them in the backpack I'd retrieved and laid the photo on top. My priority was to get far away from the camp. Just because there was no one now, didn't mean it would stay that way.

Mutt and I made our way out of the caves, quickly circumvented the rest of the camp and hightailed it back to the mountain track where I'd left Kayleigh. The rest of the pack followed.

I took the reins, and we quietly melted back into the forest.

"Where had we made the biggest difference?"

Hours later I was still racking my brain trying to recall what they could have meant. It had to have been something I'd discussed with the team or where we'd worked together. With Jonah, Aaliyah, Sly. They were the ones still in the camp who I shared the most memories with, one of which had left the message. And Ebony of course, but she hadn't been there, she was still somewhere else, but that didn't mean she wasn't involved.

I couldn't for the life of me remember. So, I just gave up and lay my head on the makeshift cushion in the new den I'd fabricated in the bowels of a massive hollow tree. I wasn't scared anyone would surprise me while I slept. The pack would alert me. Feeling safer than I had for a long time, I quickly descended into a dreamless slumber. Halfway through the night Mutt joined me, and we shared the bedding, our body heat warming the small area and each other.

With newfound peace and energy, I turned my thoughts back to the mystery early next morning. Where?

I replayed the times we'd celebrated our success in my mind. First since the invasion, but when I drew a blank there, I let my mind wander further back. The ranch, when I'd returned from Taxore after my abduction, Los Angeles.

One place stood out. Both because of the impact it represented and because it was within a hundred miles of where I was. Whoever had left the note, knew my only form of transport was horseback. They wouldn't have suggested I travel the length or breadth of the country. It had to be approachable.

I reasoned it would be the location where we'd exposed The Establishment. The mansion where they'd convened almost a year ago. It wouldn't be easy to find anything or anyone there—it was a big area—but that wouldn't stop me trying. I decided I would determine how to find any new signs when I got there.

It took us more than a week to traverse the distance. Our progress was hindered by the thick forests, deep early snow and the fact that I wanted to avoid any human contact. I had no idea how I would be welcomed, my face—minus the thick beard—was plastered over every stream and TV program. Taxore was seriously looking for me and the promise of a big reward would be too much for many humans to resist. Thankfully, they hadn't announced that I was an alien. Probably because they expected humans to kill anything that came from Taxore. I didn't disagree. It was the same reason why Aaliyah, Tajan and I had kept our heritage under wraps in the compound.

The one exception to my isolation, was the day before I reached the mansion. Kayleigh started to limp and upon investigation I determined she'd bruised the underside of her right front hoof. She wouldn't be able to go far, and I needed tools to open what I expected was a small abscess just under the surface. We'd barely passed a cabin, and I reluctantly decided to backtrack, hoping the off-grid locality would work in my favour.

Loud dog barks and a shotgun barrel greeted me as I slowly led the limping horse into the small clearing to the front of the cabin.

'That's far enough,' a female voice called out. She shouted at the dogs, and they were silenced.

I stopped.

'What do you want?'

'My horse is lame, she has a hoof abscess,' I answered with my hands up. 'I need tools to help her.'

The silence was only broken by a lonely bird call.

'Throw out your weapons.'

'I don't have any.'

The barrel wavered.

'What kind of fool goes into the wilderness without a gun?' she asked incredulously.

I shrugged and my lips pulled into a strained smile. 'This kind.'

The silence felt heavy in the cold mountain air. I waited. Mutt was somewhere in the trees. I'd left him there so as not to alarm the inhabitants of the cabin. He had that effect on most people. The rest of the pack were further back.

Slowly the door opened, and a woman emerged, the shotgun still pointed directly at me.

'Walk forward,' she ordered.

I complied, coaxing Kayleigh to put weight on her sore foot.

'Mum. The horse is limping.' A second voice came from behind the woman and a girl of no more than ten came forward. She raced down the two steps and over to Kayleigh, completely oblivious of any danger.

'Mitzi!' Her mother lowered the shotgun and tried to grab the child as she rushed past. She missed and a small cry escaped her lips.

Kayleigh lowered her massive head and nudged the child, who instantly giggled in reply.

My arms were still up in the air. I wanted to show I was no threat.

'Move away from the horse,' the woman approached, the shotgun again levelled at my middle region.

I gave the reins to the girl and stepped back a few paces.

Kayleigh glanced at me for a second and neighed softly. Then she turned her attention back to her new friend.

'We must help her, mum. She's in pain.'

The dilemma was visible in the strained features on the mother's face. Her nostrils flared slightly as she looked from me to her daughter and the horse, and back again.

A big sigh indicated a decision had been made and she lowered the gun again, flicking the safety back.

'Could you step back a few more paces?'

I complied and lowered my hands. She eyed me suspiciously then turned her attention to Kayleigh who strategically neighed her best imitation of utter pain.

'Let her walk, Mitzi,' she indicated to her daughter.

The girl pulled at the reins and coaxed Kayleigh to walk. She took a few steps, her balance off because of the limp. It was decidedly worse that when we'd walked up, and I was certain she was overdoing the pain. I had to stop my lips from pulling into a smile. Looked like she'd made her choice. I couldn't blame her; we'd covered a lot of distance, and she was up for a rest.

'See, Mum?'

The woman nodded her head and stroked Kayleigh's neck. She lifted the painful hoof and held it up to examine the underside, knocking on the hard surface. At one spot, Kayleigh whimpered and pulled her hoof slightly. The woman put the hoof back down and patted Kayleigh's neck again.

'You're right,' she said to me. 'She has a hoof abscess. We'll need to bleed it.'

'Thank you,' I answered.

She looked at me, bit her underlip and finally just shrugged.

'Come on,' she suggested as she bent to pick up the shot

gun. 'Let's bring her into the barn.' She broke the shotgun open and held it in the crook of her arm.

I followed Mitzi and the limping Kayleigh, the woman brought up the rear.

The barn was warm and welcoming. Mitzi stopped in the centre of the building and her mother walked to the right where I saw a rack of tools. They included hammers and even farrier's knives. Understandable, this far away from civilisation, farmers would have to do most chores themselves and needed the correct tools. It was what I'd hoped for.

An hour later the horse's hoof had been taken care of, and she was munching happily on fresh smelling hay while Mitzi stood on a crate to brush her, chattering away merrily.

Mandy, the mother, and I sat on hay bales drinking fresh coffee. I was grateful for the warm brew that I'd missed for more than ten days. Cold that I hadn't felt in my bones dissipated and left me with a soft internal glow.

'What are you doing in the forest at this time of the year?' Mandy asked.

'Trying to find my friends.'

'Same question.'

I laughed. 'You really don't want to know,' I suggested.

'Anything to do with the battle that took place on the other side of the mountains last year?'

'Maybe.'

She nodded. 'Figures.'

There were no more questions for a while.

'So just passing through, huh?'

'Yes.'

'She's not going anywhere,' she commented with a nod towards Kayleigh. 'Not with her hoof like that.'

'No.' I'd come to the same conclusion.

Mitzi's chattering made me wonder whether I would ever be able to get my horse to come anywhere with me anymore. She was nickering softly in answer to Mitzi's prattling.

'So, what will you do?'

'Could she stay with you?'

'Until she's better?'

'Yes, or maybe longer. If I don't come back.'

'Are you sure?' Mandy turned to look at Kayleigh.

I'd noticed that there were no mechanical farm tools like tractors in the barn. It wouldn't help, petrol was hard to get and just about everyone had run out. The invaders kept a close lid on the depots. Once she'd recovered, Kayleigh would be a great asset to help with the heavy chores. The two quarter horses were strong but not equipped to pull the old plough I saw in the corner.

'Yeah,' I answered. 'Something tells me she's better off here.' I smiled. 'And I wouldn't want to come between those two.' I nodded in their direction.

'Thank you,' Mandy said softly.

'You're welcome. I should thank you for not shooting me.'

We both laughed.

'You can stay here till the morning if you want.'

'It's ok. I'd like to get across the next hill before dark if possible.'

'But you're on your own.' Mitzi had finished brushing Kayleigh and joined us. 'You can't go all alone, there are bears and cougars.' She looked at her mother beseechingly.

'I'm not alone,' I answered to Mandy's surprise. 'My dogs are out there. They'll join me as soon as I leave here.'

'You have dogs?'

'Yes,' I answered. 'I didn't want to alarm you, so they stayed back in the trees.'

I stood up and put my coat on again. My gloves followed and the knitted cap I wore.

'Thank you again,' I smiled towards them.

Kneeling down I looked intently at Mitzi. 'I'm counting on you to take care of Kayleigh. Can you do that?'

She nodded vigorously.

I stood up again and nodded at her mother, stroked and thanked Kayleigh for one last time, then turned and left the barn.

At the edge of the woods Mutt and the pack joined me and I looked back. Mitzi waved and I returned the gesture.

We turned and melted into the dark forest.

I'd miss Kayleigh. Not just as a means of transport. The stubborn, recalcitrant horse felt like family. But I took comfort in the realisation that she had a great new home with a little girl who already adored her.

One of my biggest dilemmas had been what I would do with Kayleigh if I found anyone at the hotel. I'd figured whoever left the message most likely wouldn't have a spare oversized horsebox to transport her to wherever we would be going to.

It had worked out well in the end.

If, that is, I found anyone.

Chapter Eighteen

The familiar area, and the possibility of reconnecting with my friends sent tingles of anticipation through my body. Would there be anyone here? And if so, who? Or had I just imagined it all.

The mansion seemed deserted from the distance I kept between me and the building. I was halfway up the mountain, in a thick copse of trees. I'd scaled the biggest one to get a good view of the area. Thick forests obscured most of the expanse, but the mansion and other related buildings were clearly visible.

My vigilance lasted for three hours. I descended back to the pine-needle coated floor just before the sun set. There were no signs of humans, or Taxorians for that matter. I was convinced of their absence when I spotted a pack of wolves roaming the area in between the entrance and the outbuilding. They wouldn't be there if there was any kind of humanoid threat and definitely not act as relaxed as they'd seemed through the high-powered binoculars I'd brought back from the cave.

I absentmindedly stroked Mutt's head. He was relieved I was finally back near him on firm ground. I'd noticed a definite reluctance to let me out of his direct proximity. I guess he didn't want to lose me too. We'd become close in the past weeks, and I couldn't imagine life without this massive, dangerous looking canine.

The pack had joined us, and they waited for me to decide what to do. It was late, the sun was going down and the forest would be pitch black within an hour. It made sense to stay where we were and continue our search tomorrow. I didn't want to bump into anyone in the night.

I refrained from lighting a fire and we huddled down in the lieu of a short cliff edge in a natural depression. At least it kept out the freezing wind. The dogs curled up close and Mutt stayed a small distance out, clearly on guard. At some point through the night, he switched places with one of the other canines and joined me on the bed of pine needles.

The morning air was crisp, and a light snow had settled on the pack's fur. They seemed oblivious to the cold and yawned as the sun slowly rose in the sky. I stretched my limbs to stimulate the blood circulation and express the stiffness that had settled in my muscles during the night. My joints creaked and protested but reluctantly complied. Slowly I warmed up.

After a meagre meal of dried meat, we set off to explore the area around the mansion. The air was cold, early snow was imminent, and I pulled my coat collar up to try to keep the chill out. It didn't work. At least it was dry. The snow on the ground was still minimal and didn't hinder our progress much, though it was slippery in places.

The thick shrubs and fir trees shielded us from most of the cold wind and we were able to circumvent more than half of the terrain before one of the dogs barked softly. It had taken us most of the day, but I wanted to be very careful.

I pulled out the binoculars and observed the building from the new angle. Still nothing. Some of the windows on this side were broken and one door stood askew. Animals probably, I figured. Humans would close the door against the wintery climate if they'd taken residence. There were no signs that anyone had been here in a long time. I swivelled the binoculars to the left from where we'd just come, and further to the right, more to the back of the building. There was a small construction to the side of the main structure. There were closed shutters on the windows, and the big barn-like door was closed. A light flurry of snow had coated the walkway up to the building and I noticed soft indentations that could be footprints walking away from the doors. It was difficult to see from that distance.

I was reluctant to move too quickly. Nervous goosebumps ran up my arms at the thought that this may one of my friends, but cold stabs in my gut warned me it could be someone else. Someone I didn't want to run in to.

There was no choice, I had to get closer.

We carefully moved further through the trees, me now acutely aware of the footprints we left behind in the softly dropping snow.

Mutt's nose was close to the ground, he and the other dogs had found a scent. They moved out from the shrubs into the trees and sped up. I followed as quickly as I could, still trying to keep one eye on the surroundings. We wove between the trees up the side of the hill until we reached the crest of a small hill to the side of the hotel grounds, with our backs to the buildings. I called the pack back with a whistle to make sure we didn't suddenly break our cover.

Mutt joined me and whimpered softly.

He'd recognised the scent.

His tail wagged slowly from side to side reinforcing my idea that we were on to something good. I crept up over the ridge and looked down into the valley below. There was nothing to be seen. Not even with the binoculars. My spirits took a nosedive as the idea occurred that maybe it had been an old scent. I had no idea how long anything like that would be traceable. Maybe there was no one here and I'd just imagined the message. Maybe it didn't mean anything, or a different place. Negative thoughts reigned supreme in my mind as I scanned the area.

I turned back to the pack. They were still positive.

Slowly we made our way down the hillside through the shrubs and trees to where a small stream trickled down a waterfall of stones. The water was clear as glass and we drank it quickly. I refilled the flask I carried. It paid to take advantage of what nature offered; we had no way of knowing what would be around the next corner.

That valley produced no definite clues, but the dogs were clearly still following the scent.

At one point we neared a clearing where the stream widened into a small pond. Mutt's tail wagged harder, something I'd never seen when he was tracking. He was usually one-hundred percent focus and concentration. Now he resembled a puppy, his movements erratic and jumpy.

I called softly as he pushed through the undergrowth to a tiny glade. For the first time since Kate died, he ignored me.

The scent must be stronger.

Mutt stood in the centre of the clearing; his nose close to the ground. He raised his head and looked around, softly whimpering, his ears revolving to pick up any sounds. One by one the other three dogs joined him and stood waiting for whatever they'd followed to show itself.

Nothing stirred.

I stayed where I was, still not fully happy with the circumstances but unable to change them. I had no real weapons. No guns, just a hunting knife. It wouldn't do much good against any adversary.

Nothing happened for a while.

The shrubs opposite from where I was moved. Mutt let off a short bark, his tail and rear end wagging stupidly. The rest of them followed suit. My gaze alternated between the dog and the shrubs. Shivers crept up my spine and sent goosebumps all over my body.

The branches parted and a familiar form stepped out, Mutt jumped up from his position and raced over.

I let the pent-up breath out and slowly stood up.

Aaliyah was petting Mutt as he pushed himself up against her legs, The other dogs ran around them in excitement. Then one stopped and looked back at the spot where Aaliyah had emerged. He stared at the area until another person stepped out of the shadows.

The big man walked over to where my dog lay on its back enjoying a tummy rub, something he never let anyone do. Well, no men. I'd seen Kate do it, and now Aaliyah. Mutt surely had a preference for women. I smiled, warmth filling my body as I took a step forward to the edge of the clearing.

'You coming out? Or is this your version of hide and seek?' The big man's deep voice and humorous tone felt like music to my ears. He knew I was near; Mutt was a dead giveaway.

I stepped out into the clearing and Aaliyah stood up, a massive smile on her face, mirrored by that of Jonah and myself. Pin pricks at the back of my eyes informed me I was in danger of shedding happy tears. I swallowed hard and bridged the distance before I lost control. It wouldn't do to cry.

They both hugged me, even Aaliyah. I only thought afterwards how uncharacteristic that had been for her. Jonah was more outgoing; he wore his feelings on his sleeve, and he was relieved and happy to see me. Well, it was mutual.

'So, you figured it out, huh?' he jested.

'Was there any doubt?' I asked, slightly stung by his insinuation that I wouldn't have been able to.

'Only whether you would want to come,' Aaliyah interjected. 'But I'm happy you did.'

'You ok now?' The big man asked, concern once again his main feature.

'Better,' I answered truthfully. I still had a lot to deal with, but finding my friends again was the first step.

'Looks like you got yourself a pack,' he commented.

'Yeah. You know Mutt was with me when I left, the others joined us when I visited the compound.'

'There are going to be some great reunions,' Aaliyah smiled. 'Humans love their dogs.'

'And they should. This lot is the reason I'm still alive.'

Jonah looked around the clearing, then up at the white sky. There was more snow on the way. A lot more.

'We need to get out of here, before we make too many tracks,' he suggested.

I nodded, ready to start hiking up the mountain again.

'The truck is in a building to the side of the abandoned mansion,' Jonah answered. Ahh, that explained the footprints.

I gathered the pack, and we quickly moved to the structure, circumvented the main building and retrieved a beaten-up pickup from the barn. Before long we were all bundled up in the double cabin of the vehicle grateful for the warmth. The dogs curled up on the floor with Mutt on the seat next to me and fell asleep. I relished the heat coming from the vents, it was the first real warmth since Maddy's barn yesterday and my shivers told me it was decidedly better that outside. I felt my face turn red from the warmth and the satisfaction of once again being among friends.

Chapter Nineteen

'Where are we going?'

I woke up to the renewed motion of the truck. The comforting warmth of the car had done its work and I'd fallen asleep almost immediately once we were out of the thick forest.

I looked out the window. It was pitch black and I estimated it to be about four in the morning. There had been a change in driver and Aaliyah sat behind the wheel with the big man asleep against the passenger door.

'A mountain compound, most of it underground,' she answered, glancing in the rearview mirror.

In a mountain, sounded good. It would be difficult to find us if we were deep inside a rock enclosure, though underground was not something I was looking forward to. I wasn't too fond of tight spaces.

'Was it already there?'

'Yes, it was some kind of semi-military site. It's where they kept any proof of extraterrestrial life they had.'

I raised my brow. 'Area 51?'

Aaliyah laughed. 'No, that was a decoy. Something they wanted to be found so no one would look further.'

I nodded. 'It worked.'

'Hell, yeah.' The big man had woken up and joined in the conversation. 'This place is off the map. No one knows about it. Not even the president.'

'Sounds like a film I saw a long time ago,' I remarked.

Jonah chuckled. 'Sometimes it's better to hide in plain sight. Though I wouldn't call this anything plain.'

'Need I ask how you found it?'

'Ebony.'

I nodded. Trust her to find a place that didn't exist.

Another thought crossed my mind. 'Was it inhabited?'

Johan shot a glance to Aaliyah before he answered. Hmm, there was tension there. I took that as a yes.

'There's a military resistance group there. We've more or less joined them.'

'More or less?'

'Well, we keep our distance a bit, but we work together, and they agreed to let us live there.'

'Did they have a choice?'

Aaliyah laughed. 'Not really. Thanks to Ebony.'

'Okay.' The word was drawn out, showing my curiosity. 'Tell me.'

'Ebony contacted them on their secure network,' the big man picked up the narrative. 'It scared the shit out of them. They thought they were invisible. She knows one of the geeks there. He convinced the leaders it would be in their best intention to welcome us.'

I laughed. Good old Ebony. No matter that she was now underground somewhere, we could still count on her and her reputation to open doors.

There was something in the strained way Jonah laughed

that alerted me. I cocked my head in question. He glanced at Aaliyah who nudged him with her elbow to continue.

'The people there are a mix of special forces, some kind of Marines and regular folks.'

'And I'm guessing there are issues with the military types?'

He nodded.

'They didn't take too kindly to being blackmailed,' Aaliyah answered for him.

'Blackmail?'

'That's how they call it. We've been fighting an uphill battle against some of them since then.'

That tempered my feelings of relief.

'But it's a great base from which to launch attacks,' Aaliyah added. 'And we're doing our best to blend in.'

This time my laughter was silent. I couldn't just see the big man trying to blend in anywhere. It was impossible. He wasn't the blend-in type, and he had a distinctly non-compromising mindset. One I'd encountered way too often.

'It's one group in particular,' Aaliyah continued. 'The Marines. They think they own the place, which of course doesn't go down well with the Special Forces that originally formed the security for the base. Finder's-keeper's doesn't really cover it.'

'The Marines were our ticket in though, some of them had ties with Sly. From when he was in the services.'

'But they don't want us?'

'Nope. They like to decide who gets access and who doesn't.' Jonah explained.

'And how do you handle that?' I asked what was bothering me.

'Carefully,' Aaliyah answered.

So, when will we arrive there?' I asked after a few minutes silence. 'I assume we're going there.'

'We are,' Aaliyah replied. Jonah had fallen back to sleep, his snores loud in the small, contained area.

'It will take a few days. We must be careful, only travel at night and over small roads.'

'We're still enemy number one, I guess.'

'Exactly. That's part of what makes us so popular.'

It took two days, the trip long and laborious. We stayed at abandoned buildings or in densely wooded areas by day and took the backroads at night. The dogs were getting restless, especially Mutt. He wasn't used to being confined in a small space for so long. I tried to alleviate his restlessness by taking them for walks whenever I could, but it was nothing like the big open spaces we'd had the weeks before.

Tension among the people was growing too. I've never been one for prolonged close contact and this was way too close for way too long. Jonah and Aaliyah were better at ignoring it. They'd been hiding out at the motel for three days before I got there. Add two days to get there and they'd had more than enough practice. I was still getting used to the proximity of others after my self-imposed isolation, and even though I was grateful they'd waited for me, it wasn't easy.

'Do they know about us?' I asked Aaliyah.

'Our origin?'

I nodded.

'No, we thought it was prudent not to tell them that detail, what, with the animosity.'

It figured; we would stay under wraps again. Only a

select few of the old team knew the truth, best not to make it common knowledge.

'Do they mount offensives from the mountain?'

'Some, but not many. They've done a few missions, as they call them. Mostly far away. They want to keep the location hidden for as long as possible. It's extremely well concealed and they're reluctant to chance anything. But there's a real tension there. People don't accept the military regime and some want to act.'

'Sounds like a happy place,' I said sarcastically, eliciting laughter from Aaliyah.

'Yeah, something like that.'

'This one of their trucks?'

'Yes. It is.'

'How did you get them to loan it to you?'

'Jonah convinced them.'

Now it was my turn to laugh. I could image how that had gone down. The big man was very convincing when he wanted to be.

'They didn't have a death wish then?'

'Nope.'

The forests and mountains made way for desert and endless long drives over a scenery that hardly changed. The slopes in the distance seemed just as far away the next day and we trudged on. Jonah refilled the tanks from hidden jerry cans mounted in the pickup's load bed to keep us going. We could hardly stop for gas, not that there was any easily available.

'The base is well stocked with all kinds of gear, weapons, food and petrol,' Jonah explained when I asked.

'It's like Christmas in there. The place was made to withstand a nuclear war with a direct hit and has enough provisions to last them for at least a decade. It makes you wonder how they kept it secret for so long.'

'Are you sure they did?' I asked.

Aaliyah turned to look at me. Jonah, from behind the wheel observed me in the mirror. 'What do you mean?'

'I wouldn't put it past them to have found it and infiltrated the place.'

'A sobering thought,' Jonah commented. 'But how do we contend with that?'

'I don't know,' I answered truthfully. 'But we must tread carefully. My father is a resourceful man. He had the vice president in his pocket all that time, and who knows who else. We can't be sure he doesn't know.'

'You think he'd leave them here waiting for us to come around?'

I shrugged.

'Let's keep our ears and eyes open,' Aaliyah suggested. 'Trust no one.'

'I never do.' Jonah remarked. I nodded. No, neither did I.

I sat back in the seat, absentmindedly rubbing Mutt's head. He felt my apprehension and moved closer. The dog was becoming an extension of me, he was so attuned to my emotions. Not for the first time, I was grateful for the moment Kate had rescued my canine best friend.

'We're coming up on the dirt road,' Jonah said. 'Hold on to your hats, folks. It's going to be a bumpy ride.'

That turned out to be the understatement of the year. Jonah slowed the car to a brisk walk, manoeuvring it over the stones and avoiding the big holes in what looked like a little used track. It was basically a wild run, frequented by elk and maybe wild horses. The truck pushed through the tight corners, the branches screeching across the paint as we passed. I looked behind me where the shrubs readjusted back to their original form, effectively hiding the path. Up in front of us was the exact same outlook. I had no idea how Jonah was navigating. I couldn't even see the track.

More bumps and jolts later we circumvented the peak and came up into a narrow chasm between the mountain we were on and its sister. The car barely fit between the sheer walls and Jonah slowed down even more.

After more than an hour of agonising and sometimes death-defying manoeuvres we turned another tight corner and drove onto a ledge that widened out allowing me to finally breathe again. I envied the dogs, they were blissfully unaware of the dangerous trip we'd just taken, all of them asleep on the floor or the back seat next to me.

A cave opened in the sheer cliff structure and Jonah turned the wheel, coaching the pickup into the black cavern. He switched on the lights and slowly made his way deeper into the mountain.

There were occasional side tunnels that appeared in the headlights, but Jonah kept going on what I expected was the main track. A fork in the distance forced him to choose and he took the left one. I saw lights up ahead and Jonah slowed even more. Another turn and the tunnel opened to what looked like a natural cavern, except for the illumination that was situated every ten metres at a hight of two meters from the floor. They ringed the whole cave, casting strange and haunting shadows.

The car stopped and we disembarked. The dogs were instantly alert, Mutt by my side. Jonah and Aaliyah pulled their bags from the pickup, I slung mine over my shoulder and followed them to what looked like a solid wall.

One of the pack put his nose to the ground and snarled at a crack just above the floor. A hissing sound started, and Mutt growled loudly. Jonah and Aaliyah remained calm, so I followed their example. The hissing increased and slowly a large portion of the wall we stood in front of moved to the right. A hidden door. Great.

Jonah stepped over the threshold, and we followed into a three-metre wide and two-and-a-half metre high tunnel. It slanted slightly downwards, and I could feel my calf muscles working hard to keep upright. In parts, Jonah even had to duck when the ceiling lowered. The dogs proceeded us, their noses down to the ground and the hackles on their backs raised. They were nervous and that rubbed off on me. Aaliyah must have noticed, she glanced over at me and smiled reassuringly.

Yeah, I thought to myself, relax. But somehow, I didn't feel comfortable deep underground. It had taken a while for me to get acclimatised to the caves in our previous camp and the underground garage before that. This was much more claustrophobic. Awesome.

We walked up to a large metal door, marking the end of the natural part of the mountain. I stood between Jonah and Aaliyah and waited for whatever would happen. Mutt stood next to me, the deep rumbling of his growl actually comforting me.

The door split and both parts moved sideways, opening to a setting I will never forget.

The bright lights were intense after the subtle illumination in the tunnel. I blinked hard to focus my eyes.

The doors had opened into a massive man-made cavern. The hard walls had been blasted out of the mountain itself and were supported in places with steel constructions. It was at least three stories high and maybe a hundred metres from side to side. The bustle of people going about their business on all kinds of vehicles and on foot seemed so foreign after the silence of the past weeks that I almost stepped back into the comforting dark of the tunnel.

Directly opposite us was a line of soldiers. Their desert camouflage clothing was the exact same tone as the cavern walls. The uniform down to the boots were military standard, as were the weapons they held pointed at us. Fierce hard faces stared at me from behind the fully automatic weapons and clearly showed me we were not welcome, or at least I wasn't.

Mutt growled loudly. I placed my hand on his shoulder, the muscles below my fingers were tense, ready to jump forward if anyone moved. He reacted immediately to the loaded tension that fouled the otherwise clean and fresh air.

Jonah hadn't exaggerated. The place was state-of-the-art. And the soldiers were hostile and rigid.

'You found him.' The man in the middle of the line addressed Jonah, his voice as cold as his stare.

The big man didn't answer.

'The dogs can't come in,' the soldier continued.

'They go where I go,' I answered.

'Then you go out as well.'

We had ourselves a stand-off, and Mutt's dangerous countenance wasn't helping much.

'Is that even a dog?' One of the others asked.

'Why don't you come and find out,' I answered, the tension getting to me. They obviously didn't want me here and the feeling was mutual. Mutt lowered his head, and the growl intensified.

No one moved.

Smart choice.

A familiar voice broke the loaded silence. 'Stand down, Nathan.'

Sly's stern features were a breath of fresh air in the not-so-welcome party, and I was happy to see him.

'This is Gabriel. The one I told you about.'

The leader—Nathan—looked me over with a countenance I recognised from my father's disapproving looks. I realised I must look like a bum, my hair and beard wild and unkept. I hadn't cleaned myself fully in weeks, the weather too cold to bathe in any of the streams I'd encountered on my trip. Jonah had given me clean clothes and I'd washed my face, hands and arms before we left, but that had been it.

'The dogs go back up,' Nathan announced nodding to one of his soldiers. The man stepped forward hesitantly towards Mutt and me.

'I wouldn't try that,' Sly announced.

He stopped in his tracks, anxiously looking from Nathan, to Sly and back to Mutt.

'That dog will kill you. He's more or less attached to Gabe at the hip. You won't be able to separate them. Believe me, we've tried.' Sly's lips pulled into an infrequent smile. 'And the other ones belong to some of the families we brought. They'll take care of them.'

I thought Nathan was going to continue the hard tone, but he relented unexpectedly.

'They'll feed them from their own rations.' He needed the final word.

Whatever.

Sly walked up to me, one eye still on Mutt, and extended his hand. I shook it gratefully and smiled back at him. He was a welcome face in the otherwise hostile environment.

He wrinkled his nose. 'Come on, I'll show you to the shower. You stink.'

My laugher cut through Mutt's anger, and he relaxed, the hackles on his back receding.

'And that monster,' Sly added.

'Good luck with that,' I commented. Mutt did what he wanted, and I had my doubts a bath would be on that list.

Sly, Jonah, Aaliyah and I walked through a gap in the line and the pack followed.

Our small procession traversed the enormous cavern and made our way down one of the lesser tunnels that opened at intervals on either side.

Chapter Twenty

'What's the history between you and Colonel Ridgeback?' I asked Sly as we walked down yet another long grey corridor. It was impossible to keep my bearings, so I just gave up, this place was a labyrinth.

'I used to be his CO,' Sly announced. 'Pulled him out of some tight spots.'

'So, he owes you?'

'He does. With his life.'

Good hold to have on someone, especially if it was such an obnoxious bastard like Nathan. That kind of personality combined with the weapons he had access to made me nervous.

'He's not as bad as he pretends to be,' Sly added.

'Well, he does a good job of masking that.'

'He's an arrogant piece of shit,' Jonah added his ten cents.

'It's a difficult job,' Sly tried. 'The people here need discipline, otherwise it would all quickly descend into anarchy.'

Yeah, but do they need a tyrant?' Aaliyah asked.

'Is he solely in charge?' I wondered out loud.

'No, there's a committee. They rely on his advice and his expertise, but he doesn't decide on his own. It's a form of democracy.'

'It doesn't trickle down,' Jonah added. 'He rules this place with an iron hand. Him and the other Jarheads.'

'Jarheads?'

Another name for a Marine,' Aaliyah explained and shrugged.

We passed many closed doors and one or two new corridors. This place was a real rabbits warren, and I was totally lost.

'How the hell do you find your way around here?' I asked exasperated and even a bit claustrophobic.

'The signs on the wall.' Sly indicated small images painted on the wall every ten metres and at each intersection. 'The top one shows you which level you're on. Blue is level three.'

'Three underground?'

'Not really underground. We're probably still above the forest floor, but the third level within the mountain.

'The second icon, the green circle here, shows you're in the Eastern section. The number behind it gives the coordinates. This place is basically built up like any US town. Vertical and horizontal streets that are identified by numbers.'

'What about the red triangle below that?' The image was on its side, making it look like an arrowhead.

'That shows which direction has the closest exit out into the forest.'

That figured. There had to be more than just the entrance we came in. The vehicles I'd seen in the big hall would never have been able to negotiate the track and the tight corners we came through.

'How many?'

'Seven in total. Three of which are small, like the one you came in on. Two, I wouldn't advise anyone to try. One big one on the mountains lee side and the biggest entrance out two miles into the desert.'

'None of which are visible from the outside.'

'We sure hope not.'

'Some complex.'

'Hell yeah, this place is an architectural wonder,' Jonah chimed in.

We continued onwards and finally the tunnel opened into a larger space. The high ceiling, even though it was hewn out of the mountain, seemed less oppressive. I could breathe again.

I looked around. Lights high up on the walls imitated natural glows and gave off a soft radiance that resembled outside. Softly whirring vents at regular intervals sent in fresh air that even had that tang of fir trees. Doors led off the space into what I expected were private quarters. One or two were open and offered a glimpse of bunk beds and tables. The people here were non-military, and some of them were familiar from the old compound. A long table with folding chairs stood in the centre of the space, to the right of what resembled a small kitchen. The appliances were rudimentary, but workable. Three people were busy there, one juggling pans, another cutting vegetables and the third peeling potatoes into a bucket of water.

'He's back!' I heard from the side and turned to see Caleb and Nasheed approach with big smiles on their faces. We clasped arms and did the typical man-hug that humans seemed to like. It felt good to see them. We'd become good friends over the last year and even Mutt seemed happy to see them again. Nasheed patted his head, Caleb was more careful, not entirely comfortable with the large canine.

'Good to see you again, man,' Nasheed said.

'Good to be back among friends.' I smiled. 'Though I'm not sure about this place.' My gaze roamed the cavern.

'Claustrophobic?' Caleb laughed.

'I just don't like the idea that the whole mountain can come down on us.'

'It won't,' Sly commented. 'This place is bomb proof.'

'Great.'

They all laughed at my expense. I tried to join in, but it wasn't heartfelt. This place gave me the creeps. I didn't like the containment. It felt too much like a dungeon. But that was probably just me being dramatic.

Sly walked on to a closed door on the right which he opened and pushed inwards to allow me to enter the small room. There was little comfort, but it was practical. A bunk bed with a metal trunk at the end, a small table holding a jug of water and a few glasses, and two folding chairs against the wall.

'We have communal showers in the last door on the left. You can use them for five minutes max every day. Shampoo and soap are there as well as towels. Any belongings you put in the trunk and lock it. That's the extent of privacy around here though.'

The bottom bunk was clearly occupied, the sheets pulled down to the end. There were two mattresses which seemed strange to me until I noticed how the trunk was positioned strategically to extend the sleeping area. There was only one man who needed that length, and I deduced my new bunk buddy was the big man.

It was clean, practical. More comfort than I'd had in the

past weeks camping out in self-made lean-to's and hollow trees. The only thing missing was what I wanted most, a window to the outside. Bummer, not an option.

Mutt pushed up against me a soft whine escaping his mouth.

'I know, buddy. But this is it for now.'

'They'll probably want to have the dogs in the pens across the main cave,' Sly suggested carefully. I refrained from answering. Mutt wasn't going anywhere.

'Showers,' Aaliyah suggested.

I smiled. I could probably use some soap. Quite a lot to be honest.

Jonah handed me more clean clothes and cocked his head to the left. 'You're not sleeping here smelling like that.'

I took his offer and hung my head in mock shame as I walked out the door towards the showers.

Mutt followed me, though I wasn't sure how far that would last.

An hour later, we all sat at the communal table eating a simple but nourishing meal. I'd used my full five minutes in the shower and another five Jonah donated. Mutt had declined further cleaning after the first drenching and no one felt inclined to force him, not after he bared his teeth. He was under the table, happily munching on one of the moose bones the cook had given him. The rest of the pack had found their families and were enjoying tearful reunions.

'A definite improvement,' Aaliyah remarked nudging me.

'Let's burn the old clothes,' the big man suggested.

'And the towels.'

I laughed along with them. The water running off my body had been dark brown, especially once I washed my hair and beard. It made me wonder how Aaliyah and Jonah had coped in the tight confines of the car. My only hope was that the dogs had smelled worse than I had.

It felt good to be clean and among friends. So good that I almost felt at home. Almost.

My first night in the mountain was better than I'd expected. The fatigue and gratification that I'd found my friends offered me the peace I needed to sleep soundly. I wasn't even that bothered by the location. Mutt, as usual, lay at the bottom of the bed. He couldn't get up onto the top bunk and he was definitely not amused, but he finally complied and slept with one eye on the door.

Feeling a lot better, we joined the team at the breakfast table.

'You look like a different person from yesterday,' Caleb commented.

'I feel like one,' I admitted.

I scoffed down everything that was put in front of me, making sure I reserved some for Mutt. Nathan's comment that he had to eat from my rations still rang in my ears.

'What do we do now?' I asked after everyone was finished.

'There will be a communal meeting in two days, they organise these to let everyone speak their mind,' Jonah explained. 'Happens once a fortnight.'

'We usually just listen,' Sly added. 'It's a fountain of information.'

'Anything in the works right now?' the big man asked.

'No,' Sly answered. 'There was an attack on a fuel depot while you were away. That's the last action they organised.'

'How does that usually work?'

'The Marines, some of the Special Forces and occasionally some of our team join forces. The plans are made by the Marines, though with Lady E's influence we've been given more say in the whole thing.'

'They must love that,' I said sipping my coffee. Man, I'd missed the warmth of the dark beans.

'They're ecstatic.'

The laughter belied the comment.

'Nathan was never good at sharing command,' Sly mused.

'How was he at following it?' I asked.

Sly shrugged and shook his head at the same time. That good, huh?

Chapter Twenty-One

The days passed slowly in the compound and once again my claustrophobic tendencies came into play. The rest were obviously more used to the confinement. Mutt and I took every chance we could get to go up to the surface. And that was exactly what got us into trouble.

Nathan's face was bright red, the veins to the side of his temples throbbing with rage. He clenched his fists until the knuckles were white. I had to stop myself from laughing when the thought occurred to me that he might just explode, he was that tense. It wasn't the time for mirth, so I reluctantly, and with great difficulty, held my features in a stern look.

The Marine was embroiled in a loud shouting match with the big man.

'He can't go out,' Nathan exclaimed.

'I don't see why not.' Jonah stood to his full height; his arms crossed over his wide chest staring down the much smaller man. I have to hand it to Nathan, he didn't flinch. Just stayed up close. He was a head smaller than Jonah and even though he was fit and lean, he would fit twice in the big man. My friend had the nickname for a reason.

'He's on probation,' Nathan declared exasperated.

Jonah raised an eyebrow. 'Probation?'

'You know the rules. When someone new comes here, they are on probation. They can't leave the compound without a hood. We must be sure they are trustworthy. A plant could alert our enemies if he knew where we are.'

'Gabriel already knows where we are,' Jonah answered calmly.

If he'd been riled before Jonah's last comment, he was now in overdrive. His mouth opened in disbelief and his face became even redder.

'How can he know that? Have you told him?' He looked at me, Sly—sitting at the table behind us—and then back to Jonah.

'I didn't have to. He saw where we were,' the big man continued.

'You didn't hood him?'

'No.'

Sly stood up from his chair with a sigh and walked the few steps until he stood perpendicular to both men. He pulled his lips together into a thin line and regarded Jonah from under his eyebrows. Then he turned to the fuming Marine.

'Nathan, calm down.'

'Calm down?' he almost screamed, his nostrils flaring and breath coming in bursts. 'How can I, when this group of yours brazenly defies every single rule we have.'

Sly sighed again and even rolled his eyes slightly.

'Nathan. Stop!' He enunciated each word carefully and with considerable force.

'We are aware of the rules,' he began.

'And we follow the sensible ones,' the big man inter-jected, which earned him a stern look from Sly.

'We have followed the rules,' Sly began again, daring Jonah to interrupt. My friend declined. 'Even the probation, for most of our people.'

'It's for everyone,' Nathan stated loudly.

'I disagree.' Sly's face was calm and collected but his demeanour clearly suggested that Nathan back off. The temperature in the room had gone down a few degrees.

'There are certain exceptions.'

Nathan's attempt to react was silenced by Sly's raised hand and side glance.

'The people who started the whole resistance you are now part of, they are exempt. That's Jonah, Gabriel, Aaliyah and Lady E, as well as Caleb, Nasheed and myself. Unless you want to take that up with her?'

He was silent.

'I have worked with them all on multiple missions and found them to be our greatest allies. Lady E vetted them long ago, and she pronounced them trustworthy. Now that's good enough for me. If you want to take that up with her, be my guest.'

Ebony clearly had more clout than either Jonah or me because Nathan backed down. He cast a last look at me, shooting daggers from his eyes. I shrugged and raised my eyebrow. His call.

'This isn't the last we'll talk about this,' he announced.

'Yes, it is.' Sly was clearly tiring of the conversation.

With a last glare at me and Mutt, Nathan left us.

Jonah and I could hardly conceal our smiles.

'You two,' Sly berated us. 'Will be the death of me.' He looked at Jonah intently. 'You need to stop riling him.'

'But it's so much fun,' Jonah answered for both of us. I decided to stay silent.

Sly cocked his head in answer and Jonah laughed and nodded.

Yeah, right. He would stop. No way.

In the meantime, Mutt and I would be out in the fresh air as much as possible.

Chapter Twenty-Two

Our core team was gathered in Jonah and my room. We wanted some privacy, one of the things in short supply in our new base.

Nasheed and Caleb sat on the bottom bunk, Tajan on the top one, Sly and Aaliyah had confiscated the folding chairs and Jonah stood between the table and the wall, his large bulk leaning against the hard stone surface. I had my back to the door. Mostly because it was the only place left to stand, but also to stop anyone from coming in. Mutt lay at my feet. I was counting on him to alert me if anyone approached our quarters.

Despite our attempts, we still didn't fit in with the rest of the inhabitants. It was a combination of mistrust, need for control and plain fear on both sides. And probably just simple stubbornness from us. We weren't used to following other people's orders. Jonah and I had major authority issues and Aaliyah just plain ignored them. Nathan had a massive chip on his shoulder when it came to Jonah and not a day passed when he didn't blow up about something the big man had or hadn't done. To be fair, Jonah loved baiting him.

Life in the compound was frankly boring and both the big man and me were starting to go stir crazy. Not a good situation when one is six-foot-four and two-hundred-forty pounds of bad attitude and the other is basically an irrational immortal, hell bent on revenge. It was a recipe for disaster. That was why Sly had convened the impromptu meeting. We were headed for a major confrontation and that wouldn't benefit anyone.

Though it might be fun.

Could liven things up a bit.

Anyway, we were there to generate ideas for future missions. These would be detailed out and Sly would propose them at the next meeting. Something had to happen to alleviate the tension that was building and focussing that on the enemy seemed like a no-brainer.

Sly took the floor, which was just as well.

'We need to find someone outside of this place that you two can vent your frustrations on.' He looked pertinently at Jonah and me.

Jonah raised his eyebrows in mock shock and pointed his finger to his chest while he silently mouthed the universal sign for innocence: "Moi?". Sly observed him over his glasses and the big man zipped his lips.

I stayed silent. Sly was right, we were frustrated. But not just the two of us. We all were. It had been a long time since we'd been on any kind of mission. I, myself, felt totally useless to the cause and needed to do something before my feelings of guilt combusted. I saw the same in others.

'We need to get our teeth into something,' Aaliyah remarked. 'Hit the enemy where it hurts.'

'I agree,' Sly answered. Everyone heard the unspoken "but".

'Yeah, but how?' Caleb filled in the open space. 'Last time we tried to liberate prisoners they blew them up. We can't endanger anyone like that again. And we're not familiar with what's near here.'

'What's the last info we got from Ebs?' Jonah asked from the wall.

'Cal-Tan's hold on the world is almost complete.' Sly relayed the bad news. 'The last major resistance in Russia has been annihilated and any sedition is fractured and ineffective. Though Lady E does want to follow up on a few leads she has. Seems some of the previous secret services like the KGB and Mossad have gone underground and could still be functional in a coordinated revolt. The biggest problem is how to contact them.'

I felt a spark of excitement that there could be bases like this one scattered over the world. Sly's next announcement brought back all the confusion I'd felt earlier.

'Cal-Tan is still sending masses of people through the transportation hubs. Mainly young men, with occasionally young women. Lady E estimates that more than seven million have been sent to another dimension by now.'

'Seven million?'

Sly nodded to his son. 'And there are another five million in the compounds worldwide, waiting for their turn.'

'What I don't understand is what Cal-Tan is doing with all the grunts,' I said. 'The numbers are ridiculous; he can't handle that many in the slave trade. There must be more to this than just pure profit.'

'What are you thinking?' Aaliyah joined in the conversation.

'It must be something in the Thirty-eighth. Something massive.'

'Like what?'

I shrugged and shook my head. I had no idea.

'Is there any way we can find out?' Sly suggested. That might point us to opportunities. If we know what he's trying to achieve, maybe we can sabotage that.'

'I don't see how,' Jonah remarked. 'Unless we could involve the insurgents on Taxore.'

I stayed silent. Up till now no one was aware of my mother's involvement in the resistance on Taxore. They knew I had connections to the resistance, but not how close they were to me.

'How can we do that without exposing you, Tajan or Aaliyah? There's no other explanation for a contact in Taxore.' Caleb noted. He was right. There would be no reason why anyone within these mountain walls would have contacts to the invaders dimension, other than that they were aliens themselves.

'We might have to go through Ebony,' I suggested carefully.

Sly's head shot around to me. 'You will not endanger her!' His voice was dark and dangerous.

'I have no intention of doing that,' I assured him with just as much intensity, my feelings hurt that he could even contemplate such a thing. 'She's family to me too, you know. To all of us. I would rather walk unarmed towards Cal-Tan than do anything that could risk her safety.'

He'd hit a nerve. A very sensitive one after Kate's death. I still blamed myself for her demise and probably would for the rest of my life.

He nodded and his features softened. 'I know, sorry, Gabe.'

My feelings weren't placated as quickly as that, and I had to stop myself from adding anything to my earlier outburst.

'How could she contact anyone?' Caleb asked. 'With Tajan here, she doesn't have any contacts within Taxore.'

'No, but I might,' I surprised them all.

'Are you still in contact with Taxore?' Aaliyah asked.

'I haven't heard from them for a long time,' I answered. 'And I didn't want to put them in any danger, so I refrained from trying. I'm not sure the method we used is even an option at the moment. With all the changes that have been made to life on Earth.'

'There is still a semblance of normal life,' Sly mused. 'It's only skin deep, but many of the old things are still working in a slimmed down or adapted manner. What do you need?'

'Newspapers.' I surprised them.

'Newspapers?'

I nodded.

'There are still some, though they are state owned now. That means they're censored.' Sly pointed out. 'I'm not sure which part of the newspaper you would need.'

'The personal ads.'

'We couldn't set up an ad from here,' Aaliyah pointed out. 'Nathan won't allow any communications to the outside.'

'No, And with reason.' Sly stood up for his former protege.

'That's where Ebony comes in,' I explained. 'She could find a way to clandestinely take out an ad and follow the replies.'

'It's not without risk,' Sly pointed out.

'Life hasn't been without risk since the invasion,' Jonah

pointed out. 'We will have to take risks to do anything. I'm sure Ebs is very aware of them.' Sly nodded.

'And that she won't let that stop her for doing her part,' I added.

'She has to stay safe.' Sly's love for his adopted daughter was evident.

'She won't.' Jonah answered softly. 'It's not in her genes. Or in the way she was brought up.'

'He's right,' Caleb said softly. 'You taught us to help. To stand up for others. That's what she does.'

Sly sniffed and rubbed his nose with his hand, he was conflicted. He loved her to death, like we all did, and he knew as no other how stubborn she could be.

'Why don't we let her decide?' Jonah suggested.

'That is just what I'm afraid of,' Sly replied. 'I know what she'll decide.'

'Oh, come on Dad, have you ever been able to stop her from doing what she thinks is right?'

Sly smiled. Ebony never took "no" for an answer. She lived her own life. That was what had made her what she was.

'So how are we going to contact her?' Jonah asked. 'Without Nathan knowing what it's about.'

He was right, up to now the contact with Ebony was through the resident nerd and he was on Nathan's crew. The guy thought he was speaking to a middle-aged white nerd; the deep fake identity Ebony had built to hide her true person. Only Nathan knew who it really was behind the face.

'We'll have to go off-base.' Sly uttered the words I'd hoped to hear today.

Now that was an idea that got my blood pumping. I

could see the big man's enthusiasm through his carefully controlled facial features. He hadn't had any personal contact with her for weeks now. Not since before we left our previous compound in the forests. He was looking forward to seeing his love.

Chapter Twenty-Three

We decided to meet in a secure location, if there were such a thing. It was the closest to safe for all parties that we could come to.

Sly and Nathan had argued extensively before the Marine finally gave in and let us leave the compound.

'Make sure no one finds you,' he ordered redundantly. 'No one, absolutely no one, should be able to find this place. If I see any sign of you being followed when you come back, I'll have you shot. I will not endanger the inhabitants here.'

His face was bright red with anger and concern. I understood to a point, but in my opinion his isolation tactics weren't helping to oppose the enemy. He was keeping the people relatively safe, but at what cost? They were just as much prisoners as the grunts in the holding facilities. Okay, maybe not, but you get the picture. No-one could leave. The survival of the base rested completely on secrecy, and everyone knew how fragile that was.

We were a recalcitrant bunch, and we hadn't made his

life easy. On the other hand, we'd given him access to information he would otherwise have missed and that not only helped to make the base safe, it also opened opportunities to hit back at our common enemy.

We camouflaged our latest trip as a fact-finding mission for a future attack. The committee had finally agreed to let us go. It had taken a lot of diplomacy from Sly and Aaliyah, with Jonah and me relegated to silent observers. I think the added pressure of almost a hundred people who were starting to rebel helped as well. They had a powder keg in the mountain. One that was on the brink of explosion.

We'd exaggerated the need for the recon. Ebony's team had somehow already gathered all the necessary information to mount an attack and the only thing we wanted to really do there was check the accuracy. I was convinced it would be exactly as we expected, but we needed to veil our real reason for the outing.

Sly had conveyed a coded message to Ebony through the resident nerd, and we'd received coded coordinates of the intended target. We would meet somewhere before that.

Mutt, Jonah, Caleb and I set off in the same pickup that I'd arrived in. Sly reluctantly stayed in the mountain. He wanted to monitor from there, not entirely sure about Nathan and whether he would let us back in after our trip.

Our intended target was a repurposed factory. Ebony had found out that it produced the collars we'd seen on the prisoners earlier. Anything we could do to minimise the use of such deadly items would be a major benefit. Many of the supplies used for the transportation and incarceration of the grunts were now produced on Earth. It made sense. Only the explosive substance yeraah and the ore miscian were transported in. The mechanics, electronics, and the enhanced polyester and collars themselves were fabricated in hundreds of plants world-wide. With an estimated transportation of two hundred thousand grunts a month and many more in the holding facilities, the demand was enormous.

Ebony had the original blueprints of the factory and though we expected there to be adaptations to fabricate the new product, the bones of the place would probably still be close to the original plans.

She'd indicated that further details would be imminent. I expected the use of drones to find out the finer points of the vast complex.

Because of our head start, we had the time to do a detour. Sly had effectively cut out any chance of others joining our recognisance, we didn't want any snoops. Not with what we were planning. Ebony was still under water. Other than Nathan, no one knew she was behind the technological wonders, and we wanted to keep it that way.

We'd found an abandoned motel. It wasn't an anomaly. Most of the hospitality buildings were deserted, their function completely obsolete in the new reality. Ebony's team had sent a drone to scout the location and there hadn't been any signs of human or Taxorian presence in three days. We assumed—even though we stayed alert—that there was no one there and it would be reasonably safe.

We arrived early in the evening, just as the sun painted the sky bright red drawing long shadows from the neglected buildings.

The paint flaked off the originally pueblo style walls displaying the concrete modular elements below. Arches and Spanish tiles hinted at old glory though there was little left to entice visitors to the broken-down buildings. Most of the windows had been thrown in, shards of glass still in the frames. Graffiti adorned the walls. Lots of it targeted at the invaders.

We approached carefully, driving in a large arc before we finally parked our pickup under an awning at the back of the motel. Once we were satisfied no one was there, we conscientiously explored every room of the two extensions that flanked the central structure. No one. A rat or two, and some signs of long-gone occupancy, but nothing more. Mutt proved once more to be indispensable. His nose was constantly on the ground, sniffing out any sign of either human or Taxorian. He surprised a family of rodents but that was all he found.

We approached the main part of the complex where the original office and reception had been. It was there that we found the rest. There were four of them, three bodyguards and Ebony herself. Up till that last moment I don't think either Jonah or I had really believed she would be there and that we would see her again.

The big man rushed over, discarding his ever-present axe as he swept her up in his massive arms. he swung her around and pressed his face into her still colourful hair. I saw the tears stream down both their faces; made even more precious by the bliss they portrayed.

A massive stab hit my heart. I was happy for them, but their elation stressed my own loss. I missed Kate with a vengeance, each and every day, but never so much as at that precise moment. It felt debilitating. My breath halting and shallow. I was close to hyperventilating.

I admonished myself for my self-pity and pushed myself to be happy for the big man. But it was difficult.

I felt my heart jump when Ebony spied me in the room, only then understanding how much I'd missed her.

She came over to me and hugged me. Then took my hands in hers and squeezed them.

'I'm so sorry about Kate, Gabe. I wish I'd been there to support you.' There were tears in her eyes and I felt mine do the same.

I couldn't talk so I just pulled her into an embrace. We had a comfortable intimacy that filled me with warmth. It was exactly what I needed.

I reluctantly let her go and she joined a beaming Jonah again and snaked her arms around his waist. He kissed the top of her head and wrapped his big arm around her. I was still envious of their closeness, their love, but it felt good. I'd finally experienced the same, something I hadn't achieved in the hundreds of years before I met Kate. Her warmth filled me, and at the same time left a hollow empty hole in my hearts. Losing Kate had been the most intensive loss I had ever experienced. It was a pain even my mother's teaching couldn't alleviate. I hurt intensely each day and wanted to cry every night. Only my innate need for revenge spurred me on.

'It's so good to see you all,' Ebony broke the silence. She included all of us, even the tail wagging Mutt. As usual, he'd completely done a one-eighty for a pretty face.

'It's been too long,' Caleb voiced what we were all thinking as he hugged his adopted sister.

'How have you been?' I asked.

She looked around. 'Ok, under the circumstances.'

'No one looking for you?'

'No more than usual,' she laughed. It occurred to me that I still didn't know what she did for a living. But whatever it was, it helped us in our cause.

'I have missed you all,' she added.

We all agreed, and the conversation turned to friendly banter.

Caleb took me by the arm, 'Gabe, let's go and check the other rooms.'

'What? Now?'

'Yes, now.' He glanced back at Jonah and at Ebony.

I was slow to understand, then I finally got it. They wanted some alone time. I smiled a bit to camouflage my uneasiness. Both Ebony and the big man were smiling too.

Caleb and I left the room and proceeded towards where Ebony's guards were gathered around a large thermos of coffee.

'Who am I contacting?' Ebony asked me as we sat in front of the small fire early morning of next day. Jonah and Caleb were checking the perimeter alarms we'd set up to make sure no one would accidentally barge into our camp site.

I looked up from the embers. I'd expected her to ask, even practiced what I would say. Something in the line of "I can't tell you" or another lame excuse.

I looked her in the eye and answered truthfully, surprising even myself: 'My mother.'

'That explains why you never wanted to talk about it,' she commented. 'Your mother is in the resistance?'

'Yes, she is.'

'And when did you find out?'

'Last time I was there.'

'Ahh, she was the one who helped you escape?'

It wasn't really a question. I wasn't surprised, Ebony

could connect the dots like no other. She also understood the implications.

'That must have been quite a shock.'

'Understatement of the year,' I smiled. 'She's been fighting my father for centuries. Undermining his authority right under his nose.'

'Brave woman.'

'You have no idea,' I answered. 'And neither did I,' I added, the guilty feeling that I should have known resurfacing.

'You must be so proud of her, and she of you.'

I smiled and nodded. No more needed to be said. A warm glow started in my chest at the thought of my mother the last time we spoke. She'd expressed her pride at my rebellion, at my goals. I hadn't been able to say how mutual that was, so shocked by her revelations.

Ebony broached a subject that haunted me every night. 'Are you convinced your father doesn't know?'

I voiced the conclusion I'd come to, one that made sense and was something I could live with. 'Yes. He would kill her if he found out. It would be the ultimate betrayal, even worse than mine. So it's imperative he never does.'

Ebony nodded. 'Then we have to make sure he can't. Is there anyone else who knows? Like Aaliyah?'

'I'm not sure. She might, she's surprised me before, but she's never given any indication that she does.'

'No one else?'

'No. I didn't dare tell anyone. It's not that I don't trust them. I do, with my life.'

'But not with hers.'

I shrugged.

'It's understandable. I think I'd do the same.'

'She has to stay invisible,' I implored. 'Cal-Tan would

make an example of her in the worst possible way. She has already sacrificed her whole life for me, for the resistance. I can't endanger her anymore.'

'We won't.' Ebony made it a collective action, and I was grateful for that.

'What made you want to contact Taxore now?' Ebony brought the conversation back to the reason we'd met up.

'We need to know why Cal-Tan is sending so many people off-world, where he's sending them to and for what? I think the destination is the Thirty-eighth dimension. It's the only thing that makes sense with these kinds of numbers.'

'Why is that relevant at this point in the struggle?'

'It could give us some insight on the total numbers he's working with. And how badly he needs labour. That, in turn, will give us an indication on how far he's willing to go.'

'Do you think he will keep his word and bring them back after five years?

'Not a chance.' I answered resolutely. 'People want to believe him. That makes them complacent. They don't want to antagonise the invaders and have basically accepted their rule. That will last until they are faced with the betrayal and his lies, and then it will be too late. The sooner we can inform them, the less established his rule will be.'

'It will give us a way to show they're not to be trusted.'

'Exactly.'

'All the information we can get will help us.'

She observed me closely. 'How bad is it, do you think?'

'What?' I tried.

'The resistance. Here on Earth.'

'Bad. The groups are fragmented, scattered over the country. And everywhere else. There's little cooperation and everyone is basically taking care of themselves. The base we've joined is more concerned with staying invisible than in launching any kind of resistance.

'Survival.'

I nodded. 'And that's exactly what Cal-Tan wants. As long as he can keep us separated, he'll have rendered most of the resistance futile.'

'Divide and conquer?'

'Yes. And keep everyone silent.'

'Silence is such a valuable weapon,' Ebony commented.

'The biggest.'

We fell silent, both lost in our own contemplations.

'How do you contact the Taxorian resistance?' Ebony asked after a few minutes.

'It's a variation of an old trick mum taught me. A code in a text. We adapted it to an ad in a newspaper here. I'm just not sure the newspaper is even still available or that there is anyone checking it who can pass the message on to Taxore. It's a hell of a risk. We need to make sure neither side can be traced.'

I filled Ebony in on the details of the strange code and the communication forms. She agreed to find out what she could about the Earthen side. There was however no way any of us could check on Taxore. It would stay a major risk; one I still wasn't completely convinced we should really chance. Not with my mother's life in the balance.

We also agreed that she wouldn't tell anyone about my mother. It was just too perilous.

Jonah and Caleb joined us and dumped a new stock of dead branches for the flames. We sat around the welcome heat and mused over what was to come.

'It's so frustrating,' Caleb told his adopted sister. 'We can't launch attacks on holding facilities because of the collars, and Nathan, the leader at the base, is reluctant to try any offensive on anything else. We're basically stuck. And it's driving us all nuts. The place is a powder keg waiting to explode.'

'It's like that everywhere,' Ebony answered. 'Cal-Tan's division tactics are working. No one really dares to oppose the invaders.'

'The message was clear enough. If you do, you die. You and everyone around you.'

'There must be something we can do,' I said exasperated. 'We can't just let Earth accept what's happening. He'll run it to the ground.'

'I'll try to find more resistance groups,' Ebony suggested. 'Then maybe we can make some initial connections. I'm looking across the borders, even to Europe and Asia. The only way we'll be able to make a difference is with a coordinated approach.'

'But why would they listen to us anyway?' Caleb lamented.

'We're the ones that exposed The Establishment,' Jonah answered.

'Not sure that's a good thing to mention, big man.' Ebony took Jonah's hand. 'There are a lot of people out there that lay the blame for the invasion with that.'

'That's short sighted. Cal-Tan would have invaded anyway.'

'Yes. We know that. But they don't. And there's no way we can convince them without revealing Gabe and Aaliyah's origin. Under the circumstances we want to avoid that. There would be a witch hunt.'

He nodded reluctantly.

For us, exposing The Establishment had been a major success, one that had carried us forward for a while. The invasion had already been in my father's plans, I was certain of that. Otherwise, how would he have been ready to harvest the hundreds of thousand, even millions, of grunts he seemed to need. That wouldn't have worked with the reincarnation method. There was no way he would be able to transport that many people without invading Earth. But Ebony was right. We wouldn't be able to explain the nuances without exposing ourselves.

Cooperation with other resistance groups seemed like the best way to go. But it had major risks. What if they had been infiltrated? Not every group had a tech wizard like we did. Our screening was basically foolproof. It would take time and a lot of effort by Ebony and her team to first find, then evaluate, more potential allies.

We left again next day, secure in the knowledge Ebony was doing all she could to help our case while keeping safe herself.

Chapter Twenty-Four

Taxore

The witch-hunt was in full swing on Taxore. Cal-Tan knew there was a traitor in the ranks, he just didn't know where, and that was driving him crazy. Not a good state of mind for a volatile psychopath.

One person was totally enjoying the paranoia. Ibrahim had free rein over the investigations, and he used this to fulfil his most brutal cravings. For him, there was no distinction between status, gender or connections. If his gaze fell on someone, they were done for. He honed his torture skills on the victims, enhanced by age-old Hashta techniques and had the time of his new life. Even in a group of killers, he stood out in imagination and dedication to inflicting unthinkable pain.

Many died at his hands. Some he surmised were even part of the Taxorian resistance. They died horribly, but to his amusement, none of them talked. One by one their lives terminated with their secrets intact. He was no closer to finding the traitor than before. He didn't care. It offered him an endless supply of victims. But he was aware that Cal-Tan wanted results and how volatile his temper was. He had no intension of ending up as a subject for Hashta torture himself.

Cal-Tan was in everything but formality the ruler of Taxore. His power and the dimension's dependency pushed him into a position where he literally determined what the dimension did.

Sure, the council had tried to intervene. Their attempts to hold on to their power had been quashed by Hashta visits to their families. Close family members had disappeared. Others had encountered strange accidents debilitating them or even killing the weaker ones. Never obvious, but still clear. No one crossed Cal-Tan.

The enormous threats endangering the first dimension were mounting. Cal-Tan had a solution, or so he claimed. Survival won, freedom lost, as it so often does. Like the humans, the Taxorians traded their independence for a chance to endure and weather the storm that faced their world. The masses rallied behind Cal-Tan, ensuring his grasp for power was guaranteed.

His hold on the planet was absolute. He tolerated no opposition, no questions and only accepted complete and utter compliance.

He was on a clock.

Cal-Tan had a plan, and no one—absolutely no one—would come between that and its fulfilment.

Chapter Twenty-Five

And then there was Michael and his untimely death.

The worst part had been the wait. The endless period between death and reincarnation. Michael had never felt so alone, so forsaken, so abandoned.

Time didn't exist in the vacuum between life and death. There was no sense of it, yet it was endless. Initially, his mind had been blissfully dormant, his essence floating on a river of peace. The longer he stayed in that void, the more his consciousness became aware. And the more he knew what was happening or in his case, wasn't. He felt the minutes as hours, days as years. Without the presence of time everything is infinite. And empty. He was lost. Waiting on what more and more seemed would never happen.

The realisation was the worst. They knew he was there, in limbo. They had to. His wakening mind reminded him of how the procedure worked. The essence was captured and temporarily stored awaiting the pre-growth. Only this wasn't temporary. It was infinite, and with it came the understanding that he had been forsaken, abandoned. Fully aware of his precarious situation; his dependency on someone flicking a switch, he understood his long wait was intentional.

This was yet another torture his father made him endure.

He had failed him. He deserved what Cal-Tan handed him.

The terror he felt was worse than anything anyone, including his father, had ever rained down on him. Never mind Ibrahim with his psychotic love of pain. The demeaning glances of Cal-Tan would be a walk in the park compared with what he endured in the emptiness. Even the possibility of the Hashta's knives was preferable to the emptiness and rejection that filled his every pore.

When the prayed for reincarnation finally came, he was reluctant. Was this just another step in the endless torture he was sentenced to endure? Was it even real? Or just another figment of his terrified imagination?

He was conflicted, torn between trepidation and elation that his prayers had been heard, that there was someone out there who loved him. Someone who had taken upon themselves the task of reincarnating his essence into a new body. The thought warmed him. The prospect of taking another breath. Of holding his mother.

But there was also the apprehension, What would await him when he woke up? Why had they continued the process, after all that time? Had Cal-Tan had a change of heart? Or was this just another step in the endless torment the man rained down on his progeny.

He opened his eyes and found out.

Chapter Twenty-Six

Like always, he felt ten years old again.

A small child in the presence of his father, the important head of the family, and so much more. Only this time there was something else mixed in with the trepidation and the fear. For the first time in his life there was the seed of resentment.

It was such a foreign feeling for Michael that he initially repelled it. All his life he'd lived for his father's approval. That had been his only goal. Now it seemed corrupted. The edges slowly rotting away, brown and powdery. It felt strange. The man he'd put on a pedestal for so long was tainted, his image blurring. It gave Michael a welcome feeling of freedom and at the same time one of enormous loss. It had been his foundation and now that was crumbling, endangering his mental stability.

For the first time in his long existence, he looked up at the man opposite him. He dared to look him in the eye.

It wasn't lost on Cal-Tan.

He attributed it to the new body. A reincarnation, along

with the obvious disadvantages of getting used to the new form, also gave the owner a renewed sense of life and self. That often translated into a feeling of immortality, they'd conquered death, they felt they could do anything. Time for a reality check. He'd given Michael life—again—and he could take it away. It was time his son understood that.

'You've failed me, Michael.' He went right in, straight for the jugulars. 'You had a simple task. Make sure The Establishment follows my guidelines. Once again you let your younger brother take control of what was mine. Because of your inadequacy, I had to move the invasion up in time. It resulted in more fatalities and so, more costs.'

Each word felt like a stab directly into Michael's hearts. He flinched visibly at his father's rejection. Yes, it was more of what he'd experienced most of his life, but it still hurt, badly.

'How difficult is it to best your brother? You are the eldest, you should be able to successfully trump anything he does. Yet again, and again, he is the victorious one.' Cal-Tan rubbed in the already existing sibling rivalry. 'He is a flea in my pelt. An irritation. Something that should have been taken care of long ago. Since he returned to Earth, he has increased his rebellion and even the invasion has not stopped him. He makes me look bad. My son, my apparent heir, betrayed me.'

Michael recoiled internally at his father's words. He was the heir. Not Gabriel. He was the eldest. He had always been the loyal son.

'I reincarnated you,' his father continued. 'I decided to give you another chance, not that you deserve it. You have one more opportunity to redeem yourself and show that you are worthy of my trust.'

His words registered with Michael. Part of him felt the

stirrings of elation. His father had not written him off. A small voice at the back of his mind, one he had never given any attention to before, asked why he still believed Cal-Tan. Why he would even bother to try and please a man who would never, ever, give him the respect he deserved. Previously, he'd ignored the recalcitrant thoughts. But now, after the long, endless and terrifying wait in the emptiness, he let the words register. This was the man who had left him there. He had abandoned his own son into nothingness. Michael had suffered beyond imagination in the twilight between life and death. And that was all down to the man who—once again—now criticised his every move.

How was it his fault that Gabriel had brought down The Establishment? Had he not died to protect his father's interests? If there were any fault, then it lay with the man standing to his father's right. The place where he himself should be. Ibrahim. The butcher. A reincarnated grunt. How could he listen to him instead of his own blood? Yet he did. Cal-Tan's paranoia was pushing his own family away. And the Hashta had successfully filled the void that was left behind.

'I can take that life away as easily as I granted it,' his father continued.

So take it, Michael wanted to shout out. Life as it was now, wasn't worth living. His father had damned him to hell with the reincarnation. He had taken away that one thing that Michael had, himself. What could he do that was worse than that?

'You will bring me Gabriel. Dead or alive. Preferably breathing so that I can extract my revenge on him.'

Gabriel again. Michale was sick of even the mention of his brother. He was the bane of his existence. Without him, life would have been different, better. But no, Gabriel had taken away any chance of that, and still he managed to thwart Michael at every turn.

'It is the one and only reason I brought you back. You breathe to catch him. That is the way you will redeem yourself for the failure that you are.'

Michael wanted to scream. Would the man never stop? He understood. No need to keep rubbing it in. It wasn't like he could escape the quest, or his brother. He would capture him. Not for his father, for his own closure. To rid himself of the endless comparison and rejection. So that he could finally find rest. Then he would let the butcher have him, there would be no clemency for his brother next time they met.

'You will go back to Earth with Ibrahim, and you will bring me what I require.'

'You will not disappoint me again, Michael.' It wasn't a question.

He was dismissed.

Cal-Tan turned his back on his son and sat down again at his desk, supposedly studying more important aspects of his busy schedule.

Chapter Twenty-Seven

'Michael.'

Ibrahim's laugh was cold and mirthless.

Michael refrained from answering and did his best to ignore him. He continued to walk the long corridor from his father's office to his own quarters.

Ibrahim caught up with him and adapted his pace to the smaller man. 'Your father really did a good one on you this time. He out-did himself.' He was enjoying this.

Michael felt the hairs in his neck stand up. He wanted to act, to wipe that smirk off the butcher's face. The need almost overwhelmed him, but he knew he was no match for Ibrahim. His new body was fit and strong, but the reincarnation was too fresh, and he lacked the energy or the coordination. Muscles were slow to react, almost as though the synopsis in his body hadn't woken up yet.

There was nothing he could do. Not yet.

'No way you can escape your failure this time.' Ibrahim's words brought him out of his reverie.

He stopped and confronted his new tormentor. 'And whose fault do you think that is?' Michael couldn't stop himself. 'This is all because of you.'

Ibrahim crossed his arms over his chest and looked down at Michael with a patronising stare. 'Of course it is.' Sarcasm dripped off the butcher's reply. 'You're incapable of taking responsibility.'

Michael's face coloured purple with his rage. 'You threw me to the lions. Pushed me in front of Aaliyah. It was your job to protect me.' He felt vindicated. The Hashta was there as a bodyguard, he was the one who had failed.

The smile on Ibrahim's face showed his amusement. 'It was my job to protect your father's best interests.'

'I am my father's interest.' Michale shouted.

Ibrahim's lips pulled up into a vicious line that sent new shivers up Michale's spine. 'Yeah. Look in the mirror when you say that.'

The silence could be cut with a knife, Michael had no answer. His body shook with rage, his hands balled into fists, the nails cutting into his palms. He felt the heat wash over him like a wave, pushing his common sense to the background and urging him to attack the butcher and cut that infuriating pretentious smirk off his features.

'You may want to check with dear old dad,' Ibrahim pushed the spike deeper.

Michael closed his eyes, he knew it showed his inner conflict, but there was nothing else he could do to quell the emotions deep inside him. He couldn't win this fight, and deep down he was sure his father wouldn't even punish Ibrahim if the man hurt or even killed him. The old man had been clear in his rhetoric. He had no love for Michael. That much was abundantly clear. Otherwise, he wouldn't have treated him the way he had and let him linger so long in the darkness of death. And then he had woken him, which was even worse. He'd reincarnated his eldest son into a hell so bad he almost wanted to go back to the emptiness. At least there he could fool himself that there had been love, there had been caring. Now he knew. He was a pawn. Nothing more.

'No. I didn't think so.' Ibrahim's words pulled him out of his contemplations. 'Face it Michael. You never were and never will be his favourite. Your failure is a disgrace.'

'You can't talk to me like that?' The anger was still in Michael's words, but the power had fled him.

'Why not. It's not like he cares what happens to you. You're expendable. Unlike Gabriel. He doesn't give a shit what I do to you. And if you disagree, go complain to your father, by all means. See how far that gets you.'

The butcher invaded Michael's space, his face up too close. Michael took an involuntary step backwards until his back almost touched the wall and raised his hands up in front of his chest to ward off the threat.

'One of these days, your father is going to tire of watching you fail. He's still amused, but that won't last. And then he'll hand you over to me and we will finally see what you're made of.'

Michael pulled back as far as he could in absolute terror, The anger fled him, and he felt the muscles in his body tense for what he knew was a flight reaction. The utter malevolence that seeped out of the butcher was terrifying and there was no way he could keep his act together. Not under the pressure of the impending bloody and excruciating death he saw mirrored in the dark eyes of the Hashta.

Ibrahim pushed him in the chest with one finger

knocking him over, and left the corridor, his cold laughter following him.

Michael sat on the floor, unsuccessfully attempting to hold back the tears. He felt so small, so insignificant and just as lost as he had in the void.

Chapter Twenty-Eight

'Get out!' Michael shouted. 'All of you, except him.' He pointed to Ibrahim.

The others looked at Ibrahim for guidance. He nodded to them, and they left the room.

Ibrahim observed the angry man in front of him. Michael's face was bright purple, his nostrils flaring and his lips pulled tightly in a hard line. He stood up straighter than the last time they'd met two days before, with the muscles in his shoulders tense. Frankly, he looked ready to pounce.

Ibrahim casually crossed his arms over his chest and stared Michael in the eye. This time the man didn't avoid the direct eye contact; he was just too mad. There was a stalemate. The Hashta waited patiently, comfortable in the silence.

'I was just with my mother,' Michael barely managed to articulate the words through his anger.

Again, Ibrahim didn't react.'

'She's wounded. Her shoulder is dislocated, and she has a multitude of bruises and contusions.'

Ibrahim shrugged his shoulders, further aggravating Michael.

'What the hell did you do?' Michael shouted; all reservations gone.

'We talked.'

'You talked! You tortured her.' He took a step forward, bringing himself dangerously close.

Again, Ibrahim shrugged, not in the least impressed with Michael's outburst.

'Don't you ever, EVER, touch my mother again.' Michael pointed his finger at Ibrahim to make his point, he stopped just short of poking the butcher in the chest.

It amused the other man who chuckled softly. Just loud enough for Michael to hear.

'What do you think my father will say about this?' Michael strove to gain the upper hand.

Ibrahim raised an eyebrow and looked at the smaller man incredulously. 'Are you really that naive Michael?'

Michael was flustered. This was not the reaction he'd expected. He thought the mere mention of his father would make Ibrahim shudder, or at the least apologise.

'What do you mean?' the power in his voice was lost as he started to doubt himself.

Ibrahim huffed his disgust. 'Where do you think the order came from?'

A physical blow couldn't have had a bigger impact on Michael. He flinched visibly, his eyes opening to the max. The earlier blush in his features paled with the realisation that not only had his father condoned the torture, he'd arranged it. His mind couldn't process the understanding.

He stammered. 'My father would never hurt her.' Even he didn't believe his statement.

Ibrahim cocked his head and stared at Michael; his

voice full of contempt. 'Are you blind? Beating her is his idea of foreplay.'

'She's the mother of his children.' It sounded weak, pathetic.

'Yes, and one of them now leads the resistance on Earth.' The butcher's words were cold, the danger clear.

Ibrahim uncrossed his arms and pushed himself up from the table he was resting against. He stepped towards Michal, stopping only half a metre from him. The presence of the tall dark man dressed completely in black was intimidating. His earlier courage fled him, and it took all his resolve to stay put. His body screamed at him to move backwards and keep the distance much, much larger.

'How can my father ever suspect her of anything? She has supported him throughout his life. She's never even contradicted him.'

'Someone helped Gabriel to escape,' Ibrahim continued.

Michael willed his body not to react and stayed silent.

'We will find out who that was, and we will catch him or her,' Ibrahim continued. 'There is a traitor within the palace. Someone who defies Cal-Tan. He—or she—aided Gabriel in his escape, killed the guards and assisted in his return to Earth where he subsequently exposed The Establishment.'

Micheal cringed inside but managed to keep his face straight.

He'd hoped the invasion and the Thirty-eighth would distract any attention from Gabriel's magical escape. He'd killed the guards so no one would be able to identify him. In his naive mind, Cal-Tan would never, never, suspect anyone from the family. And now his actions had resulted in his mother's torture. A stab of pain hit his hearts. Had it been his fault? Was that true? Was the pain she had endured a direct result of his actions? Actions that had once again failed miserably. It had been his intent to ultimately hunt down and kill Gabriel himself. Get to him before the butcher did. Before unspeakable torture would be rained down on his infuriating brother. His mother would have grieved, but his actions would have made the loss bearable for her. At least he would have made it quick and clean. An easy death. Practically painless. All to relieve her pain. And now, he was the reason she had even more.

'We will find whoever aided him,' the venom in Ibrahim's voice brought Michael back to the present. 'And whoever that is will wish they had never been born.' He stepped even closer to emphasis the point.

Micheal stayed silent. He didn't trust his nerves to answer, the butcher would pick up on the stress in his voice. He was barely holding himself together. For the first time he was grateful for the newness of his body. The synapses were still sluggish and slow to react. That gave him that split second respite to stop some of the unintended reactions. Hopefully it would be enough.

Ibrahim slapped him on the side of his left shoulder. 'Don't worry, she didn't have anything to say. Nothing interesting anyway.' His version of a smile pulled his lips into a thin hard line. Michael couldn't resist the shiver that went through his body, and he inadvertently pulled his hand upwards to ward off the daemon.

'Well, not yet,' Ibrahim added as he stared into Michael's eyes.

Michael could barely stay upright. He hated himself for it, but lowered his eyes, unable to guarantee that the Hashta wouldn't see his guilt there

With a last laugh, Ibrahim left the room.

Michael stayed where he was. Upright. He didn't trust his body to move, scared his legs wouldn't hold his weight. What should have been a rightful accusation had turned into a nightmare.

They were looking for Gabriel's liberator. For him. He would have to tread even more carefully, not make any waves. Make sure there was no reason for Ibrahim to suspect him. If Cal-Tan was prepared to let the Hashta torture his wife, someone beyond reproach, then he would have no qualms about his son.

He shuffled towards the chair, sat down and put his head in his hands until the shaking stopped.

Chapter Twenty-Nine

Earth

The news was terrible.

The worst.

Ebony had been captured.

We'd lost our friend, our family member, our tech wizard. She should have been untouchable and had been for so long that we barely entertained the idea anymore. She was so adept at staying hidden, doing her business without the lime-lights, and though the possibility had existed as a nightmare scenario in back of our minds, we'd never really contemplated the possibility.

The big man exploded.

'Where is she?'

We couldn't answer. We only had a short cryptic message from Sly. "We've been attacked, and the prize has been captured." He was on the way back to the mountain compound. Because of the security here and the secrecy that had to be maintained, there was no further contact.

The message was all we had. And we individually filled in the many gaps in the story. None of which had a happy ending or were based on more than conjecture.

Jonah wanted to storm out and race to where she'd been taken, but we didn't even know where that was. Sly, Nasheed and Caleb had left the compound seventy-two hours ago for a meeting with Ebony and some of her team. She'd informed us they'd made mind-blowing advances, ones she couldn't share on our secure communication. A face-to-face had been the only real option. Now it had been the worst one.

'You have to wait, Jonah,' I tried, my hand on his arm. He shrugged me off and grabbed his axe, slotting the blade pieces in place to form the formidable weapon. That was bad. He never did that inside the mountain. It was one of the concessions he'd finally agreed with Nathan. All that was out the window now. Ebony was the only thing on his mind.

'We don't know what happened,' Aaliyah joined in. 'We have to wait for Sly.'

'Hell no! We could be too late if don't act now.'

'Act on what?' Aaliyah and I alternated. We had to calm the big man down. The mood he was in now was suicidal and that wouldn't help Ebony in any way.

'If they have her, they know who she is.' The voice came from the corner. Our eyes turned in unison to Tajan. The small man wilted under Jonah's intense stare but held his ground.

'That means they will want to keep her alive,' he concluded.

That outcome had a massive impact on my anxiety. I looked at Jonah and saw he was contemplating the information as well.

'What do you mean?' he asked Tajan, his voice never losing the hard edge. I pitied the small man. Jonah was a true force of nature.

'They know how good she is. How important. They will want to convince her to change sides.'

'She'd never do that.' The implied threat was like a shout in the silence.

'No, of course she wouldn't. But it will give her time. Give us time to find a way to free her.'

He was right.

The more value she had for them, the longer she would live and the best chance we had of an escape attempt.

'He has a point,' I offered, trying to placate the big man to the point that he would see reason.

We were still a way off.

I could see the cogs in Jonah's mind work. The battle between mind and heart raged in his features. I wished I could help more, but there was no suggestion I could propose that would help. I agreed with Tajan. My father, and dare I say the butcher, would recognise the diamond they had in their hands. Why otherwise would they have let her live? The impression I got from the little information we had was that she had been the target.

But there was nothing we could do now, not until Sly arrived back at base.

It was a long wait, the worst time of our lives.

I missed Kate with a vengeance. She would have been able to at least temper the anxiety I felt. Her absence was even more pronounced now than in the past weeks. I felt I knew what Jonah was going through, and I didn't envy him.

Twelve hours after the message, the pickup limped into the mountain. One wheel had a distinct wobble, and the windscreen had been shattered by what looked like gunfire.

Sly's stern visage behind the remaining shards was tanta-
mount to the difficult journey he and two others had
endured.

We rushed to the vehicle and carefully manhandled the
unconscious girl I knew as Pigtails from the backseat. She
was moved to a gurney and sped off to the medical unit in
one of the caves behind us. Her companion, another of
Ebony's tech team, followed close to the medics, holding her
hand.

Sly remained behind.

He was battered and bruised; the discolouration's clearly
visible even on his dark skin. There was a big scab on the
top of his shaved head and the shirt below that side of his
body was saturated with blood. His left hand was tucked
into his shirt at the wrist, the arm slack and the upper part
bent at an unnatural angle.

'You need medical attention,' one of the remaining
medics suggested.

'Later.'

The medic gauged his chances of success and came to
the right conclusion. 'Come see us as soon as possible. We
need to set that arm.'

Sly nodded but didn't look at him. He was focussed on
the big man.

'They knew she was there.' His voice was saturated with
the rage that shone in his eyes. 'And who she is.'

'An ambush?' I asked.

Sly turned his face to Aaliyah and me, registering our
presence for the first time.

He nodded.

'You fought.' Not a question, just a prompt to continue.

'We did what we could. They came prepared. When we
arrived at the rendezvous point, they'd just attacked

Ebony's party. I don't think they expected us, but her guards were already dead or dying, Melanie and Todd were pinned down, trying to help Ebony. We pushed to free her, but they overwhelmed us easily with superior fire power.'

He lowered his eyes. There was more.

I looked back at the pickup, then at the ramp up the mountain. No one else had followed. No other vehicles.

'Where are the rest?' I asked carefully. 'Nasheed, Caleb?'

'They've been taken.'

We had no words. It was even worse than I'd imagined.

I couldn't imagine Sly's pain. Not only his adopted daughter, but his son and a valued friend were in the hands of the invaders. There was nothing helpful I could say, so I stayed silent.

'Where did they take them?' Jonah asked.

Sly lowered his gaze and shook his head dejectedly. 'I don't know.'

I was crestfallen.

'How did you escape?' Jonah asked without judgement.

'Once they had Ebony, the invaders blew up the building,' Sly continued his narrative. 'I was knocked out by the debris falling all around me. When I came to, I was buried under two feet of rubbish. I managed to push it up with my right arm and my feet without it all collapsing. I stumbled out and had difficulty getting my bearings. I heard a noise from the right and saw Todd frantically digging in the debris. He was trying to get Melanie out.'

Sly took a deep breath.

'There was no one else. The place was deserted. I staggered towards Todd and helped him dig her out. She was unconscious. She's stayed that way. I have no idea whether she'll wake up. She was pretty banged up. Todd and I hunted for others, but we only found corpses.'

The chill in my spine had extended to the rest of my body. Jonah's brow creased more than I thought possible with every word. His shoulders were tense, and his hands gripped into fists, the knuckles white with the effort.

'We couldn't find Ebony, Nasheed or Caleb. We have to conclude they've been taken.'

The big block of concrete that was poised on the edge of my emotions sank heavily into my gut.

'We searched. There was no trace.' Sly's voice faltered, and he was in danger of breaking down. Aaliyah snaked her arm around his waist and squeezed him in support. He looked at her with gratitude in his tear-filled eyes. I'd never seen the man so vulnerable. But his emotions were just mirroring ours. We were all on the verge of panic. This was family, all three of them.

'We need to find them,' Jonah's whispered voice broke the silence.

'How?' Aaliyah asked. The big man had no answer.

'We have to talk to Todd, see if he saw anything while I was out cold,' Sly suggested.

'First, you need to get your arm looked at,' Jonah announced. 'You're no use to Ebony with one arm.'

It was hard, but it was just what Sly needed. He nodded and we all made our way to the hospital department in the vast mountain compound.

The doctor pronounced Melanie to be in a stable condition then set the break in Sly's arm. She had to pull the two edges of the break together and the pain must have been enormous. Sly's face turned a sickly grey and sweat dripped off his scalp, but he never called out. He just endured. The doctor cleaned the cut on his head and added two stitches.

Later that day we were gathered around his bed in the sickbay. It was a compromise Sly had to agree to. The initial blast, the trauma, blood loss and the long journey behind the wheel back to the compound had taken its toll and Sly was prescribed bedrest. The doctor had won the argument and Sly was stuck in the room for at least one night. He was in the room next to where Melanie rested, and we spoke in soft voices to not wake her.

Sly wore his guilty feelings on his sleeve. His concern for his family was etched in the deep lines of his brow and the tightness of his lips.

He was deaf to our reassurance that there was nothing he could have done. It clearly aggravated him. He felt helpless.

Todd joined us and asked Sly how he was.

'I'll live. How's Melanie?'

'One of the beams knocked her out. The doctor has sedated her for now, but she doesn't think there is any real damage to her body. She couldn't say anything about her mind. We'll have to wait until Melanie wakes up for that.'

'Does she think there's brain damage?'

'She doesn't know. Not without a scan, and that's not an option.'

The sickbay was quite well equipped, but it was by no means a fully functioning hospital. There was a handheld echo machine, old x-ray equipment but no MRI or anything of that magnitude.

'What happened?' I asked Todd.

'I'm not sure. It happened so quickly.' He sniffed loudly, the memories hard to relive. 'There was nothing on the radar as we approached the abandoned store. I sent up a drone, just to be sure and that came back negative too, so we proceeded. We did take precautions.' He looked at us helplessly, begging for forgiveness,

I nodded. So did Sly, urging the tech guy on.

'We'd barely entered the building when they surrounded us. There were too many. They targeted the guards, killing them immediately and we all rushed for the little cover we could find. It wasn't enough and they pulled us out from where we hid. Lady E and Melanie fought them. They landed some good kicks and punches, but the grunts overwhelmed them by sheer numbers. I hit one, but he just turned around like he hadn't felt it and smashed his weapon in my gut. I doubled over, retching on the floor. When I looked up, I saw they'd restrained Lady E. Melanie was still fighting—she's a hell of a fighter—but one of them was training a gun on her. I rushed him from behind and we tumbled to the floor. He got up and trained his gun on me. I tried to reach one of our guard's weapons, but it was too far from where I'd hit the ground.'

He paused for a moment. 'Just as he was about to fire, Sly and the others came in, guns blazing. The invaders were forced backwards, but they pulled Lady E with them out through the door at the back off the room. Then they threw some kind of explosive at us. We dove for cover and the first blast rang out.'

'I heard Lady E scream out to us to get the hell out. The invaders came back in the room, threw more explosives at the walls and the ceiling, grenades I expect, and everything just went to hell. The building collapsed, the ceiling came down and buried me. Next thing I knew it was quiet, and I sat up in the debris. I saw Melanie and started to dig her out. Then Sly came to help me.'

'Did you hear anything that could be a clue to where they've taken her, or the others?' Jonah asked.

Todd shook his head, close to tears.

I placed my hand on his shoulder in support.

He looked up, anguish in his eyes and the slump of his shoulders.

'There was nothing you could have done, Todd,' I whispered.

He tried to nod, but it wasn't with conviction, and he bent forward his head in his hands while he wept.

Chapter Thirty

'Ebony!'

She turned to the voice, momentarily stunned to see Gabriel in the corridor outside the make-shift cell.

Her emotions soured. He was there to get her out, to save her. A massive smile adorned her lips, and she took a step forward to the bars.

But something stopped her. A cold shiver ran up her spine and nestled in the back of her head.

Something was wrong.

The man in front of her stopped his advance, faltering slightly, his lack of confidence seeping through the carefully created facade.

Ebony observed him in detail, her analytical mind already investigating the reasons why she was reluctant to take his outstretched hand.

His face was so familiar, so welcome. But there was something about his posture. It was off. She couldn't put into words what it was exactly, but whatever it was, it was setting off alarm bells.

He cocked his head in surprise, his hand still outstretched towards her.

She remained stationary a metre from the bars.

He pulled a key from his pocket, turned the lock and opened the door for her.

'Ebony?' he repeated.

The voice. It was like Gabriel's. Similar but not quite identical. Like his aura.

His demeanour was different too, nothing she could put a finger on, but it enforced her conviction that things were not as they seemed.

'Ed?'

His brow crunched in question. For a fleeting moment she saw uncertainty in his eyes at the old nickname. He didn't recognise it.

She turned her back to him, walked back to the bunkbed and sat down.

'Ebony. What are you doing. It's me, Gabriel.' He stepped up to the open doorway but remained on the other side.

The more he spoke, the more evident it became that this definitely was not her friend. Who it was, was not relevant.

After the initial shock Ebony found she wasn't surprised. Not really. The Taxorians had the technology to grow a body based on DNA. Like Jonah's grunt body, it would be externally identical to the host's form. But mannerisms and demeanour were more difficult to duplicate. They were determined by the essence as much as the body. The voice was different too. Maybe not the timbre, but certainly the tone. And he hadn't recognised the nickname.

Whoever this was, it wasn't Gabriel.

The implications struck her immediately. She hadn't been fooled, but she was more observant than most. This development was devastating. An imposter would be able to infiltrate the resistance and expose everything. It would mean the end of the struggle for freedom.

The man continued to address her, anxiety now creeping into his voice.

Ebony looked up, her eyes full of anger and contempt. 'I don't know you,' she answered

'Don't be silly, Ebony. It's me. Gabriel. I've come to get you out of here. But we need to hurry.'

He turned sideways to her, gesturing with his hand that she hurry.

'I don't know you,' she repeated.

The door to the corridor outside the row of cells opened and Ebony heard strong footsteps enter the room

'Bravo,' Ibrahim said as he walked into the room, clapping his hands in mock tribute to her ingenuity. 'What gave him away?'

She observed the Hashta approaching the still open cell door.

'Everything.' Her tone was full of disdain. For Ibrahim, and for this apparition. She stood up and turned her back on them, pushing the point home.

Ibrahim cocked his head in dismissal and the imposter left the room, his eyes averted in defeat.

The Hashta walked into her cell and stopped just inside the door. Ebony remained where she was.

'Welcome to our humble abode,' he continued.

Ebony refrained from any acknowledgement, aware that her first reactions would determine the power balance in whatever was to come. She had no illusions. Gabriel—the real Gabriel—had been clear in his recounts of Hashta brutality. That she was female would make no difference to the butcher. He would torture her as easily as one of the men.

An unbidden worry resurfaced, and she wondered what had happened to the others. Had they been captured too? Were they alive? How many? And who?

She couldn't let her emotions weaken her and pushed them to the background as she had so many times as a child. Steeling herself for whatever was to come, she silently vowed to hold out as long as possible. Ebony had no misconceptions. This would be hell.

She turned to face her nemesis.

The smile on Ibrahim's face momentarily sent shivers up her spine, but she quashed any visible reaction and stared at the cold dark eyes of the Hashta. She recognised the psychopath in their depths. That and endless pain and suffering to come.

He stepped to the side to let her pass and with an exaggerated mock etiquette indicated she should leave the cell.

The goosebumps continued until she'd passed him and left the room of cells. She expected him to grab her from behind at any moment and the pain to commence.

Chapter Thirty-One

The interrogation room was more comfortable, with a heavy wooden table and two reasonably comfortable chairs. Ebony took the one opposite the door and sat down.

Ibrahim followed suite and placed his considerable bulk in the seat opposite her. Another black clad figure joined them in the room and closed the door. He stood to the right of the opening with his back to the wall, and observed her unabashedly, seemingly amused by her neon-coloured hair.

'You are a formidable fighter,' Ibrahim broke the silence.

She refrained from comment.

'For your size, you pack a punch. You brought down some of the best.'

Ebony stared at him, her eyes never leaving his. Ibrahim's intimidation tactics weren't working. At least not externally. The butterflies in her stomach were doing over-time, but she refused to show any fear.

Ebony knew who he was, she'd recognised him the moment he stepped in the door. This was the man who instilled terror in Gabriel, not a mean task. She understood. He looked like a lion ready to pounce.

Her training kicked in and she pushed the nerves to the background. She'd fought bullies in the cages before. As one of few women in the circuit, she'd taken on men as well as women. Her small stature fooled them into complacency, and they often hit the mat within seconds. She was a power-house, and she knew it.

Her mind was already contemplating the options she had.

By his demeanour, she assumed he already knew who she was, and what her role was in the struggle. There would be no pulling the wool over this one's eyes with a tearful, fragile performance. He recognised the fighter in her. The warrior.

So, she had to think of something else.

Ebony wouldn't let doubt wiggle its way into her resolve. She would get out of here. One way or the other. And if she were to die, she'd take as many with her as she could.

The silence continued.

Ibrahim pulled his lips into a sinister smile. His eyes had a mixture of admiration and slight irritation. He pulled a photo out of his cape and slide it, face up, over the table to her.

Ebony glanced down at the image, but didn't touch it.

She knew the two people locked in combat in a cage fight. One was a large Samoan by the name of Sione and the other—the obvious victor—was the unmistakable form of Jonah. She gauged the photo to be at least two years old based on the tattoos and scars. That would make it around when they met.

'You know this man?'

'Which one?' she taunted defiantly.

Ibrahim laughed. 'I'll take that as a yes.'

His mirth was short-lived, and the smile reverted to a cold scowl.

'Where do you know him from?'

'Cage fighting.'

'That you participated in yourself.' He pushed another photo over the table, this one a close up of a fight she'd won. The third photo showed Jonah congratulating her after the fight.

She remained silent.

'I want to know where he is,' he stated menacingly.

Ebony continued to hold his gaze. 'So do I. He owes me money.'

Ibrahim gathered the photos and replaced them in his cloak. 'Let's try a different subject, shall we?'

In the absence of an answer, he continued.

'We found Taxorian technology in your home.'

No reaction.

'Where did you get that from?'

'Black market.'

'That kind of technology is not available there. We checked.'

'Not anymore. I bought it.'

Again, that creepy laugh.

'You're a resourceful young woman. Silent, but resourceful.'

He gestured to the man at the door who left the room and returned minutes later with a jug of water and two plastic beakers which he placed on the table in front of Ibrahim.

'You must be thirsty,' the Hashta announced as he poured water into both containers and took one. He sipped the liquid and observed Ebony. She stayed in exactly the same position, refusing to acknowledge his offer.

'When Gabriel infiltrated our Mosque, he did so with an ironclad identity. We checked background information going as far back as his implied childhood. It was foolproof. A masterpiece of engineering. I always wanted to meet the genius behind that feat.' There was genuine admiration in his eyes.

'And now here you are; sitting across from me,' he continued, oblivious to her silence.'

'You're the computer expert,' he stated. 'You orchestrated Gabriel's identity. You're that genius.'

Ebony chose to remain silent, her eyes glued to his, no emotion visible in her features.

'I'm so pleased to finally meet you.' He held out his hand in greeting.

Ebony's gaze went from his features to the outstretched hand, and back up again. The utter disdain in her face would have made a lesser man tremble. With Ibrahim, it amused him. He pulled his hand back and crossed his arms.

'Our cause could use your talents,' he suggested.

Ebony huffed.

'You'd be an enormous asset to us. And it would benefit you as well.' Ibrahim continued his monologue. 'You are on the wrong side. This resistance is destined to burn. It's just a matter of time and it would be such a waste to squander such talents.'

Ebony felt strengthened in the realisation that Ibrahim wanted her alive for the time being. She recognised it was a challenge for him to turn her to his cause.'

'I admire your loyalty, Ebony. But your defiance is useless. I already know what I need to. Your comrades were less steadfast. One, regrettably, is no longer among us. The other, you will see again tomorrow when we try this conversation again.'

Ebony's heart sank. One was dead? Who? She didn't have to ask how. The smirk on the butcher's face said it all.

'I will ask you to join us again tomorrow. A continued silence will mean unbearable suffering for your comrade. Think on it tonight. Decide what your loyalty is worth and to whom. As an incentive I will allow you to see who has survived, for now.'

Ibrahim stood up, picked up the jug and walked out of the room, followed by his henchman.

Ebony stayed in the exact same position, with the same outward demeanour. This place was rigged with cameras. They would be watching her for any reaction. It must all be kept bottled up inside.

Internally she was heart-broken. One dead, the other soon to be.

Ebony had been separated from Nasheed and Caleb as soon as they had been kidnapped. She hoped the three of them were the only ones who had been kidnapped, but there was no way she could be sure. She was spirited off to a modified warehouse whereas Nasheed and Caleb were taken somewhere else, she didn't know where.

More than an hour passed before the door opened and two guards came in with a large portable screen on a wheeled frame, the kind used in conference rooms. They plugged it in and turned it on. She saw an empty room, four cold grey walls with one small rectangle window up high near the ceiling opposite the door. There was no furniture other than an identical screen, no carpets. It was just an empty room. In a previous life it had probably been a storage space. The walls still showed signs of racks or cupboards that had once been there. She assumed that the camera was in the same kind of monitor as she had in her room. They had made a connection to another location. Shivers ran up her spine at what she expected would happen.

The door opened and Caleb was unceremoniously thrown into the room. Ebony couldn't help herself and she rushed to the screen where she saw the moaning bundle on the floor.

'Caleb!'

He didn't react to the sound of her voice, his eyes open and empty. His face pulled into a mask of terror.

'Caleb,' she repeated softly and carefully touched the screen.

He pulled back as though bitten and braced himself against the door, a soft whimper escaped his lips, and he stared right though the screen, not registering anything other than absolute horror. Whatever he'd endured had closed his mind down out of pure survival instinct.

Ebony tried again and softly crooned his name.

'Caleb,' she whispered. 'It's me, Ebony. I'm here. Caleb, can you see me. Look at the screen.'

Slowly her soft voice registered, and Caleb turned his face towards the screen. His eyes were still vacant, but his brow was creased as though he was desperately trying to remember something. Maybe who she was.

'I'm here,' she continued. 'On the screen.' The tears were threatening to push through, but she wanted to stay strong for him. 'It's Ebony, Caleb. Please let me help you.'

He seemed to recognise something in her and his eyes roamed her face. Slowly he held out his hand towards the screen. Ebony put hers on her screen and was almost floored by a stab of pain that she couldn't actually touch Caleb, support him, console him.

'Eb?' The word was so soft, she had to strain to hear him.

'I'm here.'

'Eb?' Now stronger but filled with pain and anguish.

'Yes.'

'He's dead,' Caleb stammered, his face contouring in absolute agony. 'He's dead.' He pulled back from the screen and wrung his hands as he slowly sank to his knees again.

She didn't know what to say.

Tears flowed without restraint from his eyes, dripping to his clenched fingers and the floor beneath.

'He... he...' the words were unspeakable, pain and torment stealing his breath. 'I tried... I tried to make them stop. But...'

He raised his head and looked at her with a need that almost took her breath away. Heaving breaths accompanied his tears and he completely let himself go, howling his torment.

Ebony put her arms around herself and softly rocked from side to side filled with heartache at her impotence to help either of her friends. she had no idea what had happened to Nasheed, but it had been bad. Terrible, to have this effect on her adopted brother—the always tough, stern and unbreakable Caleb. It shook her to her core.

Ibrahim left them connected through technology for a little longer but returned at the moment two Hashta grabbed Caleb and dragged him screaming out of the room.

Her anger overflowed and Ebony lashed out at the guards that came in to remove the screen from her cell. She landed some debilitating kicks before a hard fist connected to her jaw and she sank to the floor, the sound of Caleb's terrified screams on the disappearing screen ringing in her ears.

————————

They came for her early next morning. The sky was still dark and speckled with stars as they manhandled her out of the holding facility. Her hands and feet were secured with police-issue tie wraps, she was hoisted over the second Hashta's shoulder and unceremoniously dumped in the back of a hermetically closed van. He pulled a black cloth bag over her head and pushed her hard up against the side of the vehicle, then secured her with more restraints. They were taking no chances with her.

Barely able to breathe through the itchy and musty material, Ebony lost all feeling for her surroundings. She was unable to keep track of the turns the van made and soon her senses and concentration were centred around blocking the pain of her uncomfortable journey. The cold metal floor of the vehicle offered no buffer against the frequent bumps that slapped her body hard against the surface as the driver sped away into the night.

Despite her training, Ebony was terrified. What had they done to Caleb? Would they bring her to him to watch him being tortured? Or killed? Or would the butcher turn his sadistic talents to her?

Chapter Thirty-Two

The sound was deafening, enhanced by the total silence within the holding facility.

Hundreds of Harley-Davidson bikes surrounded the building and threw up large clouds of dust as they slipped on the sand, revving their engines to maximum. The deep roar reverberated in the walls of the mainly wooden structure.

Caleb opened his eyes and concentrated. Bikers, they'd come. Were they here to help the prisoners? Or had they thrown their allegiance in with the aliens. He couldn't believe that. Their mindset was freedom, the aliens were a massive threat to the biker lifestyle, everything they lived for.

He shuffled over the floor to the wall, anxious to hear more of the comforting rumble. They were his brothers. For the first time in days, he let a glimmer of hope glow within him.

Shots were fired, Caleb couldn't determine where from, were those the guards? Or the bikers firing at them. Probably both, though the alien weapons made a different, more distinctive sound. There was no lull in the circling motion of the bikes, so he concluded it hadn't had the intended effect.

He looked around him in the small box room for something he could use to defend himself if the guards came for him. The twenty by ten-foot room was barren, the only item a chair that'd been bolted to the floor. The extensive bloodstains on and around the simple wooden piece of furniture sent a pang of agony through him. That was where they'd tortured Nasheed. Where the butcher had slowly peeled the skin off his body inch by inch. The images were branded into Caleb's retinas. Even with his eyes closed he relived the torture.

They'd held his face close to Nasheed and forced him to watch. His eyes were taped open, his head in a vice. The sounds were even worse. The screams. Nasheed had tried to stifle them, but it was impossible. The butcher returning to the open wounds time and again.

The same bastards brought him back to the torture chamber after he was pulled from Ebony's virtual embrace.

'Tomorrow, this,' Ibrahim indicated the blood, Nasheed's blood. 'This will be yours. Your blood will run freely like that of your brother. You know what will happen. Think about it. Is your silence worth the pain?'

Caleb shook his head to clear his thoughts. He had to pull himself together. But the grin of anticipation that had adorned Ibrahim's features filled him with terror.

His body shook with fear, the adrenaline rushing to every fibre of his body.

'Use it,' he said out loud.

'Use it!'

'USE IT!' with every shout he regained more of his strength. Terror became anger, rage that he could use. If they came for him now, he would fight. Let them kill him, it would be on his terms, and he would take at least a few and that black clad bastard with him.

Caleb walked to the chair and kicked it hard, and again. His martial arts training cantered the full force of his kicks to the fragile side of the chair. It creaked loudly. He intensified his assault.

Finally, he heard what he'd been waiting for; a loud creaking sound as the legs of the chair splintered just above the bolts holding them to the floor. He hit it once more and the object disintegrated into multiple pieces.

Caleb picked up one of the legs, its end now a vicious spike of splinters, and part of the backrest that looked solid. He tested their weight in his hands and swung them around.

They would do.

Whoever came in that door would feel his wrath.

More shots were fired, and the deep rumbling of the bikes came nearer, echoing in the hallways. They were in the building. He heard the unmistakable sound of breaking glass and smelled petroleum and, more alarming, fire. The structure was wooden, old and most likely extremely flammable.

He tried the door. Pulled hard at the doorknob and even kicked the lower partition. He had to get out of what again was becoming a death trap. Caleb took a step back and braced himself to hurl his body against the door. He knew the damage wouldn't be optimal because the door opened inwards, but maybe he could disjoint the hinges. He was about to rush forward when he saw the doorknob turn and heard someone push hard against the frame on the outside.

'Is there anyone in there?' A voice shouted. 'I'll get you out.'

Fear gripped Caleb and he hesitated. Should he call out? Was this yet another torture?

The person banged on the door hard. 'Hallo? Anyone there?'

'Yes!' Caleb called back deciding he had nothing to lose.

Again, the man pushed against the door, without success.

'Stand back, I'll kick it in.'

Caleb stepped back and took up a position to the side of the door, ready to pounce on whoever came through the opening. He had no idea whether it was friend or foe, and he wasn't taking any chances.

He'd decided to fight his way out, no matter what happened. Anything was better than the fate Nasheed had undergone. Something the butcher had indicated waited for him at daybreak.

He heard whoever was outside take a step back and then an enormous crash as the lower half of the door splintered. A second kick to the lock threw the shattered door into the room on what remained of its hinges.

Caleb waited patiently, his breaths deep, noiseless and calm. He tensed his body to jump at the perceived threat and waited.

'Come on out,' the voice shouted. 'We have to get out of here before the place goes up in flames or the bastards come back.'

Caleb stayed put.

'Whatever. You're on your own,' the voice said and moved away.

Caleb listened to the steps retreat out of the corridor. In the distance he heard gun fire over the still thundering noise of the big engines. The fighting had intensified as had the fire and smoke.

He knelt down and carefully looked out of the door opening. The hallway was empty. Still keeping low, he shuffled out of the room and down the dark hallway away from the flames that blocked the hallway on the left. The headlights of the circling bikes lit up the corridor in front of him at intervals and he was able to glance outside through the few remaining windows.

Pandemonium greeted him. What looked like hundreds of bikers drove their big machines in and out of the complex, brandishing guns and occasionally some kind of Molotov cocktail. There were dead humans and aliens all around, most shot, but some hacked to death. He identified one of the Hashta that had tortured his friend on the floor in a steadily expanding pool of purple blood. The torturer coughed up blood from the many bullets that had riddled his torso. Next to him Caleb saw the large, curved sword the man had brandished many times.

Caleb climbed through the broken window and made his way to the downed alien, oblivious to any danger that might pose. He was single minded. His attention focussed only on the man on the ground staring up at him.

The Hashta glanced at his sword, then back to the approaching Caleb. He tried to move his body and crawl towards his weapon, but the damage he'd incurred was too extensive. A smile pulled his lips into a grimace, and he lay back to wait for the inevitable.

Caleb picked up the heavy weapon. The heft was large, and he held it in both hands as he advanced on his target.

'I enjoyed playing with your friend.' The words were barely coherent. The Hashta's laughter at the danger approaching him ended in rattled coughs as the dark purple blood filled his mouth.

'You can only kill this one form,' he continued. 'I will come back and finish what I started. I have done it before.'

The blade came down with a vengeance severing the man's right arm.

'Not this time.' Caleb shouted.

He hacked at the alien methodically, his anger at the atrocities he'd been forced to watch guiding his strikes. He found release in the blade and continued long after the last rattled breath escaped the Hashta's lips. Until he finally felt utter and complete fatigue replace the madness.

He looked down at what he'd done. There was no remorse. The bastard had deserved it, and he was dying anyway. Caleb reached down to the folds of the bloody robe and pulled out the transporter. He threw it to the ground and smashed it, severing the connection between the Hashta's life essence and Taxore. This bastard would never come back. No reincarnation for him this time.

His fury temporarily sated; Caleb looked at his surroundings. There were less bikes, many had left, and he heard approaching heavy vehicles in the distance. He ran over to one of the bikers who indicated he jump on the back quickly. They had to leave. He grabbed an automatic gun from one of the dead and threw his leg over the bike. He'd barely put his feet on the steps when the biker took off with screeching tires. The bike slipped on the wet stadium grass but got a hold and raced through one of the burning entrances.

Chapter Thirty-Three

The fresh air was a godsend after the stuffy bag.

Ebony inhaled as much as her lungs would take. The deprivation had been almost unbearable, and she couldn't stop herself from gulping down the oxygen. They'd manhandled her sore form from the back of the van and dumped her unceremoniously on the chair before they removed the hood.

The room was warmed by hazy sunlight that streamed in through ceiling high windows. It was welcome, though she expected it to be temporary at most. It was a large, square, formal room in what appeared to be an old building built in a rather ostentatious manor-house style. The lack of sounds from outside informed her they were not in a town or city but more in the suburbs, most likely in a wealthy part of wherever it was.

Decadent paintings featuring stern looking men and women from a bygone era reinforced the idea that it was some kind of family mansion that had been repurposed.

The chair she was on had been pulled about a metre from a massive inlaid table. Seven other chairs flanked each side of the rectangle and two§ of them were occupied. Her gaze didn't linger with the occupants, she wanted to portray an uninterested countenance. Two guards were stationed beside the door to her left. Looking up she noticed glass or crystal chandeliers and an ornate high ceiling. Soft rugs and a hefty, solid oak gentleman's desk completed the look. She reverted her gaze back to the people in front of her.

They hadn't removed the restraints, just the hood. She tested the cuffs, there was no movement there, so she just stared at a spot on the wall opposite her.

'I hope you're comfortable,' the butcher's words cut through the silence. He sat to the right of her, his tall frame at ease in the chair and his long legs almost touching hers.

Ebony looked up at him and raised an eyebrow. She refrained from answering.

'I was told you had quite a bumpy ride.' The glint in his eye belied his implied concern.

Ebony knew the discomfort had been intentional, so she refrained from answering. She was covered in bruises and chaffing from the jarring trip but refused to acknowledge the pain she felt.

Her stare was designed to intimidate. His reaction—amusement—pissed her off even more.

'I'm sorry you had to be brought here under those dire circumstances.' The second voice came from the man on her left. He was seated in the first chair on that side of the vast table, nursing a large tumbler of caramel brown liquid. The bottle of expensive whisky and a tray of glasses were placed on the table just behind him.

Ebony slowly turned her face towards him. She knew

who he was. The handsome face, the stark violet eyes, the disengaging smile. It had been splayed over every stream and plastered over every building since he took up office as the governor. This was Man-Kayl.

She settled her scrutinising gaze on him, but still didn't answer verbally.

His reaction was to chuckle and broaden his smile. He nodded at Ibrahim. 'She is exactly like you said. A tiny pocket rocket. Impressive for such a small creature.'

The creature part registered with Ebony. No matter what he said in public, this Taxorian viewed humans as inferior beings. Assets. Under these circumstance, it showed.

She put on her most disinterested and disapproving face, causing him to chuckle even more.

'I love it,' Man-Kayl commented. 'Such a firecracker.'

His grasp of English was excellent, there was hardly an accent, and his word choice showed he was acutely aware of the language and its usage.

She turned her gaze back to the spot on the wall.

'You led us on a wild goose chase, Ebony. I must say I like a challenge, and you certainly offered me one.' Man-Kayl's chuckles were starting to irritate her.

'Is Caleb here?' She broke her self-imposed silence, her question aimed at Ibrahim, ignoring Man-Kayl.

'No,' he answered coldly. 'There's no use in transporting a corpse.'

A stab of pain threatened to cleave her heart. Caleb was dead? She kept her features blank and emotionless, even though she was dying inside.

'I must say he lasted longer than I'd expected,' the butcher continued, his eyes locked with hers. 'After what he experienced with the other one. What was his name? Ah yes, Nasheed. I assumed he would fold quickly. He knew what was coming.'

Again, she refrained from a reply. Her heart was breaking but another, less emotional voice at the back of her consciousness suggested he was bluffing. He wouldn't have killed Caleb. Not yet. He was the leverage they would need to bring down her defences. The butcher was too professional to accidentally kill him, so she concluded that he'd escaped in some way.

That thought gave her new-found energy and strength. It must have showed in her eyes, because Ibrahim's lips curled up in a thin smile.

'Let's take this conversation in another more pleasant direction, shall we?' Man-Kayl also deduced that the bluff had been successfully called.

'We have an offer, Ebony,' he continued unperturbed by her demeanour. 'One that I think is very interesting.'

She turned her head slightly to observe him.

'We know who you are.' No surprises there, she'd deduced that.

'You may wonder how we finally found you, well that's quite a story.'

The guy loved to hear his own voice, in contrast to Ebony and judging by the barely hidden look of contempt on Ibrahim's face, the others in the room.

'We have allies in your military, and they gave us full disclosure on their suppliers. One of which was a certain software genius responsible for many exciting inventions. We followed the mirage of false personas and finally found the source of the best technological mind mankind has, you.' He pointed to her, his face a mixture of bullshit and barely veiled admiration. She got that a lot, especially with myogenic idiots and was totally unimpressed.

'One thing we hadn't counted on was that this investigation would collide with another,' Ibrahim interrupted, and continued the narrative. 'For the past two years we have been searching for the brain behind Gabriel's efforts. Our investigation led us to a middle-aged white man who turned out to be an elaborate scam. Can you imagine our exhilaration when we found out we were looking at the same person in both probes.'

She could only keep silent. They were happy enough to spill their information.

In the almost certain knowledge that Caleb had escaped, she'd shifted her view from lasting as long as possible to getting out of there. She would escape—one way or the other—and any information these idiots wanted to give her would go along.

'You led us around the bush for a long time,' Man-Kayl interjected. 'But we found you. As we always do.'

Yeah, right, she thought. They'd been lucky. That was all.

Ebony's main concern was which military had gone over to the Taxorian side. Information on the mountain compound was hidden deep within the secret military vaults. It was on such a need-to-know basis that not even the president had known about it. None of them had. So, unless they'd turned a very specific five-star general, they were still in the dark about where the guys were.

'We have a proposal,' Man-Kayl finally came to the point. 'We want you to join our ranks. Work with us.'

'Why would I do that?'

'It will be very beneficial for you. You would be rich beyond compare.'

'I have enough money.'

He seemed flustered. Most humans were susceptible to

money. He tried more status enhancing options that made absolutely no impression on Ebony, and she made sure it showed.

Ibrahim was amused. With every suggestion he saw the frustration in Man-Kayl grow. There was no love lost between those two. She guessed Man-Kayl saw Ibrahim as a brainless butcher. A tool to use when needed but otherwise to be detested. She knew he was wrong. The Hashta was cleaver. Way too astute. He was the quintessential manipulator and doing a good job on the governor as well. He was a dangerously intellectual psychopath, and all the more threatening for that.

'You will have unlimited access to Taxorian technology,' Ibrahim interrupted the Governor again.

Man-Kayl's face flushed deep purple, and he was about to protest the disrespectful breach, but Ibrahim just held up his hand and stopped any reply. Ebony laughed internally. These two were quite the puppet show.

'Your work would expand with leaps and bounds. Think of the limitless possibilities. You've seen what our scientists are capable of, now imagine what heights you could reach if you combined your intellect with theirs.'

She was impressed. He'd certainly found the one aspect that could have made her susceptible to their offer. She wasn't of course but decided to play along. Not give in straight away, that would seem too suspicious. He wouldn't believe that.

She let her features show an inkling of interest then abruptly shut it off and ignored him again. It would be enough for him to think he had a way in. Enough to buy time.

She knew something they didn't. Something that would

allow the others to find her, if that is, anyone from her team was still alive.

'We would prefer to convince you to offer your services voluntarily, but if need-be we will revert to, shall were say, more convincing methods.' There was a twinkle in his eye.

She didn't even flinch, he was impressed. Ibrahim was looking forward to subjecting the little firecracker to his best interrogation talents. He decided to up the pressure.

'All we need is your mind and maybe one arm, though preferably two. Your legs are superfluous.'

'Is that really necessary, Ibrahim?' Man-Kayl interrupted.

She saw a flash of anger in Ibrahim's dark countenance. He wasn't amused by Man-Kayl's interference in his interrogation tactics. It took him a lot of effort to stay even barely civil. But he had to be careful, this was Cal-Tan's official ambassador. He couldn't just be rid of him.

'It is important to be clear,' he answered with clipped, aggressive words. Their venom registered and Man-Kayl nodded his agreement. He sat back in his chair to watch the further proceedings.

The exchange wasn't lost on Ebony, she'd felt the tension between the two men and was acutely aware of the power struggle. It also confirmed for her that Ibrahim's words would not be enacted exactly as he threatened. She didn't think torture was completely off the table. But it wouldn't be as extensive as the butcher wanted her to believe.

She decided to see if she could rile him even more. Widen the gap between him and the governor, up the aggravation.

'That's a funny thing coming from you,' she said.

'And what do you mean by that?' He was amused, with an edge.

'Who are you pretending to be now?'

'My current name is Ibrahim, or Pad-Rim if you prefer. That is a title bestowed on me by Cal-Tan.' He looked snug. 'It means butcher. Killer.'

'The correct translation would be animal slaughterer, the lowest caste on Taxore, the unclean, and I believe it's generally used as an insult,' she answered with a straight face.

He stared at her, anger flitting momentarily over his face, but he recovered quickly.

Ebony made a point of looking at Man-Kayl and Ibrahim followed suit. He only just registered the broad smile on the governor's features before Man-Kayl rearranged his features. The anger returned and this time Ibrahim made no effort to conceal it.

'It's appropriate,' she commented, holding his stare. 'You are and have always been no more than a psycho. A slave to your own bloody urges. You may wear Hashta garb, but it doesn't make you a Taxorian. You're just a grunt in a slightly better body. What did he promise you? That you'd get a real body if you did what he asked? He's manipulating you just as much as anyone else. You're nothing, Julius, Nothing more than you ever were as a human.' The use of his birth name registered but before he could react the governor interjected.

'You were human?' Man-Kayl asked, surprised.

'Don't pay any attention to what she says,' Ibrahim tried. 'It's a ploy to instigate.'

But the damage was done. She had planted the seed of dissent. Man-Kayl was a Taxorian supremacist. Her risk had paid off. His respect for this Hashta—not big to start with—had diminished drastically and it showed on his face and the way he pushed his chair back from the table.

He stood up, turned to the guards and issued an order. 'Bring her to the cell. Lock her up.'

Ibrahim stood to his full height but didn't intervene. He glanced at Ebony. She saw anger there but also a small glint of respect at how she'd played the governor to achieve what she wanted; an end to the interrogation.

Chapter Thirty-Four

Caleb made it to the safe house.

He contacted us through the network. Jonah and one of Sly's men picked him up, They drove three hours over back roads and bush in the pitch black without headlights. The driver used Ebony and Tajan's night goggles. They stayed out in the desert for an additional three hours before they continued to the entrance of the tunnels. We'd agreed on a total radio silence until they were underground.

The rest of us were waiting in the meeting room, where an anxious Sly paced up and down nervously. The intercom in his hand pinged and we turned to the door, anxious to see our friends.

Jonah came through first and held the door open for Caleb. The young man limped painfully, favouring his left leg. His face was a mass of bruises, the right eye swollen shut. Dried blood coated the side of his head and stained his shirt dark red. He looked terrible.

Silence reigned as we took in the terrible state he was in

in. Sly rushed forward and gently touched his son's face. 'My god. What have they done to you? he whispered.

Caleb looked past his father. Intense and pure hatred burned in his one open eye as he looked straight at me. The vehemence shocked me, and I was taken aback. My brow crunched in question.

Sly moved back a step and followed his son's gaze, as surprised as I was at the enmity his son portrayed.

All eyes were suddenly on me.

'Why don't you ask him?' Caleb spat out as he lifted his left arm and pointed directly at me.

Sly looked from me to Caleb and back to me again.

I shook my head. I had no idea what Caleb was talking about.

The silence was total. No one moved a muscle or made a sound.

'What do you mean,' Sly asked his son softly.

Caleb turned to his father. 'Him' then back to me. 'Why don't you ask him what happened. To Nasheed. And to me.'

'Gabriel?' Sly's question was aimed at me.

'I don't know what he's talking about.' I answered.

'Like hell you don't,' Caleb shouted. He suddenly lunged forward flailing his arms at me in a frenzied attack. I stepped back as Jonah took hold of him and held him back. Caleb's energy was short-lived, and he sagged into the big man's arms.

Aaliyah pulled up a chair and Jonah softly lowered his charge to the seat. 'Easy, buddy.'

I stayed put.

I didn't know what else to do.

Goosebumps ran up and down my arms from the intense stares of the people in the room. The people I called my friends. The way they looked at me made me feel distinctly unpleasant. Sure, we were all paranoid since the invasion. But this was ridiculous.

Sly knelt beside his son. 'Why would Gabriel know?' he asked softly, his hand on Caleb's knee.

'Because he was there,' he answered as he bent over to put his head in his hands.

Sly glanced at me, his face a mass of questions.

I could only shake my head in complete bewilderment.

The animosity towards me could be cut with a knife, the only exceptions Jonah and Aaliyah.

'Son,' Sly carefully prompted. 'Are you sure?'

What the hell? What does he mean, was Caleb sure? Of course not. It was preposterous.

The young man looked up deflated. 'It was him.'

All eyes turned to me again.

'He stood against the wall while that butcher took Nasheed's eyes out. He didn't say a word, never tried to intervene. He just stood there and watched.'

'I wasn't there.' I stated resolutely.

'Nasheed called out to you. He begged you to make it stop. You did nothing.'

'No.'

'When Ibrahim started to flay him, you turned and left. No stomach for that, huh.'

His words cut deep as he explained what had happened to our brother, our friend.

'Ibrahim made me watch. The whole thing. Until Nasheed finally died. It took hours.'

I closed my eyes, images of my cousins resurfaced, and I shuddered at the tremendous pain and suffering Nasheed had experienced at the hands of the Hashta.

'I knew it was my turn. But he wanted me alive. To use

me as leverage, for Ebony. He was going to torture me in front of her, to break her. And me.'

He looked up at me again. 'It was him.'

'It wasn't.' I answered softly. 'I don't know what you think you saw, Caleb. But it wasn't me.'

'My son is not a liar.' There was an edge to Sly's voice, the tone dangerous.

'I'm not implying he is. Maybe the pain and the shock made someone who resembled me look like me.' It even sounded weak to me.

'I know what I saw.'

Sly stood up, his broken arm hindering his movement.

'Where were you yesterday, Gabe?'

I stared at him incredulously,

'Surely, you're not implying I would do such a thing?'

'Answer the question. Where were you?'

'Here, in my quarters. And on guard duty, like everyone else. I also helped in the kitchen.'

'Can anyone vouch for you?'

'I was alone in my room, other than that yes, lots of people can here in the compound. How could I have been in LA?'

'Transportation,' Caleb stated. 'You transported there and back.'

'Take his weapons,' Sly commanded.

'What?' I exclaimed.

'And his transporter.'

Tyrone stepped forward.

'Are you shitting me? You can't seriously believe that I'd betray you all. That I'd be instrumental in Ebony's capture. Or this abomination that happened. Not after all this time.'

Sly's eyes were cold and hard. 'Your escape from Taxore was always suspicious. It was too much a stretch that

Michael, your enemy of hundreds of years, would break you out of the cell.'

'What the hell?'

'And you wouldn't kill him at the mansion. It's all making sense now.'

My indignation rose to a boiling point. Who the fuck did Sly think he was to accuse me of something like this? I threw my life away for this cause. I loved this family. Ebony, Jonah, Nasheed, all of them. And now Sly was accusing me of betraying them all. My righteous anger spurred me on to demand an apology but was cut short by Jonah.

'Gabe,'

I stopped and gazed at him, momentarily freed of my indignation.

'Give Tyrone your weapons and transporter.'

I was about to vent my anger on him when he shook his head.

'Don't make this situation any worse than it already is.'

'I wasn't there,' I repeated.

'No. But someone was, and we have to get to the bottom of it. In the meantime, we need to keep you here. Seconded, so we can be sure it's someone else.'

Sly was about to say something but he caught Jonah's stern glance.

'Cal-Tan is up to something, and we need to find out what it is.'

'You do?' I said softly. 'Without me?'

'For now,' Aaliyah chimed in. 'It's the only way.'

Common sense slowly edged its way into my consciousness and pushed the anger to a more manageable proportion.

Jonah had to defuse the volatile atmosphere in the room. I understood that.

One-by-one I slowly and carefully unsheathed the two short swords strapped to my back and handed them over to Jonah. He passed them on to Tyrone. The transporter followed.

I felt deflated. The animosity weighed heavily on my shoulders. People I'd considered my allies, my friends, brothers even, now branded me as a traitor.

This had my father's name written all over it.

He'd done it again.

Once again, he was one up on me.

Chapter Thirty-Five

Aaliyah came to the cell door sporting a tray of food for me and my dog.

Mutt wagged his tail, as always happy to see her. He too was behind bars with me. It was deemed too dangerous for him to be on the other side, given the circumstances. I could relate.

She stroked his head through the bars.

'Did you have a pre-growth,' she asked out of the blue.

'What?' I asked between bites.

'A pre-growth. Did you have one back home?'

I stayed silent, munching on the bread, just nodded.

'For emergencies?'

An idea started to form in my mind. She waited patiently until I caught up with her line of thought.

'Yes,' I answered softly.

The penny dropped. 'He's using it,' I concluded.

She nodded.

'He's put a grunt in my pre-growth and is passing it off as me.'

It all fell into place. Chills ran up and down my spine with the realisation of what my father had done.

'I'd forgotten about it. I assumed Cal-Tan would have destroyed it. But of course, he didn't. He's going to use it against us.'

She nodded again.

I pushed the tray of food to the side, no longer interested in sustenance. My appetite had dissipated into thin air. Mutt had no such reservations.

Aaliyah came back half an hour later with Jonah. She'd obviously told him about her theory, and he looked decidedly more optimistic than last time I saw him.

'It sounds plausible,' he commented, his hand stroking his beard in thought.

'What do you mean: plausible. It's what's happening. You don't really believe it was me, do you?'

'Gabriel, slow down, will you. It's a theory. A good one, but nothing conclusive yet.'

I was about to protest, my feelings hurt by the continued mistrust, when I caught a glimpse of Aaliyah slowly shaking her head. She was right. Nothing had changed yet.

There were still bars between us. Our revelation hadn't freed me and by the look of things it wouldn't happen in a hurry.

I felt deflated again. What else did they need than this explanation?

Proof. I thought.

Sometimes I forgot where I was.

'What do we do now?' I asked disheartened.

'We take it slow.' The big man answered with exactly what I'd expected him to say.

'They wouldn't believe us,' Aaliyah chimed in. 'It would be too much of a stretch for them.'

I knew what she was referring to, and had to—albeit reluctantly—agree with her.

'They have to come to the conclusion by themselves.'

'How? Not many know about pre-growths.'

The group around us were a combination of our old gang; Ebony's people, us and the new group. This last crowd was completely unaware of Aaliyah, Tajan and my lineage. They presumed us human; we didn't correct them. Aliens among them would be too much to accept in the aftermath of the invasion. Taxorians were the enemy, there would be no room for acceptance of like-minded rebels from the other dimension.

Thankfully, even with the recent developments, Sly and the guys had chosen to keep that small detail under wraps.

Our brother rebels were aware of Taxorian technology like transportation, and they knew we had access to it. But they thought that was the result of seized machines and our in-house computer wizard. Not many knew that was Ebony, but we could hardly hide all the tech, it gave us too much of an edge on the enemy.

Pre-growths would be far above human imagination. It would cause more questions, and our secret would be out.

Thankfully, the only ones who know about Nasheed were our small group. I'd been taken to the cells in a remote part of the complex and most of the people here were still unaware of the whole situation.

'Our first focus now is to rescue Ebony,' Jonah broke the loaded silence. 'They know about her. That she's the genius behind our efforts.'

My gut sank. I was clinging on to the hope she was still incognito.

'Nasheed,' Jonah added, his eyes soft.

I nodded. 'No one can withstand the Hashta,' I

answered. 'They can wring the truth out of a stone. He couldn't have done anything else. He had to.'

'Caleb told us even more details of what happened to Nasheed, and to him,' Aaliyah announced. 'He insisted that Nasheed hadn't given away this location.'

Jonah's face clouded over in rage. Understandable. The brutality of the Hashta knew no bounds. They lived to inflict pain. 'He will be avenged,' he added with an intensity we all felt.

A dark face hovered unbidden in my mind's eye. One that brought unfathomable rage and fear at the same time.

Ibrahim. The devil himself, if ever there was one.

And there was no getting rid of him, we kept running into the psychopath.

'Maybe we can do both at the same time,' Aaliyah suggested. 'We need to defuse the situation with Gabriel before the team will trust us all again. That has precedent.'

'Ebony,' Jonah stated resolutely.

'Ebony will have a much better chance if we are all helping to liberate her. Sly won't let me, and maybe not even you join any mission as long as this hangs over us all.'

The big man was hesitant, but his softening features showed he agreed with the sentiment.

'How?'

'We need to get Caleb to recant his accusation.'

Jonah huffed. 'Little chance of that happening.'

'Let me do my thing,' Aaliyah requested. 'What's there to lose?'

I shrugged. If there was anything she could do, I was up for it, if it was quick, and we could embark on our rescue mission a.s.a.p.

Jonah nodded.

'Okay.' Aaliyah smiled. 'This is how I want to proceed.'

Chapter Thirty-Six

The team had collected in the small meeting room again.

Caleb sat with Sly, two others were on one side of the room glaring at me as I stood against the opposite wall, my hands cuffed behind my back and two more armed guards, also from Sly's team, flanking me. Jonah stood to the side of them. Aaliyah had placed herself in between the two groups. In the background Tajan was silent, hunched over in a chair trying to be completely invisible.

The tension in the room was palatable and made the air taste stale. Emotions were raw and the urge to act was prevalent.

I kept my eyes downcast to avoid triggering the already volatile situation, but also so I could keep my own rage under control. The animosity towards me had hit me like a brick wall when I was hustled into the room and I had to push my anger and indignation to the background to try to understand their perspective, especially with our newfound theory.

Sly squeezed his son's shoulder and moved to the side.

He walked towards Aaliyah. I hazarded a glance, caught his eyes and was surprised not to see the bloody murder that echoed in those of the other humans. I concluded that Aaliyah had shared her rationale with him, and he was at least receptive enough to entertain the idea.

Caleb and the rest were glaring at me, and I lowered my gaze again, studiously observing a speck of dust on the floor. How the hell would we be able to convince the team that I hadn't been anywhere near the terrible murder. I had to trust that Aaliyah would take care of this, and I would once again be reinstated in my previous position of trust. Sly's seemingly softer countenance made me slightly more hopeful.

'Emotions are running high,' Sly started. Caleb opened his mouth to say something but was silenced by his father's stern visage. 'There will be a time where we can let our anger dictate our actions.'

He looked each one in the eye.

'Now is not that time.'

Protests rang out from many of the team but were silenced when Sly once again held up his hand.

'Now, we have to get to the bottom of what happened and how Gabriel is involved.'

'He's a traitor!' Caleb shouted out, jumping to his feet. 'He's the reason Nasheed is dead. He just stood there. Did nothing.' Tears streamed down his face.

Sly indicated to those around Caleb to help him back into his chair.

'If that is the case,' he continued. 'Then justice will be served.'

A large block of concrete settled in my gut at Sly's words and his accompanying look. Seems he wasn't as convinced as I'd hoped.

'We'll look at the evidence before us,' he started his report. 'Then we'll decide.'

I looked at Aaliyah, my gut turning over. The edges of her lips pulled up in a slight smile and she nodded almost imperceptibly.

'Jonah, Dennis and I went over the surveillance material,' Sly continued. 'Gabriel was in the kitchen, helping as he stated, from ten in the morning up till three. Then the streams show him walking guard duty in his station at the eastern entrance.'

'He tampered with the streams,' Caleb shouted.

'We investigated that. The streams have not been falsified.'

I started to feel better, the heavy weight in my insides lifting slightly. But the apprehension was still there.

'That leaves a period from ten at night to seven the next day.' Sly stated coldly as he looked at me. 'When you said you were in your quarters.'

I nodded. Saying anything now wouldn't help. It was a start, but I saw the big gaping hole in my alibi. Nine whole hours.

'Do you have any idea at what time you were tortured?' Jonah asked Caleb. 'And when Nasheed was killed.'

'Slaughtered!'

The big man nodded. 'Slaughtered.'

Caleb sat back in his chair and slowly shook his head as he contemplated Jonah's question.

'No. I don't know. They wouldn't let us sleep. I lost all perception of time.'

'Understandable,' Aaliyah joined in the conversation, her voice softer than I'd ever heard. 'Maybe we could go back in your memories and take it from when you were captured. It might help.'

Caleb stared at her as though he hadn't seen her in the room before. His attention had been focused entirely on me, and now he observed her like she was a ghost. Confusion creased his brow and fire returned in his eyes, 'Are you insinuating I'm lying? Or insane.'

'Neither of them,' she answered holding his eyes. 'You have experienced terrible trauma that no one should have to endure. The images you were forced to watch will be branded on your consciousness for the rest of your life. It is a pain no one can take away from you.' Her voice was sympathetic, the tone warm.

Aaliyah walked over to stand in front of Caleb. She sank down to her knee in front of him and placed her hand softly on his knee. I expected him to push her away, but he didn't.

'You have every right to be angry,' she continued, her voice almost a whisper. 'Every right to want revenge, to demand it. I would, we all would. We all do.' Aaliyah waved her arm at the others, including them in the exchange.

'Our first urge is to act.' She very effectively pulled the whole team into the feeling of association. 'We're all seeing red. We want, no we need, to strike out at the monsters that did this to our friend, our brother.'

Part of me wondered how this was actually helping me, she was digging deep into the vengeance temperament.

'But revenge will only be achieved if we punish the right people.'

Caleb looked at her, his face a mixture of pain and anger, but there was also a spark of understanding there, and dare I say it; doubt. 'I know what I saw.'

She nodded. 'You do. And you know much more than you can now see through the righteous anger you are experiencing. After what you witnessed anyone's mind would shut down. It's survival. The way your body and your mind protect you. You remember what you can handle.'

The room was absolutely silent. I hardly dared to breath. No one did.

Aaliyah took Caleb's hands in hers and squeezed. 'Caleb, will you let me help you to see details that might elude you now in all this pain? I can help you remember.'

'I know what I saw,' he repeated softly.'

'Yes, you do. I can help you see the missing parts that you need to start healing. You must know exactly what happened, Caleb, or it will never release you. It will haunt you forever, invade your days and feature in your nightmares. You need this to at some time be able to let it go and find your closure.'

You could have heard a pin drop.

No one moved. We all waited for Caleb to decide.

'I don't want to relive it,' he whispered.

'I know,' she answered softly. 'And I will try to ease you around the worst images. But you must confront it, Caleb. You are not alone here; we will support you. We won't let you go through this on your own. If you share, it will lighten the burden. Please, let us help you.'

Conflict raged inside Caleb, his features alternating between anger and fear. Beads of sweat appeared on his face with the effort of his decision. I was afraid it was just too much. No one in their right mind would want to think about the torture again. I knew, when I'd come back from Taxore it had kept me awake for months. And that was just the anticipation of what could have happened, not what he was forced to watch. My future hung in the balance, but my heart went out to Caleb. I realised I couldn't blame him if he declined.

The silence was total.

'How?' Caleb whispered.

'We walk through it, like it's a film, a very bad, terrible film.'

Sly came up behind his son and placed his hand on his shoulders in support. Caleb sniffed loudly and there was an almost imperceptible acknowledgement.

Aaliyah nodded to Sly and focussed on his son. 'Please look into my eyes, Caleb.'

He did so with a massive sigh, leaning into his father's hand, giving up the fight.

'Now close your eyes. I'm here. I'll hold your hands throughout the whole process, and your father is here, we all are.'

I marvelled at the peace that descended into Caleb's form with Aaliyah's soft words and his submission.

'When you're ready,' she continued. 'Go back to the time you were in the room with Nasheed. You've been captured and are alone in the room with him.'

He flinched and opened his eyes. Aaliyah squeezed his hands again. 'In your own time.'

He visibly struggled to relax his shoulders and closed his eyes again. After what seemed like a long time, he nodded.

'Are you there?'

A reluctant nod was accompanied by a full body shiver.

'Try to step out of your body and stand to the side of the room. Somewhere where you can see the door, maybe with your back to the wall. Somewhere where you feel safe. You are an observer now.'

Caleb's brow creased and the eyes fluttered behind the closed lids. This continued for more than two minutes, then his features relaxed a bit, and he nodded, his eyes still firmly shut.

'Where are you? Can you tell me what you see?'

Caleb coughed softly to clear his throat.

'It's a small room. Depressing and close.'

'Is there a window?' Aaliyah steered him away from the feelings of dread.

'A small one. On the right, about six foot up from the floor.'

'Can you see outside through the window?'

'Yes.'

'What do you see?'

'I see blue skies. And some grey clouds. A bird that flew over.'

My breath fluttered; it had been daytime.

'What does the ceiling look like?' Aaliyah steered him to describe more of the surroundings.

'It's an old industrial building. There are metal beams with chains dropping down.' He swallowed audibly.

'How many doors are there?' Again, she led him away from what instilled his fear.

'Just the one.'

'Are you alone?'

'No. Nasheed is there with me. I'm hanging from chains over the beam. My feet can only just touch the floor. Nasheed is chained to a chair that's been bolted to the floor.'

'You're an observer now, Caleb. Feel yourself in the third person. Like a film. You're not experiencing it as one of the victims.'

He struggled to keep his fear in check.

'Do you see anyone else?'

'No. Not anymore.'

'How long has it been just the two of you?'

'I don't know. Time is meaningless here.' His voice took on an anxious tone.

'No worries, it's not important. Just focus on what you see when you look in the room from your perch against the wall.' She continuously reinforced that he was only there as an onlooker. She had to keep him removed from the trepidation.

Caleb stiffened.

'What's happening?' Aaliyah asked calmly, her hands still holding Caleb's.

'I can hear people behind the door. They're going to come in.'

'Breathe deeply, Caleb. You are watching it from the sidelines. Let it happen and keep breathing. It's a film. We can stop it whenever we want.'

Caleb took a deep breath and nodded.

'The door is opening?' Aaliyah prompted him.

He nodded and took another deep breath.

'The door is opening, and I can see several men there.' The tension in his body increased.

'How does the door open?' Aaliyah attempted to relieve the building stress. 'Does it open to the hallway or does the door open into the room?'

Caleb cocked his head as though he was contemplating her words. 'It opens into the room.'

'Is there someone in the doorway?'

'Yes.'

The creases in his brow deepened again and he clutched onto Aaliyah's hands. Whoever it was, this person invoked terror in Caleb.

'It's him,' he whispered.

'The Hashta?'

A small nod. A tear escaped from Caleb's eye and slid down his cheek.

'How tall is he?' Aaliyah asked.

'What?' Caleb opened his eyes and stared at her.

'How tall is he?' she repeated.

Caleb calmed and closed his eyes again. He concentrated on his memories.

'About my height. Six-four.'

'And what is he wearing?'

'Black. He's in all black.'

'A shirt?'

'Yes.'

With every detail, Caleb relaxed, dissecting the terrifying image into small, acceptable parts. It dampened the overall terror.

I marvelled at what Aaliyah was doing as she led Caleb through every minutia of the man I'd identified as Ishmael. My heart went out to Caleb and Nasheed. I understood the terror they had gone through.

Everyone in the room was mesmerised by Aaliyah's exchange with Caleb.

He finished his description of Ishmael and passed on to a second Hastah who had entered the room behind the sadistic torturer.

'Is there anyone else?' Aaliyah asked when he had finished describing him.

I waited with bated breath. This was where it would get dangerous for me.

'Yes.' Caleb's voice hardened.

'Please keep your eyes closed, Caleb. You're doing great. Can you describe the next person?' Aaliyah promoted.

'It's Gabriel,' Caleb spat out. He kept his eyes shut but I could feel the daggers he sent my way. His body tensed again.

'Can you describe him?'

'What?' he exclaimed staring at her incredulously. 'It's him. You know what he looks like.'

'I do. But please tell me. What was he wearing? Start at the feet.'

Reluctantly he closed his eyes again and concentrated.

'Black jeans, cowboy boots.'

'Are there any distinguishing patterns or details on the boots?' she encouraged him.

I thought he was going to throw in the towel, but he took another deep breath, and I could see the rapid eye movement behind the closed lids.

'They look like some kind of skin. Crocodile or something like that.'

'What colour?'

'Red and black.'

I didn't own cowboy boots, and these colours were very not me.

'Please move up and describe exactly what you see, all the details are important.'

Caleb described the clothes in minutia, every time he was in danger of opening his eyes, Aaliyah asked another detailed question to distract his attention from the person itself. He recalled an amazing amount of particulars and my gut fluttered with every new one.

'His face.' They had finally reached the most important part off the description.

'It's Gabriel.' Caleb's voice was resolute.

'What's his hair colour?'

He frowned.

'Please Caleb. What's his hair colour?'

'Black mostly.'

'How long is his hair?'

'Cropped. Just over his ears.'

Sly looked at me. His brow creased in surprise. My hair was shoulder length.

'And his eyes?'

'Brown, dark brown. But I can see the edge of the contacts. There is a different colour underneath. I just can't see which one.'

'Never mind. It's going well. Concentrate on his other features. His nose.'

'Straight. I can see it's straight.'

'And his mouth?'

'The lips are tense. Like they're full of tension.'

'Go on.'

'His nostrils are flaring all the time. He keeps glancing at the first guy.'

'Is that guy talking?'

'Yes.' The tension was back with a vengeance.

'Don't listen to the words, Caleb. Watch the third man. Watch Gabriel.'

My stomach turned when she named me as the third person, but she shot me a glance to stay silent.

'How does he react to the situation?'

'He looks like he's going to throw up.' The contempt showed clearly in his tone.

'What's he doing?'

'He's fidgeting. Biting his upper lip. He keeps rubbing his chin with his hand.'

'Which hand?'

'His right hand.'

'Over a scar?'

Caleb hesitated. 'There's no scar.'

'Are you sure?'

'Yes. I can see his chin clear as day.'

'His clean-shaven chin?'

'Yes. It's there.' He raised his hand as thought to point.

Everyone turned to stare at me.

'Caleb. Are you absolutely sure?'

Caleb opens his eyes, his features pained that she asked him again. 'Of course I am. Are you doubting me.'

'No Caleb.' She squeezed his hands. 'I'm sure that is exactly what you saw.' Then she slowly turned her head to look at me. Caleb followed her gaze, and his eyes opened in sheer shock.

'It's not possible,' he whispered. 'He can't have grown it that quick.'

No one spoke.

'It's not real. His beard isn't real.' He pointed at me.

Sly squeezed his son's shoulder and came over to me. He stood to the side so Caleb could view what he was about to do and yanked hard on my full seven-month-old beard.

It hurt.

'It's impossible.' Caleb whispered.

'It's real,' Sly answered the unspoken question.

'It must be an alien thing. They can grow their beard quickly, and his hair.' He was grasping at straws, and we all knew it. I understood and my heart went out to him.

'I saw him. I'm not delusional.'

Aaliyah turned his face back to her. 'No one is saying you imagined any of this, Caleb. You saw someone. You saw Gabriel. But it wasn't him.'

'It has to be. There's only one.'

'I wish that were true,' Jonah exclaimed to everyone's surprise. 'There's something we need to tell you. Something you're going to find hard to believe.'

Five minutes later he had explained about the pre-growths. The outcome was complete confusion. Sure, they knew about the reincarnation technology, they'd seen it first-hand. But the idea that we were proposing seemed one step too far.

'Are you saying this is a clone?' Sly voiced everyone's question.

'Not exactly a clone,' Aaliyah answered. 'It's more a spare body.'

'Handy.' Sly's comment was seeped in sarcasm. 'Wasn't there a film about that?' he asked the still flustered Caleb.

'Yes, something about an island,' Jonah answered for him. 'Only these copies are empty.'

'What do you mean; empty?'

'There's no soul. No living entity. It's no more than a vessel.'

'And now you're saying that his father,' Sly pointed to me. 'Has taken Gabe's spare body and filled it with someone else?'

'Yes.'

It wasn't lost on me that Sly used the abbreviation of my name. There was some relaxation there.

I was still cuffed but allowed to sit down and listen to the discussion. Aaliyah, Jonah and I had decided earlier that I would refrain from talking. They wouldn't be inclined to believe me anyway, not till I was fully exonerated.

'Probably a confident. Or one of the humans that helped The Establishment.'

'How do you figure that?'

'Well, it must be someone loyal to their cause. Someone they can trust. I don't think it will be just any old grunt. They wouldn't be able to control him.'

'Can they do that with anyone? Just put someone else in the body.'

'Not really, no,' Aaliyah answered. 'The pre-growths are grown from the DNA of the person they are intended for. It helps with the life essence's acceptance. If it is reincarnated into a non-compliant body, they run the risk of alienating the essence. It basically rejects the body and ultimately must be either extracted again, or it will end up killing itself and the body.'

'And that's what could be happening here?'

'Well, it's Gabe's pre-growth, so anyone else will not be fully compatible.'

'He didn't seem sick or anything like that,' Caleb stated.

'Could be very fresh,' Aaliyah proposed. 'The body might initially function, but it will not function as the original.'

'It sounds like a particularly bad movie,' Sly decided.

A smile pulled Jonah's lips to a friendly countenance. I was finally starting to believe that we could convince the team.

'So, you're saying that a second Gabe was there. And that was what I saw?' Caleb mused.

'Yes,' Aaliyah agreed. 'And because they don't know our Gabe has grown a beard or hasn't cut his hair for ages, they couldn't have duplicated that. The pre-growths are pristine versions of us. They have no scars, no broken bones, no health issues, no long hair.'

'Like with me,' Jonah added. 'When I was reincarnated in a grunt body, they moulded it after me, but the tattoos and the scars aren't part of my DNA, so they weren't in that version.'

'Jonah's alien body deteriorated very quickly, can we expect this body to waste away as well?' Sly asked.

'No, this one is of a much better quality. Grunts are created with a termination date. An expensive pre-growth is tailored to be an improvement of the original. It will be an upgrade. But if we take into account the essence isn't a real fit, then we can expect it to be more fragile.'

There were nods all around. The team remembered the volatile period when Jonah's essence was housed in a grunt's body.

Aaliyah took Caleb's hand in hers. 'I'm sorry I had to take you through the memories, it must have been horrendous.'

He nodded. 'I'm glad you did. I was so positive it was Gabe.' He looked at me with a hint of an apology in his face. I just nodded and shrugged my shoulders.

'There was no way you could have known otherwise,' Aaliyah added.

Sly stood up and walked over to me. He gestured for me to stand and turn around. I felt the handcuffs drop and relief flooded over me. He believed us. He believed Caleb.

'So now what do we do?' Sly asked the sixty-four-thousand-dollar-question.

'We liberate Ebony,' Jonah answered.

'And we avenge Nasheed.' I added.

Chapter Thirty-Seven

'Give me the laptop,' Pigtails said. I should call her by her real name: Melanie, but Pigtails had stuck in the period we were on a need-to-know basis. She was one of Ebony's team of geniuses, the geek squad as they called themselves.

Todd handed it to her and her fingers flew over the keyboard.

'What are you doing?' Sly asked.

'She has a sleeper,' Melanie answered without taking her eyes off the tablet.

'A what?'

'A sleeper. It a dormant tag.'

'It's like a chip, but this one can send out a signal.' Tajan added excitedly.

'How will that help?' Jonah asked.

The small man was almost jumping with excitement 'We can trace her.'

His enthusiasm spread quickly around the group. We'd been racking our brains on how to find our friend. She could be anywhere. Caleb had seen her last in the stadium where he'd been interrogated and Nasheed murdered. But to his dismay. she wasn't among the people freed by the bikers. He'd checked.

'She's more valuable to them alive,' Aaliyah consoled him, but it only barely pushed away the worry in all of us.

With no idea how to solve the conundrum we'd placed our hope on Ebony's team. If anyone could find her, they could. At least that was what we'd hoped.

Melanie had been injured in the kidnap and brought to the Mountain in a coma. Thankfully the doctor had ruled out any life-threatening injuries and an hour ago she had regained consciousness.

We all stood around her bed as she worked the tablet.

'Where is the tag?' Jonah asked. 'Not in her clothes I imagine.'

'Under the skin. Just below the epidermis.' She didn't even look up. 'But we need to be careful. It's dormant now and we'll have to activate it to be able to determine where she is. Ping it.'

I was instantly aware of the risks. 'Will that endanger her?'

She finally raised her head. 'Might. It's untraceable now because it doesn't send out any pulses. We don't know whether the invaders will be monitoring the frequencies.'

That clearly put a spanner in the works. We had no idea under which circumstances Ebony was being held, and whether activating the tag would alert the Taxorians to our presence.'

'There's another thing you must know,' the girl added. 'She's alive.'

'How do you know?'

'If the subject dies, then the tag is automatically triggered and will send out a signal. We haven't received one, so that means she's still breathing.'

I felt some of the tension in my neck muscles slowly diminish. At least that was good news, She was still alive. But it also brought home the fact that we had no idea where she was and what state she was in.

I saw the same questions on the faces of the others. The big man was bordering on panic, something I'd never seen before, not even when his own life had been in the balance.

'Will she know?' Sly asked. 'If we activate the tag.'

'Yes, she'll feel it. A very small vibration. She designed that explicitly so the subject would know they were being pinged. We also have a version without that specific parameter.'

'Then she'll know that we're looking for her, and that we can find out her location.' Jonah latched on to the idea.

'Yes, but we have no way of knowing whether anyone else will notice.'

'Is it visible for others? Through the skin?'

Pigtails shook her head. 'No, the only way anyone will know is if they pick up the frequency. That's why we would have to do it quickly, for just a minute amount of time.'

'We might have to take that chance.' Jonah came to the same conclusion.

'I'll have to run a few tests,' Melanie announced as she swung her legs over the bed side, ready to leave. 'I'll let you know when we're ready.'

With that she and Tajan left the sickbay, the hospital gown she wore flapping open at the back as she carefully walked out of the room, supported by Tajan.

Early morning next day we were gathered in the makeshift lab Tajan had created. It was secure and there would be no one eavesdropping. We wanted to find out as many details as possible before we involved anyone from the mountain.

'Do we have everything we need to start up the signal?' Sly questioned.

Tajan and Melanie nodded in unison. Their smiles were hesitant and that rubbed off on us. I wanted to be optimistic, but it was so difficult when we couldn't see what our actions would potentially cause. We'd reasoned that an early morning activation might be our best bet. We hoped that she was being held in civil circumstances and that they let her sleep. Somewhere between six and seven seemed like a good time.

Melanie looked up at us and on Sly's nod tapped her screen.

The signal was in short bursts and would end after ten seconds.

No one breathed.

Melanie's fingers flew over the keyboard, and we watched the screen for any signs that the software had picked up a location.

A sickening thought crossed my mind, surely, they hadn't taken her to Taxore? It wouldn't be logical, ultimately it would kill her. They could try to reincarnate her once she was dead, but they had to know that she would resist, and they'd lose her. You couldn't force an essence to reincarnate. It had to be the subject's choice.

Melanie's assurance that she was still alive had pulled me through the night, but it hadn't soothed the nightmares of what might have happened to my little friend at the hands of the Hashta.

Chapter Thirty-Eight

'She's in the Holmby Hills in L.A,' Melanie stated, breaking the loaded silence. 'And her bodily functions are good.' There was a collective sigh of relief as we all started to breathe again.

A map appeared on the screen behind her. It was an arial video showing vast mansions hugging the side of the hills overlooking Los Angeles. The centre of the image was filled with an insane building.

'This house, simply known as The Manor is one of the largest in L.A,' Melanie led us through the images. The previous owners left the U.S as soon as the invasion started, and it's been re-purposed as the Taxorian Governor's residence. I guess they like ostentatious stuff.'

The image zoomed in and showed the vast extent of the buildings on a site that could have housed more than a hundred.

A former YouTube film showed a glimpse of the Manor's interior. The opulence continued in every room. There was something minimalistic and still very stylish about the interior design. Yes, it was too much, but in a very classy way.

I wondered what would be left of it now the Taxorians had confiscated the property. I guess, with Ebony there, we'd find out.

'We have the blueprints of the buildings,' Melanie continued. 'That is not to say that the current inhabitants haven't changed anything. There's no way we can find any information about that.'

'That means we will be going in blind in that regard,' Sly added. 'It's the invader's headquarters. We won't be able to fly any drones over the complex to gather more intel. The place will be rigged with all kinds of extra security, and they would probably see it a mile off.

'Do we know if Man-Kayl is present?' Jonah asked. There was a glint in his eye that told me he would love to meet the man and relieve him of his head.

'We don't.'

Bummer. The governor frequently travelled all over the world and between dimensions, so the odds had been small.

'The place is crawling with security,' Melanie continued.

Understandable if it was the official residence.

'It also has its own small transport hub. Nothing like the ones we've occasionally targeted, this one is for individual transports.'

That made sense too. Man-Kayl would have to report to Cal-Tan on a regular basis and that would mean face-to-face meetings. My father's intimidation tactics relied on him personally staring someone down. For that he needed his own location. A soft chuckle almost escaped my lips at the thought of the governor's visits to my father. They would be far from pleasant with all the disruptions the insurgence was causing.

'Is there a chance they'll transport her to Taxore?' Sly asked.

I shook my head. 'No, they need her expertise, so they want her alive. The air on Taxore is toxic for humans, it would kill her.'

'Then they could reincarnate her, couldn't they?'

'They could, but they would never know whether her intellect would survive fully or that she would want to be reincarnated, she knows how it works. It's a fifty-fifty chance and I don't think they'll want to risk that.'

His face showed I wasn't as convincing as he would have like me to be. My opinion was based on the assumption that now they knew Ebony was the brains behind our resistance they would appreciate her genius, and she would be too valuable to chance anything drastic. There was a small chance they would expunge their anger on the one person of our team they had. I hoped her intellect would be more of an attraction than her pain.

'So how are we going to get her out?' Jonah broke the silence that had ensured.

There were a lot of shrugs. No brilliant ideas, yet. We would think of something. We had to. She was family. I took another sip of the strong black coffee. It warmed me, but didn't help in the idea department.

'You have the blueprints, right?' Aaliyah asked Melanie again.

She nodded.

'Show me.'

Melanie's fingers flew over the tablet and the image on the large screen changed. It showed the architectural designs of the vast mansion. Room after room after room was constructed in the chateau style building.

'What do we know about it?' Aaliyah requested.

'It was originally built for the Spelling family,' Melanie explained. 'The producer. There are 123 rooms in the complex. Most of them are arranged in a flattened off horseshoe with two wings extending off the central entrance. The grounds are extensive, four-point-seven acres of land, and the floor space measures more than fifty-six-thousand feet. It includes a tennis court, swimming pool, indoor bowling alley, cinema and spa.'

'Do we know where the transporter is located?'

'In the end of the right-hand wing. The last room bordering on the pool'

'And Ebony?'

'Last time we pinged she was here.' Melanie pointed to a room more than halfway out in the right wing.

I wasn't sure how this information would help us, but watched Aaliyah take in every word as she stood close to the screen. She scrutinised the plans until her gaze landed on one specific part, the swimming pool.

'There's only one way in,' she said as she turned back towards us. 'Transportation.'

'Through their hub?' Jonah was confused.

'No. Our handhelds. Like when we exposed The Establishment.'

Ok, daring. But I could follow her reasoning. A frontal assault on the heavily guarded complex would be suicidal. The plans showed there were other mansions close by, but all were separated by walls.

'We can expect the invaders to have fortified the walls,' Aaliyah read my mind. 'They will also have all their security facing the external threats. That's where they think we'll come from. I'm banking on the idea that their internal focus is minimal.'

'You propose to transport into the grounds? I asked.

She nodded. 'Here.' She pointed to the pool house that was separated from their personal hub by the swimming pool.

'The normal electric waves issues by the transportation hub will mask the intrusion and from there I can find Ebony.'

'I'll go with you,' Jonah offered.

'Me too,' Sly chimed in.

'No,' she answered adamantly. 'Other than Ebony, there probably won't be any humans in the complex. I expect they'll have specific detectors all around that monitor human movement. You'd be way too conspicuous, even if they can't physically see you. It has to be me.'

'I can join you,' I suggested.

'It would be better if you stayed here, Gabe.'

I raised an eyebrow.

'We have no idea whether your double is there. That would complicate things.'

'And,' Sly added. 'Nathan won't let you out of the mountain. Not with the double.'

I was about to protest, but common sense prevailed, and I understood their reasoning. It pissed me off, but they had a point.

'I'll go in alone,' Aaliyah continued. 'The governor is bound to have Taxorian servants, so I can pose as one of them and find Ebony.'

'How will you both get out?' The big man questioned.

'Same way.'

'Has she ever transported?' Sly asked.

Aaliyah looked at me, I shook my head, then at Jonah, he shrugged.

She turned to Tajan. 'Did she ever experiment herself

with the transport amulets? While you both were working on them?'

The small man shook his head. 'No, she didn't attempt it herself.'

I felt dejected. Transporting a human was a risky business. We'd seen that last year when we prepared for the attack on The Establishment. It worked, but only if the human was in good health and even then, it could screw up their bodies for a while.

'Did she have a regular physical?' I asked.

'We all did,' Melanie answered. 'It was mandatory. I can find her last one.'

Again, her fingers worked their magic and a health report issued by our "company" physician doctor Patil appeared on screen.

We all scrutinised the information, most of it not making any sense to me.

'She has a perfect report,' Melanie said what we all wanted to hear.

'Won't you be recognised?' I asked worried.

'I can help you with a disguise,' Melanie offered.

Aaliyah smiled her thanks. 'Then that's decided.'

Chapter Thirty-Nine

Ebony was tired of waiting.

Her enormous intellect made her impatient. Why had Man-Kayl left her here alone for so long, and the butcher, where had he gone? And most important, where were her team? She'd felt the soft vibrations when they pinged the sleeper. First yesterday morning, and now about thirty minutes ago. She deduced that they were near, the first ping had offered the overall area, the second had been to determine precisely what her location was within the building. They were coming for her, she was certain.

The room she was kept in was luxurious. A vast calming space with beautiful furniture, it had been a guest bedroom in past times. The en-suite bathroom offered all the amenities she needed. They'd removed most of the furniture and anything she could use to escape and topped that off with a constant guard who accompanied her everywhere. There was no privacy for her anymore. The man they'd assigned wasn't just any old grunt, he was a full blown Hashta.

This one was older than Ibrahim, his face sporting the

traditional scars of honour. He was a hardened warrior who'd seen his fair share of combat. She didn't make the mistake of underestimating him. He would be a formidable opponent, especially with the large, curved sword he wore on his belt and the short one on his chest. He seemed to totally ignore her, but she knew this was definitely not the case.

They fed her three times a day with quality food. Nothing that she could in any way use, so not hot or hard, but tasty. Ebony reasoned that starving herself wouldn't help her. She didn't expect them to conceal any drugs in the food, at least not now. Ibrahim had been gone for more than two days and Man-Kayl since yesterday midday. She was sure they'd left the building, to where was unknown. But the lack of renewed interrogation suggested it was something important.

That gave her hope, combined with the soft vibration she'd felt just under the skin of her belly button where the tag was.

Ebony racked her brain trying to come up with the escape plan. Her captors hadn't bothered to hide where she was and through the ceiling high windows she recognised the mansion as the former Spelling extravaganza. The place was legendary. She also knew it was set in large grounds and surrounded by high walls, no doubt one of the reasons why the governor had chosen this as his residence. Soldiers routinely patrolled outside, and she couldn't see a way anyone could get into the complex. The fire power was overwhelming, and she expected the surveillance of the property boundaries to be so extensive that no one could approach it unnoticed.

'How does that work?' She asked her guard. She was

bored and had decided to sow the seeds of dissent where possible.

He looked up at her, still nothing readable on his features. He refrained from commenting.

'I mean, you look like you're a big man in the Hashta. The scars on your face, they're traditional aren't they, the sign of a powerful man.' Ebony continued to talk. His stare remained locked on her face.

'So how come you bow to a grunt?'

That hit a nerve. His eyes narrowed ever so slightly, but enough to register if you were looking for it.

'Ibrahim, he's a reincarnated human. You know that, right?'

Again, that small indication of anger, hmm, maybe he hadn't. Anyway, it pissed him off.

'How can you accept that? He's not even Taxorian. Just a would-be Hashta, yet he commands you.'

'Shut up,' he whispered. 'If you value your life.'

She held up her hands in mock surprise. 'I'm sorry. I didn't know it was such a sensitive subject.' Her eyes belied the apology, and he was acutely aware of how he'd let his emotions show.

She smiled at him sweetly, which only made it worse. He turned his head and stared out of the window.

They sat in silence for the better part of an hour.

A knock at the door alerted her to yet another meal. She estimated the time to be about six-thirty, and her empty stomach growled in anticipation.

The Hashta stared at her again.

'I know, stay where I am,' she said with an exaggerated sigh.

There was absolutely nothing she could read from his

face. No emotion, nothing. He stared at her again, then backed away and turned to the door behind him. He stood at a ninety-degree angle to the sofa where she sat, so he could keep an eye on her and open the door at the same time.

Ebony saw a young woman standing demurely in the doorway, she hung her head, not seeking eye contact with the Hashta and mumbled something about dinner in a Taxorian dialect Ebony wasn't familiar with. He pulled the covers off the food on the trolly and looked intently at this evening's offerings. Sublime smells reached Ebony, and her gut growled in appreciation. They had some cook here.

His attention returned to the woman, she flinched visibly under the attention, acutely aware of who she was talking to. Her demeanour was one of utter respect combined with mind blowing terror. Exactly what pushed the Hashta's buttons. He stood up straight and motioned her into the room, pointing to the coffee table in front of the sofa. The poor girl trembled as she passed by him, and he closed the door.

Her bent over figure was between Ebony and the Hashta as she carefully placed the bowls of food on the table. He shouted something and she recoiled as though struck. She quickened her pace and placed the last plate with flatbread on the table, then glanced up. Her eyes met Ebony's who struggled not to show any signs of surprise. It was Aaliyah.

Suitably chastened, or so it seemed, Aaliyah pushed the trolly towards the small side table where the Hashta ate. She quickly piled his food onto the surface, bowed and backed away.

Secure in his knowledge that the servant was terrified, he sat down to eat his dinner, keeping an eye on Ebony. His back was to the door, and he nodded slightly when he heard the expected click of the lock. Engrossed in his meal he failed to notice the servant had not left the room and that two daggers had materialised in her hands. Aaliyah crept up behind the Hashta and pounced at the last possible moment. She jumped on his back and drove her daggers deep into his two hearts. He tried to stand up, but the damage had been done and he slowly crumpled to the floor. Aaliyah pulled her weapons from the body and slit his throat almost to the bone for good measure. She had to be completely sure he was dead. The pool of purple blood steadily expanding beneath him confirmed that.

Ebony stayed where she was, still shocked her friend was here. How had she managed to gain entrance. She'd obviously played the role of servant, but it still didn't explain how she'd gotten this far. Or how they would get out.

'We need to leave,' Aaliyah announced,

'Hell yeah. But how?'

'Same way I came in, we transport.' She handed Ebony an amulet.

Ebony stared at the delicate technology she held in her hand. Transport. Shit.

'You can do it, Ebs,' Aaliyah coached. 'It's the only way.'

Ebony nodded. Her mind agreed, her nerves didn't.

'It will be alright; I've programmed the coordinates, and we'll materialise outside the grounds. They are waiting for us there.'

She nodded again.

'On three, turn the dial as far as it will go.'

Ebony wanted to hold on to her friend, but she knew that was impossible. It would interfere with the transport, maybe even merge part of their DNA. Separation was key here.

Aaliyah took her arm and squeezed it in support, then let go.

Ebony drew in a deep breath, nodded again and stood up straight.

'One. Two. Three!'

On the last number she closed her eyes, turned the dial with all her might and felt her body pull in directions it wasn't supposed to go. She wanted to scream and turn the dial back again, but her mind held her back. It would be temporary. Seconds at most. Let yourself go; she told herself. Exactly as she had when the others practiced. She'd been able to explain the working to them than, reality however, was a lot different and she felt the panic rise.

Before it took hold, she felt herself fall. Her legs buckled, but strong arms caught her and held her close.

'Ebs, you did it,' Jonah whispered.

She looked up too quickly, and the nausea swept over her like a tsunami. Pushing to the side, she emptied her stomach. It was pitifully little, but the bile had to be expunged. Once done, the weakness returned, and she let herself be picked up and carried towards a waiting pickup truck. Jonah carefully sat her on the back seat and jumped in after her. Aaliyah sat next to the driver, they took off without lights and slowly navigated the back streets of Los Angeles out into the wilds beyond.

She was free.

Chapter Forty

The transporter hummed; a form materialised slowly on the small transport hub. The engineer behind the controls was conflicted. Should he rush to help? He decided to stay where he was, reluctant to acknowledge the unexpected event.

In the centre if the hub the figure was on his hands and knees in the transporter gasping for breath. He tried to push himself up off the floor, clearly struggling. Moments later, Michael materialised just seconds after the Hashta stumbled off the pad, gripping the table for support.

The new arrival looked at Ibrahim with amusement clear in his features. The butcher was in a bad state, his grey skin worse than pale and emphasised by his original complexion.

'It's started, hasn't it?' Michael stated happily.

Ibrahim looked up, his eyes shot daggers at Michael and the transport technician, but he was unable to do more. The table barely held him upright, his legs shaking beneath the wide black robes. Bile threatened to escape his mouth as it came in waves. His body was racked with shivers and pain that radiated from his hearts out to the ends of his extremities. He literally felt as though he'd been pulled apart and haphazardly put back together. His gaze moved from Michael to the technician. The man shuddered clearly under his scrutiny, as well he should. He would pay for Ibrahim's discomfort.

Michael's laugh sounds over the transport's deep hum, his amusement rattled Ibrahim almost as much as the weakness in his body. Another form materialised slowly. Man-Kayl joined them back on Earth. His features were hard, his anger at the abuse he'd encountered on Taxore brimming over. He looked from the amusement on Michael's face to the hunched form of the Hashta.

Michael stood with his arms crossed looking down on Ibrahim with delight.

'You don't know, do you?' Michael taunted. Man-Kayl watched the proceedings with interest and enjoyment.

Ibrahim's voice was cold, the tremble barely audible. 'I'll humour you. Know what?'

'That your body is only temporary.'

Ibrahim stood up to his full hight and pushed himself off the table, the effort almost collapsing him again. Slowly, with extreme effort, he rightened his spine and stared both men in the eye, daring them to comment on his unexpected weakness.

'A grunt body isn't made for transportation,' Michael continued. 'And how many times have you done that? Ten, twenty. More?' He was clearly enjoying himself. A small smile pulled at the edges of Man-Kayl's lips as he understood what his fellow Taxorian was saying. He stared at the Hashta, who now seemed less imposing, less of a threat.

The butcher refrained from answering.

'It's degenerating. Breaking itself down. Your days are numbered,' Michael concluded happily.

Ibrahim looked from him to Man-Kayl. He placed his hand on the pommel of his curved sword, taking energy from the knowledge that he would easily best these two, even in his current state.

'Grunt bodies aren't made for longevity. If my father told you it was immortal, surely you didn't believe him. Did you?'

Ibrahim stayed silent, he didn't have to answer vocally, his anger was clear in the balled fists and the hard lines in his brow. His nostrils flared with the effort not to quench his rage on the two Taxorians.

Michel's eyebrow raised and he glanced at Man-Kayl, his surprise mirrored. 'Oh, my goodness. you did. You actually believed the nonsense he told you. You are not immortal, and you never will be. This body you have now has a used-by-date and you're speedily reaching that. Not exactly what you were led to believe, right. That's what he does. He pulls you along in his schemes and plays you. You, my friend, are dying. Again.'

The butcher was almost at eruption point, the only thing holding him back was the prolonged weakness in his limbs.

Man-Kayl added his ten cents. 'Surely you didn't think we would be so stupid to really grant you so much power. Did you?' Disdain smothered the governor's tone.

'You're even more stupid than I thought.'

The two men left, their laughter stabbing Ibrahim's ego.

He turned his face to the one person still in the room, the technician.

The poor man stepped back, terror opening his eyes to

what could happen. He fled the transport hub and slammed the door behind him. His screams could be heard while he ran for his life.

Ibrahim stayed behind. He leant back against the table, his anger the only thing holding him up. Tremors racked his body, and his breath came in bursts. He felt both his hearts pounding in his chest. He'd known something was wrong. Every transport left him with an unmistakable fatigue. He'd regaled it to the back of his mind, convinced it was temporary.

What if they were right?

Of course they were.

Cal-Tan wasn't the partner-in-crime he'd viewed him to be. The man would never share power. He would always make sure he had and kept the upper hand. Ibrahim reluctantly admitted he had underestimated the tyrant. Something he'd never expected. The small dictator was cleverer than he'd expected. Well, he just had to catch up and stay one step ahead. His first point of call would be the medical wing in this ostentatious building. He would persuade the resident Taxorian doctor to reveal what he knew about his current body, and the alternatives that he could exploit.

A few minutes later, he'd regained enough control and energy to push himself up from the table. The first steps were hesitant, unbalanced and wavering. With each following one, he felt his energy and stability increase, fuelled by an anger that filled his body with heat and pushed the blood through his veins.

No one. No one! Screwed him over. Not even Cal-Tan.

He stretched his shoulders back, improving circulation. A smile started to form on his lips at the thought of his next interrogation. Ebony would fold. He would make sure of that. They always did. She was a firecracker. Strong and determined. But he knew ways to break anyone, even her.

Ibrahim opened the door and walked out of the transport hub, his strides strong and no hint left of the weakness he'd experienced just minutes ago.

Chapter Forty-One

Bodies littered the floor. Purple blood splattered on the white furniture in the bedroom the butcher had left Ebony in and made it the stuff of nightmares.

The Hashta Aaliyah had dispatched had been joined by other bloody corpses. All the guards that had been on duty lay dead at Ibrahim's feet. His anger had known no boundaries, and the brutality was excessive, even for him.

Three other Hashta stood near, awaiting new orders. They had participated in the interrogations on Ibrahim's orders, though they drew the line at the butcher's suggestion that they should do the same with the remaining two Hashta. They argued the two had accompanied Ibrahim to Taxore and were therefore nowhere near when the breakout happened.

Ibrahim was reasonably certain there had been no inside traitor, not that it mattered anymore, any potential candidates were dead now anyway.

He washed his hands in the water bowl on the table, colouring the water bright purple. His rage at the escape and the hazing by Michael had dissipated to a manageable level. He could think straight. How was he going to broach the subject with Cal-Tan? It would not be received well, so he had to make sure the blame fell on someone else's shoulders, or more appropriately, neck.

Man-Kayl was the obvious target. The butcher had hoped to find a way to finger Michael for this one, but for now, he needed him. Cal-Tan had made it perfectly clear his eldest son would play a major role in capturing not only his brother but the rest of the motley crew of insurgents. He would have to let him live a little longer. Besides, the blame fell easily on the governor's shoulders. He was responsible for Earth. This had happened in his house. Ibrahim was Cal-Tan's eyes and ears, and he had already sown the seeds with the tyrant. Whispers of Man-Kayl's misuse of governmental powers, secret stashes of art and other valuables, and inadequate reactions to the attacks had already undermined his position, and with that his life expectancy.

Ibrahim was a master of instigation and paranoid Cal-Tan was all to happy to listen.

Michael's words at the transportation hub necessitated a new plan. Yes, this body would deteriorate. But there were others.

Ibrahim's visit to the medic had resulted in bad news and in opportunities.

'There is a difference between reincarnation for Taxorians and for aliens,' the physician had started his narrative. 'The bodies we use,' emphasis on the "we". 'Are grown from our DNA. Taxorian DNA. There is no contamination. The reincarnation fits the essence, and the bodies have been enhanced by deleting any markers for illness.'

His patronising tone almost cost him his head, but Ibrahim needed to hear more, which gave him some respite.

'Humans,' again that derogatory tone. 'Their DNA contaminates the building blocks of the grunt's body. It is necessary for the acceptance of the new form, but it has detrimental effects on the quality of the new growth.'

'Are all humans reincarnated into the same quality body?' Ibrahim asked, ignoring the insults.

'No. Some are higher quality. The standard grunt,' he looked at Ibrahim down his nose. Quite a dangerous thing to do with a Hashta, but his disdain was so overwhelming he couldn't hide his abhorrence.

'The standard grunt has a body with a limited life expectancy. They need to be strong for the sale, last a few years of hard labour and then deteriorate. It's basic economics. No one makes a product that lasts forever. It would kill the commercial opportunities.'

The coldness with which he referred to humans registered with Ibrahim. He would take care of the doctor at a later date. Rub his derogatory tone in his dying face.

'Then there are the humans that have been granted a "ticket-to-heaven". They have had at least some value for Taxore, either in harvesting grunts or infiltrating power points we wish to own. Their bodies will live longer. On Taxore as well. But even that is temporary. We have no use for humans in our society.'

'Are there more?'

'This is enough. We have no wish to keep human reincarnations in our society.'

Ibrahim ignored the barely veiled insult born of Taxorian supposed superiority.

'Can humans be reincarnated in the bodies you use for your own kind?'

The doctor's brows raised in clear contempt. 'Why would they?'

'Hypothetically.'

The physician eyed him warily.

'No. That is impossible. There would be no recognition. The body would not accept the essence.'

'So, you've tried the procedure?' Ibrahim raised an eyebrow.

'Of course not. That would be an abomination.' The doctor was truly shocked at the mere thought. What registered with Ibrahim was that it had not been proven impossible.

He was enjoying his new life and was not inclined to stop any time soon. If that necessitated another reincarnation, then so be it.

Chapter Forty-Two

We didn't think it could get any worse.

Boy, were we wrong.

Cal-Tan upped the ante when he decided there were too many useless humans taking up Earth's natural resources. It drove home how totally psychotic he was. His one and only perspective was business. Strong young grunts were his goal, and anyone not involved in securing those assets was redundant and therefore expendable.

It was exactly as cold as it sounds. And it sickened me to my core.

Numbers.

Business.

Humans were resources, nothing else.

He started with older women. They were—as Man-Kayl called it—euthanised. The manner in which it was accomplished had at least a hint of empathy in that they died in a deep sleep, they weren't shot or poisoned. Families were allowed brief goodbyes, but any females over sixty world-wide was destined to be discarded. I didn't mistake the way they died as anything humane; it was just common Taxorian sense to minimise the risk of extra insurrection. Humans were attached to their mothers, their grandmothers, and killing them brutally would exponentially increase the unrest. It was bad enough for business as it was.

The streams explained it all in cold Taxorian logic. Earth had limited resources; they should be used for the useful humans. Those who could not work or breed, no longer fell under that description. Elderly men had a short respite, until they too were no longer fertile.

The sick or handicapped were next to be ranked. Their future depended on their age, the hereditary of their illness and the strength of their essence. The invaders differentiated with young men who could be reincarnated, they were administered nanites before euthanasia. Anyone with a "blemish" as Man-Kayl called them, didn't stand a chance.

And still mankind stayed silent to the ongoing apocalypse. With the previous concessions Earth had made there was no room anymore for negotiations with Cal-Tan. The early acceptance came back to bite them, hard. We'd predicted it, but it was happening a lot earlier than I'd imagined. My father wasn't known for patience, but this was quick by any standards. Whatever he was using the grunts for, the timelines had just sped up aggressively.

The few resistance groups left, ramped up their efforts but they were helpless as long as the majority accepted the abuse rained down on them. It felt more and more like a lost cause.

Naturally, that had repercussion on the atmosphere in the mountain, it was loaded with emotions. Every stream magnified the helplessness and anger we endured in equal measures. We felt useless.

There were some positives in the past weeks, but even they were tainted.

Ebony and her team had set up their new laboratory using the facilities already available in the mountain supplemented with what she'd retrieved from the secret lower levels. She refused to share information about what was there with anyone but Tajan, her technical shadow and the geek squad.

'I'm still cataloguing everything,' she told us at dinner one night when the subject was broached again.

'Don't you trust us?' The big man clearly felt personally rebutted by her reluctance to share.

She glanced at him and sighed audibly, apparently the subject had been discussed before between them.

Her unspoken words reverberated between them, "don't go there, not now." I could hear in my mind.

Jonah's face was flushed, and he opened his mouth to answer, but rethought his actions and clamped his lips shut. Instead, he crossed his big arms over his chest and sat back in his chair, brooding.

Great, just what we needed. When he had a bad mood, everyone suffered.

He wasn't the only one difficult to be around.

Mutt was the only one who wanted to be anywhere near me, my disposition was that bad. I scowled at everyone and everything, challenging even the big man's malevolence. Yes, my self-depreciation and guilt were back with a vengeance. I abhorred the devastation my fellow Taxorians rained down on Earth, on my new home. My new family.

Aaliyah was the one to break me out of my vicious circle one evening after another of my particularly obnoxious shows of self-pity and anger.

'If your life is so meaningless now, why don't you just

end it? Why don't you just go kill yourself?' she asked after my dramatic ranting.

I was taken aback by her frankness and the dispassionate way she voiced her suggestion.

The others, Jonah, Sly and Caleb, mirrored my bewilderment initially, then lowered their eyes. I glanced at them, one by one, and beneath their embarrassment I saw the seeds of maybe even agreement in the silence.

'You're no use to us the way you are now,' she continued, oblivious to the knives she drove deep into my hearts. 'Yes, Taxorians did this. Are doing it. And like me, you know this is only the beginning. It's going to get a lot worse. Unless we stop them.'

'How?' I retorted loudly, finally finding my voice. The rage inside me wanted to strike out, physically hit whatever was near, preferably Aaliyah at that moment. Though the others were also in the firing line.

'By pulling together,' her tone matched mine. The volume quickly echoing in the small room. 'By doing anything other than drowning in self-pity.'

'Is that what you think I'm doing?' I shouted.

'Yes! Clearly.' She crossed her arms over her chest and stared me in the eye, daring me to disagree.

Which, of course I did. Okay, I was depressed, who wouldn't be. But she was overdoing it. Exaggerating exponentially.

Wasn't she?

I looked at the rest again. First with anger, then slowly shifting more to desperation.

Jonah raised an eyebrow. Sly cocked his head and shrugged.

Surely not. I wasn't that bad.

My thoughts went back to the past week. How I'd

reacted to everyone and everything. It had been bad. No, I had been. Was.

I hung my head in defeat.

'These murderers, they're my people too, you know.' Aaliyah's anger had dissipated with mine.

I hadn't realised she would be hurting and guilt stricken, like me. My self-pity had been so absolute I acted as though I was the only one involved here. These people, our team, my family, they'd all lost. Their kin had lost. Their existence was in the balance and here I was once again, feeling sorry for myself.

A stab of pain shot through me and my legs shook with the emotion.

Kate.

I missed her with a vengeance that immobilised me. She'd kept me stable. Without her, I'd fallen back into my self-destructive predispositions. And in doing so, I'd ignored everyone else's agony.

Aaliyah was hurting just as much as I was. Only she was doing a better job handling it. Her pain and guilt were translated into actions, mine had been useless self-pity.

I nodded my defeat. They were right and this intervention—how painful and confronting in the chosen manner—had been necessary.

Aaliyah came up to me and placed her hand on my arm.

'We all miss her, Gabe,' she announced softly, the emotion in her voice pushing the tears I withheld so vehemently back to the foreground. 'Maybe it's time to celebrate her life instead of lamenting over her death.'

Her words were so soft, yet they cut me straight to my core. She was so right, so terribly right. I looked at her through watery eyes and slowly nodded.

She pulled me into an unexpected embrace, and I held on for dear life.

I felt more hands on my shoulders and my back in support.

This was family.

'Good to have you back, bud,' Jonah broke the silence with words that filled me with warmth and love, pushing the pain to a more bearable level.

Chapter Forty-Three

The sun rose and warmed the ledge Aaliyah sat on, and I joined her. The heat from the rays and the smell of the forest invigorated me. An existence underground wasn't my idea of living. I needed the air, the sun, the wind. Next to me I saw the effect mirrored in Aaliyah. Her eyes were closed and her face turned towards the welcome rays. Mutt lay down next to me, his eyes shut and a soft rumble of contentment coming from his big chest.

Nathan had given up on this control. He tried to keep us from the surface, without success. There were concessions we had to make here, we knew that. This was not one of them.

The wind brought the scent of water and early snow to us, the tang was refreshing, and I inhaled the cool mountain air. Birds chattered in the treetops, and I heard the braying of elk from deep within the woods to the right. There was a clearing there, one the bucks used to challenge each other.

I'd taken control again and dressed in clean clothes without the holes that had been customary in the past weeks. I'd even cut my hair to a more reasonable length and tidied up my beard. It actually made me feel better to pay attention to how I looked.

Aaliyah looked me up and down before nodding her appreciation for my new look.

'Thank you for yesterday,' I broke the silence.

She turned her face to me and opened her eyes, the brows raised. 'For what?'

'The intervention.'

She nodded.

'It can't have been easy.'

I laughed. 'Heck no, but I needed it.'

'No contest there.'

Mutt raised his snout at our laughter, I swear I could see a smile on his lips too.

'I couldn't see what I was doing,' I mused. 'The anger took over and I just let it. There didn't seem to be any reason not to.'

'Not without Kate?'

I nodded. The emptiness within me had won out in the past weeks. I couldn't see any way forward.

Aaliyah turned back to the forest, she sat up and stared into the sun.

'I'm happy not to know how it feels,' she commented. 'Love like that.'

I knew what she was referring to.

I sniffed in the cool air.

'I thought like that too,' I continued, sharing what had always been private; my emotions. 'I wished for a second that I'd never experienced the depth of feelings I had—have —for Kate. But that would leave a massive hole in my hearts. In my soul, if you like. Yes, the pain is unbearable sometimes. It makes me want to give up, stop living. But then I remember what it felt like before she died. I was whole. Complete. Bigger and better than I ever thought possible.'

She placed her hand on my lower arm in support.

'But even though I hurt. I'm still happy I did experience how good it felt. Humans have a saying "It's better to have loved and lost, then never to have loved at all." I know it's a cliche, but it's true. I am a better man because of her. Because I opened my hearts to someone else. That cannot be closed anymore. It has made me understand others, their loves, their lives and their loss. I needed that. It's part of me, like she always will be.'

It felt good to unburden myself. There were no tears, not this time. I could feel the loss without the rage and the emptiness. She was physically gone, lost to my arms. But forever in my hearts. I finally understood what humans meant with a soul. It was what made a person whole. Made them able to make good choices for themselves and others. It was an integral part of humanity. And now of me.

'I feel blessed she was here and showed me what I could be.'

'She did have a good influence on you.'

We were comfortable in the silence that followed. Mutt placed his head on my thigh, and I felt his warmth both inside and on my skin.

'Do you think you'll ever find that again?'

I shrugged. 'I don't know. Maybe. I never thought I would experience it at all, so who's to say I won't do it again. At least I'm open to it now.'

'But isn't the pain of your loss too great? Doesn't that shut you down?'

'It could, but I don't think it works that way. Not with me. I know now what it looks like. What love feels like. It's something I've been searching for my entire life, but I never knew how to recognise what was right in front of me. I do now. Her presence will always stay with me, like a ray of warmth that keeps the cold from taking over my mind and body.' I pointed to the sun. It felt the same.

'And that's good?'

I nodded and squeezed her hand. 'Yes, it's good.'

Chapter Forty-Four

Nathan had to concede. He couldn't close the mountain off any longer.

People were dying by their thousands outside and we had the facilities to at least offer sanctuary to some of them.

The call to open the doors came from the mountain's residents. They had families outside. Families that were in grave danger. Somehow, the invaders had been able to construct a list of people with family ties to identified rebels. Just a hint of rebellion was enough to be branded as such and more and more news reached us of horrendous slaughter wrought on their kin. The message the invaders sent in blood had a massive impact on everyone and terror gripped their heart when another coded message came through cataloguing more atrocities.

Daily public streams were watched with heavy hearts. They had a simple but very effective format. First one or two mock trials—lasting no more than minutes—where captured resistance fighters were sentenced to death. The executions were televised with horrendous detail. These scenes were generally too much for anyone to watch. But what came next was enough to stay the heart of every community member with kin outside the mountain. A list appeared on the stream. The death list. The names of hundreds, maybe even thousands of humans that had been executed in the past twenty-four hours. The background of the projected names was a collage of bloody photos bringing home the impact of the texts.

More times than I care to remember, I'd been in the central area when the stream was aired only to hear gut-wrenching screams when a name or a body was recognised. It was heartbreaking.

Something had to give, or there would be mutiny.

Unused rooms in the vast complex were prepared for new inhabitants and frequent missions were executed to bring the families into their new home.

There were rules.

We were all very aware of the tender balance between compassion for the families and safety for all of us. A process was set up where inhabitants could apply for reunion with their kin. Direct kin in the first and second line only. They were vetted by Ebony and her team. Beside the requesters, the potential joiners had to be supported by two other current citizens. Once agreement had been reached more rules came into place. The potentials wouldn't know of their rescue in advance, there were no messages sent, no communication. They would be lifted from their beds and whisked off in the night, a hood over their heads to disorientate them about the location. Each was allowed one backpack of personal belongings, including their clothes. They were not allowed to bring any technology, no phones, nothing. No manner in which they could be tracked or traced.

They were scanned before they stepped into the vehicles. Anyone who didn't pass it one hundred percent, was left behind. It was brutal. But necessary.

The new recruits stayed in the mountain for the first two months. They were not allowed out, unless on a mission and even then hooded until at a safe distance.

The prisoners we encountered in our missions occasionally became recruits. Young men and women ready to be transported off-world. They were subjected to even more ruthless checks. Anyone already tagged or who'd been administered nanites was refused. They couldn't join us. We helped them where possible to flee from where they'd been incarcerated, but there was no way they would be allowed to return with us.

Incidentally, someone managed to contact the council, usually through secret communication channels. These were generally military people. They were vetted to the maximum and initially had to stay in another location for at least two months before they were allowed to join us in the mountain. The hoods and other rules were applicable for them as well. No exceptions.

It was harsh.

But it was unavoidable.

This place, what it stood for and what it could mean, was just too important.

Chapter Forty-Five

The first things Ebony had improved when she came to the mountain, were IT and security. She basically took over the computer rooms and organised them according to her requirements. Some of the IT guys sputtered briefly, but a short discussion and some hard glances later, and they capitulated to her superior knowledge. She had that effect on technical people. They clearly acknowledged their master.

The processes and procedure were left alone, Ebony focussed on the area around the mountain. Up till now, we'd relied on advance warmings within a perimeter of five miles, but that wasn't enough for her.

'We need to extend the boundaries,' she argued with Nathan. 'To at least forty miles, preferably more. That way we can follow whatever comes into the area and determine the risk before they come anywhere near the mountain. That will reduce the chance of them homing in on us.'

'We don't have the materials,' Nathan shouted. The man had two tones, directive and angry. Both were getting on my nerves. I observed Ebony. Even though she was outwardly calm and answered the man's questions with a patience I didn't have, I noticed a definite edge to some of her answers. Nathan was blissfully unaware and continued on his pathetic road of destruction. He wouldn't win the argument. No one did. Not with Ebony. I chuckled at the idea. Even the big man had found out to his detriment that opposition was useless. If she was convinced of a route, then nothing—absolutely nothing—would deter her from her intended result.

Nathan had yet to learn that snippet of information. I had no doubt he would, quicker than he'd imagined.

'Where would we get the supplies?' he tried to sway Ebony. Good luck with that.

'In the lower levels,' she answered calmly, the edge more pronounced.

'What lower levels.'

She pointed to the floor.

Nathan's brow creased and he cocked his head in question. 'Here?'

She nodded.

'You already have what you need?'

Again, a nod.

'But there's nothing there,' he spluttered, trying desperately to keep what he thought was the upper hand. I felt for him. The poor man had never had that, not even close.

Ebony just cocked her head and blinked slowly; the smile still plastered on her lips.

'You have to let me know what's in the lower levels,' he tried. 'I should know.'

I almost laughed out loud. He really didn't understand Ebony's clout. She was in charge. Had been remotely and definitely was now she'd joined us in the mountain.

Ebony just stared at him.

It was enough.

'I can't give you anyone from my people to set it all up.' He thought he'd found a new control.

'I don't need them. My team is perfectly able to do it. Probably better.'

The jab landed. Nathan's face flushed bright red, but there was nothing more he could do. She'd parried every one of his arguments and he had none left.

He turned and stamped out of the room.

Ebony turned to her team who could barely hide their amusement. 'Get it done please, Melanie.'

'Of course, Lady E.'

A week later, the additional security had been put in place, and I was back in the command centre.

The cave we were in was enormous. Twenty metres square and at least two stories high. The floor space was taken up by twelve desks each surrounded on three sides by banks of screens. At the back of the cave, I recognised the familiar wall of screens that Ebony had also used in the many headquarters we'd had before the invasion. I counted twelve big-screens wide and four high, so forty-eight in total. It eluded me how anyone could keep an eye on the information on so many different views. There were streams from the multitude of cameras that littered the area in a radius of twenty miles from the mountain. After that, the movement-triggered cameras were less frequent but still covered all regular access routes for more than fifty miles. Other screens showed alternating TV channels, most of them regulated by the invaders. The content was often horrific with close ups of executions, interchanged with Man-Kayl's latest heated speech or more new laws and regulations. Still more screens showed data streaming so fast I couldn't read most of it.

I counted five of Ebony's geek squad manning the desks, supplemented with the previous IT team, most of which had a hard time keeping up with the tempo now Ebony was in charge. She was up-and-running like before, filling me with renewed hope for the future. Her presence here boosted all our moral, mine was no exception.

'Lady E?' Melanie called out.

Ebony turned towards her; her head cocked in question.

'Bogies area sixteen,' she continued.

'Show me.'

The four centre screens went black making room for a new vista spanning all of them. I took a few steps closer and peered at the evolving scene.

Initially, nothing jumped out at me, it was a wide-angle view of the desert. Then something caught my eye. A movement at the edge of the screen, hardly visible.

'Zoom in, please,' Ebony requested.

The image blurred slightly then focussed on what was now visible as a human form. The camouflage uniform hid him, or her, well and only the slight shift in shadows made it possible to single out that it was a soldier.

'Another one at three o'clock,' Todd declared. The screens to the right lit up with more views of the valley. I identified the second soldier, then another. Todd highlighted the figures, making it easier for us to follow their movement.

'How many in total?'

'Three,' Melanie stated. 'No, Wait. Four.'

Ebony waited for possible adaptations, when none came, she nodded.

Okay, four soldiers. The big question was of course not only who they were, but where their loyalty lay.

'Two male and two female,' Todd declared.

I focussed on the figures. Yes, two of them were slightly smaller and moved with more fluidity. All four traversed the area carefully but with a determination I associated with humans. Still didn't answer the question whether they were aligned with the invaders though.

Ebony glanced at me. 'Get Nathan here please, Gabriel.'

I nodded and left the computer room to find the military man and inform him of our visitors.

Ten minutes later, Nathan, his second in command John, Sly, Aaliyah, Jonah and I were transfixed by the images on the screens. Ebony's team utilised the whole bank of screens and followed the four soldiers from different angles.

'Where are they?' Nathan asked, his voice more subdued than the previous time he'd been in the command centre. Just this one occasion had proved Ebony's point and her added value.

'Thirty-three miles west,' Todd answered. 'In the Pinbone valley.'

The technicians had named every valley and peak with their own labels to be able to identify each square mile of the territory around the mountain. They had carefully catalogued it with the use of data from the archives, occasional careful drone flights and of course the input when the cameras were positioned.

'Direction?'

'On a chartered course that will bring them to within ten miles of the mountain.'

Too close for comfort.

I glanced at Jonah and caught his eye. The concern in his creased brow mirrored my own.

Nathan's eyes were glued to the scene.

'They move like Marines,' Sly remarked.

Nathan nodded.

'Intercept?'

'What's the ETA for ten miles out?'

'At the speed they're going and taking into account that it's almost sundown, probably mid-day Thursday.' John suggested.

It was Tuesday. That would allow for a ten mile hike each day.

'Keep an eye on them and we decide tomorrow,' Nathan declared.

'No vehicles?' Jonah asked.

'We haven't identified any within the security radius,' Melanie declared. 'Could be further out, and they abandoned it.'

It sounded plausible. We were hundreds of miles from any inhabited areas and getting as far as they were on foot would be impossible, even for a seasoned Marine. Whatever vehicle had brought them this far could have run out of gas.

'We're scanning all other areas,' Ebony stated. 'Just in case this isn't the whole group.'

Next day, we decided to intercept.

Ebony had run closeups of the soldier's faces through the face recognition software she'd unearthed. Two came up blank, the others were identified as Marines, one—Callum — had been in John's boot camp on Paris Island.

The soldiers had unexpectedly turned back on their tracks and regrouped with a fifth member at a small camp. The long-distance camera could barely make out the military man under a camouflage net.

Ebony took the stage. 'There was one more person with the supplies and a vehicle. This morning, they all left on foot, retracing where they walked yesterday. The big difference was that they were carrying backpacks and not trying to be as stealthy.'

'Yesterday was a recon,' Sly added.

The soldiers came into view, walking in line. The first two were in full gear, the third carried nothing on his back, leant on a makeshift crutch and walked with obvious difficulty over the uneven terrain. The last two once again were packing. Their progress was slow, often stopping to rest the wounded man. At one point the sun reflected off a splint around his lower leg and ankle. With their current tactic, they wouldn't make as much progress as we'd initially calculated, so Sly and Nathan decided to try a different approach.

Our team was put together. Sly, Nathan and Jonah joined seven more soldiers, including John and Steve the medic. Aaliyah and I were not allowed to accompany them which resulted in heated arguments.

'We can't run the risk of exposing you,' Sly challenged us in the privacy of our own quarters. 'If they turn out to be hostile and one of you is wounded, even slightly, then the cat will be out of the bag.'

'We'll make sure we aren't,' Aaliyah protested.

'Not good enough. I won't endanger the whole team. If word gets out there'll be mutiny here, you know that.'

'I won't just sit here and wait.'

She was adamant. I shared her sentiment, but Sly's

reasoning rang true, and I had to reluctantly agree with him. The place was a powder keg anyway. We—mostly Mutt and me—were not popular with a large portion of the mountain's inhabitants. They objected to the perceived freedom we'd garnered for ourselves. We didn't follow all the rules, only the ones we agreed with and now Ebony had effectively taken over the whole mountain. We challenged the order; the one thing they thought kept them alive. Our constant urge to take on missions endangered them all, or so they reasoned.

It made sense for us to stay in the mountain. We would be able to follow the proceedings from the computer room, not that the idea helped to placate Aaliyah. She stormed out of the room. Sly looked at me for my reaction, I just shrugged my shoulders and nodded.

'Don't get killed,' I said in general, my lips attempting to smile but failing badly.

I left to find my fellow Taxorian and make sure she didn't do anything rash.

I found her on the ledge we frequented on the sheer side of the mountain. There was only one way in or out, through the small cave and a labyrinth of corridors. From the outside not even a mountain goat would be able to traverse the overhang and steep mountain wall. There were no hand holds, no outcrops. It was as though someone had cut through the rock like a hot knife through butter.

'You were uncharacteristically quiet,' she accused me.

'Well, Sly had a point. We can't risk adding to the tension already here.'

She opened her mouth to protest but decided against it.

'I don't want to be here either,' I continued. 'But it makes sense.'

There was an almost imperceivable nod as she stared out to the dark forests. The sun was setting between two peaks and coloured the rocky sides with a deep glow. Snow on the highest areas mirrored the waning light and gave the place something magical.

Three hours later found us back in the command centre. Just because we couldn't be in the action didn't mean we weren't invested. Aaliyah's face was still set to dangerous, and the rest rightfully avoided her. I stood in the open space between the desks and observed what was happening on the screens. Multiple different perceptions gave us a good idea of what the team would be up against.

The soldiers had once again split up to recon the area, exactly as Nathan had predicted, leaving the wounded man behind in a secluded spot at the end of where they'd come to the day before. He was well camouflaged between shrubs and the rest made their way in the general direction that would bring them past our mountain.

Our team approached the area from two sides. One group of three focussed on capturing the wounded man, the others made sure they were hidden in the area around the makeshift campsite. They would ambush the rest when they returned. Ebony's team kept them all up to date on the movements of the advance soldiers with our complicated system of clicks and individual words. If anyone homed in on the signals, they wouldn't be able to make head or tail of the noises. It was a combination of morse code and an audio version of braille.

The sun was at its zenith heating the desert to a heady forty degrees, even in the shade it had the expected result on the wounded man and the team crept up on the sleeping soldier without issues. They subdued him easily before he could alert his companions. Steve administered to the man's ankle and gave him pain killers. He and John stayed with the wounded soldier until the rest came back three hours later.

They came single file down the track, one of the women on point. Callum was second. We counted on him recognising John and defusing the situation.

It was tense. They immediately fanned out and dove for cover as soon as the point alerted them to strangers in the camp. John called out to Callum, naming himself and the bootcamp they'd shared. He held up his hands, clearly unarmed. The wounded man also called out that he was okay and that the strangers had treated his wounds.

The stalemate seemed to last forever, but finally Callum stood up, much to the point's disagreement. She shouted at him, but he took the first steps towards the shade where John, Steve and his companion were. His weapon was still pointed at John, who continued to address him and hold up his hands.

After a tense few minutes, the two men clasped arms, and I released my pent-up breath. Callum called back to the rest, we couldn't hear what he said, but they reluctantly stood up and glanced at each other. The weapons weren't lowered. The second female shrugged her shoulders, slung her weapon over her shoulder and walked to the shade. The other two followed.

John spoke to Callum who turned and scanned the area, his features suddenly worried and hard and his M27 once again ready to fire. More assurance from John, and he lowered the weapon again.

John whistled and the rest of our team emerged from their hiding places surrounding the scene. There were additional tense moments, but John handled it well.

A collective sigh of release in the command centre accompanied the realisation that the whole mission had been achieved without one shot fired. I turned from the screens and nodded to Ebony. The smile on her face mirrored mine. It had gone down much better than I could have imagined.

Chapter Forty-Six

As usual, the teams brought the hooded visitors back to the mountain in a very round-about route to confuse them of our location. The fact that one of them had been recognised by John wasn't enough to sway the suspicion, especially because one of the women; Liz and one of the men; Neil, hadn't turned up in Ebony's database. Two of Nathan's men had returned to the hidden Humvee with jerry cans of diesel. They scanned the vehicle for trackers, removed even the broken one, then brought the vehicle back to our HQ. It was stored in a second garage three miles outside the mountain.

Mark had been whisked off to the infirmary by the doctor. The rest received a good meal and fresh coffee in a small room off the garage. We'd deduced that the mountains inhabitants would be curious and possibly overwhelming, so we'd decided to isolate the visitors until further notice. Ebony also wanted to observe them, looking for any disconcerting signs. She wasn't happy with the new recruits. The lack of information rubbed her the wrong way.

The hairs on my arms tingled with the loaded atmosphere. Though thankful that Mark was now undergoing medical care, his friends were wary. They'd been brought to what for them was basically a prison of sorts. Their weapons had been confiscated and the hoods brought home the dependent position they found themselves in. Liz's eyes jittered around the room barely landing on anyone for more than a second. Her hands fidgeted with the mug, and she was yet to take a sip of the hot brew.

Her chair was close to Callum who seemed blissfully unaware of his colleague's tension. He was locked in a happy trek down memory lane with John, bringing up wild tales of their time in Boot Camp. Neil and Serena, the last two of the group, alternated between listening to their friend's banter and glancing at the strange band of revolutionaries who now controlled their life expectation.

We turned as one to the door where the doctor stood.

'Your friend is resting,' she announced. 'His ankle is broken, and I've set it. He'll be in plaster for the coming six weeks and need physio for at least another six weeks after that. He did extra damage walking on the foot. The splint helped, but I can't be sure there won't be any lasting trauma.'

'Thank you, doctor,' Callum answered.

'What kind of trauma?' Neil asked.

'There may be some residual tenderness in the bone and the ligaments have been stretched beyond their normal elasticity, so he may need additional surgery later on.'

'Fat chance of that,' Liz stated.

I understood her sentiment. With the invasion all medical care had been taken over by the invaders and only the procedures deemed absolutely necessary by the new masters were executed. A young man with a leg issue would mean termination and reincarnation. Bottom line, it was less costly.

'Nothing more I can do now,' the doctor continued.

'We're very grateful for all you've done,' Callum quickly answered with a glare at Liz. She was unimpressed.

The doctor nodded and left, the atmosphere in the room tainted by Liz's bad mood.

I struggled to find a reason. Until that is, I glanced at Aaliyah who was in an animated conversation with Callum. She hung on his every word, laughing at jokes and smiling often.

She was flirting.

Shit.

Not the most appropriate course of action, not when it was quite clear that Callum and Liz were a couple. I mean, even I saw that. The female Marine shot dagger glares at Aaliyah who completely ignored her. Callum seemed vaguely aware that there was something wrong, but he clearly enjoyed the attention.

I tried to catch Aaliyah's eye, but she stubbornly refused to look my way.

Jonah and Ebony were huddled in whispered conversation in the corner. He glanced at the unfolding scene and walked up to Aaliyah and tapped her on the shoulder.

'Can I have a word, Aaliyah?'

Her features instantly changed into a frown. 'Now?'

'Now.'

She turned back to Callum and smiled seductively again, then followed Jonah out of the room. Callum watched her go, then doubled up from an elbow in his ribs and the dark glower from his girlfriend.

I hoped the big man would be able to talk sense into

Aaliyah, but I doubted it. She could be exceptionally stubborn, and I imagined part of her current actions were just plain revenge for not taking her on the mission. She was bored, and now she was transferring her energy into something else, something that could turn around and bite us.

Chapter Forty-Seven

'There's an alien among us.'

A voice carried through the caverns and resonated loudly, like the owner had used a bullhorn. The resulting loaded silence was as powerful as the shout itself.

I looked over the large group of people who had convened in the meeting hall. Many of the adults were there, though mainly the men. Their features were pulled in hard visages and angry scowls. The atmosphere in the area changed from a musty, but calming earthen essence into a heavy oxygen-depleted pressure where the tension could be cut with a knife.

People I counted not as friends exactly, but at least as good acquaintances glared at us with an animosity that took me back. It was bound to happen at some time, and we'd even broached the subject at our inner circle meeting two days ago. The consensus then had been that this was not the right time to offer the information. Aliens were the enemy. They'd invaded Earth, killed these people's kin. It was just too raw.

Now we'd waited too long, and it was out of our hands. We didn't react.

'There's an alien here,' the man who shouted earlier repeated. 'And you know who he is.' He pointed to us sitting around the conference table.

His words caused a surge forward in the line of people. They took two steps towards where we were and, for a moment there, I thought they might rush in through the wide opening and attack us.

Jonah calmly stood up, lifted his ever-present axe handle from its perch up against the wall behind him, released the blade shards with a resounding clang and walked from the table out to the challenging mob.

They stopped their advance. The casually held weapon of destruction and relaxed features of the big man weren't fooling anyone.

'Who are you?' he addressed the spokesman, stopping two metres from him.

'Gregg,' the man answered, his bravura dented. 'I'm Gregg.'

He stood up straight and tried to stare Jonah down, kind of difficult if you're a head shorter. He didn't stand a chance, and the big man raised an eyebrow as he let the pommel of the axe bang on the floor. Gregg couldn't help himself and looked down at the possible cause of his imminent demise, his courage clearly failed him.

'Hi, Gregg,' Jonah exaggerated the name and spoke clearly and slowly. 'You seem to be the representative of this fine gathering of people here. Is that right.'

'Uh, yeah.' He looked around at the others, they nodded slightly, anxiety pushing their anger back.

The impending threat was clear. Jonah's prowess with the axe was legendary, and the sound of the blades extending out from the heft had resounded clearly throughout the cavern, alerting everyone that it was ready for duty. No one moved. Many forgot to breathe.

We just waited, curious to see how this would progress.

Jonah sniffed his clear disdain and picked up the fully extended weapon again. He hefted it from one hand to the other while he stared in Gregg's eyes the whole time. Beads of sweat congealed on the smaller man's forehead, and I noticed a definite shake in his frame. My big friend's intimidation tactics were clearly working, and not only on Gregg. Others had shuffled back a step, leaving him standing alone to confront Jonah. Not a place anyone in their right mind wanted to be.

'And what was it you wanted to talk to us about?' Jonah called him out.

Gregg swallowed hard, his gaze flitting from Jonah's face to the massive weapon he held.

'Yeah, uh. We wanted to ask you something.'

'Ask us?' There was amusement in Jonah's tone. 'Now that sounds a lot better than your first demand.' He spat out the last word.

The rest of our inner circle walked out of the meeting recess and stood in a semi-circle facing the mob. Sly walked over to where Jonah and Gregg had their stand-off. He put his hand on the big man's arm and nodded to him, then walked one more step until he was standing to the side, halfway between them.

'Now, Gregg,' he faced the smaller man. 'Shall we start all over again? I'm sure you didn't want to antagonise Jonah here.'

Gregg was quick to shake his head vehemently. 'Hell no. I just wanted to know, uh, we wanted to know something.'

'And what was that?'

'I—we—heard there was an alien here,' he stammered, then pulled himself together again and stood up straight, his defiance once again resurfacing now Sly was there.

'Who told you that?' Sly asked.

'Doesn't matter.' Gregg glanced back at the people behind him, taking strength from them. 'We want to know. We have a right to know who the alien is.'

'You have a right,' Sly echoed. 'How do you figure that?'

'We're all here risking our lives to fight the invaders.'

'All of us are,' Sly remarked calmly.

'That's what I said.'

'All of us.'

Gregg's annoyance at what he clearly perceived as Sly's dallying was clear. He pulled his brow down, so it hooded his eyes.

'That's what I said, old man. All of us. Are you deaf?'

I hid my smile behind my hand. Gregg was walking on non-existence ice, and it was cracking like heck. You did not address Sly in that manner and walk away.

Sure enough, Sly looked up from under his brow at Gregg and stared at him. The audacity quickly turned to uncertainty and Gregg glanced around for some support. Not going to happen. All he encountered were amused grins from us and terrified ones from his former backers.

'Uh. I didn't mean that in a bad way,' he stammered.

'How else could you mean it?' Sly asked calmly, which was probably even more terrifying. I wondered which adversary was better, Sly or Jonah. It seemed good old Gregg had navigated from the pan into the fire.

'I just, uhhh, well thought you hadn't understood.'

'I think it's you that has an issue with comprehending what's going on here,' Sly answered, his visage still stern.

'So, once again. ALL of us here are risking our lives to fight the invaders?'

Gregg nodded. No more than that. He didn't dare.

'If there is an alien among us,' Sly continued. 'And I'm not saying there is. Then the alien is risking everything as well.' I was grateful that he kept the discussion to one alien. That was bad enough.

Gregg opened his mouth to contest when Jonah coughed softly. One glance at the big man and his axe convinced him silence was still the way to go.

You could hear the cogs turning in the mob's brains. Sure, it was a difficult thing to get their mind around, and their emotions. Aliens were the enemy. The flash invasion had overwhelmed and devastated everyone in its wake. There wasn't a family that hadn't lost someone, either dead or taken. It was raw. Sentiments were the same. I couldn't blame them for the mob mentality, they wanted to lash out, especially when someone like Gregg instigated the barely suppressed rage.

'How do we know the alien's not going to betray us?' Gregg wasn't finished.

Did the guy have a death wish?

'The alien could just be biding his time so their soldiers can get us all.'

I glanced at the others, there were occasional nods.

'Setting us up for the invaders,' the instigator continued, urged on by the agreement he saw in his fellow humans. 'They can't be trusted. They're aliens. They will always choose their own above us.'

'Like you would?' Jonah remarked casually, again leaning the big axe on its pommel while he slowly turned it. The blades caught the lights and reflected into the mob, emphasising the weapon's presence.

'Every species puts their own first.' Gregg's voice was growing in tone and volume again. He was back on his soapbox, inciting the mob. 'It's natural. Why would any of them want to help us? We're just cattle to them. Assets to be exploited. Money in the bank.'

'Not all the Taxorians agree with what's happening. Not all are slavers,' Aaliyah stated.

'Of course they are. It's inbred in them. They've done this for centuries.'

'You seem to know a lot about the Taxorians,' Jonah remarked calmly.

Sweat drops formed on his brow and he stammered. 'What I saw on the streams,' Gregg quickly recovered. 'That guy, the leader.'

'Cal-Tan.'

'Yeah, the dude in the fancy shirt. He said they'd done it for hundreds, or thousands of years.'

I glanced at Aaliyah. That didn't sound like my father. He wasn't about to own up to anything like that. Made me wonder where Gregg had accumulated all this knowledge.

'They've been kidnapping humans for all that time, and now they want to either kill or transport everyone out of here. Earth will be empty. No humans left anymore. If they continue like this.'

'Might be better for the planet,' Jonah remarked laconically.

'We're all either going to die or become slaves.'

The murmurs increased. His words were having an adverse effect on the group again, and they became more animated. The general consensus was turning back to all aliens being the enemy.

'No, we're not,' Jonah declared. 'Not as long as we're all here and fighting them.'

'But what about the alien among us?' A voice asked from the crowd.

'Yeah, how do you know he's trustworthy?'

'Because he saved my life. Multiple times,' Jonah answered, his body still relaxed but his words loaded. 'And yours.'

'Not mine!' Gregg pulled the conversation back to him.

I wondered what his agenda was. How would he benefit from outing Aaliyah, Tajan or me?

'Yes.' Jonah's tone was hard and uncompromising. 'Yours as well.'

'We have a right to know,' the voices from the mob continued to demand.

I glanced at Aaliyah; she was about to step forward. I shook my head softly.

'You do,' I answered. 'Not because of Gregg here. Or the nonsense he's spewing.'

'So, who is it?'

I registered that the expectation was still that there was just one and someone else than had addressed them up to that point.

'You're looking at him,' I answered as calmly as possible. I'd decided at the start of the confrontation that I would be the only one put in the crosshairs. Aaliyah and Tajan had to stay under wraps. For now.

My confession, if you could call it that, unnerved the mob. Their surprise and disbelief were complete.

They all knew what I'd done to help the rebels. What I'd lost. Kate, everything. I looked at them one by one, my eyes catching theirs and daring them to say something. All declined, most lowered their gaze in shame.

I left my spot at the side of the doorway and walked into

the small space between the mob and our inner circle, closely followed by the extremely agitated Mutt.

'Here I am,' I challenged them. 'I'm the alien, and if you don't believe me, watch this.' I punctured the skin on my arm and held it up to clearly show the purple blood.

'I've been with you from the start of the rebellion. Part of the group fighting Cal-Tan from long before that. If you have doubts about my loyalty, speak up.'

'Gabriel was the first who rebelled. He was the one who exposed The Establishment.' Jonah picked up his axe and moved to my side. 'He risked not only his life, but everything he had to help us and show the world what was happening right in front of their eyes. He revealed that HUMANS were working with the aliens to kill and enslave our young men. What we know, is because of him. He's fought against his own kind, against his own kin, time and time again.'

Jonah walked up closer to the crowd. As one, they stepped back, fear and shame on their faces.

'Gabriel killed his brother to save me,' he challenged Gregg directly. 'His younger brother.'

He let that land.

'Do you know what that means? How much he's suffered for us?'

Gregg couldn't hold his stare. I wasn't surprised, the big man was intense.

'He lost the woman he loved.'

A stab hit me hard at the reference to Kate and I shuddered visibly.

'He's lost more than you have. There's no way he will ever be able to go home or see what's left of his family. He gave all that up to help you. To save your pathetic ass.' He prodded Gregg in the chest so hard the smaller man was pushed back a step.

Jonah looked at the mob, he spread his left arm and waved it over them all.

'He gave it up, all of it, his future, his past, his family, all of it. For you,' he repeated.

There was total silence.

'And you dare to doubt his loyalty?' The tone was dangerous. Threatening.

The big man picked up the axe. 'Well, any of you who want to get to Gabriel, will have to go through me.'

'And me,' Caleb echoed as he moved to stand next to me.

His support surprised and warmed me. He was the last one I'd expected to have at my back.

'And me.' Sly stepped up to my other side.

One by one, all the inner circle declared their commitment to me. Others in the mob slowly either stepped back or moved sheepishly to our side until Gregg stood alone.

The silence and tension could be cut with a blunt knife. All resentment had shifted from the aliens, from me to Gregg. The big man smiled—not in a good way—and took a deep breath.

'So,' his voice had an edge you could wound yourself on. 'We've answered your question. You now know who the alien is and where our knowledge of Taxore comes from.'

The guy's skin turned a sickly grey colour as he shrank under the big man's glare,

'The only question that remains is: where does yours come from?'

From the corner of my eye, I saw Liz and Neil lounging at the back of the area watching the proceedings. Was it my imagination, or did I detect a glint of amusement in the woman's eye.

She was observant.

A shiver started at the bottom of my spine and travelled up to end in a stabbing pain at the back of my skull. Liz glanced from me to the right, I followed her gaze and saw it land on Aaliyah. She whispered something to her companion, her face close to his ear and he too observed my Taxorian friend. He nodded slowly, then looked at me.

The shivers were intensifying, they were putting two and two together. I realised how often Aaliyah and I separated ourselves from the rest and just enjoyed each other's company. We also sparred together in the gym, it made sense, we were much stronger than humans and it was difficult to hold your punches, especially for Aaliyah. Her temper was even more volatile than mine and she quickly rolled over to excess.

We'd have to be careful.

They knew about me. The rest had to stay under cover.

It resonated with me that Neil and Liz were the two Marines Ebony still had doubts about. Couldn't be worse.

Next day we reconvened, just the inner circle, to discuss what had happened and how that could change the status quo after Gregg's announcement.

'We scanned him again,' Tajan offered. 'No tags or anything. No tickets.'

'So he was sent in cold, without back-up?'

'Looks that way,' Aaliyah answered.

I pursed my lips and pulled down the edges in thought. 'They expected us to scan for electronics.'

'Yes. It makes sense. They know we're in the resistance.' Aaliyah voiced what I was thinking.

'Did he get out at all?' I wanted to know whether our location had been compromised. 'Since he came here.'

'No. He was still on probation. He's only been here for three weeks.'

Relief spread through my tense shoulders.

'How did he get through the security?' Sly asked the group.

'They have some fancy background builders,' Caleb answered. 'Ebony scanned him fully, like she does with all of them. He came up squeaky clean. At least for any contact with Taxorian forces.'

'We're going to have to be even more careful,' Sly voiced what we were all thinking. 'They're getting better.'

'Yes,' Jonah chimed in. 'And throwing more resources into capturing us.'

'We're a flea in Cal-Tan's pelt. An irritating itch he wants to get rid of.' I could imagine how my father viewed us. We were a bump on his road to whatever he wanted to achieve. If it hadn't been for me and his hatred for his wayward son, then I think he wouldn't even have bothered. But he had to make an example of my betrayal. One way or the other, he needed to capture me again and show everyone what happened to disloyal Taxorians. I had no illusions about how he would make the example stick.

'What about Carol and Steve?' Aaliyah asked. 'They vouched for Gregg, he's Carol's nephew.'

'They're devastated,' Caleb answered. 'Just the thought that he could betray us is killing them.'

'Are we sure they're not just good actors?' Sly asked the question that was foremost in my mind. I didn't want to be so suspicious, but I'd talked to Gregg after he came, and no alarm bells rang then. He was good.

'They aren't,' Jonah assured me. 'I vouched for them.'

That was good enough for me.

'What are we going to do with him?'

Lots of shrugs. We would deal with Gregg later. For now, he would be incarcerated in our deepest dungeons.

'Is it safe to stay here?' Aaliyah questioned.

Sly shrugged. 'We can never be sure. So, Lady E is looking for a new location, just in case.'

We might have to move again.

Made sense, but I wasn't looking forward to it. Losing this place with all its assets would be a big blow to the cause.

Chapter Forty-Eight

'What if we used Cal-Tan's strategy against him?' Ebony suggested.

After her escape, she'd joined us for good.

I loved having her near, we all did. Jonah positively beamed, a massive smile on his face every day since she'd come. I was happy for them, kind of jealous and sad that Kate wasn't with us as well, but I didn't deny them their bliss.

My brow creased, what did Ebony mean? I wasn't the only one confused and shared the same questioning features with the big man and Caleb. Only Sly seemed to have an inkling.

His stern features had softened in the past weeks with Ebony's arrival. It suited him.

'He reincarnated your pre-growth,' she addressed me directly. 'Then tried to pass him off as you.'

A niggling feeling started at the base of my spine. My mind was starting to connect the dots, and I wasn't sure I liked the outcome.

'So, what if we pass you off as the double?' She'd said it.

'Infiltrate them?' Jonah asked.

She nodded, a smile lighting up her face. Other's picked up on the idea.

'Then we would know what the invaders are planning,' Sly added.

'And maybe even finally find out why Cal-Tan needs all these people.'

Sly turned to Aaliyah. 'You said earlier that they'd never been interested in women before?'

'They weren't. My father never reincarnated females, there was no market for them.'

'What about Cal-Tan?' he asked me. The answer was the same. I shook my head, not trusting my voice to stay level. It was bad enough that I wanted to keep the shivers I felt in every cell of my body a secret.

'So why are they doing that now?' The sixty-four-thousand-dollar question. 'What changed?'

'If we find out, it could be important to the whole reason why Earth was invaded.'

They talked on for a while, I stayed out of the conversation, just nodding and shaking my head whenever appropriate.

I didn't share their elation. Jonah was the one exception; he was silent too.

Yes, it was an option. One that had possibilities. We'd been looking for a way in for a long time. Ebony had failed to hack into the invader's data, and it frustrated her and Tajan no end.

But it would mean I would be under cover again. Playing someone who was playing me. Someone who had an advantage I wouldn't have, he knew the people on both sides. Sure, he was going in with some blind spots, but I would be completely blind. There was a difference. A very big difference. He knew who he was playing. I didn't.

Ebs noticed.

Of course she did.

She walked up to me and looked at me intently. I cocked my head and shrugged.

'I can understand you're not keen, Gabriel,' she said softly, just loud enough to stop the others chattering. 'It would be you in the crosshairs again.'

I nodded.

'And this time would be even more dangerous.'

She looked at the others, then back to me.

'I'm sorry.' She took my hands. 'I should have spoken to you first, before I suggested it.'

'It's ok,' I answered with a small smile. 'It is a good idea. And that's something we really need at this moment. I just don't know whether I can do it.'

'Can or want?' Sly asked.

I turned to look at him. There was no malice in his features, it was just a simple question.

'Both, if I'm honest.'

'I don't think it's feasible,' Jonah joined in. 'We don't know who this person is, who he knows. He's a complete anomaly and sending Gabriel in to try and take his place would be like blindfolding him.'

'We know how he acts,' Sly continued, reluctant to give up on the idea.

'No,' the big man countered. 'We know how he acts when he's impersonating Gabe. Not in his normal day to day life. For all we know he could be a snivelling little shit or an arrogant megalomaniac. It's too risky.'

I was eternally grateful to the big man. He voiced my exact hesitation. Blind wouldn't cover it.

'You're right,' Sly conceded, looking at me slightly apologetically. 'It seemed like a good idea on the surface, but on reflection it would unnecessarily endanger you.'

'So, what do we do now?' Caleb asked.

There were a lot of shrugs. We were out of ideas. Again.

The mood in the room darkened.

'We can't just sit on our hands here while they're transporting thousands a day off-world,' Caleb announced.

'We don't have to.' Tajan had come into the room silently, as was his pattern. The small mousy man had a massive smile on his face, all the more apparent because of the scowls and down-pulled lips of the others in the room. He walked towards Ebony and handed her a tablet.

She read the contents, and her brow raised. Slowly the edges of her lips pulled up in a smile she beamed at the small man who instantly blushed under the praise.

'Tajan has done it,' she claimed enthusiastically.

I moved closer. Nervous energy once again filling my body.

'He's decoded the collars.' She paused for effect. 'We can remove them. Free the prisoners.'

No one spoke, we all looked at Tajan who again blushed under the attention.

Finally, we had good news.

Chapter Forty-Nine

After they cracked the code, Tajan and Ebony made great progress, and we started planning new missions to liberate the intended grunts. We already had locations, Ebony had catalogued them long ago and kept up with any changes just in case.

Nathan and his lieutenants joined our inner circle for the planning and together we plotted seven initial attacks coordinated to happen at the exact same time. Surprise would be our biggest ally, and we needed to make the most of it. We didn't expect the invaders to be able to make changes to the software quickly once they found out what we were capable of. Besides, Tajan and Ebony had the bones of the code, and any adaptations would be easy to follow, at least that's what they told me.

This first attack had to be a big one. Any others would be more difficult. The best way to take advantage of the new options was to look further than just our team, even globally. Not everyone agreed and we argued the merits of sharing our technology with other underground resistance groups.

'We can't run the risk of any of the other teams being infiltrated,' Nathan argued.

'Only the ones we're sure of,' Ebony countered. 'The ones we've vetted.'

'We don't know them.'

'We know there are many groups out there. And there are people in lots of them we do know.'

'How do we know who we can trust?' He wouldn't back down.

'We already have trusted people all over the world,' Ebony surprised all of us.

'This isn't just a local war,' Sly joined in. 'It's a global fight. There are transport hubs all over the world where hundreds of thousands are sent to another dimension. We can't keep this technology to ourselves.'

He was right. Our segregation from the outside world made us short-sighted. We had to look globally.

'There's an added benefit to that,' I suggested. 'If we can coordinate a global attack, we'll make it much more difficult for them to react swiftly. We'll attack them in multiple places and divide their attention. Make the most of the surprise.'

'We don't have the contacts,' Nathan was adamant.

'You don't.' Ebony shut him up, her patience spent. 'I do.'

He physically pulled back; his eyebrows creased in disbelief.

'How?' was all he could say.

'I have contacts, Nathan. You knew that.'

'Yes, here. But I assumed they were only local to the US.'

'Kind of short-sighted,' Jonah commented. He was masking his surprise better than the rest of us. The only others not showing any signs of astonishment were Sly, Caleb and Tajan.

'My reach goes beyond the country borders, Nathan, and we will involve global resistance in this mission. I'll share the technology.'

He took a breath to counter her but noticed the big man move closer.

'How?' he asked. 'How did you get the contacts, the power.' His eyes swung from her to Jonah and back again.

'Now that is on a need-to-know basis,' she answered. 'And you don't.'

Hours later, we'd set out the bones of a global attack plan. It hadn't really been contested by Nathan, he saw the merits. I think it was more the lack of control that was bothering him. He'd run the compound since the invasion and done a good job keeping the place and its inhabitants secure. He wasn't a man of action, reluctant to endanger what had been set up, he avoided risks. I could understand that. My father would love to get his hands on the people here. Most of them were prime workers. Young, strong. Just what he needed. People here looked to Nathan to keep them safe and sound. Our group had put a spanner in those works. We'd brought the fighting mentality. It stirred kindred emotions in many of his soldiers and they itched to make a difference and engage the enemy. It was, after all, what they'd joined the military for. Our idea quickly gained momentum with Nathan's lieutenants, and he finally conceded that we had the opening we needed.

Now was the time to look beyond our safe-haven. We were here to fight. To disrupt the harvesting and ultimately defeat Taxore.

Yes, I dream big.

There would be no respite for us until we'd confronted and beaten my father.

Chapter Fifty

'I have something to tell you,' Ebony announced at dinner.

Jonah, Sly, Caleb, Tajan, Aaliyah, Melanie, Todd and I were seated around the small table in Jonah and Ebony's quarters. Sly had cooked and we'd just demolished two trays of his legendary lasagna. Even with the restrictions we faced in the mountain compound he managed to cook like a chef. The food was happily devoured, and we all sat back with full stomachs.

I was intrigued. What could she mean? The question was mirrored on Aaliyah's features.

'I think it's time you know what I do for a living.' Ebony's voice had a hint of mirth. 'We're all family here and there should be no secrets.'

I loved the way our group of misfits had indeed become a close-knit family and felt privileged to be counted as one of them. We might have different origins, even be different species, but this lot was more my family than what I'd left behind on Taxore, with the exception of my mother.

Yes, it had puzzled me how she'd amassed her seemingly

endless fortune that built her organisation and supported our cause, not to mention the clout she seemed to have in even the strangest places.

'After Sly and his family found me, I finally started my new, more normal life.' Ebony continued. 'There were difficult moments.' She smiled at Sly. 'But they gave me the love and belonging I'd never had. My wild nature found a home and calmed a bit.'

'Yeah, a bit,' Caleb echoed, his words eliciting laughs all around.

'They sent me to MIT. I tried to behave there, but away from the order of our home, I rebelled again. I fell in with the wrong crowd of nerds, probably because I was bored. The curriculum didn't challenge me, and I was looking for more adventurous things to keep me interested. Anyway, they were hackers. And not the ethical kind.'

I pulled the water jug towards me and refilled my glass. This promised to be very interesting.

'At first, we hacked into all the major companies and played pranks. Nothing really impactful or damaging. We were just having fun.'

Her smile faded as she continued.

'It all became a lot darker when Whitney joined us. She was a seasoned anarchist, hellbent on inflicting as much damage on the government as she could. Initially, I stayed clear of her, but she intrigued me. Her monologues became famous at our frequent binge-drinking sessions and slowly she started to influence us all, me included.'

I glanced at the rest. Caleb and Sly were slowly nodding, they of course were familiar with the story. for the rest of us it was an eyeopener.

'We joined her and started to hack government systems. First just to prove we could, but later to do damage. I'm not proud of it, but at the time it seemed legitimate with what they were doing to the people through taxation and the justice system.'

She sighed.

'Anyway, to cut a long story short, we were caught. We hacked into one system too many and they arrested us. The army immediately flew us off to a military facility somewhere and I felt terrible. Sly and Latitia both worked two jobs to get me through college and uni, and I'd made a mess of it. You could say it woke me up. So when the time came for me to be interrogated by the army, I resolved to take the full blame for my stupid adolescent actions.'

'They left me alone in the cell for the night and when they came in the morning, I was quite teary and dejected. They led me to an office where a three-star general proceeded to lecture me about the ethics of what I'd done. I sat there and took it all in. Then he surprised me. I thought he would send me off to prison for treason or something like that, instead he offered me a job.'

A small laugh escaped Jonah's lips.

She turned to him. 'Yeah. That was what I thought. That it was a joke. But it wasn't. It was the start of my covert employment.'

'I saw the potential and I've worked for the US government and Nato on and off since that fateful day. Many of the patents I created are military based. They and my civilian inventions financed the tech company and the production company I clandestinely have. Or should I say, had, under the current circumstances. Every different line of work required a new identity and background which I easily created. The warren of identities is a form of security in itself, shielding me from enemies and allies alike. I've lived so many secret lives with all the personas I created that I sometimes forget who I really am.'

I was glued to her every word.

'I've been party to a lot of secrets, military and political. I know where the skeletons are buried and who threw in the dirt. It gives me an edge. They know I know, but not what measures I've taken to secure my life, so they're careful not to antagonise me. Basically, it gives me a very untraditional position in this country's security.'

She looked around and waved her hand at the walls surrounding us. 'Take this facility for instance. Part of it is my design. I knew where it was and what it was, and more importantly how few people know of its existence. This place makes black ops look like child's play. There are secrets here even Nathan has no knowledge of, and he's the custodian. Like the weapons and technology hidden deep in the mountain that he can't access.'

'But you can?' Jonah asked incredulously.

She nodded.

'That's where you were this morning?' The big man concluded.

'Yes. I had to be sure it was all undisturbed.'

I felt a tingling of anticipation in my spine. This could be the game changer we so desperately needed.

'And it will help us win this war against the invaders.' Ebony confirmed my deductions.

We let that sink in. The last part had been a surprise for Sly and Caleb as well as for us.

In a strange way, it all made sense. As a genius she'd been a bigger asset to the military if she worked with them than rotting in a jail somewhere. I smiled. She'd no doubt manipulated them to further her own goals. Used them as they thought they were using her. And when they finally realised how powerful she'd become it was too late.

She was truly a master strategist.

And again, the future was looking better because of her.

Later that night I was still mulling over the implications of what Ebony had told us when she walked into the kitchen for a drink.

'Tea?' I asked. 'There's some in the pot. I just brewed it.'

'Thanks.'

She poured herself a cup and topped off mine, then sat down opposite me.

'Penny for your thoughts.'

'I was just thinking about what you said earlier,' I answered.

'Were you surprised?'

'Yes. Though I feel I shouldn't be.'

'Didn't you ever wonder?'

'Where you got the funds and power from? Yes. I did. But that was your business, not mine.'

She was amused and smiled while she took a sip of the warm brew.

'Where did you think it came from?'

I cocked my head and blushed a bit. 'Um, I thought you were involved in maybe less than legal enterprises.'

She laughed warmly. Then surprised me yet again.

'You'd be right,' she commented. 'Some of them aren't above board.'

Chapter Fifty-One

Two days later Ebony had aligned with resistance groups in twelve countries world-wide. Arrangements had been made for a coordinated attack and the interference software for the collars had been shared with local geniuses Ebony trusted. Our team had modified military wrist computers to emit a signal that would counter that of the invaders. As an added bonus, it also unlocked the collars, and they could easily and safely be removed. We had strict orders to leave all collars behind because they were most likely tagged with location software. Each of us had the small computer on our wrists and we set off in the middle of the night to the designated locations.

Ebony stayed back at the compound from where she would coordinate the global attack. The countries participating included the UK, France, Russia, China, Japan, Australia, Brazil and Germany. If successful, it would definitely knock a dent in my father's plans.

This coordinated attack marked the first time resistance teams from multiple countries worked closely together. Only

Ebony's legendary status within the underground high-tech community made it possible. That and I suspected her reputation in less than legal areas. All in all, it was a monumental occasion.

Our target was a holding facility a day's drive from the mountain. We'd set off almost immediately after the hardware had been distributed and our intricate coded communication method kept us up to date on what was happening worldwide.

We estimated there were almost one-hundred and twenty prisoners in the compound which was defended by no more than ten grunts. The collars had made them complacent. They assumed we didn't dare mount a release attempt after the initial disasters with the collars.

Our team was ten strong. Jonah, Caleb, Aaliyah and I were joined by Nathan and five of his soldiers. I'd reluctantly left Mutt behind because of the distance and multiple objections of the soldiers. They had issues with him, I suspected they were just plain scared. The way he looked right through them didn't help, but hey, that's their problem. It was the first time we'd been separated since Kate died, and it had been necessary to lock him in the big kennels just to stop him from jumping on the truck with me. He would be alright, just pissed off that he'd been left behind. I didn't envy Jackson who would have to feed him and clean the kennel while I was gone.

We arrived at the area of the holding facility before dawn on the second day. We would be attacking in daylight. Not ideal, but with a worldwide coordinated mission it was inevitable not all teams would be able to use the cover of darkness. We'd drawn the short straw because of a mass transportation planned in the UK that we wanted to counter.

The attack was just an hour away and we stayed hidden in an old, abandoned factory complex. The three pickups were concealed under camouflage nets in one of the hollow buildings. We could see the facility through the broken windows using binoculars and nothing seemed out of the ordinary.

Even in our mountain compound, most of the inhabitants were unaware of our mission, and those that were didn't know it was global. We still dispensed information on a need-to-know basis. They would find out after the fact. After the scene with Gregg, trust was hard to come by. Better safe than sorry. Man-Kayl would no doubt have the full force of his technical staff working on our location and scanning for communications.

The holding facility consisted of seven buildings, six of them held the prisoners and the last one housed the kitchen, staff and supplies. They were arranged in a square with the housing buildings perpendicular to the larger municipal building. A three-metre-high electric fence surrounded the complex. There were no dogs, my kind generally doesn't know how to handle them, besides they were confident in their superiority under the given circumstances. No one would dare to free prisoners if they exploded when they reached the gate. It defeated the objective. And then there was the mentality of the prisoners themselves. Every time a new batch of prisoners were incarcerated at the facility the invaders held a demonstration. Thankfully not with a human, but the message was just as clear when the collar was put on a pig. It effectively made the prisoners their own wardens and no one dared attempt an escape. That was why it was so important the software not only nullified the explosive character of the collars but also opened them. We didn't expect anyone would dare walk out of the compound wearing it.

The first signal finally came, and we made our way through heavy brush that covered the flat area between the deserted factory and the holding facility. We kept our silhouettes low to the ground which made the one-kilometre trek slow and uncomfortable. Daylight didn't help. I hoped the guards were as complacent as we expected and that they didn't bother with regular surveillance. They would be focussed on the inside of the facility, at least that was what we were counting on. Stealth must have been difficult for Jonah. The big man stood out, even hunched over as he was.

We slowly made progress and spread out around the fence. The electricity would be turned off remotely at the grid by Ebony's team, which would give us the opportunity to cut the fence and enter the grounds. Jonah, Nathan and I would mount the frontal assault and rush in the front gate. Simultaneously we would activate the jamming software and if all went well, might get some help from the prisoners themselves as soon as the collars fell off.

The countdown had started, and we waited with bated breath.

This was it. We were in action again. I felt the thrill of the anticipated battle. I relished the fight to release my pent-up anger and energy before it all boiled over. These invaders would pay for everything that had happened in the past months. I know, they weren't personally responsible for the specific pain I'd experienced, but they were guilty by association, and they were in the wrong place at the wrong time.

My bloodlust was set to purple, and nothing would stop me now.

The sound was almost inaudible—just a slight frizzle—as the electricity died. It was our signal, and we rushed to the gate. The lock had opened when the current was cut and we quickly made our way towards the municipal building, already firing at the figures behind the windows. Answering fire forced us to find what little cover we could. More barrages from all sides pulled the defenders in all directions, and we continued towards the entrance. Jonah lined up with the door and fired the handheld rocket launcher resting on his shoulder. The blast disintegrated the entrance which allowed Nathan and I to rush through the now gaping hole in the building. Heavy return fire from the windows held the big man back until another rocket blasted the defenders to smithereens.

Screams sounded throughout the complex and we entered the buildings to absolute chaos. I took a moment to look around. Bodies lay strewn on the floor, most in puddles of purple blood. I saw two dead humans and another wounded, his leg a mass of red blood. Discarded collars were everywhere, confirming the software worked. A group of prisoners to my right had cornered a guard and were engaged in hand-to-hand combat wielding whatever they could find as a weapon. The grunt succumbed to the superior numbers and the violent rage of the humans. He didn't stand a chance.

The whole fight was over within minutes. No invaders were spared, there was just too much anger. Mine wasn't sated; I hadn't been able to actually fight anyone. It was a disappointment, though I reminded myself this was about freeing the prisoners, not fulfilling my dark desires. It didn't help. I was still riled up.

The buildings were targeted after all the invaders had all

died. It was necessary, the prisoners had all that pent up rage and energy that needed an outlet.

Our team stood in a row, shoulder to shoulder until their anger dissipated. Slowly, they calmed down and their attention turned to us. There was an uncomfortable moment when I almost expected them to attack our group, but it passed when they realised we were the reason they were now free.

There was an impasse. No one moved.

Finaly, Jonah stepped forward, the rocket launcher still resting nonchalantly on his left shoulder and his trusty axe in his right hand. He made an imposing figure with his height and wild looks, and the former prisoners were suitably impressed.

'You're free to go,' Jonah shouted so all of them could hear. His booming voice carried, and all eyes were turned his way. 'Use the compound's vehicles or go on foot. Avoid towns and cities until you reach somewhere where you can hide. There are phones with GPS in the bag you will be issued, that you can use but do so sparingly. You don't want to be re-captured.'

The prisoners looked at each other is disbelief.

'Where are we supposed to go?' one of them asked. 'Can't we come with you?'

'No,' Jonah was firm. 'We don't have the capacity to house and feed everyone.'

'But they'll be back for us,' another stated nervously. 'They'll swamp this area before we can get anywhere.'

'Don't be too sure about that,' Nathan answered. 'There have been simultaneous attacks on many facilities that will have disrupted the enemy's logistical abilities. They can't be everywhere at the same time.'

'More near here?'

'More everywhere. In and outside of the US.'

There were nods of appreciation all around and even a few careful smiles.

'What if we want to help?'

'We can't take in new people,' Nathan was adamant. Something we'd agreed on earlier.

'See what you can do to help people where you end up,' he suggested. 'You can help in many different ways but keep your eyes open. Make sure you stay safe.'

'What about weapons?' Another asked.

'You can take whatever you find in the compound and from the guards. Distribute it amongst yourselves.'

'When are you leaving?'

'Now.'

With that last comment, we turned, split up and made our way out of the buildings back to where we'd hidden our vehicles. I glanced back, some of the prisoners were still milling around flustered by their suddenly changed circumstances. The man who'd spoken up had taken control of the others and was clearly giving order to the chaos. They would make it, most of them. It was inevitable that some would be re-captured, but we couldn't guarantee safety for everyone. At least they could give it a hell of a try.

Our team reached our vehicle, and we piled into the pickup, throwing our weapons in the back and hiding them from view. We didn't expect to encounter anyone, but a car full of heavily armed people would be very conspicuous. With the current bounties on our heads, it would be too much of an incentive for most people to ignore.

We made it back to the mountain two days later. The attacks had heightened the invaders lock down and we had to be extra careful. We drove by night and hid in the daytime. No warmth from a fire made it uncomfortable but we hardly noticed, still full of euphoria with the success of our mission. A coded sequence of beeps had informed us that the other attacks had gone well, and we basked in our success.

Back at the mountain Ebony brought us up to speed on the results worldwide.

The coordinated attacks had put a big dent in the invader's plans. Worldwide more than three-hundred-thousand prisoners had been freed. Yes, they would kidnap others, but it would take them valuable time and manpower. And they would have to find a solution to the now useless collars.

As expected, Man-Kayl reacted angrily, his face on every stream announcing that the bounty on rebels had been doubled and anyone found hiding the insurgents would be executed on sight, without a trial.

We'd expected the invaders to retaliate, it was inevitable. It had been the subject of heated discussions within the council before they gave us the all clear to organise the missions. It hurt, but other than just sitting on our hands, there was no avoiding it.

There was a general feeling of elation, not just in the mountain, but world-wide. It was possible to hurt the enemy.

Chapter Fifty-Two

After the last successful mission, the invaders clamped down heavily on the resistance. They launched worldwide attacks on suspected locations and picked up the families of identified resistance fighters to hold them hostage. In addition, they rounded up new prisoners to transport to wherever they were sending them.

We figured they would expect further attacks on more holding facilities, so we decided to steer clear of those. The most logical next target was the transport facilities themselves, actually a suggestion from Ebony's counterpart in China. It was decided, Ebony set up the next coordinated attack and we were once again underway to our new objective.

The main transport centre in the western part of the US was located just west of Las Vegas near Blue Diamond on the edge of the Red Rock National Park. We were north of Vegas and even though the distance was less than two hundred miles, we decided to take our time for security reasons and left two days in advance of the agreed attacks.

The area we traversed was mainly desert which made any kind of vehicle extremely conspicuous. Travelling by night was a must and so was keeping to the back roads.

The four vehicles in our team all left the mountain at intervals of three hours and would individually make their way to the arranged coordinates. Ours was the third one, and it took all my non-existent patience to wait until our waiting time was up. We, Jonah, Aaliyah, Sly and I, left in an extended pickup. We needed the extra space to haul the massive rocket launchers Ebony had uncovered in one of the underground arms depots in the mountain. As she'd indicated, the place was a treasure trove of weapons.

Nathan was familiar with the launchers and became the designated shooter, much to Jonah's dismay.

'How difficult can it be?' The big man lamented. 'I can shoot it.'

'No.' Nathan answered categorically. 'You can't, not without endangering everyone within a ten-metre radius.

Sly urged the big man to let it go and issued him with a GAU heavy machine gun, which mollified him to the point that he decided to join us.

The rocket launcher would blast a hole in the transporter itself, rendering it useless. We hoped the parts would need to be brought in from Taxore and the simultaneous destruction of transporter hubs worldwide would hinder the repairs.

A smile came to my lips just thinking about how my father would react. He would be livid. Then I remembered he always made someone pay for it and that took all the elation away. There would be collateral damage, it could not be avoided in this kind of war.

The trip was uneventful, and we joined the others at the predetermined coordinates. Three of the teams had arrived without any issues, only the fourth had to hide for a few hours when they almost encountered a patrol.

The team counted eleven; our core group, Nathan and five Marines, most of which had been on the other missions with us, including Callum. We knew we could rely on each other and even the Marines had to agree we held up our end of the fight. There was a grudging respect growing on all sides.

We spread out and made our way stealthily from the fringe of the trees where we'd hidden the vehicles, through the waist high brush of the desert, towards the complex. The rocket launcher was carried by alternating pairs of Marines. It was too heavy to lug for one man and Jonah had his hands full with the heavy-duty machine gun. I offered to help, but they put me on the outside of our line and the launcher was to stay in the centre.

The slowly rising sun expelled the cold of the desert night. A light haze helped shield us as we crawled the last hundred metres until most of us were only a short distance from the compound.

Nathan would set off rapid fire targeting the transporter, the main gate and the building we'd identified as the invader's barracks. We hoped most of the troops would still be sleeping and that we could surprise them. Aaliyah, two Marines and I would attack from the left, Jonah and another Marine from the right. The rest would help Nathan devastate the transporter with the rocket launcher. We wanted maximum damage.

We waited for the signal. Again, all the attacks were coordinated. Maximum impact.

It finally came when the first rocket hissed past us and impacted the building twenty metres from the gate. It was a direct hit, sending debris metres high into the air. The second and third rockets were underway before the dust settled and devastated the gate and the barracks. More rockets hit the hub in rapid succession and blew out almost every window in the entire complex. Machine gun fire announced Jonah's arrival and we stormed into the complex from the left side.

We sustained return fire from the guards, lots of which was aimed at Nathan who continued to fire rockets with devastating precision. One of the Marines next to me was hit by the laser beam of an invader who materialised out of the dust cloud thrown up by the impacts. The grunt raced at us with no regard for his own life, shooting around him with a wide arc. I ducked under the laser and fired my own automatic weapon into his advancing form. He shuddered at the impact but renewed his advance, impervious to pain. I continued to shoot him, aiming at both hearts and his head.

Aaliyah pounced on him from the back and drove both of her knives deep into his chest. He finally fell to the ground and died. More grunts appeared and we had our hands full. Rapid machine gun fire came closer, and Jonah's big form made short work of them. Even they were helpless against the heavy-duty gun.

The fight continued for a few minutes more. Flames lit up the early morning where the rockets had set fire to the buildings. We pushed further into the complex, finishing off grunts where we could find them.

I heard screams originating from a building to the left of the demolished hub and signalled to Aaliyah and the Marines. The horrific sight we encountered brought us to a standstill. A Hashta was slaughtering prisoners, hacking into them with his long, curved sword. For a moment I thought it might be Ibrahim, but this man was shorter and stockier.

We rushed in and attacked him, Aaliyah and I working in tandem to land blows and cuts with our own weapons. She was too close for me to use my machine gun, so I pulled the two swords from their sheaths on my back. Jonah joined us and discarded his gun in favour of the axe. The three of us mounted a constant barrage and finally managed to gain the upper hand. The Hashta was a formidable fighter, but he didn't stand a chance against the three of us. Jonah dispatched him with a two-handed swipe of the axe, decapitating him.

Aaliyah and I turned our attention to the prisoners, while Jonah retrieved his machine gun.

There were cells all along the walls of the building. In each one I estimated there to be at least fifteen people, mainly young men. The last cell held five young women. In total, I counted more than fifty humans destined for the transporter. One of the cells was open and bodies littered the floor. This was where the Hashta had started his bloody undertaking to dispatch as many humans as possible.

Soft whimpering pulled my gaze from the bodies to three humans huddled at the back of the cell. I called out to them to leave the cell. They refused. I could understand the hesitation. First the Hashta had attacked them, and then two sword wielding fighters and a giant with a double headed axe appeared out of nowhere. They were terrified.

Aaliyah joined me and softly tried to coax the humans from the cells. I re-sheathed my swords and attempted to help.

A woman's voice rang out shouting names as she pushed past me into the death cell. She rushed to one of the men cowering behind the bunks, enveloping him in her arms.

Another man ran to the entrance of the cell and called out. These three were clearly related.

We urged them to leave the cell. We all had to get out of the complex as soon as possible. The attack had no doubt been registered and troops would be underway. Thankfully, the transporter itself had been completely demolished, and my father's people couldn't transport into the melee.

Outside, we joined the rest of our team. Nathan and his band of Marines had entered the complex and made their way towards us.

Steve, the medic, was slowly making his way past the human casualties outside. He'd already determined there were no wounded still alive within the cells. He reached the three siblings who we'd seen in the cell. He hesitated for a second, glanced back at us them moved quickly towards them. The young man was still catatonic as far as I could see, he stared into infinity, not registering anything. The second male stood behind him, his hands on his sibling's shoulders in support and the woman was on her knees in front of them holding his hands.

Steve examined the young man carefully and talked to the family. I couldn't hear what they said but the interaction and the way he pointed back at us made me curious. The young woman stood up and turned, she held her hand over her mouth, her eyes open in surprise. Steve took her arm and led her back. I thought to us, but they continued towards where Nathan was issuing orders to gather everyone together.

'Sir,' the medic called out when they were close.

Nathan turned, irritated that he'd been interrupted. His words stuck in his throat as he recognised the young women. She hesitated for a second then rushed forward and ran into his arms. He held her tightly and stroked her hair, showing an empathy I'd never seen in the man.

Steve joined them and spoke softly to Nathan, causing

him to turn his head towards the girl's siblings. He took her hand and walked over quickly, embracing them in turn.

The medic slowly left them and went to assist another prisoner who'd been wounded.

They were Nathan's nephews and niece. His sister's children. It was a tearful reunion, especially when Nathan was informed of their parent's demise. It's cold, but my father has no use for middle-aged humans, so they had been killed. I felt the pain even from this distance. The otherwise so strict and military Nathan was clearly affected by the news and he and the siblings hugged each other in support while tears flowed on all their faces. All except the catatonic young man. He'd closed himself off from the world and stared into the void he'd made for himself. The presence of the Hashta and the scene in the cells gave me an indication of what would have caused him to retreat from consciousness.

I turned away from the family scene to give them some privacy.

We had to get these people out of the complex. Our intelligence had suggested there wouldn't be prisoners in the compound. We hadn't counted on civilians. But now we were here, we had to at least help them to escape.

Four of the Marines had retrieved the vehicles, and we proceeded to load as many people as we could in the truck beds. We would take them to the reservation close by, that would give them at least a small chance of escape.

Nathan helped his family into the pickup he came in on. Steve had sedated the young man, and he was lifted into the back seat where he lay with his head on his sister's lap.

Fifteen minutes later, the overfull pick-ups were driving in different directions away from the totally demolished transport hub.

We sped across the desert, hoping to convene again at the reservation.

An hour later Jonah's long range Walkie Talkie signalled that one of the pickups had left their passengers in an abandoned motel just outside the reservation lands. Ten minutes later, the second message announced a similar wording. We stopped at an empty cabin in the forest where we gave our passengers whatever we had in rations, some weapons and blankets. With the emotional goodbyes and "thank you's" I felt cold and angry. Jonah and I had travelled with the prisoners in the truck bed, and they'd told us their stories. Most of them were in some way related to people suspected of being in the resistance. They'd been pulled from their beds in the middle of the night and herded out of their homes. Any family members the invaders couldn't use were executed in front of their kin. Mothers, fathers, even children. They made no exceptions. I shivered at the callousness, the total lack of empathy. This had my father's name written all over it and I was equal measures ashamed and angry.

We left the cabin in silence. What could we say. All of us experienced the same resentment and rage. Every time we encountered the impact of Cal-Tan's actions it enhanced our commitment to bring him down. To end the reign of terror he perpetuated.

Late in the evening we arrived back at the mountain. Nathan's vehicle was the only one still to come in, and we all waited with bated breath, there hadn't been any contact since we'd seen them at the hub. Their pickup came down the ramp ninety minutes later. Nathan jumped out of the passenger seat and immediately opened the back doors. He'd brought his family with him, I guess I'd expected that, and the woman stepped out, still holding the hood she'd worn for the last hours. Her brother was still seated, and he removed his, blinking in the sudden light. The medic had accompanied them and the youngest was still sedated.

We'd arranged a stretcher and the doctor as soon as we were back anticipating their arrival, and she immediately went to help. She examined the young man while he was still in the vehicle, then signalled he could be moved to the stretcher, after which the small procession left in the general direction of the infirmary, closely followed by other two siblings. Nathan stayed behind, we had to debrief, and he was a major part of that.

'You ok?' I asked.

He looked at me, trying to gauge whether I was sincere or not, decided I was, and nodded.

We all moved to the large office where coffee and sandwiches waited.

Chapter Fifty-Three

Ibrahim again.

He'd been at the transportation hub where he and the other Hashta had interrogated the family's older brother in front of his male siblings. The torture had been extreme, even for the Butcher and left Manny, completely cut off from the world. He would need extensive psychological help for a very long time to snap out of the fortress he'd encased himself in. The elder brother—David—though clearly impacted by the experience, was stronger both physically and mentally. Their sister, Elaine, had been spared the torture. She told us Manny had always been a very sensitive boy. The death of their parents, the torture and murder of his brother and the bloody scene in the cells had pushed him over the edge.

I cursed the butcher for the thousandth time. Not that it helped anyone now, but I vowed to end his life any way possible. He was responsible for such pain and anguish that he had no place in this dimension or the next. I wasn't the only one with dark thoughts. Jonah and Aaliyah made the same promise. The biggest issue we had was finding him. He appeared out of nowhere and disappeared just as easily, leaving a trail of blood and gore wherever he went.

Nathan's mentality changed entirely. His earlier hesitation to act vanished with the arrival of his kin. The details of the family's experiences hardened his opinion of the invaders. He turned his "safety-first" attitude into a "let's get them" one, actively promoting missions to undermine the Taxorians. After an initial difficult moment when he fixated on Aaliyah, Tajan and me, Sly spoke with him and he had to agree not all aliens were invaders.

I understood his projected hatred. We were close by, within his reach. He'd lost three members of his family, and the others were scarred for life. But we were also on his side. The righteous side.

We welcomed his changed demeanour towards missions, and our compound slowly became the base for the extensive rebellion we'd envisioned. The Marines and soldiers were a fantastic addition to our original team. Couple that with the plethora of weapons in the mountain and Ebony's international contacts and we were really becoming a force to be reckoned with.

We mounted different attacks in the three weeks that followed the transport hub mission. The supply of new parts for the hub was under constant fire and we managed to delay the repairs. We raided Taxorian warehouses of almost anything we could use varying from food to weapons parts, nothing was safe from us. In addition to our forays, we regularly participated in global missions to undermine the invaders.

Success followed us most of the times. Occasionally, the invaders drove us away before we completed the mission, but those were exceptions to the new order. Violence during the attacks increased exponentially on both sides as the odds became even higher than before. As a rule, we killed every invader we found, and they returned the favour; we lost three of our own, with two more wounded in our ranks. The doctor had her hands full.

David wanted to participate in the missions and after yet another argument with his uncle he finally managed to convince Nathan he would be an asset and could take care of himself. True to form, Nathan hooded his nephew when we left the mountain to blow up a long-distance goods train line. He was predictably making a point that I should have been hooded when I came. Internally, I laughed at the sentiment. Externally, I ignored it, like I had the guideline.

I'd passed all the guidelines except for the one about the hood. Nathan's family flew through all of them with flying colours. Well, yippee. Good for them.

David proved to be a good addition to the mission, like the team of Marines we'd brought back earlier. Ebony still didn't trust them all and they too were hooded in transport. Once David managed to overcome his initial nervousness, he attacked the invaders with a zeal I admired.

We celebrated that night with some of the supplies we'd taken from the targeted warehouse. There was a collection of expensive wines and hard liquor that had probably been destined for the governor's palace or maybe even Taxore. David and his sister joined us and quickly became part of the banter that was common with us.

Manny was still in the sick bay, still closed off to everyone and living in his own world. Not even Elaine had been able to break through the walls he'd erected. The doctor informed Nathan there was very little anyone could do other than wait, and even then, the predictions were guarded.

Chapter Fifty-Four

'Is everything in place?' Ibrahim's mood was at an all-time low.

Cal-Tan had chewed into him with a vengeance, attributing some of the current failures to him and seriously pissing him off, so someone had to pay.

The obvious target was Michael. He was near and the snivelling bastard had gloated at the last meeting when his father demanded results from the butcher as well as from the governor.

Man-Kayl was a lost cause, so there was no fun in pushing him any further into the massive hole he'd dug for himself. The fool had made promises to the tyrant. Ones he could never deliver. Stupid. Arrogant. And now it was only a question of time before it cost him his life. Cal-Tan did not accept failure. Ibrahim would make sure he was Cal-Tan's first choice to dispatch the obnoxious governor. He would enjoy that and make it last.

Michael raised an eyebrow, an amused tilt to his lips while he observed the tall Hashta. He had thoroughly

329

enjoyed Cal-Tan's derogatory comments aimed at the elevated grunt. Oh sure, he was aware of the danger the man posed, and that it grew exponentially when he was pissed off, but it was soooo much fun to rile him.

What could the butcher do? Kill him? Cal-Tan needed him, he was an integral element in the old man's plan. Even Ibrahim couldn't touch him now. Michael revelled in the new value he had to his father.

No matter what had happened, or what he had done, he still wanted his father's approval. Still yearned for his acceptance. Maybe not as much as earlier, or so he wanted to believe. There were doubts. Niggling questions at the back of his mind. But he pushed those back, unwilling to let them taint the feelings of self-respect that grew with his father's attention. It was built into his very DNA.

He had a way to redeem himself for previous fiascos.

He would not fail. Not this time.

He would finally deliver his rebellious brother to face his fate. This time he wouldn't let his emotions get in the way. He would kill Gabriel, drive his swords deep into his hearts. It was imperative that he finish the job before the butcher got to Gabriel, before he found out who had helped him escape from the cell on Taxore. Michael's continued existence relied on it.

And now he had a plan.

A master plan. All the pawns were in place. The information was impeccable, and he'd gone over the details so often he could see them in his sleep. The waiting was over. It would finally happen.

The plan had been a while in the making, it was complex and necessitated a lot of preparation. Part of which he'd regrettably had to rely on Ibrahim for. That was the one aspect he was nervous about; it was out of his control. It was also crucial to the success.

'If you did your job,' he retorted. 'Then there is nothing to worry about.' The intended stab landed, and Ibrahim's eyes flashed with anger.

The Hashta refrained from answering. He would not give Michael that pleasure.

He had prepared the pawn in the plan. Tortured him to complete subjugation. The pawn would not disappoint. He was mentally unable to do anything other than what he'd been charged to do. The absolute terror Ibrahim had installed in the man would guide his actions that, in turn, would finally mean the downfall of the resistance, the re-capture of Ebony and the death of multiple humans and Taxorians that stood in Ibrahim's way.

He too had a clearly defined purpose. A far-reaching plan that would ultimately put him in the palace, on the throne, where he would reign supreme. Cal-Tan and his brood's control over Taxore and Earth by proxy had run its course, it was time for a new leader. Time to let the blood flow.

A stab of exquisite pain shot through his chest. He welcomed it, a reminder of the deadline he lived with. The body was deteriorating fast on Earth. He managed to hide it well, with the exception of transports, but he felt it inti-mately, his hearts beating louder in his ears and no longer in sync. On Taxore he would have more time, the body was designed for that atmosphere. Poisonous fumes that charac-terised the dimension actually aided the longevity of the pre-growth. He had to go back, but first, there was business to take care of on Earth.

Chapter Fifty-Five

We'd become smug in our success and our complacency cost us dearly.

It had been a difficult mission, with devastating results.

We'd lost two Marines at the scene. One from the group Jonah, Aaliyah and I were in, and another from one of the other teams. There were more wounded. Some of them critically. Steve had administered to them as well as he could, but he was restricted in what medical supplies he'd brought with him. Those were quickly depleted.

One of the wounded lay on the back seat of our pickup, Aaliyah tried to keep him as comfortable as possible on the bumpy trip back to the mountain. His pale features winced with every jolt the car made, until even that stopped. Aaliyah placed her fingers on the jugular coating them with the soldier's blood that ran freely from the wound on his head and saturated the makeshift bandage Steve had applied. She waited for a few moments, then shook her head. Another fatality. Shit.

Aaliyah stretched her arm, the one that had been hit

during the mission. The intention had been to free a group of humans Man-Kayl had branded as traitors. We were too late. Their mangled bodies were strewn all over the town square. Most sported sword wounds, some burns, one or two were even missing a large part of their skin. All signs the Hashta had been involved.

They had been brutally slaughtered to make a point. There was nothing left of the "reasonable" facade the invaders had originally portrayed. Their true nature had come out as the result of the world-wide insurgence. The successes of the past months had enraged my father beyond reason. Man-Kayl's new orders were to quell the revolution or die trying. Ibrahim and his Hashta had been elevated to a higher status and basically ruled Earth, leaving the governor scrambling to literally save his own skin. More troops were brought in on the remaining trans-porters, their one and only goal to find and kill as many revolutionaries as possible. They made an example of everyone they caught, and other humans who were simply in the wrong place at the wrong time. The bloodbaths were streamed live over every medium available to them and had the intended result; humans cowered, and the revolution stalled.

As we'd walked through the slaughter I felt my blood boil.

'Don't blame yourself, Gabe.' The big man read my features like an open book. 'It's not your fault. Or mine.'

I nodded absentmindedly. Yeah, sure. Then why did it feel like it was?

We walked in silence, taking in the grisly scene.

A movement to our left brought us all back into fight mode, our guns levelled at what could be the enemy. Instead, an old woman stumbled into the square.

I glanced at Aaliyah, like me she was uncertain what to do.

The mumbling figure cut a crazy path through the dead bodies; her own legs barely able to function. Wayne, one of the Marines, slung his gun over his shoulder and went to help her.

A heavy block of stone landed in my gut. there was something wrong here, even more than the atrocities that had taken place. I swivelled my head around, scrutinising the area beyond the seventy-by-seventy metre square. It was bordered by two- or three-story buildings on three sides, with the widest road leading in on the fourth. Little or no room between the houses made the whole place claustro-phobic. I couldn't see movement behind any of the windows. Open doors on more than one shop or home made me very uneasy. The place looked deserted, not strange under the circumstances, but still eerie and sinister.

The other side of the square was a mirror image. No people. No movements.

Wayne approached the woman, his hands held out to catch her. She raised her head and looked directly at him. Her eyes opened in shock, and she raised her hands up as she took a hesitant step backwards. Her scream broke the silence and resonated in my ears.

'Get away from me.' She stumbled back. Wayne tried to comfort her, but she only screamed louder.

'This is because of you!' She shouted. 'You did this!'

'No, no,' Wayne tried. 'We're here to help you.'

'You killed them all!' she continued.

Under the blood and grime, I saw she wasn't as old as I'd initially thought. Maybe mid-forties, but wounded and broken, like the bodies beneath our feet, only still breathing, barely.'

Our attention was so focussed on the woman that we'd ignored the buildings.

A blue laser beam hit Wayne squarely in the chest throwing him backwards. He was dead before he hit the ground. More beams announced that the shooter wasn't alone. The woman's screams were silenced when the next one hit her, exploding the side of her head.

We ducked and raced for the closest cover we could find; a space under the wooden podium the torturers had used for their bloody lesson. From the relative safety of the structure, I counted three beams in the buildings on the left. Three invaders. The Marines gestured they would take the other ones on the right.

I signalled to Jonah and, under the protective fire of the rest of our team, we moved quickly behind the structure and through the covered arches of the shops at the back of the square. The Marines did the same on the other side. We approached the left side of the area and rushed up to the relative safety of the buildings where we flattened our bodies against the structures.

Jonah took the first building we'd identified and within seconds a scream accompanied by a loud thud announced that one of the grunts was down. I jumped through the big shop window of the second building, shattering it into a million small pieces, and mowed the area with my machine gun. A blue beam narrowly missed me as it moved haphazardly in the dying grunt's hands. I'd landed badly on a hard surface, probably the solid marble counter, and felt a searing pain in my hip. I pushed the agony to the back of my consciousness and struggled to get back on my feet. I had a job to do. Healing would come later.

I advanced slowly on the last building, and hopefully the last grunt. Aaliyah beat me to it and jumped through the door into the front room of the house. She easily dispatched the grunt and turned to me when another door opened, and a second grunt shot her. The laser hit her upper arm and threw her backwards. Jonah stormed in from the back of the building and drove his axe deep into the figure's neck, almost severing the head.

The silence was complete, the only noise my hearts beating loudly in my ears. I scanned the room, nothing. No more grunts. They'd probably left them here to dissuade the locals from burying their dead. The lesson Ibrahim wanted to portray wasn't over yet. The bodies would have been left to rot, the ultimate insult.

Aaliyah stood up, her arm dangling at her side. Jonah raised an eyebrow and nodded at the purple blood that soaked the still smouldering sleeve.

'It looks worse than it is,' she remarked, dismissing his concern.

Outside the gun fire had stilled. We hoped because our teams had prevailed.

'We'd better get out of here,' I suggested. The sound of the battle could have alerted other grunts if they were near.

We gathered our wounded and dead, and left the square, There was nothing we could do there.

Failure hung heavily on our shoulders as we split up and left the grizzly scene. No one spoke. What was there to say? We'd been too late.

The woman's words cut deep. She was right. No, we hadn't been the ones with the swords or the firepower, but they'd been slaughtered as a retribution for our attacks. Indirectly, we were responsible, and it split my hearts to know that—other than stopping our endeavours—there was nothing we could do. Collateral damage. The words were so easy to say, but so difficult to live with.

It took us longer than we wanted, but with the wounded Marine now dead we had no rush to get back. Safety was once again paramount, and we hid during the day in a deep forest until the sun went down. Driving along the dirt roads without our lights was dangerous, but the alternative was even more perilous.

An hour after midnight we navigated the final stretch and drove through the hidden tunnel down into the bowels of the mountain we called home.

I opened the passenger door and stepped out into the relative calm of the parking area. My demeanour was at an all-time low. The dulled pain in my hip flared up again with the movement after the long and cramped drive. I gasped as a red-hot poker shot from the top of my hip down into my right leg causing me to almost crumble.

'You okay?' The big man had noticed. Of course he had.

'Yeah,' I lied. 'Cramps.'

His raised eyebrow showed he didn't believe me, but he left it at that. I'd heal, he knew that. It was just a question of time.

I pulled myself together and stood up straight, banishing the pain back to the box in my mind that had helped me through my bullied childhood on Taxore.

I walked around the car and joined the big man and Aaliyah where they were in a heated conversation with Nathan. He glanced my way and immediately stopped talking. I saw confusion in his features, in the creased brow and the slanted head.

'Where did you come from?' he asked.

The surprise was now with me. What kind of question was that? He knew I'd accompanied the team on this mission.

'The pickup,' I answered.

'You went back up to the surface?'

'What?'

'And you two.' He gestured at Jonah and me. 'I thought you'd had a fight.'

I looked at the big man. He was as confused as I was, his brow creased.

'What the hell are you talking about?' he demanded roughly.

'He said you'd had a fight,' Nathan continued, pointing at me. 'That was why he'd left your team.'

'Gabe has been with me all the time,' Jonah answered angrily. 'There was no fight.'

The Marine turned back to me. 'You came back two hours ago.' He could barely contain his anger. 'With team Delta. You said you'd changed teams because Jonah pissed you off and you wanted nothing more to do with him.'

'That's bullshit.'

His shoulders tensed and he automatically balled his fists. 'Are you calling me a liar?'

'Guys. Guys!' Aaliyah's voice halted the growing tension. 'Stop!'

My bad mood was in great danger of overflowing. I didn't need this bullshit. But the concern in her face stopped me from stomping off.

'What?' The big man was just as angry as I was.

'He's here,' she answered, her face pale.

'Who's here?' Nathan asked.

I stared at her. She nodded her head.

The penny dropped.

'The pre-growth,' I almost whispered.

'The what?'

'The double.' Jonah had connected the dots as well.

My blood ran cold, I could feel it in every fibre of my body. Aaliyah was right. The pre-growth was here. He'd infiltrated the mountain posing as me in one of the other teams.

A tingle started at the base of my spine that quickly enveloped my whole body. Heat radiated from the rage that boiled up from my gut.

He was here.

My copy was here, in the mountain.

'Shit.' Nathan finally understood.

We grabbed our weapons from the pickup.

'Where did you see him last?' Jonah shouted at Nathan.

'He came in with the Delta team. Joined in the debrief and then left for his—your—quarters.'

'What was he wearing?' Aaliyah asked, ever the practical one.

Nathan looked me over. 'The same as him,' he answered. 'Black jeans, black sweater.'

I cursed my generic taste in clothes. There was nothing distinctive about what I wore.

I turned towards the corridors but Jonah's hand on my chest stopped me. 'Stay here, Gabe. We need to know which one is the real one.'

I wanted to protest, but deep down I knew he was right. The imposter had fooled even Nathan. He was my copy, down to the finest detail. And with the same clothes, there would be no way to know which one was which.

'Stay with Gabriel,' Nathan ordered one of his men and rushed off to our quarters with Aaliyah, Sly and Jonah hot on his heels.

Momentarily defeated by common sense, I stayed behind.

A soft bark alerted me to the dogs in the kennels at the

back off the vast area. I stepped forward, ready to free Mutt
when a scream behind me caused me to turn on my heels.

Chapter Fifty-Six

The soldier stood five metres from me, two swords pierced his chest and blood streamed from his body to pool on the hard concrete floor. Behind the dying man, I saw a vicious grimace on my own face.

He'd been here all the time.

Hidden somewhere between all the vehicles, waiting for a chance to attack.

Instantly, I knew I was his intended target.

He'd done all this to kill me.

He pulled the swords out of the body in one quick action. The soldier fell to the ground in a bloody pile. My double stepped over the corpse and advanced on me.

My gun was still in the car, along with my swords. I felt naked. Glancing around, I slowly stepped backwards as I frantically searched for something I could use to defend myself. I feigned to the left and rushed the other way back to the passenger side of the pickup I'd just left. The double rushed me, swinging the swords in lethal arcs. It took all my fighting experience to avoid them, the sound of the swishing metal sinister as it passed millimetres from my head.

I reached the open car door and held it between us while I frantically reached in with my left-hand groping for my weapons. My adversary knew I was unarmed and obviously wanted to keep it that way. He kicked the door viciously and it slammed into my already painful hip. With only one hand I couldn't protect my body from the onslaught and the air was forced out of my lungs with the onset of pure agony in my hip. But I had no time to worry about that. I pushed the door out with both hands and it connected briefly with the copy's chin, pushing him back for a second. It was enough for me to roll over backwards on the back seat, grab my swords and kick open the opposite door with my good leg. I half fell out of the pickup and only just managed to stay upright as new stabs of pain racked my lower body. Stumbling back, I put some distance between myself and the car creating enough room to swing my own swords. The double rushed around the pickup and attacked me ferociously again.

The incessant barking of the dogs had alerted the others, and they came rushing back to the parking area. They stopped as soon as they saw the scene unfold. I wanted to scream at them to come and help but they were still far away, and I could see the confusion on their features.

The fight intensified when he attacked again, swinging the swords like a master. I countered. The clash of the metal resounded loudly in the hollow cave, even over stemming the constant barking of the caged dogs.

They were all confused. Dogs and humans alike.

I couldn't blame them. Both of us were me. On the outside. In essence, there was just one. But how the hell were they supposed to know which one it was?

The double made use of the confusion and kicked me again, this time in the upper thigh on the side where my hip was damaged. I stumbled backward, barely staying on my feet. With a vicious scream he intensified his attack, swinging the swords first to my lower body, then up to my head, forcing me to a full defence. I couldn't attack myself, too embroiled in staying alive. I stepped backwards; my leg almost crumbling.

Our swords clashed again, this time to my advantage, and I was able to shatter one of his. However, the force of the contact almost threw my own weapon out of my own hand. My hip was killing me, the pain almost too much to bear. He noticed and high kicked my upper arm and the sword flew out of my temporarily paralysed hand. That evened the odds and the weapons, each of us had one left.

He raised his sword again, I blocked him, our weapons clashing over my head. That opened up my lower body to a renewed onslaught. He kicked me hard in the wounded hip and I fell over backwards. My lame arm bucked under me, and I fell down, completely open to his attack. I'd dropped my last weapon trying to break my fall and now I was unarmed.

I lay on the ground, my leg totally debilitated by the blows to my hip and my arm not much better. I couldn't even scramble backwards. He stood over me, his hands holding his remaining sword up over his head when a shot knocked it out of his hands.

Jonah lowered his gun, unsure which of us he should target. Instead, he'd shot the blade out of my nemesis's hands. He advanced on us quickly, followed by the others. They stopped a few metres from the two of us.

No one moved.

Then my copy dove to the side in an attempt to regain

his sword. He never made it; Jonah's kick sent him back three metres. Caleb and the big man grabbed him.

'Let me go, Jonah,' the double shouted. 'It's me. He's the imposter.'

I couldn't believe the man. He was still perpetuating his deceit.

Jonah looked to me, then to Caleb and back at the man he held. The rest joined them, all equally bewildered. I couldn't blame them. We were exact copies. And he kept shouting he was the real one.

Their faces were characterised by utter confusion.

'He's lying,' I shouted over the double's incessant ranting. 'Don't believe him. He's the pre-growth, big man.'

My friends were at a loss, they argued amongst themselves and failed to see the smirk on my double's features.

We had a stalemate. There was no way I could prove I was the real one.

Or was there?

I had an idea, or at least the beginnings of one. I honestly couldn't predict how it would turn out. I only had what I hoped would happen and held on to that.

I caught Aaliyah's eye. She stood to the back of the group, more in the centre of the vast area.

I mouthed a word silently to her, a name. Then again, the same one, and cocked my head to the back of the hall where the dog kennels were. I kept repeating it, my voice wouldn't carry in the turmoil, so I hoped against hope that she would follow my reasoning.

Her features were confused at first, then her eyes opened wide at what I prayed was understanding and she rushed to where the dogs were barking frantically.

One was silent. The one I wanted her to free.

Mutt.

'Stop!' She shouted loud enough to stay everyone in their tracks.

She pressed the clasp on the door down and pushed it open.

Nothing happened.

Mutt stayed where he was, observing first me, then the other one, and back again.

Time stood still. I couldn't breathe. Surely, he would know. He wouldn't be restricted by appearance and expectations or deceit.

Mutt stood up and stepped forward agonisingly slowly and made his way to the now open doorway. One of the other dogs barked but was instantly silenced with a short growl from his alpha. He advanced out into the area in front of the pens. I saw everyone, human and alien alike, step backwards to let him pass.

Finally, I understood the pure power that radiated from this dog. Weapons were lowered after his glare, people rightfully gauging their odds. He would get to them before they even fired a shot and even if they did, there was no guarantee it would stop him. Mutt was imposing and frightening to everyone. Except me. He was my dog, my friend. I was completely positive he would know who his buddy was, and whom the foe.

Jonah and Caleb let go of the double's arms, both waiting for the outcome of the test that would give them all clarity.

I glanced at my mirror image. His gaze alternated between me and the approaching canine. I saw beads of sweat on his forehead, and an almost imperceptible shake in his frame. He recovered, stood up straight and stared at what I was sure was his impending doom.

Mutt lowered his head and observed us intently with his

black eyes, his lips flaring to catch a scent, a deep growl escaped from his lips as he stepped towards my double. The sound reverberated in the silence, and I felt it in my very bones. For me it was reassuring, for everyone else it gave new meaning to the word menacing.

The double took a deep breath with quivering nostrils and held himself upright in an attempt to make himself taller. The dog still looked from one to the other.

I became acutely aware of my vulnerability lying on the floor, but I trusted Mutt.

He advanced on me.

For a second I thought I'd made a mistake.

Then he rushed forward and took up a position between me and the other, his rear to me and his wide-open maw pointed at the double.

The fake couldn't help himself; he took two steps back. Mutt advanced on stiff legs, the deep growl now constant. No barks, just that terrifying deep, murderous and primal growl.

It was clear. He'd made his choice.

I silently thanked Kate. Her humanity had saved Mutt and now he saved me. Again.

'Down!' he tried. Mutt continued his advance. 'Down, Mutt!'

The imposter stood his ground and tried to stare down the canine. That in itself was enough to show he was the copy, no one in his right mind would attempt anything as stupid as that. Not with my dog.

With a last growl, Mutt launched himself at the man and threw him back onto his butt. He held his arm in his jaws and bit hard. Purple blood stained his teeth as he forced his point.

I had to intervene. Sure, he deserved it, but I needed to know who he was.

'Mutt!' I shouted over the growls. 'Here!'

He reluctantly let go and backed away until he was by my side. I placed my hand on his neck and felt the course hairs that stood on end.

He'd come through for me.

Of course he had.

He had my back.

I felt an enormous rush of emotion that I could call this fantastic animal my friend.

Chapter Fifty-Seven

My arm was still in a sling. The bone had a fracture, but nothing major. The same applied for my hip, though no bones were damaged there. I had to rest it for a while, but with my healing abilities I figured it would be functional by end of day tomorrow. Till then it was a bother. The cuts and other bruises had faded and were no more than a memory.

It was time.

Time to face him again.

My double.

Only now on my terms.

They'd put him in one of the containment cells, but not before they scanned him for any kind of location device. Just as well, because they found one hidden under the skin of his left arm. The doctor removed it and stitched up the mauled arm with a dose of local anaesthetic. If it had been up to me, I wouldn't have given him anything. He didn't flinch, not that he could; shackled and restrained in Jonah's killing bear hug. One of the soldiers had taken the tag and driven away to mask our location. The jamming technology Ebony had reinstated in the mountain rendered it useless twenty miles out, but whoever was on the other end would find the silence even more suspicious. The soldier would drive further up into the mountains, then onwards and finally to Canada, where he would dispose of the tag. During the drive he would put it in a reinforced lead container every now and then for a few hours to copy the silence period when the double had been within our base. We hoped this would disorientate the invaders and they would ultimately put the blackouts down to bad reception and magnetic waves in the mountains. There was some truth to the myths that the area around us interfered with technology. It wasn't alien technology, just Earth's natural magnetic rays that were concentrated around Area 51 and the proximity of the tectonic plates.

Jonah came for Mutt and me, and we walked through the labyrinth of corridors until we came to the lift. A short dip of two underground floors brought us to the cells. It felt cooler there, or was that just my imagination. The air was clear and fresh, the ventilation reached down into even the deepest levels of the old military base.

'How did it feel?' Jonah asked as we turned yet another corner. 'To fight someone like that?'

'It was surreal, weird doesn't cover it. I felt like I was actually fighting myself.'

'You were, for all intents and purposes. He is you.'

'Only on the outside,' I stated with more anger than I wanted. I had to distance myself from whoever was in the cell. What he'd done wasn't on my slate. Sure, mine was covered in blood, both red and purple. But this man, he'd killed so many. Not only the soldier earlier today, he was just as responsible for Nasheed's torture as Ibrahim.

'That's what I meant,' Jonah quickly answered, defusing the situation.

I nodded my apology. My nerves were shot, and I jumped at everything. I knew his comment hadn't been meant as criticism. He was probably just as flustered as I was. It's not often you get to see two identical versions of one of your friends, one of which is your enemy.

A thought crossed my mind. 'It's like the opposite of what happened to you,' I said. 'You were looking at a body in the mirror that wasn't yours. I'm looking at a body that is mine but not me.'

'Seems we've experienced all the options,' he laughed.

We walked on in comfortable silence.

'Do you have any idea who he is?' The big man asked.

I shook my head. The only contact up to now had been during the fight, and that hadn't rung any bells. Something niggled at the back of my mind about that, but it wasn't anything definitive. I was missing a connection. Something I felt I should have known.

'It must be a confident, Cal-Tan's staunch supporter. He wouldn't have risked just any old essence or a human one,' Jonah deduced. 'The guy had to die voluntarily for this.'

I nodded my agreement.

Is there anyone you can think of who's that dedicated?'

'No,' I answered. 'But maybe it's not dedication, more greed. That might persuade some of the people in his inner circle.'

'And then he promises them their own body back after all this?'

'Probably.'

'Reincarnation is no picnic,' the big man mused. 'It would have to be one greedy individual.'

'Well, there's no shortage of those around Cal-Tan.'

The big man's features turned to storm, nothing left of the humour of seconds before.

'There's another thing we have to investigate,' Jonah commented. 'The double knew his way around the mountain, he was familiar with who's who, he knew you were gone and what you were wearing, not to mention he even knew your dog's name.'

He had come to the same conclusion I had.

'He had inside help. There's a mole.'

I nodded. The man knew too much for it to be a coincidence and he'd been able to fool everyone he met, including the ever-paranoid Nathan. No way that could have been a fluke.

We had a traitor in our ranks.

It was sobering.

Minutes later, we reached our destination. Too soon for my liking, but there was no postponing the inevitable anymore.

'You ready?' The big man asked outside a thick metal door.

'Hell, no,' I answered truthfully. 'But let's get it done.'

My legs felt as though they were encased in concrete, heavy and cumbersome, unwilling to move. The muscles locked and my nerves danced a merry jig as I tried to convince myself to take another step. Jonah pulled the door open, and I stood on the threshold for a few seconds, filling my lungs with a deep breath.

The room was relatively big, about seven metres by ten, the rear part of which was taken up by a cell. The bars stretched from one side of the room to the other, effectively halving the space. Grey walls on all sides and a concrete floor were broken by sparse furniture. In the cell that consisted of a bed, a bolted-down desk, a lavatory behind a low half-wall offering very little privacy, and on this side of the bars; a table with three chairs in the middle of the space. There were no windows—we were deep under-ground—but the air-conditioning kept the place well-venti-lated and the air fresh. Led lights lit up the room and the figure sitting on the bed. Two armed guards stood just inside the door on either side of the opening.

In contrast to earlier that day, I had the time to really observe the man in front of me.

It was like looking in a mirror.

We were identical.

Of course we were. This was my pre-growth. It was created for me, made from me. Grown from my own DNA.

We were even dressed in similar clothing. Black jeans and a black sweater, my usual attire. It crossed my mind again that he'd known that. Was acutely aware of my habits.

The experience was so surreal it took my breath away. Here was a mirror image of me, just without a mirror.

I had to stop myself from reaching out and touching the apparition, just to see whether it was real. Whether any of this was.

A deep growl brought me back from my internal musing. Mutt's opinion hadn't changed, he didn't like the imposter. Well, I fully agreed with the sentiment, even without knowing who he was. This man had a lot of my friend's blood on his hands, either directly or indirectly. He would be held accountable; I would make sure of that.

The double sat comfortably on the bed with his back to the wall, observing me just as much as I did him. His nostrils flared in anger when his gaze strayed to Mutt. The dog answered the unspoken threat with another deep growl of his own. The bite marks on the man's arm had already scabbed over and were healing rapidly, the stitches redundant. Mutt announced with a deep rumbling that he was more than willing to create new wounds.

We locked eyes. The prisoner and me.

Deep tingles ran up and down my spine sending goosebumps over my whole body at the absolute malevolence that radiated from him. Whoever it was, he really had it in for me. I guess we'd screwed up his plans. Well, too bad. He'd been quite audacious coming to our headquarters; it made me wonder how he thought he was going to get out anyway? It was a dead end. How desperate was he? Or maybe suicide had been the intention all the time, like we'd reasoned, to reincarnate him in his own body once he'd achieved his mission.

'Has he said anything?' I asked the guard standing next to Jonah.

He shook his head.

I turned back to the man in the cell. He hadn't moved, his piercing eyes—well, mine actually—still shot daggers at me.

An intense feeling of dread filled me, causing my mouth to dry up. I couldn't place it other than a premonition of some kind.

'Who are you?' I voiced the one question we all had foremost in our minds.

He just observed me with a patronising look. Then stood up and advanced to the bars. He stopped a metre from them and stared intently into my eyes.

A wry smile pulled his lips back into a crooked grin that seemed familiar, but I couldn't place. I was racking my brain, but it alluded me.

Until he spoke.

'Hello, brother.'

The familiar derogative voice came from the mirror image. A voice I'd never imagined I would hear again, and definitely not in this situation, not with my face.

I was stunned.

'Michael?' I said incredulously.

More by Monique Singleton

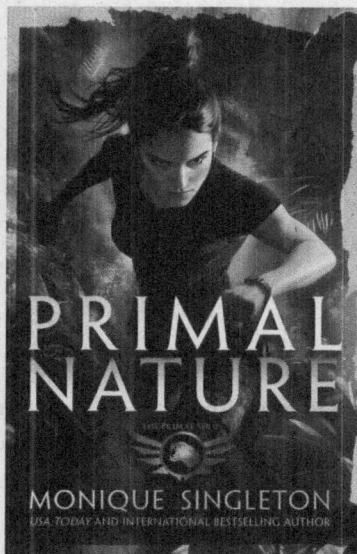

vinci-books.com/primalnature

Immortality comes at a price.

Subject 336, once a victim of sinister experiments designed to
replicate her extraordinary abilities, now grapples with the
consequences of her captors' actions. Unbeknownst to them, they
unleashed a primal force that laid waste to their facility and left her
haunted by the aftermath.

Turn the page for a free preview…

Primal Nature: Chapter One

I've lost count of how many times you've tried to kill me.

Hundreds, maybe even thousands. And not only in the course of the two global wars that so characterise the past two eras.

When will you get it through your thick heads that you cannot succeed? I'm here for as long as I want to be. You do not decide my fate. That prerogative is mine, and mine alone. I'm here to stay, I'm here for eternity.

But still, you try and every time you fail.

You're attempts can't kill me.

But man, it hurts.

Every time you shoot me, cut me, try to blow me up, it hurts, causing the pain and anger within me to build exponentially. It clouds my judgement, clouds my reserves and morals, with the expected result—I turn the tables and kill you.

I'm no stranger to pain. In the two-hundred and fifty-eight years I've lived up till now, pain has been the one constant factor.

That and death—yours, not mine.

I started off human, or at least I had no reason to think otherwise. I was born, grew older, got sick and better again —nothing unusual or even remotely interesting. All the human traits.

Until it stopped.

All of it.

I stopped growing old. I never got sick again. And life definitely got a lot more interesting.

Primal Nature: Chapter Two

I'm cynical.

Eternity does that to you.

I've seen so much evil in humans it eclipses any good that might lie dormant.

As you will have guessed, I'm not a fan. But that's mutual. You don't like me. Not after you really get to know me.

It's not that you think I'm malicious, or inherently evil or anything superficial like that. Just different, and that terrifies you. That—and jealousy—colours any relationship between you and me.

Why? Well, it's too simple to exile all myth and folklore to the realms of fantasy. True, the majority of them are ninety-nine-percent fantasy. But somewhere, deep down, there is the origin. The reason for the myth; a small wafer of truth.

And that's the really scary part.

The enormous technological advancements that characterise the last few hundred years lulled you into a sense of control. You think you can rationalise everything.

Well, you can't. There are still things in this world that defy reason; that your scientists or politicians can't explain. There are still things you can't control.

And that terrifies you.

I'm not human anymore.

That implies I once was. For the first forty years, my life was quite normal by your standards; nothing really strange or out of the ordinary.

I still don't have a definite reason why I am what I am. There was no poisonous spider, mythical animal bite, no radiation from a meteoroid as the catalyst or anything dramatic like that. Nothing that I can label "The Reason."

In my early forties my scars and wrinkles started to fade. I welcomed this and thought I was experiencing some kind of second youth due to better eating habits. Who wouldn't? At that age you begin to understand that nobody—not even you—has eternal youth and that you are starting to look remarkably like your parents did twenty-five years earlier. How's that for a nightmare? Wrinkles? Sagging figure? Cosmetic surgery comes to mind. Well anyway, I didn't need surgery. I became younger, or at the very least— didn't age.

Everyone around me of course did. My husband started off younger than me. I buried him looking like his grand-daughter.

People stalked me for an explanation. How did I do it?

Surprise quickly made way for resentment. I could at least share my secret. Let other people benefit from my "fountain of youth". I wanted to, but how could I, if I didn't know the answer myself?

I tried to find out.

One of the perks of longevity is you have ample time to learn. I studied biology, chemistry, anything that could help me understand what was going on. But the answers eluded me.

It's funny how friends and family turn into enemies when you have something they covet. Especially something as elementary as life. But be careful what you wish for. Immortality is not the eternal dream it's portrayed to be, more an eternal nightmare.

The resentment and jealousy finally drove me away from everything and everyone I knew. And that I was the subject of countless medical experiments and tests. Everyone wanted to know what stopped me from ageing. Everyone wanted a piece of me.

I was sick of it and left. Besides, everyone I really loved —every family member or friend—was already dead, even the ones born long after me. I'd said so many goodbyes, there was nothing left.

They still needed answers, so they brought me back.

There are just so many needles and tests a person can take before they snap. With me there was one too many. But instead of becoming abusive or just plain giving up, I changed. Changed in ways that defied science and belief. That was the real beginning of my exile. That was when they started to hunt me with a vengeance. It heralded my promotion from an anomaly to a major threat. In the end the whole weight of the government and military fuelled the hunt.

But even then, in those dark times, there were ways to disappear if you really wanted to.

I needed to.

Not just to evade them.

More than anything else, I had to find out and come to terms with what I was.

It would be nice to say I went to a sanctuary in Tibet, or somewhere exotic like that, where enlightened masters showed me my new path in life and my place in the universe.

But that's not how it went.

We'll pick up the story about that later. I want to finish what I see as the "management summary" first.

I've experienced things that would make you sick. Killed and healed. Loved and lost, as the clichés so eloquently say.

I've seen governments and nations come and go. Lived through both global wars in the twenty-first and twenty-second century. Come out the other side, sometimes even with a sense of direction and purpose.

In your human years, I would now be two-hundred and fifty-eight. Quite a life span. Me? I'm just beginning.

So, why am I writing this epistle? Why come out of hiding now? Well, by the time this manuscript becomes public in any way—if it ever does—I will be long gone. Back to my old ways of making myself invisible.

There have been many theories about what I am. Some extremely far-fetched, some have merit. None completely fit—save one. One reason. One explanation that sticks in my head. That just might offer the answers that I want, that I need. But I need to be sure. I need to put everything that happened to me in perspective. Review the timeline as it were. That will help me determine whether I really accept the theory as my basis. As my destiny. For that, I need to tell my story. I need to share what happened. I need to explain.

I've given up on acceptance. I have no illusion I will be one of you. Don't even want to be.

So, okay. Let's backtrack, go down memory lane. Go back to where it more or less really started.

Round about my ninety-third birthday, I was in quite a fix.

I had been the focus of medical interest and experiments for more than thirty years. Understandable—I looked the consummate thirty-four-year-old. I was in excellent health with a body to die for. Dr Karpatski, my old MD, was genuinely worried for me, he wanted to make sure I was all right. He could never have imagined the pain and torture his good intentions would cause. He and the initial scientists wanted the best: for me, and for others who could benefit from the "talents" I had.

That was the noble goal.

The other ones we will encounter further on. Be patient.

I was in and out of medical institutions, poked at, scanned, tested, and put through the mangle. I finally managed to disappear for a few years, started a new life and was subsequently kidnapped and transported to a secure facility somewhere in the Americas. There, the tests continued. That I was there against my will didn't seem to bother anyone. It was for the greater good, so I was designated a volunteer.

The first year the circumstances were reasonable. I had a "suite" of rooms and some form of privacy, however controlled. The doctors—and I use that term loosely—still wanted my cooperation.

But as time passed, the results remained slim. Somewhere down the line they decided that was my fault and subsequently tried to force me to cooperate. Problem was, I wasn't sabotaging the tests. I actually hoped they would find what they were looking for so that I could finally leave.

How's that for naivety?

I didn't know. I couldn't answer the questions. No matter how often I tried to make them understand, it didn't sink in. It was unacceptable, because that would mean they'd failed and that was not an option. There was too much at stake.

The initial group that "recruited" me still had illusions of saving mankind. Curing diseases like AIDS, Cancer and LKX-clones—quite enviable goals.

Changes in staff brought changes in incentive. Budgetary issues necessitated new partners; not so noble ones. Partners more interested in the monetary successes that could be achieved. Eternal Youth is of course the ultimate product.

The military came later on. After the cosmetic companies gave up. After the revolution started.

I see it all in my mind, clear as day. I relive what happened over and over again. And now I'll share it with you.

It's not pretty.

...You have been warned.

Primal Nature: Chapter Three

The walls of the cell closed in on her again: sickly grey, damp and covered in mould. The small window at the top right of the far wall was dirty, filled with fly shit and grime so thick it barely let in the light. Not that the speck of clouded sky did much to relieve her dark mood anyway.

The room was spartan, fifteen-by-fifteen feet, grey walls, one solid metal door, a table, and a chair—not for her, naturally.

The ever-present stench of her stale dried blood and sweat hung in the air. In an attempt to get her to cooperate they left her on her tortured feet for more than forty-eight hours. They wanted to force her to answer the questions she had no answers to.

"Big nose," as she called the eldest doctor—the one who had been there from the start more than three or four years ago—was ranting and raving again. Spittle flew from his mouth and his face was bright red. One of these days she fully expected the veins pulsating in his prominent nose to explode. That, or he would have a heart attack. She was laying bets on which would hit him first. His nose was winning, the strained skin looking ready to erupt.

It was business as usual.

The doctor, a small thin man of about fifty-five with a big chip on his shoulder, did not impress her in the least. His demeanour was of someone who desperately needed recognition but wasn't getting any, despite all his intellect and effort.

'It's you; you're doing this,' he spat. 'You refuse to let us do our work. Do you have any idea of the trouble you're getting me and the staff here into?' Pacing the small interrogation room, she felt the agitation he exuded in the air around him. She didn't react. It wouldn't do any good, not that she could be bothered anyway.

The fatigue showed on her face and in the slight tremors in her legs and torso. All she wanted to do was lie down and forget everything for a few hours. Big nose had other ideas. He had a deadline.

'We need results.' His agitation coloured his face an even darker shade of red. 'You have no idea of what will happen to us, or to you for that matter, if we don't come up with something, anything.' His breath came in frantic bursts. Saliva landed on her face again. He stood so close she was forced to inhale his stale smelling breath and body-odour as he tormented her with his relentless questions. Looking up at him, her eyes showed the contempt.

'Whatever,' she replied.

He hit her. Slapped her across the face. She didn't flinch. The increased anger caused him to shake with pure rage and utter helplessness.

'You think we're tough?'

Could his nose get any brighter?

'Well, this is a picnic to what will happen when the military takes over, and they will.'

'They will break you,' he added smugly, contorting his face into what was supposed to be a grin. Moving around the table he lowered himself into the chair and smirked at her.

The past months had been bad. All the tests ended up useless. Time and again blood and tissue was extracted, and once it left her body it died quite spectacularly. The nucleus of the cells imploded, the DNA liquefied into a brown mush and there was nothing they could learn from the samples anymore. It frustrated the hell out of the scientists.

Initially they suspected malfunction of the equipment. Then they suspected each other of sabotage. Security checks were intensified. The scientists were interrogated, which formed a short reprieve for her. Finally, they ruled out sabotage or malfunction. That left her. But how was she doing it? Was it a conscious act? How could she control her body, her cells, like that? Even after they left her body.

She was tortured, physically and mentally.

Nothing seemed too depraved for them. They placed her in a cage not even fit for a small dog. She felt degraded, less than human, less even than a lab rat. They kept her there for five days. Not letting her out, not even for toilet breaks, she lay in her own excrement. Cramped beyond compare, with no way to avoid the stink, the filth and the inevitable bugs attracted to the waste, she felt humiliated... debased. When they finally let her out, all she could do was crawl out of the muck. Her seized-up muscles wouldn't work. She just lay there while they hosed her down, too cramped and depressed to even try to resist.

But still, they didn't get any answers.

Refusing to give up, they took samples again, and again,

and again. Anaesthetic was discarded. she healed anyway, so what did it matter. Any wounds and scars were gone within twelve hours. Biopsies were taken from all major organs, except the brain and heart because they didn't want to inadvertently kill her. If she didn't comply, they strapped her to the table. The only tests that showed results were the ones documenting her increasing strength and healing capabilities. The more they cut, the quicker she healed, and the more frustrated they became, yelling at her and subjecting her to further abuse.

The door opened. The youngest doctor Hardy—the nice one—entered the dim room, unintentionally hurting her eyes with the sharp light that followed him into the dim cubicle. He looked pale. Frightened.

'He's here, Doctor Collins,' he said. 'He's waiting for you in your office.' He fidgeted uncomfortably waiting for Big-Nose to reply. 'Doctor Collins?' Sheepishly.

'Yes, yes, I heard you.' Collins zoned back from wherever he had been. Standing up he looked at her with a mixture of disgust and pity. 'You brought this upon yourself,' he whispered.

She continued to stare at the small window as the two men left the room. She didn't sit. They were watching her. She knew any deviation to the current situation would bring repercussions—painful ones. She didn't need more pain, so she just stayed upright where she was and waited.

Primal Nature: Chapter Four

Collins tried to regulate his breathing. It would not do to let the General know how much he resented losing control over the investigation. He would be the ultimate colleague, helpful to a fault. And when the General failed—which was inevitable—he would take control back. It was all a matter of patience and a straight face. There was no way in hell the military would take the credit for the project, not after all he'd invested in this undertaking.

Rounding the corner to his office, the doctor was instantly taken aback by the presence of the military force. He'd expected a small contingent of maybe two or three scientists and the General with maybe one or two additional soldiers. More than twenty people filled the hallway. The majority of them were soldiers in full battle gear. One even had a vicious looking dog straining at the leash. Heavily armed, they all turned to glare at him as he approached. The canine growled. Hanging on to the barest threads of his composure, Collins opened the door and entered his own outer office.

Sally, his assistant, immediately clamped a hand around his arm to stop him from moving on to the inner office.

'He's on the secure line and can't be disturbed,' she whispered.

Taking one more step towards the door, but reluctantly recognising the urgency in her voice, he stopped and turned. The arrogance of the man—locking him out of his own office.

He looked around the small anteroom and forced himself to calm down. He was in his own territory now.

There were much bigger windows here than in the cells, with a view of the park-like grounds around the institute. The walls were painted in a soft apricot to mimic the adobe style that was so popular in this area. In the cells the impression was of a clinical institution, far away from the inhabited world. Maybe even on an island somewhere. The truth was the institute was hidden in a beauty spa in a residential part of the suburbs; a hide-a-way for the rich. The grounds were reasonably secure. The laboratory was impenetrable, but in a non-imposing way. The paying residents were unaware of the tests performed in this part of the clinic; unbeknownst they were acting as the blissfully innocent front to it all.

That of course would all change now the military had arrived in such ridiculous numbers. What was the use of all this force? They weren't even attempting to disguise their arrival; hadn't they been briefed? There would be hell to pay.

Through the window Collins saw that the military vehicles and even more guards outside had already attracted a small group of nosy residents. The phone rang. Sally ran to her desk and pressed the button on the receiver next to her ear.

'Heaven Valley spa, Sally speaking,' she answered in a clear and composed voice. 'How can I help you?'

Even from where he stood Collins could hear the agitated voice on the other end of the line.

'Please calm down, Mr. Stark.' Susan managed to get a word in. 'The military are only here with regard to an investigation we are helping them with.'

She looked at Collins helplessly—an unspoken plea in her eyes. How could she explain the presence of such an excess of military force? As paying customers, the residents expected to be pampered and kept away from all the disquieting realities of the outside world and not to be confronted with violence or the ugly real world on their doorstep.

Collins shrugged and turned away from his assistant, leaving her to think up an acceptable story. His thoughts once again turned to the specimen; how would he be able to keep the General from finding out all there was to know about the creature? How would he keep on top of it all?

He wandered over to the door of his inner office and tried to hear what was being said on the other side. But the doors and walls were soundproofed. At his request, to offer absolute privacy when he had visitors or was entertaining. He heard nothing. Just as he turned to walk back to the water cooler, the door opened suddenly.

He was startled, and it showed.

The doorway was filled with the presence of the General.

'Ah Collins. Just the man I wanted to see.' His manner was pleasant, almost friendly. But Collins had heard stories about this man and was not about to let his defences down.

Walking past the General, he entered his own office. He hesitated for a moment. Where was he supposed to sit? The General solved the problem for him by closing the door and sitting in the leather seat behind the desk, forcing Collins to sit in the chair in front of his own desk. Both were equally aware that this was the first clash in the power struggle and that the General was now ahead by one point.

'Thank you so much for the use of your office,' he said sweetly. 'As of now these are the headquarters for the military side of the operation.'

An agitated Collins muttered, 'you're welcome.' Neither of them giving any credit to the statement. Collins felt surprised at the distance the desk and the elevated seat created making him actually feel small. Insignificant. The General observed him intently. This unsettled him even more and he felt compelled to speak.

'We weren't expecting you until next week,' he attempted feebly. 'Then we could have readied everything for you and your staff.' He refused to call them soldiers.

'No worries.' The General smiled at his discomfort. 'My men and I will feel at home here before the end of the day.'

His hard stare unnerved Collins. Silence was a mighty weapon when used correctly. Sure enough, the doctor's insecurity increased, and he flustered to take control.

'Why are all these soldiers with you?' he demanded in what he hoped was an authoritative tone. 'Our residents will need an explanation'.

The General dismissed the challenge with a wave of his hand. 'I'm sure that you will think of something, you can always blame the Revolutionaries.'

He shuffled the papers on the desk. Collins saw that many of them were test reports, MRI- and brain scans from the specimen.

'Bring me up to speed,' the General ordered. 'The results I have here are depressing, what is the status?'

The ground opened up beneath Collins. Depressing was

an understatement. In the more than four years she'd been here, no real advancement had been made.

'The specimen arrived here some four years ago; we commenced the tests...'

The General stopped him in full sentence.

'The abbreviated version please, doctor. I've read her file. What have you actually achieved in those years?' His tone was accusative.

Visibly rattled, Collins stammered. 'We've tested everything we could. We have a very competent staff, but she won't cooperate.' When cornered blame someone—or in this case—something else.

The General softened his approach. 'My dear doctor Collins, I have no doubt that you and your staff did all you could. But you must agree the results have been painfully absent, the Powers are getting nervous, they want results for their investments.'

His tactics worked; the doctor was lulled into compliance. The real enemies were the specimen and those in power. The man was so easily manipulated it was pathetic. What a schmuck.

'She thwarts all our tests.' The fatigue was back again. 'No matter what we try, we don't get any closer to the source of her healing abilities, or her longevity. She is now almost one hundred years old but looks barely thirty-five. Though we are certain the two things are related. We've found out the healing capabilities are intensifying.'

This caught the Generals attention.

Collins continued; glad he had something positive to say. 'When she came here the healing procedure took much longer than it does now. Any wounds we administer heal within twelve hours now, scars are gone within twenty-four hours.'

'Any wounds?' The General raised an eyebrow. 'Describe the extent of the injuries.'

'We tested her with inch deep scalpel cuts on her torso and her extremities; length up to ten inches. We taped the healing process. I can show you the streams if you want?' When the General didn't react, he continued. 'We also observed that her strength is increasing dramatically. She is much too strong for a female, no matter what age.'

The General was quiet throughout the rest of the narrative. He was becoming more and more interested in the side effects of what the Doctor called "the major question". The doctor and the pharmaceutical companies were only interested in marketing eternal youth. They'd pumped millions into research in the last two centuries with no obvious results, and then to everyone's surprise, this creature crossed their path—an unexpected break.

What he saw was the full potential for her; unbeatable soldiers. An immortal army capable of healing itself. The opposition—any opposition—would be stamped out. Whoever controlled her talents controlled the world. He'd always scoffed at the thought of world domination. But the idea was getting comfortably more realistic the deeper he became involved in this project. The powers-that-be had no idea what treasure they held here. All he had to do was succeed where this annoying overbearing scientist had failed.

Grab your copy...
vinci-books.com/primalnature

About the Author

USA Today bestselling author Monique Singleton writes compelling stories that mix fantasy and science fiction with realistic psychological suspense and unique insights into the minds of the main characters.

As the daughter of a British soldier and his Dutch wife, Monique was born in an English military hospital in Germany. The family toured the world where she was exposed to different cultures in many countries. Finally settling down in the Netherlands, she pursued a career in art and later in consultancy.

In 2017 Monique started to put the scenes she had running around in her head, down to paper. Scenes led to a story, the story to a book, and the first book to a series. The rest is, as we say, history. She has now penned many books in multiple series.

From her Dominion series, The Devil You Know was runner-up in the Page Turner Awards 2024 and won a Readers' Favourite 5-Star award. It also won two PenCraft awards in 2024: one for literary excellence and the Fall Seasonal Book Award.

In addition to her writing, Monique still holds down a full-time job as a business consultant. She lives in a beautiful old farmhouse in the south of Holland with her two sloppy monster dogs, a horse, and two cats.

The cats are in charge.